~~~~~~~~~~~~~~~~~~~~~~~~~~~~~~~~~~

Phoenix Hose,
Hook & Ladder

~~~~~~~~~~~~~~~~~~~~~~~~~~~~~~~~~~

A NOVEL OF PHOENIXVILLE DURING WORLD WAR I

June J. McInerney

This is a work of fiction.
Names, characters, places, and most incidents are figments of
the author's imagination. Some are based upon historical facts,
real people, places, and businesses which are used fictitiously.
Dates and times, as well as certain circumstances have been
sometimes altered in the best interests of continuity and of
telling a good story. Any resemblance to actual persons, living
or dead, local business establishments, organizations, events,
and locales is purely speculative and intentionally coincidental.

First Edition: November 2017

ISBN-10: 1979563985
ISBN-13: 978-1979563987

Cover photograph courtesy of
David Meadows, President Emeritus
Phoenix Hose, Hook & Ladder Co., No.1

Back cover picture courtesy of the author.

B'Seti Pup Publishing
Phoenixville, PA
www.BSetiPupPublishing.com

Printed in the United States of America.

To the courageous men and women of our own
Phoenix Hose, Hook & Ladder Co., No. 1
who so valiantly dedicate and risk their lives every day for the
safety and welfare of our historical community.

The battle field may have its charms,
For those who fame desire,
Go count the famous battles won,
By those who fight with fires.
LYRICS FROM "ONE OF THE BRAVEST"
BY CHARLES MCCARTHY

Rumor has it that God created firemen
so that policemen
could have their own heroes.
DAVID MEADOWS

MAY 1917

Lenny Lochmann dejectedly lumbered up the stairs of the three-story stone house on Canal Street, carefully shielding the lit candle from the many drafts that often wafted in through ceiling cracks and small and unrepaired wall crevices.

Built in 1819 of greyish-brown stone, the house was tall, narrow, dank, and dark, lacking the modern amenities of electricity and central heating. Unlike their Italian neighbors, whose homes sported well-tended grape arbors and pristine facades, Lenny and his father were too poor to afford the cost of installing the necessary wiring nor the subsequent monthly fee to use it. Nor were they able to keep up with all the on-going maintenance required to keep a hundred-year-old home in good repair.

The previous owners had come, along with other families from County Donegal fleeing one of the great Irish potato famines, to Phoenixville to help dig the Black Rock tunnel for the Philadelpia & Reading Railroad. The neighborhood they settled came to be known as Scape Level, so named from the original Erse Irish word *sceilp*, loosely translated as "rocky ground or clefts". Lenny's father, a German immigrant himself, said the area was named because of the black rock located in the area. Hence, he stated with authority, also the name of the tunnel.

Lenny really didn't care about the house's history or any other history for that matter. He totally ignored the facts that a major conflagration was being fought in Europe – *Wherever that was!* -- and that President Woodrow Wilson had finally declared war on Germany just last month.

He didn't care that a Selective Service Act had been passed and that next month all eligible men had to register to be drafted.

He didn't care about anything except himself, his own immediate surroundings, his own actions in the present and his own plans for the immediate future.

Lenny's mother died when he was eight years old. After the somber, ill-attended funeral and burial in the graveyard of Central Lutheran Church on Main Street, he banished himself to a third-floor room, sparsely furnished with a small table, rope bed with a horsehair-filled mattress, a scratched-up Windsor chair, and a squat cupboard to store his few clothes and his meager "treasures". It was his retreat from fake friends. From his father who obviously abhorred his son.

From what he perceived as the unkind world.

A hefty, hulking twenty-two-year-old, Lenny had a thick forehead, beady dark brown eyes, and a perennially greasy and unruly mop of coppery-blond hair. His overall looks, coupled with his lack of any semblance of personal hygiene, had turned away potential friends all through school. People living on Scape Level avoided him. And now, even as they approached adulthood, girls in town ran away whenever he came near. Most of the boys, too, shunned him. Except, for a while, two.

Over the years, Stanley Martinez and Edmond Hope had tried to include Lenny in their group. While he wasn't very bright or good-looking, they had noticed over the years how unkindly others spurned and rejected him. Stanley's parents, both strict Catholics, had told him to always be kind to others; to find the good in everyone. And he had tried to do just that, nearly convincing Edmond, Campbell Wheatley, Hans Gruber, and Frank LaBronsky that Lenny, despite his ugly looks, his clumsy bumbling, and his incoherent speech patterns, was "deep down inside, a good guy". With a quirky sense of humor and, from what Stanley claimed he could see, "a really great throw to second base from home plate".

But despite their many offerings of friendship, their requests that he join them in baseball games... Despite their suggestions to just "hang out", Lenny always refused. He thought Stanley, with his fancy larger-than-life Victorian house on Vanderslice Street and his father's new-found wealth cobbling shoes, didn't really like him. Lenny firmly believed Stanley felt sorry for him and was just pretending to be nice.

After years of being refused and rebuffed, Stanley and his friends finally stopped asking Lenny to join them. As a matter of fact, except for the occasional wave or half-hearted "Hello" when he shambled by, they basically ignored him, just as other Phoenixville residents did. Going about their own business; meeting for drinks after work; playing their pick-up ball games at Reeves Park on Saturday afternoons; sitting on the library steps ogling the girls as they sashayed by; meeting for beers after work at a local bar.

And that made Lenny all the more angry.

If there was one thing he hated more than people pretending to be nice to him, it was being ignored.

Lenny, too, was inordinately jealous of Edmond Hope. Jealous of his prowess on the baseball field. Jealous of his tall, lanky, robust good looks. Jealous of his courage and bravery. Jealous of his easy way with the local girls who hung adoringly on his arm and his every word. Jealous of his prestigious father, the pastor of St. Peter's, his pretty sister, whom Stanley seemed to adore.

And, most of all, jealous of Edmond's friendship with Stanley.

If he wasn't around Stanley all the time, Lenny often thought to himself, *then maybe I might have accepted Stanley's offer... played some baseball. I like baseball. I'm the best baseball player ever in Phoenixville... Better than Edmond. Better than anyone else. Anywhere. And I'm braver, too, much braver. And more handsome...*

As for the other three buddies, Lenny didn't know them well enough to form any opinions. Just the fact that they hung around Edmond and Stanley was cause enough for him to hate them. Regardless of how nice they, too, had tried to be toward him.

And so, over the years growing up, Lenny's misconceptions about Stanley and Edmond – and their friends – coupled with being spurned, had developed into a hateful grudge against them. And in the last few months, it had become a spitefully dangerous vendetta.

Just wait, he told himself. *The time will come. I will do something. Something really big,* he scowled, putting the candle on the small wooden table in his tiny room. *I have plans. Big plans. I'll show them a thing or two about being friends.*

Lenny stowed his plaid flannel jacket and hobnail boots in the cupboard and retrieved a small wooden cigar box hidden behind his one good suit.

He sat glumly on the bed and frowned.

"I'll teach them not to ignore me," he whispered, opening the box. His deep nasal gravelly voice, when louder, conjured up images of a large sick frog. He spoke slow and deliberately, as if trying to conjure up words he thought he ought to know but didn't.

"I have plans. Many plans. Big, big. Very big plans."

Now that he finally had a job as a threader and janitor at the Perseverance Knitting Mill, he had what he thought were the proper means and special tools to carry them out.

JUNE 5, 1917

"I can't do this, guys."

Stanley stood frozen on the top step of the entrance to Borough Hall, glaring with trepidation at the large white double doors. Beads of cold sweat condensed under his arms and on his palms. He rubbed his damp hands down the front of his dark green work pants, trying to ignore the small voice whispering inside his mind.

If I open the doors and go inside... my life... the very life of Stanley Francis Martinez – even if I did somehow survive... It would never be the same.

He brushed a lock of dark curly hair from his forehead. He had his Mexican father's short wiry build and dark complexion that sharply contrasted with his Irish mother's twinkling sapphire blue eyes and thin Aquiline nose.

"Hey, you chickening out on us?" Edmond Hope asked, bounding up the steps to stand next to Stanley. At least six inches taller than his friend, he was a ruddy-faced slender, but strong redhead with dark brown eyes. "We made a pack ya know," he said, rubbing his hands together, licking his lips in anticipation of the future. Edmond, Stanley knew from years of growing up together, would do anything dangerous on a dare.

"I'm breaking it."

"Why, Stan?" Edmond turned to the other three young men who clustered on the steps behind, waiting for Stanley to lead them into the building.

It was a balmy afternoon in early June of 1917; the first day of registration for the Selective Service. In April, America had declared war against the Central Powers of Germany and Austria-Hungary, joining the Allies of the Triple Entente: France, Russia, and Great Britain. To swell the ranks of the army – just a little over 150,000 in number – Congress had passed the first phase of the Selective Service Act of 1917. Men born between 1886 and 1896 were to register for the draft on or after June 5th.

Stanley had just turned twenty-one and, like other single young men his age without any dependents in Phoenixville, along with his four closest buddies, was eligible.

Edmond Hope and the three others worked in various shops of the Phoenix Iron Company and the Phoenix Bridge Company. They had collectively reasoned that now that their country was at war, it was their civic duty to defend its democracy and its freedoms against all kinds of aggression. Each had made a promise to one another to sign-up together.

Stanley, too, had initially gone along with the agreement, but, in his heart he wasn't entirely sure. Mere moments after making the pact, Stanley instantly regretted it. He ached to back out; but, to him, once his word was given, it was a matter of honor not to break it.

After the registration period ended, the local draft board, per the law, would compile a list of non-registrants who would then receive a letter postmarked from Washington, D.C demanding that they report for duty. Failure to do so was punishable by imprisonment and, in cases of flight, execution. But, now, even with the threat of being forcibly conscripted – or punished – Stanley couldn't shake his feelings of dread.

He tried to explain why he was having second and third thoughts to Edmond. As the local newspaper titled those like himself, he was, a Pacifist, like many of the local Quaker and Mennonite Phoenixville residents who did not believe in war. Of any kind. Even though his father, a Patriot, flew the Stars and

Stripes proudly in front their home, unlike the majority of residents in what *The Daily Republican* termed A FLAGLESS TOWN. He had these and other reasons not to want to enlist, but Edmond had turned a deaf ear. The opposite of Stanley, he was all too eager to sign up, to be called to serve, to be sent to war. To fight.

Perhaps, almost certainly, to be killed.

"There's no going back, Stan. You promised. We all did..." Edmond cajoled. "And you know deep down inside," he thumped Stanley's chest, "it's the right thing to do."

Stanley nodded. Despite his deeper feelings, that very morning he had, for the sake of camaraderie and solidarity with his friends, reluctantly decided to join them. Besides, his boss had said that the company – in the spirit of patriotism – would give any employee who registered the afternoon off, provided they worked that morning. Stanley and his friends jumped at the opportunity for a few extra hours of freedom. They planned, after registering, to high-tail it to Reeves Park to play a pick-up game of baseball and then visit a local bar to down a few beers.

It was, as Campbell Wheatley opined, "the perfectly agreeable winning combination."

Yet, at the last minute, notwithstanding that he couldn't, shouldn't let Edmond and the others down, Stanley had stopped at the double-doors.

After all, he thought trying to drum up the courage to go in, *it's just putting your name, my name on a list. It isn't as if I am actually signing up to fight. Is it? What else could really come of it if I just sign my name on a meaningless form? I mean... my number might not even come up...*

He rubbed his hands again down the sides of his pants, slick with grease and wood shavings from his grueling job as a pattern-maker at the foundry on north Main Street. Dirt wedged into the creases and calluses on his fingers and palms as he tried to wipe it off. Long hours of hard work had matured his body years beyond his young age.

Edmond recognized the signs of anxiety on his friend's face. He had seen it before. Unlike himself, a professed daredevil, Stanley was not one to take any chances; always seeking the safer side of any and every situation. He turned to the three other young men.

"Give him a moment..." he said. "Okay? This is a big decision..."

"Ah, geez... We all know that. C'mon," Frank LaBronsky snickered. A tall, slender lad, he worked alongside Edmond as a master puddler, forging iron in one of the massive furnaces that lined the perimeter of the steel plant. "I ain't got all day."

"And I gotta get back to work," Campbell snorted. Oldest of the five, Campbell was a descendant of the famous miner and paleontologist, Charles Disney Wheatley who had lived for many years at The Knoll, the landmark mansion off Nutt's Avenue at the south end of town.

Despite having the afternoon off, he was meticulous and conscientious. Shop #6, which he managed, had an outstanding order of rivets and spikes that held together bridge trusses and railroad ties that had to be fulfilled by tomorrow. For three years, he ran the shop like a tight ship and hadn't missed completing an order yet. It would look bad if he, the manager, was late getting back to work after he constantly demanded strict punctuality from his workers. He impatiently flipped a thick strand of straight ash-blond hair from his forehead.

"Well, if you're not going to go first," he said, brushing past Stanley, "then I will." Campbell pulled open one of the double doors and, beckoning to his friends behind him, went in. Frank followed, along with Hans Gruber, a stocky German lad, who like Stanley, was a pattern maker. The quiet type, Hans preferred actions rather than words; speaking only when he deemed it necessary. As he walked past Stanley, he paused briefly and quietly grasped his friend's shoulder.

"Thanks, Hans," Stanley tried to smile. Hans nodded thoughtfully, then went inside.

Only Edmond remained on the top step.

Stanley stood stock-still and looked intently at his best friend. He sighed. Just a half-hour ago, he and the others had jauntily walked arm-in-arm up Church Street to the polling place where the Selective Service had set up a registration area.

"We're all making a big mistake," he uttered. "*They're* making a big mistake..." broadly waving an arm in the air as if to indicate the entire world. He shook his head at the doors Frank, Campbell, and Hans had just entered. "This whole war thing... and all its senseless killing. Despite what I promised, I'm not signing up."

"But, it's the law," Edmond said, frowning at Stanley. "They'll put you in jail, ya know."

"Safer than a battlefield," Stanley retorted.

"Yeah, but... We gotta do it," Edmond averred. He paused, then elbowed Stanley's side in jest. "Hey, you afraid... or something?" He need not have asked. Stanley's face was ashen with fear, his thin dark lips clamped in both dread and fierce determination. "Hey, you really are afraid... But, Stan, you aren't gonna wind up being a coward... or anything... Are you? I mean... Being afraid... Hell, we all are... He paused. "Well, it isn't going to stop us." He hesitated. "Is it?"

Stanley did not reply. Not that he didn't want to. He just couldn't.

In his mind, he freely admitted that he was afraid; but he wasn't going to ever say it aloud. To anyone. Not even Edmond. He felt the small rivulets of panic soaking through his light blue chambray work shirt and tried to suppress the rapid flutter in his chest. He inhaled, slowly, filling his lung to capacity with the sweet late spring air, tinged with the faint odor of melting iron that constantly wafted over Phoenixville from the foundry. He slowly let out a deep breath, then shrugged his shoulders

"I can't. I just can't," he managed to say. Then, nodding slightly, he brushed past Edmond and quickly marched down the steps.

"Hey, Stan... Where're you going?!" Edmond called after him.

But Stanley didn't respond and hastened east along Church, crossed Main, heading toward Starr Street. He did not look back to see if Edmond might be following him or if he had ignored his warning and entered the make-shift local draft board office.

Stanley hoped his best friend had opted to do neither.

Once he had confirmed his decision, he tried to put it out of his mind. He had other, more important things to do than be ordered around by men he didn't know to fight a perfect stranger's battles.

In his haste to put as much distance as possible between Borough Hall and himself, Stanley hurried past the firehouse of Phoenix Hose, Hook & Ladder Co., No. 1 and the Church Street School building next door where he and Edmond attended elementary school.

When the alarm sounded, he was almost to Starr Street. Stanley stopped and turned around. Duke and Harry, massive half-breed dappled grey Percheron fire horses, were pulling a heavy combination chemical and hose wagon out of the firehouse. Six men, clad in rubber boots, heavy twilled cotton pants, canvas knee-length jackets, and red peaked metal helmets clung for dear life on the back and sides. Driven by Nathan P. White, the paid driver perched high upon the bench seat, the horses pranced down the hill toward Starr where they turned right. The apparatus was followed by six more men pulling a smaller pumper.

Stanley watched in awe as they passed, listening to the bell clang on the firehouse tower and counting the loud blasts from the Gamewell Diaphone air horn mounted high atop one of the Pipe Mill buildings. "Two long, followed by eight short..." he said out loud. "Two, eight."

As he counted the blasts, Stanley remembered that when the horn blared during school hours, he and most of the students were frightened. Though scared, Stanley was also fascinated by the horses and by the firehouse equipment. He visited Mr. White and the horses as often as he could after school; learning as much as he could about firefighting.

Knowing the young lad's fascination, Mr. White taught him as much as he could, making sure that Stanley knew the codes and their locations.

"Two, eight," Stanley counted again. "Sounded twice. Two alarms. Corner Stores," he remembered. "At least... in the general vicinity..."

It had been a while since he last visited Mr. White, Duke, and Harry. He surmised that when they returned to the firehouse after the call, Nat would probably be grateful for help cleaning tack and brushing down the horses. Stanley retraced his steps and walked through the massive doors left opened by the hastening firefighters.

Faint odors of fresh straw and old manure pervaded the large room in which four fire vehicles and the two horses were housed. Stanley sauntered by the generously-sized stalls along one wall, then past the horse-drawn hook and ladder, freshly polished and gleaming under an array of overhead lights. *Must be a small fire, if the hook and ladder isn't needed,* he surmised.

The unit Duke and Harry pull out of the firehouse that day was a combination chemical and hose wagon purchased by the company in July of 1903 from the Charles T. Holloway & Company in Baltimore for $2,000. Stanley recalled when his father took him, at the impressionable age of seven, to see the new wagon with its two tall tanks.

He had stood silently in awe holding his father's hand as the burly Fire Chief and the lanky driver patiently explained to the boy how "the apparatus" worked. Nat White pointed to the tanks and then to a reel of leather hose.

11

"The tanks each hold forty gallons of water, sixteen pounds of bicarbonate of soda, and a small bottle of sulfuric acid. That hose there, is one inch wide."

Stanley scrunched up his face in confusion. While fascinated by the large gleaming wagon, he didn't quite understand the big words the driver was using. He scratched his cheek. The Fire Chief eyes twinkled, but he did not smile.

"Inside the tanks are plungers," Mr. White continued. "When it pierces the bottle, the acid goes into the water and a chemical reaction occurs. You see? Like this." He tried to illustrate by gesturing with his hands, which only made Stanley laugh.

"What puts out fires?" he asked.

'Well, the acid and the water mix and that makes a pressurized gas called carbon dioxide. And that gas propels the mixture into the hose and then it's sprayed out onto the flames. The chemical solution is heavier than air and since a fire needs air to burn... the flames are smothered. Um, put out."

"Smothered!" Stanley exclaimed, delighted to be learning a new word. "Smothered!" The three men laughed with the young boy.

Someday, the Chief thought, this time with a smile, *he'll be a great fireman.*

Years later, while helping Mr. White with the horses after school, he learned the finer principles of the chemical reaction and how using the mixture lessened the risk of damage when just plain water was forced through the pressurized larger, 2½" hose lines.

Lost in thought, Stanley idly stared at the wall of racks and hooks where fire coats, hats, and boots were neatly arrayed. He remembered that later that day, while walking home, he had told his father, "when I grow up, I gonna be Mr. White."

He heard a muffled sneeze, then glanced at a closed door marked "Fire Chief".

Stanley gently knocked.

'Yeah?" a gruff voice asked. "Who's there?"

"I, um, Stanley Martinez.... Remember me, sir? My father was, is a friend of Mr. White." Stanley felt a bit silly talking through a door. He tried the handle, but it was locked.

"Responding to an alarm." The Chief sneezed again.

"Yeah, I know, but... I was wondering..."

Stanley shrugged his shoulders and was turning to leave when he heard a click and the door opened.

Fire Chief David Mendowski was an imposing figure, filling the whole door frame. He stood nearly six feet four inches in his stocking feet, with a shock of short-cropped dark brown hair greying at the temples. His face was as leathery and gruff-looking as a seasoned New England whale fisherman. In his late-forties, Mendowski had maintained his beefy athletic build through many years of hauling fire wagons through Borough streets and handling heavy leather hoses that spewed highly pressurized water as he fought to douse smoke and flames.

But Chief Mendowski's crusty outward appearance belied his true personality. He was, in fact, as Stanley remembered, a very kind, thoughtful person. And, except when barking orders to others while fighting fires, Mendowski was also a man of few words.

"Huh. The little kid who used to hang around?"

Stanley nodded.

"Thought so. Knew your father." He paused, appraising the young man standing before him. "Didn't grow much taller."

"No, well, I... perhaps a few inches," Stanley said, intimidated by the Chief towering over him. He was a bit taller than his father, who stood just shy of five-foot six. Growing up, he got used to being good-naturedly teased about being what Campbell called "vertically challenged." But now what he thought was a veiled taunt coming from the Fire Chief unnerved him. Stanley looked down at his hobnailed boots. He didn't see Mendowski's smile.

"You'll do," the Chief chuckled.

"What?" Stanley asked, looking up.

"Volunteer."

Mendowski pointed to a sign on the bulletin board next to his office. VOLUNTEERS URGENTLY NEEDED. Stanley scratched his temple with a forefinger. He had come to help Mr. White and the horses after the fire, as he used to do growing up. Although becoming a firefighter was his fondest ambition as a child, he wasn't sure he wanted to join yet another service he had since learned could be just as dangerous as fighting a war.

"Volunteer, sir?" he asked.

"The company. Be a firefighter." Chief Mendowski proudly tapped the badge pinned to pocket of his dark blue shirt, then sneezed. "Excuse me. Summer cold..." He blew his nose into a large linen handkerchief clutched in one hand.

Stanley nodded. "Bless you," he whispered and then frowned.

"Well? Martinez?"

"Well, I... don't know. I came here to..." carefully mulling over the possibilities in his mind. He had read the provisions of the Selective Service Act when it was first printed in *The Daily Republican*. Somewhere in the back of his mind he recalled the phrase "reasons for deferment". Professions and jobs in service to the public were listed, but he couldn't quite remember if "fireman" was one of them.

"Well," he asked tentatively. "Would being a firefighter... be much safer than being in the army?"

"You ask, Martinez. After all Nat taught you?

"Well, I...."

"Come in," Mendowski beckoned. "Let's talk."

Stanley hesitated before following the Chief back into his office.

He would remember that brief moment as one of the rare defining nexus points of his life.

Phoenix Hose, Hook & Ladder Co., No. 1, commonly called Phoenix № 1, had been organized and chartered in March 1874. Prior to then, firefighting in the Borough of Phoenixville was virtually non-existent, depending mostly on civilians with buckets of water or assistance from the Phoenix Iron Company fire brigade. When the installation of a new centralized water system was completed in 1873, the Borough Council decided it was time to organized a fire company of its own.

David Mendowski was only five at the time, but he could still recall when a used hose carriage and a 35-foot long hook and ladder truck had arrived. Perched upon his father's shoulders, he watched as two six-man teams pushed and pulled the newly-purchased used equipment down Bridge Street from the Philadelphia and Reading Railroad station to the fire company's headquarters. The building, 38-feet wide, 66-inches deep and 17-feet high, had been recently built on the lot behind Buckwalter's Store on south Main. It would be Phoenix Hose, Hook & Ladder's home for the next eight years.

Fascinated, David listened to his father's simplistic explanation of what how the hose carriage and truck were used. Nothing more than two wooden wagons with wheels especially designed to carry 1,200 feet of leather hose and four stacked ladders that were unfolded so that fireman could climb to the top floors and roof of flaming buildings. The hose, he said, required a lot of care.

"After every fire, we have to be careful drying it," Albert, the elder Mendowski said. He had joined the thirty-seven-member volunteer company, headed by its newly appointed president, Charles H. Shaffer. "We clean them, then hang it in the tower – that's why it was built – and then rub it inside and out with Neet's Foot oil. That keeps it water-tight and prevents the hose from cracking..."

"Then roll it up. Onto the wagon's big reel."

"That's right, son. So that it's ready for the next fire." He paused. "It's a tedious job, but we do it."

David was proud of his father. As he grew, he attentively listened to his father's stories of fighting fires in and around the Borough. As he grew older he knew that he, too, would one day be a member of the company. Just like his Dad.

In 1885, the officers and volunteer members of Phoenix Nº 1 marched in the Fourth of July parade along Bridge Street, up Main to Fourth Avenue, over to Starr, and back down to Bridge. The large bell atop the hose tower tolled in the distance. Albert Mendowski, now a member of the company's board, bedecked with ribbons, walked stately behind a newly acquired hose carriage. His son, David, then a strapping young lad of sixteen, with his own ribbon, marched proudly by his side.

In the course of the next twenty-five years or so, the fire company acquired various pieces of equipment, including a horse-drawn hook and ladder truck and a "Philadelphia Style" double-deck stroke pump engine that could be hooked up to a hydrant line of the Borough's water supply.

During those years, Albert Mendowski aged into retirement, finally leaving the company in 1910, the same year David, who, except for his brief stint fighting in the Spanish-American War, had nobly and heroically risen up the ranks, became the Fire Chief.

Since he joined the company, David had fought many fires, almost too numerous to count. Most of them were battled shoulder-to-shoulder with his father. Small brush fires; barn fires; houses consumed by flames caused by carelessness; stores on Bridge and Main gutted by spontaneous combustion of old newspapers, rags, and rotting supplies forgotten in dark, dank basements and drafty attics. Outhouses, the Chemical Copper Works, the Charles Bader Property on West Bridge Street. He vividly remembered the conflagration that consumed a foundry building when a worker carelessly tossed a bucket of water onto flaming puddles of coal oil, exacerbating the fire and causing it to spread to other parts of the wooden structure.

All the fires, large and small, were dangerous and not to be taken lightly.

But there was one that David found notably funny. The fire that had erupted in the Walters & Sons Ice House. Nobody knew the cause of the flames that gutted most of the establishment, but it seemed to the young firefighter at the time that the torrents of water from the melting of the ice stored on two floors of the building would have thwarted the small conflagration. But it didn't. Thank goodness no one was injured.

Fire Chief David Mendowski had to admit that through the course of his career he had seen just about everything.

Or had he?

An hour or so later, Nathan White returned with Duke and Harry. Stanley was still sitting in Chief Mendowski's office when the driver knocked and poked his head around the door.

"Sorry. Didn't realize you were busy." He paused when he saw Stanley. "Say, there. If it isn't young Stanley Martinez. Haven't see you for a while. Where've you been?"

"Hi, Mr. White. Been working as a pattern maker over at the foundry. Keeps me busy..."

"And out of trouble, I hope."

"Kinda... Yeah, well. Yes."

"And your father? I haven't see him in a while, either..."

"He's fine, Mr. White. "Still making shoes. That keeps him busy, too."

"Well now. Give him my best." He paused, then smiled. "You gonna volunteer? You'd be a natural, son. Hell, you already know your codes...."

"Today's call was two-eight," Stanley said flatly. "The Corner Stores, down Nutt's Avenue... Off Whitehorse?"

"Good memory. Yep. Nearby, at The Knoll House, the large mansion on the old Buckley estate. Paul Reeves and his family live there now."

"I know. They and their house guests come into my father's shop for custom-made shoes."

"Well, don't know much about that... but..."

"What was the fire, Nat?" Mendowski interjected. "Just the Holloway. Not the pumper?"

"Wasn't needed. It was just a small brush fire outside the garden wall. Nothing much. The chemically-treated water did the trick. Nobody hurt. Except one or two of Mrs. Reeves favorite rose bushes were singed by hot embers floating over..."

"Good news," the Chief nodded, cutting Nat short. "Log it in the book?"

White gave a mock salute. "You got it, sir." He paused, looking at Stanley. "Stop by and say hello to the boys when you're done..."

"Sure, Mr. White. Will do."

"Well, then," he said, winking and then looking at the Chief with a knowing look in his eye. "Well, then, I'll leave you two..."

"The thing is," Stanley continued trying to explain to Fire Chief Mendowski, when the driver left. "Like I was saying... I am not like the other guys, you know? I don't want to be conscripted..."

With his hands clasped in front of him, the Fire Chief quietly listened to the sinewy young lad nervously rubbing his palms up and down his thighs. He had remembered the young man as a cautious, timid but extremely curious lad who, when growing up, had often visited the horses, marveling at the firefighting equipment. *Perhaps,* he wondered, *these traits would serve him well on our force?*

"I'm not about to sign up," Stanley continued. "I was going to, but... the thought of being in the line of fire..."

"Firemen are," the Chief stated softly. "You know that." Yet, he wondered if Stanley had any real idea, other than a little boy's hero-worship of them, what firefighters really did.

"Well, I mean, it's less dangerous. Isn't it?" Stanley paused. "Is it true being a fireman will get me deferred?'

Mendowski frowned.

"From being drafted. Being in the army... You know," Stanley faltered. The Chief's reticence unnerved him. "It's not that I'm not patriotic. I mean, I love my country just as much as the next man, but...."

"Not enough to defend it?"

"Well, no... Um, yes." Stanley started to explicate that it wasn't that he wasn't eager to fight for American values. "It's just that... well more that I don't want to mindlessly march into battle on foreign soil thousands of miles away... A land, a country I don't know of, nor care about... You see, sir, I... "

"Enough," Mendowski interrupted, holding up a large, well-tanned callused hand. He silently scrutinized Stanley, recalling his own fears fighting as a young man nearly nineteen years ago in the Spanish-American war.

The United States had sent troops and ships to the island 103 miles off the coast of Florida in the valiant attempt to help liberate Cuba from the clutches of Spain. As a young infantryman, Mendowski had faced fierce gun fire as he raced behind Teddy Roosevelt up San Juan Hill on that fateful June 22, 1898 morning. Nearly to the top, he was shot in the left shoulder and was forced to sit out the remainder of the short-lived five-month conflict recuperating on a United States Naval ship patrolling Manila Bay.

Rubbing his now badly scarred upper chest he recalled the pain. He remembered how frightened he had felt when the doctor told him he was lucky. Two bullets had just barely missed his heart and one of his lungs. He understood, more than he would admit, how today young men, such as the one before him, would not want to die a needless death defending foreign soil. He

19

had welcomed the respite of being out of the line of fire and guiltily admitted he would have thoroughly enjoyed it had he not suffered continual long bouts of seasickness.

But fighting fires, dangerous fires, was just as, if not riskier than being in a major conflict. And, more often than not, they burned brighter and were deadlier than any war's enemy fire. *But how do I explain this to Stanley Martinez without scaring him off? To be honest, why would I?* There had been a recent increase in fires in and around Phoenixville the past few months. The force needed more men to fight them.

"I'll give you a chance", the Fire Chief said. "You look capable enough... even if a tad short..."

Stanley watched impatiently as the Fire Chief slowly took a large envelope from a wire basket on the left side of the desk and handed it to him. "Fill out this application. Two letters of recommendation. End of the week. Training starts a week from Monday."

"You mean...?" Stanley briefly glanced at the form. "I'll be deferred?"

"Not sure, but I'll check. Policemen are..." he shook his head. "Maybe firemen?"

It was, at the moment, all that Stanley could hope for.

"Thank you, Chief Mendowski!" he said, standing up and reaching over the desk to shake his hand.

"Your parents... Irish-Latino?"

Taken aback, Stanley smiled nervously. "Yes..." He knew very well that Chief Mendowski was quite aware of his and his parents' heritage.

"Thought so." Mendowski shook Stanley's hand. Even with his own strong grip, Stanley likened that of the Fire Chief's to a powerful steel vise.

"Your father and I... back in the day... In Cuba together."

"You were?"

"A long time ago."

"Um, can I ask…?"

"Best not" the Chief shrugged. "Thanks for coming in", he said, abruptly ushering Stanley out the door. "Nat will really appreciate your help…"

"Thank you," Stanley said again, rubbing a now slightly sore right hand. "You won't regret this… I mean, my volunteering…"

"I hope not," the Chief said, sneezing, and then closing and locking the door behind him.

Stanley and Nat White reminisced as they cleaned tack together, soaping up and drying reins, bridles, collar, pads, and breeching.

"They still know their tricks?" Stanley asked.

"A' course," White smiled, recalled how he taught Duke and Harry how to, wherever the alarm sounded, quickly unlatch and leave their stalls, positioning themselves in front of the apparatus he had indicated via hand signals. Once in place, they'd patiently wait while their harnesses descended from the ceiling and were quickly secured by Nat and his assistant.

He had also taught them a variety of skills and tricks. The pair could simultaneously mount pedestals, roll barrels and large boxes, pluck a handkerchief out of the driver's back pocket, and assist him in removing his fireman coat and boots. Duke had also perfected the task of removing Mr. White's hat and carrying it between his teeth across the room and hanging it on a peg. Harry, the brighter of the pair, had taught himself how to untie a scarf wrapped around his foreleg. He was also able to manipulate other objects, including unbaling hay and flipping sections of it into his and Duke's stalls.

The diverse variety of their tricks captivated and thrilled the hearts and imaginations of Borough children and adults alike. Including Stanley, who fondly remembered when his and Edmond's families had crammed into the back of a hay wagon and, along with other residents of Phoenixville, followed Duke and Harry as they pulled the streamer all the way from the firehouse to the Devon Horse Show and County Fair. There, they had won the Fire Horse Team competition not once, but twice. The first time in 1911 and then, again, in 1912. Stanley laughed as Mr. White recalled how the crowd had roared with cheers and applause when Duke and Harry had won.

"But...sadly," the driver said. "We just recently ordered a Brockway combination chemical, pumper, and hose car..."

"A new one to be hauled by 'the boys'?"

"No, Stanley. Unfortunately, it's gas-powered... Will be delivered in early 1918, replacing our two fine lads."

Stanley frowned in dismay. He hadn't gone to see Mr. White since he started his apprenticeship as a pattern maker at the Phoenix Iron Company. Busy with work and his new obsession with what the newspapers were now calling "The Great War", he had kept away from most of his previous interests. Or, now, as an adult, was it because he was quickly outgrowing his fascination of them?

"What will happen to Duke and Harry," he asked.

"Probably be retired to some farm... Out to pasture," White shook his head. "Doing not much of anything. Idling away. Such a waste."

"That would be such a great loss to Phoenixville."

"Well, yeah. But we have a few more months yet... And with the war on... perhaps more than that. A year or two. At best." Nat White tried to smile. But in his heart, Stanley knew, he was nearly grief-stricken.

Then and there, Stanley made a promise to himself that if he did decide to join the force – and was accepted – he'd try to do all he could to save Duke and Harry from such an ignoble end. *After all,* he thought, *after so many years of brave service to the firehouse and to the community... do they really need to be put out to pasture... Rendered useless?*

"I'll be here more often, even if I don't volunteer," he told Mr. White. "Maybe I can help with the horses... must be something I can do..."

Nathan White nodded. "Ah, yep. That'd be fine..." he said, and then continued to polish tack. "We could use the extra manpower, even if you're not part of the force."

Stanley slowly walked home, mulling over the Fire Chief's suggestion that he volunteer. It seemed like a good idea. Far better than being drafted. And if it meant deferment? By the time he had crossed the High Bridge and was headed down Vanderslice Street, he had made up his mind.

That night over dinner, Stanley tried to explain his decision to his parents.

"I mean," he once again that day attempted to say. "Why should I have to risk my life for the sake of a country mad at another for killing a prince? And the Kaiser is the grandson of Queen Victoria... Why is he fighting her? The war just doesn't make any sense to me... It's just stupid. That's what it is."

"Regardless of your feelings, Stanley, you're going to have to go," his father explained. "When they draft you, you know. It's now the law. I presume you've registered? Today was the day..."

Stanley shook his head.

"No, I didn't. I was going to... but..." He wanted to blurt out his news about meeting with Chief Mendowski and his vow about Nathan White and Duke and Harry. And since he decided to join, he also wanted to ask his father to write one of the required letters of recommendation. But his father continued to drone on.

"*Otras razones, mi hijo.* There are other reasons, my son," his father continued, breaking into his thoughts. "The sinking of the Lusitania, for one..."

Stanley squinted, then quickly responded, "A British ship in British waters..."

"But there were American passengers on board. The whole country was aghast... and appropriately quite angry. *Y con razón.*

Then there's the sabotage of the munitions depot in Jersey City..."

"No proof it was the Germans..."

"*Estoy en desacuerdo,*" Carlos paused. "But... okay. We can agree to disagree. But, what about our pride and our promises to our allies?"

"Don't you read the papers, Papi? We entered this crazy conflict as a separate diplomatic act... It has nothing to do with our basic American freedoms."

"We are defending France... over run by Kaiser Wilhelm and his allies..."

"And we're supposed to fight their battles for them? If we do it now... They'll expect us to do it in the future... every time they are threatened..."

"France came to America's aid during our fight for independence, remember?"

"And we returned the favor defeating England again in the War of 1812. That was enough. We shouldn't be doing it again," Stanley said, He angrily stabbed a small bit of potato out of the Irish stew on his plate. "At least not with my blood."

Stanley's father frowned. His son, he had to admit, was brighter than he was at his age. He was proud of him both for his accomplishments as a model student and for taking a job as a pattern maker at the steel plant. But Stanley's refusal to register for the Selective Service had dismayed him.

He is an adult, now, he sighed to himself. *Old enough to make his own decisions.* Dios mío, ¿cuándo pasó eso? *My son was just a babe in arms just a few short years ago...*

"There are certain responsibilities..." he stated flatly, silently recalling his own experiences as part of a gun crew aboard one of the Navy ships under the command of Commodore Dewey during the Spanish-American War. *What a thrill that had been*, he smiled to himself. *If only my own son, my own flesh and blood, would realize what an obligation and a privilege it is to fight for one's country...* Por su honor. *For one's honor.*

"Then as an adult, he has to make his own decisions," Stanley's mother stated, echoing his father's thoughts. "And we must abide... No, honor them. However false or misguided they are."

"It is our job to guide him..."

"Oh, for God's sake!" Stanley shouted, rising from the table, nearly crashing his plate and wine glass onto the parquet floor. "It is no longer your *job* to do anything anymore. I am twenty-one. An adult. What I choose to do, not do with my life... is MY choice" He raised a fist to his father.

"Stanley!" his mother cajoled. "Please... your manners. Show some respect. After all, he is your father."

Stanley ignored her and continued.

"Don't you understand that? Don't you even get it? I am not... I repeat... I am NOT going to fight in this, that ridiculous war," he exclaimed, pointing out the window. "I am NOT going to sign up for the draft... I refuse to be put in harm's way... To be killed for someone else's honor or pride."

"Son, Stanley..." his father tried to say, "I know how you feel, but..." Had he been young enough like his first-born, a son, he would have once again eagerly enlisted and bravely fought for the freedoms his parents had found in their adopted country and which now he and his small family enjoyed.

But that was obviously not how Stanley saw it.

"No 'buts', Papi. You've told me time and time again about your three pathetic months fighting on a ship for Cuba... Fine. You were a hero. And you did come home safe and sound... But I am not about to take that risk... to not come home. Ever. I didn't sign up and... even if I did, if am called up, I'll refuse."

"*A chara Mother Mary agus Joseph.* You'd be shot for treason," his mother stated, reverting back to Gaelic. "Better to die a hero than be killed as a coward."

"Never will happen, Momma." Lowering his voice and crisply enunciating his words, he proudly announced, "I am going to join the local fire department. Phoenix Hose, Hook and Ladder Company Number One. And if I am accepted... and pass the training course – I could be deferred from all military service."

Both of his parents looked at him in stony silence. Stanley looked from one to the other.

"I could be, right?"

"The law distinctly says 'policemen', son," his father finally said. "Not 'firemen'."

"Chief Mendowski said he'd look into it for me... Regardless, I am not joining the army. I'll... I'll figure out a way to get out of it." Stanley tossed his napkin onto his half-full plate, glaring at his father. Defying him to challenge his decision.

"Mendowski?" his father sputtered. "Fire Chief Mendowski? David Mendowski?"

"Yeah, Papi. Why?"

"*Mi hijo,*" he sighed. "You have decided to walk away from the fires of war... only to march straight into the flames of hell."

"Whatever does that mean?" Stanley demanded, turning on his heel. He remembered the Fire Chief's cautionary words before handing him the application. He shrugged his shoulders then began to walk away. He did not want to stay to listen to the answer.

His father paused, then heaved another gentle sigh, knowing Stanley would, at all costs avoid anything that would involve fighting and bloodshed. *But to volunteer to be a fireman? One of the most dangerous jobs there was?* To him, it made no sense.

He looked away from Stanley, then glanced briefly at his wife and then his daughter. He then bowed his greying head, turning his attention to the remains of his own supper.

"Fine," he said in defeat, not looking up as his son stormed out of the dining room. "He's right. He is an adult. It's his decision." He paused, and then said, "Now, Dolly, if you don't mind I'd like to finish my meal in peace."

As they ate in silence together, both of them remembered that fateful day in August of 1895 when they had met.

Carlos Méndez Martinez was the son of Mexican émigrés who had arrived in the United States in the late 1870s. Refugees from the political unrest and economic instability under the dictatorship of Porfirio Diaz, his young parents had sought asylum in San Diego, California, hoping and praying for a chance of a better life.

He was proud of being born in America; even prouder that he was now a successful businessman in the small, industrial town nestled in southeast Pennsylvania on the confluence of French Creek and the Schuylkill River.

He was even prouder of his wife.

Dolores Murphy Martinez was very much the pragmatist. Which was one of the main reasons Carlos had instantly fallen in love with her when they first met in the small lobby of the Columbia Hotel.

Fresh out of high school, he was on his way to New York, seeking a job in the big city of endless opportunities. She, a few years older and a native of Phoenixville, worked as a clerk in the accounting department of the Phoenix Bridge Company, one of the two divisions of the Phoenix Iron Company. She was in the process of delivering final bridge specs and their accompanying contract to an out-of-town client when Carlos spotted her from the other side of the lobby.

He was captivated by the tall woman with red-blond hair and slender long legs striding purposefully across the faux handwoven Persian carpet past the tall Chandlee grandfather clock toward the lobby's reservation desk. Her sparkling blue eyes were determinedly focused on her task at hand.

He had paused for just a split second, then, without considering the consequences of a male stranger approaching a woman alone in a hotel lobby, sprinted to her side. He feigned a sneeze. She turned, automatically saying, "God bless you." Then, charmed by the attentions of the younger man standing alongside her, she smiled. A bashful, somewhat beguiling grin graced his lips. Dark, curly hair just barely touched the top of his slightly fraying, but very clean white shirt collar.

"Forgive me, ma'am... er, is that, perhaps, Miss... er, um... I..." Carlos had stammered.

"Dolores Murphy," she interrupted, extending her hand. "But most call me Dolly. And you are...?"

"Carlos. Carlos Méndez Martinez. I am on my way to New York City, but... um, before I go... May I... may I," he unabashedly blurted out, "take you to dinner?"

Dolly nodded her assent.

Carlos was taken aback.

Ah, qué hermosa mujer! he thought *She doesn't even know me and yet the beautiful woman so quickly and willingly accepts an invitation to dinner? Estoy humillado.*

He eyed her critically. She was neatly attired in a tailored heavily starched cotton shirt-waisted dress; its slightly flounced hem graced the tops of high-buttoned boots. Her hair was pulled back in a loose chignon, low on the back of a slender, pale neck. She did not look to him like a "fast" or "loose" woman... a "lady of the evening..." *Yet, why is she so eager to accept me... My invitation?*

"Well, I... I mean," he stammered. 'I didn't mean to be so bold, but..."

"Nor I so forward..." she continued to smile.

He hesitated.

"Well?" she asked. "I have a few errands to run," she said, indicating the think manila legal-sized envelope in her hand. "For work, you know."

28

"Yes, yes. I understand... I shall let you go," Carlos said. Although he didn't want to. "Um, where... How...? I mean, I am new here in town and I don't know... Where?"

"Meet me here, in the lobby, at six o'clock. I know a very nice place... Do you like French food?"

"I am, um, not sure," Carlos stammered, still both aghast and astonished that this lovely beauty had, without hesitation, consented to dine with him. And this very evening, no less. He straightened his tie, admitting that he had never eaten French food or any other foreign cuisine, for that matter, other than the Mexican fare his mother had cooked.

"Well, we can change all that," Dolly smile again. "I just happen to know the maître d'... He'll take good care of us. Six, then?" she queried. The, without waiting for a response, walked away. Her light reddish hair, Carlos noted, was like a bright beacon burning into his heart over the dull, dark sea of others mingling in the hotel lobby.

My new adventure away from home, he thought, talking the two levels of the carved mahogany staircase up to his second-floor room... *Travelling to New York in search of employment. Perhaps a better life than one in California... is definitely looking up.*

Carlos and Dolly had opposing polarized natures; two fiery magnets strongly attracted to one another. While he was shy, reticent, and thoughtfully careful, she was dynamic, decisive, frank, and self-sufficient. On that night, which Carlos would later consider their first date, they dined in The Columbia Hotel's French Country Room.

"This hotel," Dolly explained while they pursued their menus, "was built in 1892 by Frank Ecock and his wife. It's now operated by their son."

Carlos smiled his acknowledgement and appreciation of the little tidbits of history she offered about Phoenixville. It was obvious she was trying to convince him to stay in town, claiming New York would just swallow Carlos whole.

"Where are you from?" she asked, delicately spooning vichyssoise away from the rim of the china soup bowl before taking a small sip.

"My parents... are from Mexico. But I was born in San Diego."

Dolly smiled, raising the spoon to her mouth.

"How fascinating," she said. "And what will take you to New York. I mean, what do you, will you *do*?"

Carlos was dazzled by her sparkling sapphire blue eyes. He could barely concentrate on the perfectly seared filet mignon on the hand-painted Limoges plate before him.

"I am a cobbler, a shoemaker."

"Oh?"

"I want to design footwear. Make my own creations and sell them in New York."

"And you think we here in Phoenixville don't need shoeing?"

"Well, I've only been in town for one day. Not long enough to know one way or the other..."

"And are you good at it? Making shoes, I mean?"

"I think so." Carlos took a small bite of his tender, rare steak, wondering how much the succulent meal was going to cost him. He had a limited amount of cash in his wallet that, with his trip costing more than he had expected so far, was quickly dwindling. *Woman like Dolly are expensive,* he thought. *Is she really what she portends to be? A virtuous woman?*

"Phoenixville is, granted, a small borough, but welcomes newcomers with open arms," Dolly was saying. Carlos instantly assumed that she had meant hers. He flushed slightly. "I mean," she quickly added, "we don't have a shoemaker in town. At least, not a really good one..."

"It doesn't strike me as being a very, um, sophisticated town," he stated.

He had hopes for the glitz and glamour of the much larger city of New York, with its newly built shops and large department stores. Macy's and Lord & Taylor's on Fifth Avenue; Alexander Turney Stewart's "Mable Palace" built in 1862 of iron and steel featuring large sheets of plate glass through which ornate displays of all sorts of sundry goods could be seen. Carlos Martinez had seen pictures of them and lithographs in California newspapers. He had visions of his own creations dancing on display in New York's upscale store windows. And then flying off the shelves; bought quicker than he could make them.

He wanted to cater to the wealthier classes and their families. Not those of steel workers and iron mongers.

"Oh, you'd be surprised," Dolly said. "We have our own seamstress shop just two doors down from here. They mimic the latest styles in their own creations. London, Paris, New York. Women come from miles around – not just from Phoenixville – just to refresh their seasonal wardrobes... I am sure they would be thrilled to have a shoemaker here that would also cater to their, ah, more expensive needs."

"I'll contemplate that," he promised, still wondering how he, having yet to make and sell a single pair of his own designer footwear, was going to cover the cost of their meal.

"And we've cotton mills and a large leather tannery..."

Carlos was distracted by the large, elderly bald man wearing a flowing paisley-patterned caftan and red beaded velvet slippers drifting toward their table. He was not used to, had never seen a man so opulently and openly attired in what he first though was a woman's dress.

"... for your raw resources, supplies," Dolly was saying. "I am sure that would fit your needs..." She paused, following Carlos' stare. "Ah, Carmine, there you are." She waved him over, then raised her cheek to be kissed by the man in the caftan.

"Dolly, Dolly, my dear," Carmine said, flicking a lock of imaginary hair from his eyes. "How wonderful to see you.

Everything is to your liking, I assume?" He glanced suspiciously at Carlos.

"Yes, yes. Everything is fine. Scrumptiously delicious as usual," she paused. "Ah, Carmine, this is my friend Carlos..."

"... Mendez Martinez," Carlos said, half standing up and bowing slightly.

"Carmine Pickering, at your service." He limply shook Carlos' proffered hand then quickly took his back.

"Carmine is the maître d' here," Dolly offered. "We're old buddies, are we not, dear Pickles?"

"Oh, please... You know how much I hate that name."

"Sorry... "

"Forgiven. Now, if you'll excuse me..." Carmine did not wait for Dolly to reply. Instead, he took a quick glance at Carlos' slightly fraying color and his tad-too-tight serge suit, then swiftly swished away to take care of three gentlemen at the entrance waiting to be seated. "Dinner, by the way," he called back over his brightly colored shoulder, "is on the house!"

"He is a bit different, but harmless. And rarely so generous," Dolly commented. "He used to be quite the miserly curmudgeon, but then he spent a few years in New Orleans running a restaurant with his, er, a partner."

"His... partner? In business?"

"Well, yes. In both, actually." She frowned at the confused look on Carlos' face. "You know.... Men who, um, love other men."

Her dinner partner turned beet red.

"I have heard, but..."

"Well, anyway," she said, glossing over his obvious embarrassment. "When he died... the partner, I mean... Carmine came back here to take up where he left off, so to speak. He's greatly changed... More mellow. And very generous..." She paused, noticing the look of chagrin on Carlos face. "Don't let that bother you... I mean, it doesn't, does it?"

"I am not sure," he frowned. Phoenixville, he was discovering in his brief time in the village, was certainly a diverse mixture of very interesting, and sometimes strange people. To change the subject he asked, "Do you dine here often?" Relieved that he wouldn't be embarrassed in front of Dolly because of lack of funds.

"Oh, why. Yes, I do. I also live here."

"What?"

"I rent a room on the third floor..."

"But isn't that a bit, um, unseemly? A woman such as yourself... I mean... you aren't, aren't..." Trying always to be a gentleman, Carlos couldn't finish his sentence.

"A woman of the night?" When Carlos flushed pink again, she continued. "No, no, of course not. But, we do have one or two of those in town... And we certainly don't need another. But, if you're interested, I am sure I could introduce..."

"No, no, that is quite all right." Stanley said, trying to change the subject yet again. "Then... Why? Here? In a hotel. Have you no family to live with?"

"No, not anymore," she said slowly, lapsing into a thick Irish brogue. "My mother died when I was fifteen or so. My father perished in the Peddler's Row fire on Holy Thursday. April 3, 1890."

"I am so sorry to hear that. My sincere condolences, Dolly."

"*Ah, lá den sórt sin brónach...*"

"*Perdóname*? Excuse me? I don't understand..."

"Oh, sorry." Dolly paused. "It's Gaelic... I often lapse into it when emotional... It means, 'It was such a sad day'."

Carlos nodded his understanding. "I do the same thing sometimes. Forget where I am and speak Spanish." They both shyly smiled. "So, now you are alone," he whispered, tempted to take her hand in his. Instead, he wiped his fingers on his linen napkin.

JUNE J. MCINERNEY

"Yes, I have no home now and no wish to go back to Ireland, where we're from... So, I got a job here as a scullery maid, working with Carmine in the kitchen. Then a year or so ago, got a job as a clerk in the accounting offices of the steel mill."

"Yes, but you're still alone. I am *preocupado*... concerned..."

"Thank you, Carlos, but you needn't worry yourself about me. I am perfectly fine..." She delicately sliced into the remains of the cordon bleu in front of her. Then, as if interviewing him for a position at the mill, asked, "Now, what about you? Tell me more about yourself."

Carlos leaned back in his chair, relieved that the very beautiful lady dining with him was not "*una prostitute* – that kind of woman".

He spent the rest of their meal relating his own story. How his parents – his mother nearly three months pregnant – had fled across the border to settle in San Diego. His schooling by the Catholic monks at the large old adobe abbey built by Spanish missionaries. His two-year apprenticeship while still in school under Juan Kadiz, learning how to tool coarse leather into soft sandals for women and sturdy shoes for men. His dream of opening his own shop one day.

"Hopefully, in New York," he excitedly concluded. "My train leaves tomorrow afternoon... I've a cousin, Manuel, waiting for me in Harlem..."

Dolly quickly put down her dessert fork, trying to hide her obvious disappointment. She refrained from saying else, lest she dim his enthusiasm for his future plans. *Yet, it would be nice if he could stay...* She thought. *One more day so we could get to know one another better..."*

Carlos frowned at her look of displeasure, not quite understanding what it meant. *Is it me? The meal? I am enjoying it. Why, suddenly, is she not?*

"Oh, I didn't mean," he tried to explain. "I mean... I mean... *Querido señor, ¿qué he dicho o hecho mal?* Is there something wrong?

"Oh, no. No. Please," Dolly said, looking up. "It's just, um. Well, it's been a long day at work, that's all." She sighed, then tried to smile.

Carlos learned back, regarding the very pretty – and smart – lady sitting across the table from him. He was very much attracted to her and, it seemed obvious, she was taking a liking to her. It would be shame, *Sería una lástima* – such a shame – if he left first thing in the morning, as planned, without another opportunity to be with her.

"One more day won't matter," he thought out loud.

"What?"

"I mean... Manuel is a very patient man and I am sure he wouldn't mind me being a day or two late."

"What are you saying, Carlos?"

"I'd like to stay another day."

"Only if you want to," Dolly said, a wane smile replacing her frown.

"Oh, but I think I do, Dolly. Want to." He realized he really couldn't bear to leave this amazingly beautiful, yet smart self-sufficient woman. At least, not just yet. "Then, it is settled," he said. "One more day won't really matter to... to him." To himself, he thought, *But perhaps one more day will matter... to us.* "I'll telegraph my cousin in the morning... assuming there is a telegraph office in this small... er... "

"Borough. It's called a Borough. And yes, we do have one. In the post office on Main Street."

"Yes, well... tomorrow is Saturday. Perhaps I could call upon you in the morning and you could show me where the post office is... Then..."

"I only have the afternoon off, Carlos. But I'll show you after work... and then... we could stroll around Reeves Park or take a trolly ride..."

"We'll do both!" Carlos grinned. "You could show me the sights of Phoenixville..." He paused. "Then I could leave on Sunday..."

But Carlos did not leave on Sunday. Nor the next day or the following week. As a matter of fact, he never even made it to New York. Instead, he stayed in the small steel town nestled in the foothills of the Appalachian Mountains, renting a very small apartment above Kettleman's General Store and Food Emporium, where he worked during the day and designed his shoes in his rooms at night.

And while it was evident that some residents of the community frowned upon a "mixed arrangement" between a taller winsome Irish lass and a tad shorter, but very handsome, Mexican *hombre,* Carlos undauntedly continued to court Dolly. They fended off jeers as they walked arm-in-arm down the street together and ignored the nervous whispering behind their backs when they dined in local restaurants. It was not unheard of in Phoenixville for people of different ethnic backgrounds to wed. It just didn't meet with everyone's approval.

Yet, despite objections from both friends and strangers, Carlos Méndez Martinez married Dolores Marie Murphy three months after they met. Just as he thought he would during the very first instant he saw her strolling across the lobby of the Columbia Hotel. Just as he had inwardly promised himself he was going to do the very first night they had dined together.

They made, a small article in *The Daily Republican* noted the afternoon after their wedding in St. Anne's Church, "a most interesting, yet handsome couple".

Carlos wasted no time in setting up shop on the north side of Bridge Street, two doors up from the Colonial Theater. As he told Dolly, "I may be a shoemaker by trade, but I am a designer in my heart." He began crafting, selling, and repairing, as he called them, foot apparel. Boots, shoes, slippers of all shapes, styles, and sizes for men, women, and children of all ages. With his shy, retiring, unassuming personality coupled with his skilled craftsmanship, he fit right into the local culture and mores of the small borough. His business, needless to say, was an instant success.

Within two years, Carlos had shod just about every other man, woman, and child in Phoenixville – and beyond. Thrifty to a fault, he had also amassed a small fortune which enabled him to build a three-story frame and stucco house in the more affluent section of The Hill on the north side of French Creek. The house on Vanderslice Street, now the home of Carlos and Dolly Martinez was large enough to accommodate their small family. Their son, Stanley, was born eleven months after their wedding. Even with the three of them occupying the home, there was still plenty of room to accommodate any of Carlos' extended families – from both San Diego and New York – should they decide to visit. He regularly wrote back to his parents, telling the about his good fortune. But his parents did not follow him east as they had originally planned to join him in his newly found largesse. They were too ensconced in San Diego where they ran their own successful bodega.

The Martinez family life in the small, close-knit community of Phoenixville was relatively quiet, except when, two years after Stanley's birth, Carlos had decided to volunteer to fight in the Spanish-American War.

"Because of my Latin background," he explained to his distraught wife, "I must defend the honor of my Cuban brothers."

"Not those of Spain?" Dolly had asked, shooing their toddling son away from the large fronds of the bushy green fern that threatened to engulf one corner of their large, ornately decorated parlor.

"My parents were from Mexico, remember," Carlos stated proudly, pronouncing the name of his native country as "Meh-he-co." He gazed longingly into his wife's sparkling blue eyes. "Their country, too, fought for independence from Spain and the oppression of dictators. You will agree, *mi querida*, I cannot sit back and watch another Latin country fighting for the same independence. I must go and help."

"But who will watch the shop while you are gone?" Dolly queried. "… Surely not me, with a toddler and… another on the way. I am an accountant, not a shoemaker, remember?"

Carlos, taken off guard, sat up straight. He had been perfectly content to have one child, a son to carry on his name. But another *bambino* on the way?

"Are you…?" he asked cautiously.

'Yes. At least four months. If not more. And this one feels… heavier, not a lively as young Stanley…"

"I had not noticed. Forgive me… but…" Then her husband smiled expansively. He rose from his seat in front of the large, stone fireplace in which a small coal fire smoldered against the chilly Spring air, crossed to her slipper chair, and hugged her.

"This is exceptional news," he said, kissing her on the forehead. "But it does not change my plans. I will arrange for Orrin Weathersby, my assistant manager, to take care of the business. He is imminently capable as well as a good cobbler. I will leave him new designs and patterns to follow… And there is enough foot apparel in stock to last throughout the summer. I shall be home by the end of the year."

Dolly sighed. "In time to meet our next child?" She reached up to caress her husband's cheek, dotted with black stubble, the beginning growth of a thin beard. "Promise to return in time?"

"I promise, *mi dulce. Te prometo.* I promise."

Within weeks of his safe return, their second child, a daughter, Rosalina Bridgette, was born. She was named, respectfully, after Carlos' and Dolly's mothers.

June 6-14, 1917

Stanley strolled into the bar of The Columbia Hotel, a favorite haunt of steel workers; puddlers, forgers, and pattern makers alike. It was where, a few nights after work and almost always after their Saturday afternoon pick-up baseball games in Reeves Park, that Stanley, Edmond, Campbell, Frank, and Hans met to hoist a few and trade jokes and stories in front of the fabled half-naked – or it is half-clad? – odalisques hand-painted on the large leaded mirror over the bar.

Edmond, Campbell, and Frank were already clutching half-full beer steins at the long, hand-carved mahogany bar. As soon as he pushed open the swinging saloon doors, his buddies began teasing Stanley about his "defection". They proudly waved their newly printed and signed draft cards at him; the ink on them barely dry.

"We are all going to be in uniform soon. Marching off to do battle," Edmond chortled, raising his foaming glass. "Give us a toast to your bonnie brave boys," he commanded others in the bar. "Unlike my good friend, Stanley, here, we are all signed up to fight for you. Aren't you all proud of that? Of us?"

A few cheers rose from the small crowd as Edmond took a deep bow. "Thank you one and all," he smiled and then took a healthy quaff. He glanced at Stanley who was gritting his teeth while waiting at the bar for a double-whiskey. Edmond's mocking boasts had grated on his nerves.

"Where's Hans?" Stanley asked, looking around the barroom. Although the most silent member of their cadre of friends,

Stanley enjoyed Hans' company. In his own quiet way, his presence was stalwartly reassuring, almost comforting. In many ways, he often enjoyed Hans more than he did Edmond, with all his braggadocio and daring bravado.

Stanley struggled to describe how he felt about the sturdy, thickset young man who had immigrated ten years ago with his family from Wittenberg, Germany. His father to work as a master puddler at one of the seven large furnaces at the steel mill; Hans, when he was old enough, became, as Stanley, did a pattern maker. He had always thought Hans as steadier; yes, surer about himself, than himself or even Edmond... but in a quiet, understated, reserved, purposeful sort of way.

"Don't know," Edmond shook his head. "Haven't seen him since we signed up this afternoon." He raised his empty stein up to Jeremy, the shy, retiring bartender, and signaled for yet another refill.

"I heard he went straight home to tell his folks," Frank stated. Like Hans' father, he had become a master puddler, but not before he worked for several years as Mr. Gruber's "rabble boy". "Proud as punch, he was." He frowned. "I'd hate to think I'd be killing them Krauts and one of them was related to Hans. I'd feel really bad about that."

"No, you wouldn't," Edmond said, slapping Frank on the back. "Krauts is Krauts, ya know. They're all alike... Dirty Germans."

"Better not let Hans hear you say that," Campbell whispered to Edmond, turning toward the swinging doors through which Hans had just stepped.

"Already did," Hans said slowly in a thick Germanic accent. He walked just as slowly up to Edmond and slammed his fist into his face. Edmond fell back against the bar, dropping his newly-filled beer stein onto the floor where it shattered and splayed cold beer onto Campbell's feet.

"I thought we were friends," Hans frowned, spitting at Edmond. He then nodded at Stanley as if to say, "that will show him" and walked back out of the bar.

"Son of a bitch," Edmond mumbled through his hands, trying to stem the blood spewing from his nose dribbling onto the chest of his denim work shirt.

"Told ya," Frank smirked.

"Shut up," Edmond sneered. "That does it... I can't wait to be called up and kill those dirty... sons of..."

Stanley put a hand on Edmond's shoulder. "Calm down, Eddie... He's our friend, remember? Regardless of his nationality... He's our friend..."

Edmond shrugged Stanley's hand away. "Not anymore," he muffled. "Not anymore."

"But, Eddie..."

"Leave me alone, you coward. Just leave me the hell alone."

Fine, Stanley thought, hurt and dismayed by his best friend's comments. *Let Eddie be called up... Let him be harnessed to a war machine... and then destroyed by it. I wash my hands of it... all of it. All of them. And him.*

Sullen, angry, and unhappy with himself, Stanley quickly finished his drink in three gulps, wished his buddies – soon, he suspected, to be his late, former buddies – a tepid "Good luck." and left.

Maybe, if he was fast enough, he could catch up with Hans and apologize for Edmond's cruel insensitivity.

He had tried once before to sign up for military service. And had failed. Perhaps, this time, he would be accepted.

A month after President Woodrow Wilson had declared war against the Central Powers, and a few days after the Selective Service Act was passed and signed into law in May, Lenny had finally realized there was something, something bad going on outside of his own internal world. *A war. A bigly war.* Determined to prove himself, he shambled into the armory of Company D on the corner of Main and Hall Streets. He wanted to, for once and for all, show his father that he really wasn't an imbecile. That he was, in fact, smart. Very smart. And brave. Very brave. Perhaps joining the National Guard infantry unit would convince him.

Captain Joe O'Donnell wasted no time in telling the strapping cumbersome young man that he was "both mentally and physically unfit for duty". The 6th Pennsylvania Infantry National Guard unit had just a week before been mustered into federal service and he and his men had a lot to do in preparation. He had no time, he sighed, for fools like the one standing in front of him.

"You have to tell me," Lenny demanded. "What's dat mean? Unfit?"

"Your reputation seems to have preceded you," the sergeant said gently, trying to persuade him to leave. Born in Phoenixville, O'Donnell, as did every other native resident, knew of the Lochmann family and Lenny's reputation as some would call an "ignorant thug". "Besides, you're in the wrong place," he said, trying to persuade Lenny to leave.

"What's dat mean?" Lenny demanded again.

"Registration does not take place until June fifth. At Borough Hall. And, as I said, you're not fit to serve, son."

"I want to serve. I want to fight."

"No. Sorry, but… there really isn't anything that I can do…"

Lenny angrily picked up a stack of papers on the desk and threw them at Captain O'Donnell.

"You sign me up, Mr. Armyman! You sign me up or I'll have my father…"

'He's probably not eligible, either." The Captain was becoming increasingly impatient. "You have to leave now, Lenny. Leave quietly, or I'll have my sergeant here physically escort you out." He nodded to the armed guard standing at the door of his office.

Lenny scowled, grabbed some of the papers and ripped them to shreds. As O'Donnell calmly watched, he threw pieces on the floor, spat on then, then shambled out the door.

"I be back!" he shouted. "I be back!"

"Dear Lord," the sergeant said. "If we accept guys like that and put 'em at the front, he'd get us all killed."

Two weeks later, on the date registration for the draft as to begin, Lenny Lochmann marched up the Borough Hall steps. He stopped when he saw Edmond Hope, Campbell Wheatley, Hans Gruber, and Frank LaBronsky exit through the double-doors, laughing together at a private joke as they passed him on their way down.

Edmond stopped and turned.

"Hey, Lenny," he said. "You gonna try and sign up?"

"Yep. You in?"

"Yep," Edmond mimicked. "I am. We all are."

"Me, too. I gonna be in, too!"

"Bet a buck they don't take you," Edmond sneered. He had hated Lenny Lochmann ever since fourth grade when he had grabbed his sister's crotch during recess. Edmond had pulled him off Rebecca, who was crying and screaming in fear, and kicked Lenny between his own legs.

"You touch her again... you come near her ever again... I'll do worse!" he had threatened, seething in anger as Lenny limped away in agony.

He had not forgotten the incident. Nor had Lenny.

"Shut up, Edmond! They take me. I know. For sure. Believe me!"

"And how, you lump of sh..."

"Shut up, Edmond," Frank nudged his friend aside. 'Leave him alone.

"I know Captain. Captain O'Donnell. He said... come back when fit," Lenny slapped his barreled chest. "I fit, now. I gonna be in. I gonna fight!"

"Sure, Lenny. Anything you say," Edmond smiled condescendingly, then, when Lenny sneered at him, walked away.

Lenny impatiently waited in line at the Selective Service registration desk. When it was his turn, he threw a crumpled-up letter at the sergeant.

The sergeant, who just happened to be Captain O'Donnell's assistant, remembered Lenny from his visit at the armory. He frowned when he saw the lummox standing in front of his desk. *Not you again.*

"My father says you have to take me!" Lenny yelled. "It says so in letter."

'Look, son. The Captain told you before, you're not fit for duty."

"I just saw him. He's in. I want in, too!"

"Who?"

"Edmond Hope. You signed up Edmond Hope. Now you sign me." Lenny thumped his chest. "I am fit, like him. More fit. See?" He flexed his biceps. "Stronger, even."

"Who? What... No, sorry. I can't do that..."

"You can! Read my letter!"

The sergeant impatiently shook his head, unfolding the letter and trying to decipher the smudged pencil scratching. "Hmm, you say your father wrote this?" the sergeant asked, looking up."

"I helped. He has broken English."

The sergeant looked at the name block printed on the bottom. "Your father registered?"

"No. Too old."

"No, son. Not for the service... But, your father is German. Right?"

"I German, too."

"Well, the law says, and I quote, 'Any persons of Germanic heritage or descent living in America must register with the United States government'."

"What dat mean?"

"It means that if your father hasn't declared he is German and has sworn that he doesn't support the Central Powers..."

Lenny started to stare beyond the sergeant, a blank look clouding his face.

"I don't think he understands what you're saying, Sarge," one of the men waiting in line stated.

"Yeah. Too many big words," another smirked.

'Look, Lenny," the sergeant said, snapping his fingers to get his attention. "You're not eligible to join the military. Okay? Now, go home."

"I not want home. I want war." Lenny straightened his shoulders and attempted a clumsy salute. "I want to make Poppa proud. I not imbecile. I soldier."

Well, you can't. And you are. And you certainly won't be, the officer thought. He carefully folded up the letter and forced it into Lenny's hand. "Go home and tell your father he has to register..."

Lenny scowled, but did not move. The sergeant nodded to two armed soldiers standing nearby. He shook his head, frowning as they escorted Lenny out the door.

Dejected once again, Lenny stood in the middle of the sidewalk in front of Borough Hall, his fists clutched at his sides, angry tears streaming down his face. He wanted to make his father proud. He wanted to be a soldier and show him that he was all grown up and not "so stupid" as his father constantly said he was.

Now, unable to join the army, he couldn't even do that.

He couldn't do anything.

He ripped up the letter he had attempted to forge with his father's signature, threw it into the gutter, stomped on it, then lumbered east toward Starr Street.

No one accepts me, he thought. *But I change all that. I make them accept me. I have plans. I make them sorry. Make them all sorry.*

The next morning on his way to work, Lenny looked for and found a clump of dog feces thoughtlessly left on the sidewalk of Morgan Street. He folded it in a large piece of wax paper he had brought for the purpose, then stuffed it into the pocket of his red and green plaid woolen jacket. He did so not out of civic pride, but because he had a plan; a use for the turd.

That afternoon, the employees on the second floor of the knitting mill couldn't figure why the cloakroom reeked of dog shit. They told Lenny, the janitor, about it. He crookedly smiled and said, "I take care of it."

On his way home, Lenny walked up South Main Street to Reeves Park. In the opposite direction of Scape Level, his journey home would add at least another mile or so to his already long walk back to the old stone house. He knew his father wouldn't care and, he reasoned, he had a few dimes jingling in his pants pocket. After his errand, he'd take the trolley across the low bridge and walk home from the last stop at the corner of High and Dayton.

Stanley and his buddies were playing baseball on the small diamond field close to Starr Street. Just as Lenny knew they would be. Just as they always did every Saturday afternoon after their morning shift at work. Edmond and Stanley were pitted against Campbell and Frank. Hans was on the mound; his turn to be the designated pitcher for both teams.

Lenny walked slowly along the wooden fence backstop behind home plate and then along the path to Third Avenue where he sat on a park bench. Watching the men play. Watching. Waiting for the right moment. Silently wishing that he could play, too.

But what he was about to do would be, he reasoned, a lot more fun.

Edmond hit a high lob into right field. Campbell, in mid-field, started running toward it, stretching out his gloved hand to catch the ball before it landed. But he wasn't quick enough. The ball bounced and skittered across the grass to where Lenny was now standing.

He picked up the ball, scuffed with many hours of being batted around, and pulled the wad of wax paper from his jacket pocket.

"Hey, Lenny!" Stanley shouted from behind home plate. "Throw the ball back!" It was the first time Stanley had acknowledged his presence or called his name in a long while. It felt good. Like maybe he was liked and accepted after all.

Maybe he let me play now, Lenny thought.

"Magic word!" Lenny shouted back, rubbing the ball vigorously with the paper.

Campbell walked over to Lenny, his gloved hand still outstretched. "C'mon, Lenny, give me the ball."

"No, not you. Stanley! Stanley ask me!"

'Yeah, but I'm right here."

"Go! Away!" Lenny spit into Campbell's glove, then yelled at Stanley again. "Magic! Word, Stanley! Magic word!"

Stanley sauntered up the first base line toward him. Edmond walked a few paces behind. His hands clenched, just in case.

"Back off, Campbell," Stanley said. "I'll handle this."

"But... "

"Yeah, you hear Stanley him," Lenny sneered, shoving Campbell away. "Back off."

"Hey, don't you go pushing me, you big lummox..."

"Who you call lummox? Smarty-pants boy?" Lenny shoved Campbell again.

Edmund stepped in front of Campbell, his fists raised in front of his face, taunting Lenny to do the same. "C'mon, dipshit, c'mon... "You want an excuse to fight?"

"You needn't fight for me, Edmond," Campbell said. "I can handle myself..."

"He's much bigger than you, Cam..." Edmond waved his fists in front of Lenny's face. "About my size. He'd cream you..."

Lenny glared at Edmond. He would like nothing better than to punch him in the face. With the dirty ball now clasped in his raised hand. But the ball was meant for Stanley.

"Okay, okay. Edmond... back off." Stanley said softly, trying to intervene. He turned to Lenny, "It's okay, Lenny." He paused, wishing his friend would stepped away. "Okay. Magic word, Lenny. Please. Please, give me the ball."

"Not yet," Lenny said, swinging at Edmond. Edmond quickly parried the blow, then punched Lenny in the gut. Lenny doubled over.

"Lenny... you, um, okay?" Stanley asked, putting his hand on Lenny's shoulder.

"I no like people..." Lenny whined. "I no like people telling me what to do..." He looked up at Edmond with fire in his eyes. "Especially you! Why you always mean to me?"

"I'm not mean to you, Lenny. Just teaching you a lesson..." Edmond stated, raising his fists again.

"Need no lessons!"

Stanley waved Edmond away.

"We just want my ball back. Okay?" he said. He stretched out his hand. "C'mon, Lenny. Just give me the ball."

"Sure," Lenny said. "Sure." Wincing, he gingerly fingered the ball, trying not to get his fingers and palm covered in the dog filth. He stood up and flicked the smeared ball high up into the air. "Here, catch, Stanley!" Stanley reached up and nimbly caught the ball in his bare hands.

"What the... hell!?!!" he exclaimed, dropping the ball. "Lenny, you dumb fuck!"

Lenny guffawed and turned.

"I no dumb fuck!" he screamed and then punched Stanley in the nose. "You dumb fuck!"

Edmond instantly went to Stanley's side, blood profusely dribbling down his chin. "Stan... you okay?"

"I... think so..."

"Tilt your head back," Edmond said, handing him his handkerchief He turned to confront Lenny, but he had already backed away and was now awkwardly running down Third Avenue toward Main.

"You dumb fuck!" Lenny yelled back. "All dumb fucks!!"

"Why you..." Edmond turned to run after Lenny.

"Let him go, Eddie," Stanley winced in pain, his voice muffled through the blood-stained bandana. "He's not worth it..."

Lenny maniacally laughed as he ran. When he reached Main, he stopped at the corner, put his beefy hands on his knees, panting heavily, his face flushed a deep red. He didn't hear the clanging bell of the trolley as it ground to a halt.

"Hey, buddy, you ridin' or what?" the conductor shouted.

"Yeah... I... coming," Lenny huffed, trying to get the words out. "Coming." He managed to climb aboard the streetcar, fish a dime out of his pants pocket, and pay the conductor. His hand, he saw, was still smeared. He grimaced again, then wiped his palm across the front of his jacket, leaving a small streak of dark brown feces on his chest. Almost as if it was a badge of honor.

"You okay, son?" the conductor frowned at him, pulling the overhead bell cord twice to signal that the streetcar was about to move.

Lenny stared blankly at the conductor. An almost angelic smile spread across his very red ruddy face. He was about to say how much he had desperately wanted to be noticed; to be accepted. And that one of his plans to be noticed and accepted had almost worked. Almost.

He had hoped Stanley would have laughed at his prank instead of yelling. *And had stopped that stupid Edmond from attacking me... hitting me... Maybe, if he did...*

"Maybe, if ask nicely, I stay to play baseball with them," Lenny said aloud. "I good at baseball. Very, very good. Best player in town. Best in county. The world. I the best."

He looked up for approval.

But not one of the riders took notice of of him. Lenny was just another rider. And the conductor had already walked to the front of the trolley and didn't hear a single word the large man-child had said. For the rest of the ride to the Northside, Lenny stared blankly out the window

Stanley stared in disgust at his hand, streaked with drying dog shit. Then he looked at the bloody handkerchief. He couldn't believe what Lenny had done. Nor could he even fathom why.

"What did I... ever do to him?" he asked, now sitting on the ground.

"Do you think it's broken?" Edmond asked

"Not sure... Sure hurts like hell, though."

"Keep your head tilted back," Campbell advised. "Maybe we should... ah, get you to the hospital?"

Stanley waved his hand. "No, no... I'll be fine."

"Yeah, sure," Edmond said, kneeling beside his friend. "Hey, is that what I think it is?"

"If it looks like... shit...?" Campbell asked.

"Yeah, it is," Stanley shook his head. "Dog shit, I hope... I'd hate to think..."

"And to think..." Campbell sighed, "to think we signed up... to go to war to defend the rights of guys like him..."

"I don't think the war is about defending our rights," Stanley muffled, his head tilted back. He waited for someone to start arguing with him. When his buddies just stood around, without saying anything, he asked, "What do we do about Lenny?"

"Well, he did do a shitty thing," Edmond tried to laugh. "Maybe we ought to show him that that's not acceptable. Not, at least, in this fair town. Whaddya say?"

"Well, I don't think we can do anything ourselves..." Frank said. "He's bigger than all of us... put together. I think this is a matter for the police."

Stanley clutched his nose and tilted his head back and groaned again.

"We can't let him get away with his nasty prank. Punching Stanley... and everything," Campbell reiterated. He paused. "Maybe the Constable could arrest him?"

"For punching out Stanley? Is that a crime?"

"Maybe not. But assault and battery is..."

"But you pushed him first," Stanley mumbled through the handkerchief "Technically speaking... He just retaliated."

"Technically, but who's to know that?" Frank suggested.

"Not me," Edmond and Campbell said in unison.

Hans, who had remained on the mound, wisely avoiding the fray, shrugged his shoulders and shook his head.

"Well, if nothing else, Ol' Tucker could reprimand Lenny," Stanley moaned.

"Yeah, scare some shit into him," Edmond said repeating his joke. "Especially since it looks like Stanley is going to be out of commission for a while..."

Frank nodded. "Then it's decided. Once we get Stanley squared away, we all go together."

June 15-30, 1917

All four of them, assembled in front of the desk of the surprised Constable Luke Tucker, nervously fidgeted. They tried desperately to mask the fears and dread steadily growing in their hearts and minds about the future. But the welfare of their own comrade in arms was now more paramount in their minds.

"Now, please tell me," Tucker asked, flipping open a small notebook on his desk and drawing a short pencil stub from his pocket. He touched the lead tip of the pencil to his tongue, then poised it over a blank page of the notepad. "What is this all about?"

Twelve years ago, with the help of the now quite elderly Faith Little, the then manager of The Columba Hotel, he had cracked the case of the murdered maid. Her body had been found slumped in a slipper chair in a second-floor room of the Columbia Hotel, strangled. An emerald and garnet necklace dangling from her outstretched hand. Since then, the small Borough of Phoenixville had not had a crime as sensational. The Constable was getting on in his own years and for once, just once, before he retired, he wanted to solve a major mystery.

Not that he wanted anything bad to happen in Phoenixville. But, still...

He looked at each one of the young men standing resolutely before him and sighed.

Probably here to file yet another annoyingly small complaint, he shrugged. *Probably nothing more important than that. It's once again just another typically boring day in the life of Luke Tucker...*

"Go ahead, tell me," he briskly asked again, his pencil poised. "What's happened?"

"You pull a stunt like that again..." he suggested an hour and half later to Lenny Lochmann in the parlor of the shabby stone house on Canal Street. The constable was standing in the middle of the room, afraid to sully his neatly pressed pants by sitting on one of the two filthy old brocade chairs facing away from an unlit fireplace. Despite the warm weather outside, he shivered in the cold inside.

Lenny was pouting, slumped on the sagging settee. His head bowed over his hands clasped tightly between his knees.

"... and you'll what?" Herman Lochmann asked gruffly in a thick German accent. He was visibly uncomfortable with an American police officer invading his home, especially when the reason was his imbecile of a son.

"We have laws in this community," Tucker said. "While slinging, um, dog..." He searched for the right word. "...stuff around isn't exactly a violation, still there is... assault and battery."

"I do nothing," Lenny said, looking at the floor. "I want play baseball with guys. They not let me."

"Where'd you get the... stuff, Lenny?"

"Off the street."

"See, officer? My son was just being mindful of this community. Need I remind you that..."

"You needn't remind me of anything, Mr. Lochmann," the policeman said. "Lenny disrespected two of his friends... And started a fight."

"I... no friends," Lenny mumbled to his feet. He was ashamed in front of his father and afraid of the policeman who, he was sure, had come to arrest him and his father just for being German.

"Whatever," Tucker said, turning to Lenny. "Listen, son. You did a vile act on public property. You assaulted two people on that property. That's something... quite nasty. Totally unacceptable and uncalled-for behavior. Do you understand that?"

"They start it," Lenny said raising his head in defiance, his eyes squinted, his mouth puckered.

"No, you first hit Edmond Hope, then punched Stanley without provocation. You broke his nose. I could arrest and incarcerate you for that. Assault and battery," he repeated. "Two counts. Do you even know or understand what that means, Lenny?" Tucker thought if he couldn't reason with Lenny, perhaps he could intimidate him into telling the truth.

"So what?"

"Tell the truth, Leonard," his father commanded. "What really happened?!"

"I told you. Edmond and Campbell come after me. All I want... play baseball. Stanley say no."

"There, officer. Lenny told you it was self-defense.

Detective Tucker sighed. "I doubt it," he muttered to himself. He knew from the sworn statements he had taken earlier that afternoon that Lenny was lying. Unabashedly lying. *Or,* he thought, *perhaps, maybe he really doesn't know the difference between truth and lies...*

"I think you're not telling the truth," Tucker said softly, trying another tack. "Why are you lying?"

"Oh, *un Himmels willen,* officer," Lenny's father erupted in his thick accent. There's a war on it Europe... *Tausande...*Thousands are being killed! Don't you have anything better to do than to come here and harass my son?"

"Well, I..." Tucker stammered, taken aback. He was not entirely sure what side Herman Lochmann was routing for – the Central Powers or the Triple Entente. He, unfortunately, suspected the former. If so, he certainly did not want to say anything to further upset the man.

Especially if, as he had presumed, Lochmann had not – yet – registered with the authorities as a German. He frowned, trying to remember if he had seen the name "Lochmann" on the list the government had sent him.

"Well, I. You. Nothing! Now, if you don't have a warrant and are finished badgering Lenny here, then I suggest that you leave my, our home. At once!"

"Fine," Tucker said. "Consider this a warning. If it happens again, I'm afraid I'm going to have to arrest him."

"*Mein Gott! Wirst du es aufgeben!* You come after my son again and... *und...*" He wanted to shout, *and I'll shoot you!* But refrained. Threatening an American police officer when he was sure his son had broken the law, would not be prudent. His silence was a stretch. Hermann Lochmann, most of his acquaintances knew was, like his son, far from cautious or discreet. Instead, he opened the broken front door and pointed. "Just... just go! Go!"

Almost as if on cue, Duke and Harry, pulling Phoenix № 1's red Holloway combination chemical and hose wagon, galloped down the narrow dirt road. Urged on by Nathan White, they were on their way to a large brush fire at the far end of Scape Level.

Lenny could hear the driver yelling encouragement to the large Percherons; the loud thudding of their massive hooves against the hard-packed clay; the shouts of "Get out of the way! Coming through! Get out of the way!" from the four firemen clinging to the wagon's sides. Lenny straightened up, a broad grin spreading on his face. He jumped up to peer out the front window to watch the fire wagon race by.

I wanna do that, he thought, remembering as a little boy telling his mother he "was going to be a fireman". She told him in her wispy German, *"Nein! Zu gefährlich."* When he had heard that Stanley had just volunteered to join the company, a pang of jealousy gripped his chest. *What was dangerous,* as his mother had said, *about fighting fires? If cowardly Stanley had volunteered? He not brave enough to hold a dirty baseball. Or fight in Reeves Park.* Lenny sneered his scorn and returned to the couch, waiting for this father to come back into the parlor.

Hermann Lochmann chased the Constable out of the house and down the stone steps. He watched as the shiny red police car followed the fire wagon up the road. He unclenched his fists, but was still scowling.

He hadn't meant for the fire, set just an hour or so ago, to be detected so soon. He had explained to Lenny that decaying shrubbery and the gnarled trucks of old trees needed to be burnt away. But that wasn't the real reason for the German setting the fire. He was hoping that the charred remains of the dying vegetation would conceal what had been buried in the field. Angry that his plan was being thwarted, he walked back into the house and slammed the broken front door behind him.

"You told him off, Papa. You really told him off," Lenny tried to smile. "And the nasty man went away." Did this mean his father really did care for him?

His father cuffed him on the side of the head and told him to wipe *"dieses dumme Grinsen – that silly smirk off your face."*

"But…"

"Dummes Dummkopf. Imbecile. You do anything else to cause the police to come here again and you'll get more than just a slap in the face. Now, *raus heir*! Get the hell out of my sight."

As Lenny cowered out into the hallway and slinked up the steps, his father frowned and shook his head, mumbling. *"Dere dumme Arsch.* That stupid, stupid dumb ass."

In his room, fondling the wooden cigar box, Lenny surmised it was Stanley and Edmond who had sic'd the police on him. If it wasn't for them, his father wouldn't have yelled at him. He hated it when his father yelled at him and called him an imbecile. It made him all the more irate.

Angry at his father. Angry at himself. Angry at Stanley.

"I glad I broke his nose!" Lenny screamed. *"Froh! Isn bin froh!"*

"Shut up, *Dummkopf!*" his father called up the stairs.

Lenny pursed his lips together and took a shiny small rectangular tin box from inside the large wooden one. He lovingly fingered the insignia etched on one side, underscored by a German phrase. He nervously slid the box open and closed it. Over and over he opened and closed the box. Each time counting the small, Sulphur-tipped wooden sticks inside. Again, and again, and again as an idea slowly began forming in his mind

I show them, he thought. *Now I have a real reason... I show them. Everyone. Even my father. I have another plan. I use it soon. If I not fight fires, I start them. Then, maybe, maybe they stop ignoring me. And accept me.*

After a hurried and harassed supper with his father of cold bratwurst and watery sauerkraut, Lenny hastily ran up the stairs to fetch his plaid jacket, the small tin box that he had kept hidden in the wooden cigar box, and the baseball bat he had stolen from the Meadow's Toy and Sporting Goods Emporium on South Main. He had first wanted to take it to one of Stanley's and Edmond's pickup games. Hoping they'd let him play. But when he was rebuffed, he decided it had a better use than swatting balls.

While his father attended services at the Central Lutheran Church, he had spent the morning sanding the shiny lacquer off its surface. Ash, he knew, did not burn as quickly as pine, of which some other baseball bats were made. No, this one would perfectly suit his purposes.

He crept down the stairs, carefully opening and closing the broken front door behind him as quietly as he could. The last thing he wanted to do was to awaken his father snoring on the frayed settee in the front room. He hastened down the dusty dirt Scape Level road that the Borough had named Canal Street. Once part of the Schuylkill Navigation System, it had long since been filled in. He slinked in the shadows, careful not to be seen as he lumbered his way into town.

Lenny, once again, had a plan, a new plan to carry out.

57

He didn't want to be deterred in the errand he was determined to make.

It was a guard who spotted the flames licking out of a top floor window of one of the long buildings of the Battery C Artillery Company armory complex just off Morgan on Buchanan Street.

"Fire! Fire!" he shouted.

Luckily, the complex was virtually empty. Those National Guard members that had been there for week-end maneuvers and training had already left to continue their civilian lives. Only the guard, a sentry, two groomsmen, and a stable hand were left to stand guard and take care of the horses that pulled the cannon-laden caissons.

One of the groomsmen continued the yelling – "Fire! Fire! Water! Buckets! Get the buckets!"—while the other raced to red call box #35 on the corner of Washington and Buchanan Streets. He tripped the lever and then hastened back to the barracks.

Running back through the training field gates, he didn't see the hefty man lurking in the shadow of the concrete wall wielding an unlit torch. Its blunt end was heavily charred. The man stared, almost mesmerized, at the flames jetting into the cloudless summer sky. But the sentry, racing from his post patrolling the field's perimeter to help man the bucket line, did.

"You there!" he shouted. "Halt! Halt!" He unslung his Arisaka Type 38 rifle from his shoulder and aimed it at the intruder. "Halt or I shoot!" But he knew he couldn't fire without proper cause or reason. Lurking was not a crime and the skulker was outside the military compound, not in it. Still, it was his duty to guard and protect his fellow artillerymen and their horses.

He inched closer to the shadowy figure, now slowly slouching away, his back turned, his broad shoulders slumped. The sentry took note of the long greasy coppery-blond hair, the frayed dusty denim blue work shirt, and the Louisville Slugger, with its burnt tip, dangling loosely from his hand.

The man did not stop as he slouched further away, hoping that at best he wouldn't be caught or, at the very worst, shot.

"Who are you?!" the guard yelled repeatedly. "Who are you?!" But his shouts were lost in the blasts of the Gamewell Diaphone fire horn and the thunder of hoof beats advancing down Buchanan. Distracted, he turned toward the sound and lurched backward out of the fire wagon's way as it barreled through the gates, cutting off his line of sight.

It gave the intruder just enough time to lumber his way across lower Bridge and disappear behind the main building of the Perseverance Mill. When the wagon had passed into the compound, the man was gone.

The guard could only shrug and later report it to Captain Whittaker.

By the time Nat White had driven Duke and Harry pulling the large combination steam-powered water pumper, hose, and ladder into the artillery training grounds, the top half of the wooden barracks had been destroyed. The lower floors were quickly being consumed. Sparks flew across the roofs of other buildings, threatening the stables and the ten horses within.

"Get them out!" Fire Chief Mendowski shouted to two of the six other firemen who had arrived pulling the hose wagon. "You!" he said, pointing to the groomsmen. "You can help! Put rags, towels, burlap bags... anything... over their eyes so they can't see the flames."

"No need," the stable hand tried to explain. "Like your guys," he said pointing to the two fire horses quietly and patiently standing by. "They're trained to be calm during commotion. Loud cannon fire and all that..."

"Doesn't matter!" the Fire Chief yelled, cutting him off. "Do as I say! Get them out! Hurry!"

It took two hours to contain the fire. By the time it was over, a barracks building was completely destroyed. But the other artillery buildings, including the stables, except for a small portion of its roof, had been saved.

Fire call 3-5. 9:30 P.M. Battery C Artillery barracks, Fire Chief Mendowski carefully noted in the fire house records. *Injuries: 0. Damage to one building: extensive.* Under *Cause:* he wrote, *Unknown.*

The Chief sat back in his chair, wiping traces of soot and ash from his forehead and cheeks. "The men in the unit are meticulous," he said aloud. "No way was this an accident."

"You thinking it's arson?" Nat White asked, strolling into Mendowski's office.

"Not sure. Maybe."

"Fire was too hot... Burned too fast to be spontaneous combustion. Had to have been artificially set, then aided. Somehow."

"Yeah, I guess. Thank goodness it didn't spread to the arsenal. We'd all be blown to smithereens." He paused, then asked, "So, your best guess? One of the soldiers? The guard?"

"No, I doubt it. A member of the unit won't do that. But... Why? Why do you ask?" He paused. Mendowski trusted Nat implicitly. He had been the paid driver for the company for more than ten years and had occasionally served as the Chief's prime confidant. "What are you thinking?"

"Could be nothing. Could be something... but while I was tending to Duke and Harry I heard one of the guards tell Captain Whitaker there was some hefty man – not a fireman or a member of the artillery unit – lurking about. I couldn't hear much over all the commotion, but the guard did say he had coppery-blond hair and was carrying what looked like a torch." He paused. "Then the Captain said something about a spy in the area..."

"A spy? What spy? A German spy? Here in Phoenixville? You can't be serious."

"Read about it in *The Daily Republican.* Didn't think much of it at the time... But now..." the wizened driver explained. "He was supposed to be a German émigré living in Wyoming for a while before offering his 'services' to the 'motherland'... Said a few residents thought they saw a German loitering around the Artillery grounds a few times."

"I missed that article. When was this?"

Nat rubbed a stubbly cheek in thought. "About a week or so ago... Gave a detailed description, too. Tall, hefty. Scowling ruddy face. Coppery-blond hair. Very much like the guy the guard described..."

"Could be anybody," Mendowski observed. "Probably not from around here."

"Oh, I don't know 'bout that... The Lochmanns up at Scape Level are German. And they both have copper-blond hair. Could be one of them."

"Lots of Germans in Phoenixville, Nat," he sighed. "We can't rashly jump to conclusions based upon hearsay. But I'll let Constable Tucker know what you've told me. Thanks."

"I could be wrong. Perhaps we'll never know. Probably just an accident," White yawned. "Well, Duke and Harry are settled in for the night. And it's getting late... I have to be back here bright and early. So... Guess I'll head out, then... Unless..."

"I'm fine."

"Well, then, have a good night, Chief."

"Yeah, you, too." He frowned, wondering if the artillery unit fire had, indeed, been "just an accident".

There was something about it that just didn't add up. And the fact that one of the Lochmanns might be a spy... *No, that isn't possible*. He knew Lenny was not bright enough to set a raging fire and then linger about the scene to watch the stables burn down. And his father was too cautious and reticent to be loitering in town, especially at the scene of what might be a crime of arson.

Chief Mendowski closed the fire record book, capped his pen, and stood up.

What does all of this mean?

But he was too tired that night to think about it any longer. *I'll figure it out in the morning.*

July **1917**

During the first week of June, British forces had begun Operation Hush, in the hopes of securing the coast of Belgium. As the days and weeks wore on, it became a futile attempt. Morale of the infantry was almost at its lowest until the early morning of June 7th when battle commenced to capture the Messines Bridge in West Flanders.

It was the second attempt to do so and General Sir Hebert Plumer was determined not only to wrest the bridge from the Germans, but to control the Messines-Wysthaete Ridge, as well. During so would augur the beginning of the end of the war. Especially with the advent of the arrival of the American Expeditionary Forces to the European Theatre of Operations.

Campbell Moore Wheatley, the tall, fair-haired distant descendant of Charles Moore Wheatley, like Edmond Hope and others in their small cadre, could not wait to be called up... to be sent to battle. He had been raised to believe in "truth, justice, and the American way". To defend them at all costs. Yet, in his mind, the United States had taken far too long to enter the war now raging across Belgium, France, Italy, and throughout Burma. Especially since, as he put it, *we're supposed to be staunch allies of England, the home of many of our ancestors.*

When he read in *The Daily Republican* that the first battle to recapture the Messines Bridge had failed and that English forces were about to overrun, it was all he could do to refrain from resigning his position as manager of Shop #6 and swim across the Atlantic Ocean to join in the fray. After all, it was not only the values and history that he had to defend, but the values and history that his father had instilled into him, as well.

It seemed that Campbell had more fealty to British soil than his family's adopted land.

That evening, when he returned to his modest lodgings on the second floor of a small twin house on Morgan Street, Campbell found a letter addressed to him slipped under his door. It was postmarked "Washington, D.C."

It was his ticket to war.

He had less than a week to settle his affairs and report for duty at Camp Dix in Wrightstown, New Jersey.

When, two weeks later, on June 25th, the first contingent of American troops landed in France, Private Campbell Wheatley, Infantryman First Class, was one of them.

"What happened to you?" Chief Mendowski asked when Stanley arrived at the fire house for his first evening of training. A thick gauze bandage was taped across his nose and his left eye was encircled with black and blue bruising.

"Broke my nose," Stanley tried to smile, handing him a large manila envelope with his completed application and two letters of recommendation. One from a former high school teacher; the other from his foreman at the foundry. His father had flat-out refused to consider the matter.

"How the hell...?"

"The teacher was easy... I was a good student. But Mr. Brundidge was not pleased. He's afraid I'd be called away from work when a fire alarm sounds..."

"I meant your nose."

"Got into a bit of a scrape last Saturday with..."

"Don't tell me. A big bruiser gave you the shiner?"

"Yeah. Lenny Lochmann."

The Chief shrugged his wide shoulders. "Figures," he sighed. "That kid is no good. Provoke him?"

"Something like that."

"How bad?"

"What?"

"Your nose. How bad?"

"Bad enough. Broken, actually. But that doesn't mean..."

"Sure as hell. You can't fight fires with a busted nose. Nor anything else, for that matter..."

Stanley shrugged his shoulders. "But I can try," he said.

"You can stay. Listen in. Watch the training exercises," Mendowski said and then changed the subject. "I spoke with Captain O'Donnell..."

"Who?"

"Officer in charge of Selective Service enlistment... Local fella, nice guy. About being deferred..."

Stanley's hopes rose. "And I will be, right?"

The Chief frowned and said, "No, afraid not. Not volunteer firemen. Only policemen. And men in jobs vital to the safety of our country..."

"But isn't being a fireman...?"

"The law doesn't see it that way. You'll have to register anyway."

"I can't... "

"You have to. O'Donnell knows about you and if you don't... well, they'll come after you." He paused. "If you don't, you'd be breaking the law. I can't have someone in the company who is illegal."

Stanley sighed. The last thing he wanted to do was give into the whims of what he thought was arbitrary and unfair authority. Yet, he didn't want to break the law just to satisfy his own, however selfish, desires. His parents had taught him better than that. And the thing he most wanted was to be a member of Phoenix Hose, Hook & Ladder Co., No. 1.

"Um, that nose of yours," the Chief smiled wanly, "I doubt they'll take you. Register, get deferred. Then serve here as a proper member of our company."

Stanley bowed his head.

"Think about it, son," the Chief said, then walked away. He waved the three other new recruits to join him by the hose wagon.

Stanley slowly followed and stood with them. Two were a few years or so younger than he; the other was probably in his mid to late forties. Robert "Doc" Kimshaw was the proprietor of the small pharmacy next to the bank on South Main Street.

"Too old to be a soldier," he nodded to Stanley. "But young enough to do my part... You?"

"I, um... Well," he stammered, trying to figure out how to explain he didn't believe in war or fighting in one and that his hopes of being deferred as a fireman had been dashed.

Chief Mendowski interrupted his thoughts.

"Okay, men, listen up. Our first three weeks are demonstrations – the basics of firefighting, learning the fire alarm codes, manning the pumpers, hooking up to hydrants, and learning to clean the equipment." He patted the hose wagon. "Tonight, you're going to learn how to clean, dry, oil, and then roll the hoses."

It was the longest speech Stanley had ever heard him say.

"Most important pieces of equipment..." the Fire Chief stated the obvious. "You can't effectively or efficiently fight fires without them."

On the second week of their arrival in France, two regiments of the American Expeditionary Forces force-marched their way to the small Belgian city of Ypres in West Flanders. They were to partake in the third battle of Ypres, also called the Battle of Passchendaele, which would claim over 300,000 lives and result in the capture of over 24,000 prisoners.

Campbell Moore Wheatley, used to no more than dirty denim work clothes and a hot bath after each day's 12-hour shift managing Shop #6 for the Phoenix Bridge Company, found himself being ordered by a crusty younger officer less educated then he to slog through mud for two days under a hot sun and in the total darkness of cold night rains. He waded through ankle-deep slime toward the sound of unseen cannons. The air rippled with random bullets whistling by. Gun fire split his eardrums and shattered what was left of his otherwise calm nerves.

He yearned for sleep. Every taut muscle in his body ached from carrying a 35-pound knapsack. He fervently wished he had never signed up to go to war. As he plodded on, he day-dreamed that he was back home in his small sitting room on Morgan Street, Phoenixville, PA, USA reading his cherished novels. Or, even, back at work. Both were infinitely more preferable than being stuck in the muck and mire of devastation in what later would become known as no-man's-land in the darkest regions of the Belgian countryside.

More than anything else, he longed to be with his buddies.

Drinking ale at The Columbia Hotel; playing baseball in Reeves Park; chiding Stanley Martinez for refusing to sign up. *He was right, he was right, he was right. But, I wonder... Had Stanley been caught avoiding the draft? In prison?* He through of his crew back in Shop #6. *Without his nagging, were they at work on time? Did they get the rivets and the trusses just right?*

And he thought of Edmond Hope's sister, Rebecca, with her long, ash-blond hair and sparkling blue eyes. And the way she had flirtatiously looked at him when she walked down Gay Street that autumn afternoon. Her arm loosely draped through the crook of a friend's elbow. The two girls giggling together over a whispered joke. His first date with her, sitting in the back of the Colonial Theatre watching a vaudeville act in which a supposed comedienne spouted inane jokes neither he nor Rebecca understood.

If I can last until Christmas – that's when they said the war will be over... and I'll be back over there, rather than over here. Home. Finally. If only I can last until then, he thought, finally falling into one of the many shallow trenches the British army had hastily dug along the border. *If I could only get some rest... Things will look better in the morning,* he thought, falling into a deep, welcomed, but troubled sleep.

At five a.m. sharp, the hard, wet leather toe of the sergeant's boot kicked him wide awake.

"Rise and shine, lazy-assed soldier! In case you're wondering, this ain't no picnic... Get up! Get your rifle! The nasty Krauts are advancing and we're going to repel them."

Campbell scrambled for his rifle, his helmet, and hefted the heavy knapsack he had used as a make-shift pillow upon his shoulder. Only to have it ripped off by the sergeant.

"You come back for it later," the gruff officer said, tossing Campbell's pack onto a pile of others heaped against a dirt wall of the trench. "You're off to kill a few Jerrys and carrying your pack will only drag you down. Get a move on, then... Hut!"

"But, my clothes... my rations... my books..."

"What?! You brought books to war?" the sergeant sneered. "What the hell did you think this would be? A class in college?" He turned to other soldiers mustering toward the trench wall. "This brain brought books to war... But, now, ain't he the idiot?"

"I only thought..."

"Listen to him. He 'thought'!"

A few of the other members of the squadron laughed. Others turned away, afraid to cross their immediate commander. They had admired Infantryman First Class Campbell for his forethought having books in his pack. Not that he'd have time to read them, but, still...

"You ain't here to think, soldier," the sergeant said, kicking Campbell's leg. "C'mon fancy pants. You're here to fight. Not to read. Now, get a move on and climb up over that wall... With the rest of your buddies."

Campbell had just enough time to urinate in a corner against a few broken wooden slats before climbing over the top. He glanced back at his abandoned knapsack – all of his worldly goods. *Who would take care of them... If?* With a sigh of regret, he shouldered is rifle and hoisted himself up and over the dirt wall and into enemy territory.

Prodded by the unrelenting Sergeant, Campbell dashed into the onslaught of enemy fire, hell bent on, hopefully, running through it to the other side. Perhaps, he hoped, to safety.

Oh, how I miss my buddies, he had thought, running forward, randomly firing his own rifle. *What if I kill someone? Someone's son? Father? Lover? What if they kill me?*

He didn't see the stray bullet that pierced through his thin tin helmet and thence through his skull. How could he have? He had been avoiding stepping on the bodies of fallen members of his unit, trying to keep pace with the sergeant running full-tilt ahead of him. He had been dodging bullets whizzing past him, each sounding vaguely familiar, like a baseball hit hard zipping toward him in center field... when he was suddenly, needlessly, hit.

I have to get through this, he told himself, falling to his knees, then, starting to lose consciousness, he finally sprawled upon his back in the deep filth and muck of war. His advancing comrades ran around and over him, ignoring his pleas for help.

Don't leave me here in the outfield, he tried to say. *Please, don't leave me. Don't leave me here to die.*

His last thoughts were of Stanley's adamant refusal at the big white doors to go inside and sign up for the Selective Service and of Rebecca's laughing, shining eyes.

He was right. She was right... I just want to go home.

Campbell's body, it was later reported, was never found.

Little did Lenny know that by punching Stanley and thus breaking his nose, he actually did him a favor.

Emboldened by the Fire Chief's stern suggestion that he register, Stanley Mendez Martinez once again stood on the steps of the Borough Hall. Once again, he faced the double-wide white doors. He took a deep breath, held it for a few seconds, slowly exhaled, and then went in.

After he carefully filled out the twelve-question registration form and stood in line for a half-hour, he found himself in front of Captain O'Donnell.

"You Stanley Martinez?" he asked.

"Yes, sir," Stanley said, wondering why the officer had asked him the obvious. "Just like it says on the form."

"Don't get smart with me, Martinez."

"Sorry, but…."

"Height? Eye color?" He looked up. "Yeah, you got hair…" He paused, then frowned. "What did you do to your face?"

"Got punched out…"

"Yeah? You sure you didn't walk into a wall on purpose to get out of the draft?"

"No." Stanley slowly shook his head. His face ached when he moved.

"Guys do that, you know."

"No, I don't…"

"Yeah? So, what happened to you?"

"I was hit by…. by a thug. Over a… a dirty baseball."

The Captain leaned back in his wooden chair, twiddling the Waterman fountain pen in his fingers. "Sounds like a stupid thing to fight over," he said.

"Yes, but, you see, Lenny… He, well, sullied up the ball and then… picked a fight."

"Lenny? A big lumbering German guy?"

"Yeah, that's him. Lenny Lochmann. You know him? Sir?"

O'Donnell sighed remembering the large illiterate young man yelling as he tried to register for the draft. He nodded.

Stanley tried to explain what had transpired that Saturday afternoon in Reeves Park. But the Captain interrupted him.

"How badly is your... nose broken? That is, I assume it's broken..."

"Yes, sir. Bad enough that Doctor Harrop says I might have difficulty breathing... sometimes. Something about a 'deviated septum' when it heals."

"Gonna be crooked then, huh?"

"I guess." Stanley touched the gauze bandage taped across his nose, then tenderly rubbed under the lid of his left eye, still half-shut with swelling."

"Eyesight affected?"

"Don't know yet, sir," Stanley said quietly. He tried to recall what the doctor had said about blunt force and sudden bruising of the sclera. "'The recovery of full former vision is usually rare' he told me.'"

"Then... this means you might not be able to serve. Actually, I do think it does mean deferment. If you could provide us with a letter from Doctor Harrop..."

"I can do that," Stanley said, almost too eagerly. A slight loss of vision and a crooked nose would be a very small price to pay for not having to risk losing his life in a meaningless war. And the nose will heal. Meaning he could still be a firefighter. "I can do that. Is tomorrow afternoon too soon?"

"Sure, son," O'Donnell said quietly. "I'll make a note on your card that you might be physically – medically unable to serve. And I'll file it right along with Lenny Lochmann's mental incapacity to be a good soldier."

Stanley nodded his thanks, but was a bit unnerved to be in the same category as Lenny. Unfit to serve.

"Don't thank me yet. It's up to the guys in Washington. You'll eventually get a letter... either way."

71

Stanley nodded again and left, hoping for the best, but fearing the worst.

Adjusting his military-issued khaki tie, the Captain wondered why it was that several of the young men of his hometown went to such great lengths, unlike him, to avoid serving their beloved country.

Edmond Hope and Stanley Martinez had been best friends ever since first grade. As they grew older, they shared an intense love of baseball, a fascination for the Wright Brothers' flying machine, a distinct love of horses and stray dogs, and were avid readers of the English penny-dreadfuls that could be purchased for a dime at Kettleman's General Store and Food Emporium.

Black Bess, the fictionalized adventures of Dick Turpin, England's famous highwayman, was Edmond's favorite. Each month, he'd covet the latest installment, vigorously acting out the various parts for Stanley as he read them aloud. Cutting the air above his head with an imaginary sword, shouting "Ya money or ya life!".

Stanley quickly learned at a very early age that Edmond delighted in and devoured all things adventurous and perilously dangerous. Which he, himself, found particularly frightening. Unlike Edmond, he favored the tamer dime novels based upon the works of Charles Dickens. He was particularly partial to *Great Expectations* and *Christmas Stories*; although, as he grew older, he found the fantasy world of Oz created by L. Frank Baum remarkably interesting.

As they grew into adulthood, the interests of the two boys began to diverge. Edmond became increasingly reckless, more and more throwing caution to the wind in just about all his endeavors. Searching for the ultimate thrill, the utmost excitement, seemed to be his topmost goal in life. Yet, under all his brash bravado, Stanley knew, lay a soft heart of gold.

Now, Stanley, on the other hand, morphed into the cautious dreamer. Like Edmond, he, too, was inwardly sensitive. But outward, he was not as brave. Far from it. He refused to take any chances unless he knew exactly what was going to happen to him.

Which was why Stanley had originally refused to register for the draft. He did not like circumstances he couldn't control nor understand; actions and events in life that he could not himself plan or anticipate. He tried many times to explain this to Edmond, who declared he was "more than just a bit excited" at the prospect of going to war.

His recklessness and disregard for safety is going to get him killed, Stanley thought as he silently listened to Edmond constantly bragging for the past few weeks in the barroom of the Columbia Hotel. And he knew, then, after he had refused to register and then stood quietly glaring at his childhood buddy, sipping his scotch at the bar, what Edmond probably thought of him. *I am now a weak-knee coward in his eyes.*

Ever since he had refused to sign up, the disagreement over Hans in the bar, and then the row with Lenny in the park, Stanley had felt a distinct distancing from Eddie. Almost as if he had a deep, dark secret he couldn't, wouldn't share; almost as if he was ashamed of – or even angry with his friend. Eddie even spent more time with Frank, now that Campbell had gone off to war, preferring LaBronsky's company over his. As if he now had more in common with Eddie than Stanley did.

Yet, despite their differences in attitudes and their surface opinions of one another – this latest rift, Stanley surmised, would soon blow over. He'd make sure of that – the two young men had been close friends in the past. Through thick and thin. Almost as if they were blood brothers. They had been too close for too long to let anything – save the tragedy of death – separate them.

And even if that ever did happen, Stanley often thought, *Edmond will always be my best buddy.*

Toward the middle of July, when his Saturday morning shift was finished, Stanley decided, *Enough of the semi-silent treatment*.

Besides, he wanted to tell Eddie about finally registering and that his medical deferment would probably come through. He wanted to share his progress in training to become a fireman. How he was about to become a full-fledged member of the company, just as soon as he learned how to quickly and efficiently set and stoke the flames under the steam pumper. He wanted to explain that when an alarm sounded, the fire had to be lit and blazing as the horse-drawn wagon sped to the scene, with steam rising, ready to spew water in high arcs when the wagon had reached the fire site.

Determined, Stanley finished his own clean-up chores in the pattern shop, then hoisted his well-worn canvas messenger bag containing a tin of half-eaten lunch, his leather baseball glove, and a few miscellaneous personal items over his shoulder. He purposefully marched across the street and walked into the open-hearth building of the iron works. Its seven massive furnaces ominously lined in a row like huge stalwart black gargoyles.

Edmond was just finishing sweeping slag away from his osn furnace, now slowly cooling down from the morning's work. He glanced over at Stanley, nodded slightly, then continued with what he was doing.

"Hey, Eddie! You wanna shag a few balls in Reeves Park?" Stanley asked, holding up a slender ash baseball bat and his old, beat-up flat leather fielding glove his father had given him on his sixth birthday.

"Don't have any balls..." Edmund muttered, continuing to sweep. Stanley wasn't sure if it was a statement or a slur. He shrugged the comment off.

"I got some money..." he said. "We could stop at Meadow's Toy and Sporting Goods Emporium to buy a couple... Whaddya say?"

Edmond looked at him askance. He was still slightly hurt by Stanley's apparent snub the night he and the gang had been celebrating registering for the draft. Especially since he had been punched in the face by Hans Gruber. He had hoped his best buddy would have sided with him. Be proud of him, rather than rejecting him for the past few weeks. Despite all his bravado, Edmond admitted he did have feelings that could easily be hurt. Especially by his closest and oldest friend.

Which was why, he had to admit to himself, he had distanced himself from Stanley.

"That is, if you're not still mad at me," Stanley said, watching Edmond shovel slag and pieces of cold iron onto a wheelbarrow. His young assistant, after scraping and shoveling ashes from the inside of the lukewarm furnace, pushed each load to a large pile at the end of furnace row. The refuse would be reused again to fuel the flames of the furnaces when they were fired up again on Monday morning.

"Nah. Why should I be? Just 'cause you mocked me a couple of times in front of our friends about me wanting to die a hero and you wanting to continue living your boring life?" Edmond smiled. "Nah. Why should I be mad?"

Stanley picked up another shovel and began to help his friend.

"We're pals – blood brothers, remember?" he said, stepping alongside Eddie to dump a shovelful of ashes and cold cinders into the wheelbarrow. He recalled their made-up secret ceremony behind the Church Street School, pricking each other's thumb and pressing them together to let their blood mingle and dry on their hands.

"Yeah, ever since we both began walking to school..."

"Well then... ya think a little thing like you going off to war would break up our friendship?"

"No, but... You were demeaning..."

"Oh, c'mon, Eddie. Don't be so sensitive. That's my job. Let's just clean this stuff up and get outta here. It's been a long week."

The weather that afternoon had turned warm and humid. After an hour or so furiously taking turns batting and catching balls on the baseball field under a hot sun and a cloudless sky, the two young men decided to take a break. They sauntered over to the monument of David Reeves and slouched against the wrought iron fence surrounding it.

Stanley looked up, recalling the history.

When the beloved owner of the Phoenix Iron Company died in 1871, many of the iron workers, touched by his gentility and fairness toward his employees, raised funds for the statue to be placed in the park whose lands he had generously donated to the Borough.

Edmond stretched out his long, lanky legs, leaned his head against the fence, and sighed.

"It's not the same without Campbell."

"Nor Frank and Hans. Where are they, by the way?"

"Don't know..." Edmond hedged.

"It's not like them to miss our regular Saturday games..."

"Listen, Stanley... I, um..." he hesitated. "How's your nose?"

Stanley rubbed the now slightly crooked side of it. "Still tender, but I can breathe without too much wheezing..."

"Well, that's good, right?"

"Sure... Eddie, is there something wrong?"

"Wrong, Nah. But... there is something I have to tell you..."

'You're marrying my sister?"

Since she was old enough to walk, Edmond had been in love with Stanley's younger sibling. Now nineteen, Rosalina Bridgette Martinez was a dark-eyed buxom beauty with long chestnut hair cascading down her back. When she turned sixteen, Edmond had asked both Stanley and his father permission to "call upon dear Rosie". He was certain that, in due time, they would be married.

But as he was about to explain to Stanley, his immediate plans for romance had changed

"No!" Edmond protested.

"What? Wait, I thought it was all settled..."

"Well, yes, but not yet, anyway..." Eddie softened. "At least... Not right away. There is something I have to do first ..."

'What is more important than marrying my sister?"

"Going to war."

"What? What are you talking about?"

"I just couldn't wait to be called up, Stan," Edmond grinned unconsciously.

Stanley looked askance at his friend.

"Yeah, we know that. But for the life of me... of you, I still don't understand why, Eddie. All the carnage... and the threat of death," he said, then paused. He reached up to catch the baseball he had tossed over his head. "But, then, you always were keen on the macabre."

"Black Bart and vicious vampires to the end," Edmond chuckled. "When my father said it would take at least three weeks or more for the selection process... I didn't believe him... But the last month, not knowing when. I just could no longer wait. And, well, Campbell got his letter rather quickly and left so suddenly..." He looked over at his friend, blithe and carefree, once again tossing the ball up.

"Well, so... did you get your letter?" Stanley asked.

"Not really... I mean... But I am going to war."

"Sure. You and all the other thousands of guys who signed up. But if you haven't been called up... Yet, then...." *We've been through all this,* he thought. *Why bring it up again? Eddie's probably destined to go to war. And I'm not. So... What?*

"Well, Stan, that's the thing." He paused, reaching up to catch the ball. "I, um, I enlisted."

"You what?!" Stanley slammed his fist into his glove. He arched his back and turned to face his life-long friend. "You're kidding, right? Tell me you're kidding."

"Listen to me, Stan," Eddie commanded. "I couldn't wait. Seriously. I joined up."

"Joined up? Joined what?!" Stanley sat up straighter, grabbing the ball from Edmond. He tightly clutched his glove and the ball in his lap. He anxiously waited, fearing what Eddie was about to say next.

"A few days ago, with Battery C," he tried to explain when Stanley looked at him blankly, a pained expression on his face. "You know... the Artillery unit of the National Guard... the armory is on Buchanan...

"I know what and where it is, Eddie. But... Why?"

"It's a swell unit. The closest thing to being in the Calvary... with horses to pull the cannons, blacksmiths to shoe them..."

"But it's just the National Guard," Stanley breathed a half-hearted sigh of relief. Not part of the regular military... Like Company D..."

"Happened back in April. They call it being 'Federalized'. And the Battery is going to be federalized... mustered into the regular army soon... and so, I thought..."

"But... that means you won't go overseas, right? Battery C will still remain part of the National Guard. Right?"

"Not for long. More and more artillery units are needed at the front. It's just a matter of time."

"But..."

"And Hans... ya ought to know... Hans joined up with me, too."

"Hans? Why... Hans? I thought you two are now sworn enemies."

"I, um, apologized for calling him a dumb Kraut and he, well... He, um, did too. In in his own way."

"So, now you two are the best of buddies? Fighting buddies? I am speechless..."

"So, he is. Or nearly..." Edmond laughed at his own joke. "That's where Hans is now... Training with them already. That's why he isn't here. And Frank..."

"Don't tell me he's..."

"Joined the Navy. He left for training facilities in Maryland last night. I would have thought they'd both have told you... but..."

"No, they didn't." Stanley was dejected and suddenly felt abandoned. All of his buddies... Gone off to war. And here he was left... a mere fireman. A trainee, at best.

He felt a pang of guilt.

But, he reasoned, at least he had finally registered and, just a day or so ago, did receive what he hoped was his letter of medical deferment. His broken nose and bruised eye, now almost healed, the letter would say, proved him not up to par for military service.

His scrap with Lenny Lochmann had saved the day.

But he wasn't yet about to tell his best friend that, as he had originally planned. Not yet, anyway. Not until he opened the confirming letter now stuffed under his socks in the top drawer of his bureau dresser.

"And... and I," Edmond continued, "have to report Monday. Bright and early... Can't wait." He waited for a response from Stanley. When none came, he sighed and stood up, eager to convince not only his friend, but, inwardly, himself.

"Imagine... me... Edmond Hope of Phoenixville. In uniform. Who'd a thought *that* would happen?" He looked up and gave the stony-faced David Reeves a smart, crisp salute. "I promise I'll do ya proud, sir."

Stanley shook his head in dismay. Why couldn't Eddie figure out a way to get out of, in his mind, a misguided commitment?

"Did you tell Rosalina yet?"

"No, I thought I'd do that tonight... I'm taking her to the Colonial. Harry Houdini, the master of escape is going to find his way out of a locked safe wrapped in heavy chains..."

"She won't be pleased," Stanley said, "she won't be pleased at all."

"Displeased at what? Seeing Houdini bust out of a safe? That's funny. You really don't know your sister very well, do you?"

Stanley winced at the truth. Then he, too, slowly stood up, brushing bits of dried grass and dead leaves from his light-weight tan denim work slacks.

"Well, since you gotta be at the armory first thing, I won't keep you."

"Nah, that's okay... Don't have to be there until Monday. I told you, you know. We still got time yet to bat a few more around." Edmond punched Stanley just below his shoulder.

"Oh... Yeah, but... Well, besides," Stanley hedged, rubbing his arm. He hated it when Edmond displayed any sort of physical force, even if it was in jest. "Mamma would have my head if I was late. You know, we have to be sitting at the dinner table on the weekends. Promptly at five. Family tradition..."

"But... I thought we'd, ya know, pop in the Mansion House... for a bite and a brewsky. Ya know, before I pick up Rosie... I mean, it is my last Saturday night as a civilian and all..."

"Sorry, pal," Stanley said quietly. "My parents are expecting me. I got to go. Besides, it's too hot anyway to play anymore." He tossed the ball back to Eddie, turned, and walked away, his shoulders sagging, down the park steps leading to the corner of Main and Second Avenue.

The squat one-story local library, built in 1902 with funds donated by Andrew Carnegie, sat stoically across the street. He recalled the many hours he and Edmond had spent there together doing research for the many English and History papers assigned to them by Mr. Ertell during high school.

Times have gone by, things have changed, he sadly mused as he hastened north on Main. He had a long walk home, along the broad street dotted with small shops and a church or two, over the High Bridge, and then left onto Vanderslice Street on his way to the Martinez's three-story brick Victorian. He had just enough time, he thought, to bathe and don his white linen summer suit and powder-blue silk tie.

And, unlike other times, he didn't want to be late.

Mamma is such a stickler for dressing up on Saturday nights and Sunday afternoons for dinner, he reflected as he half-trotted his way home. Not that he minded dressing up as a child, but it was getting to be a drag. Weekends were no longer casual. The now formal dinners – and getting ready for them – took up too much of his time. Saturday afternoon and all-day Sunday, except for mass at St. Mary's, his father's preferred church, was his only time off from work. Growing up, they were never his own to do what he wanted which, back then, as a child, he didn't mind. But now that he was an adult, he craved his own private time and space.

I should think about finding my own place...

He had been contemplating this for a while. Ever since he started his apprenticeship in Shop #3 the autumn after he had graduated from high school. After all, he was twenty-one.

Yet, he knew, if he did, he'd miss his mother's delicious home-cooked meals. But, then again, he could always stop in now and again on Sundays when his mother made her famous corned beef and cabbage. Crossing the low bridge, he could almost taste it, laced with white wine; the potatoes and cabbage topped with home-churned butter; the beef crowned with spicy French mustard. He'd bring her an assortment of Swiss chocolates – her favorite – from Henry Denfeld's confectionary store on the southeast corner of Bridge and South Main.

Stanley trudged up the hill, lost in his own thoughts, idly swinging the bat and glove slung over his shoulder.

I'm an adult now, he said to himself, repeating what his father was now often reminding him of. *Old enough to make my own decisions, however much my parents disagree.*

Now, with most of his childhood friends already enlisted or about to be called to war that they, and he, knew nothing about... They were certainly departing Phoenixville for parts unknown. And he, being hopefully deferred, would be left behind.

But I'm about to be a fireman. I am going to fight fires, he thought. *And that... I know something... a lot about.*

Opening the hinged gate to the tall picket fence surrounding his parents' front yard, he considered what would soon be his new-found status in the community.

Yes, well, he concluded, *perhaps it is time that I, too, venture toward new horizons.*

Stanley tried to explain to Carlos right after they had finished saying the customary grace around the maple-hewed table before eating, how exceptionally concerned he was that his buddy couldn't wait for the Selective Service to call him up, and had, instead, voluntarily joined Battery C.

"It was so rash of him," he said. "If only he could have told me beforehand, I might have... talked him out of it."

"Could you have?" Carlos asked, starting to carve the large roast resting before him on a hand-painted Wedgewood platter. A stack of matching Wedgewood dinner plates was on his left in front of his wife, a carafe of Madeira and four small crystal stemmed glasses on his right.

"He seemed disappointed that I was... disappointed in his decision. I think, sometimes, Eddie does things to impress me. Or for my approval."

'You're the best of friends," Dolly commented. "Of course, he'd want you to be proud of him..." She deftly put a dollop of scalloped potatoes onto his sister's plate right after Carlos put exactly three thin slices of medium-rate beef on it and then passed it over to her.

In total awe of her brother and more than just slightly afraid of their father, Rosalina had, all though her childhood, huddled away from the family in relative silence, watching rather than participating in the world around her. It seemed as if she had her own secret world of which, except, lately for the attentions of Edmond Hope, Carlos, Dolly, and Stanley had no place in or part of.

In return, her bother had stopped a long time ago trying to include his younger sister in his own life. Instead, he acknowledged Rosie's existence in the family, but refrained from going beyond the exchange of mere sibling pleasantries. There were only two things he really knew about her: Her great love of books, the only thing they shared. And, what he really couldn't quite understand – even if he was his best friend – her profound and, in his mind, inordinate affection for Edmond Hope.

They were such opposites. He with his reckless ways; she with her shy, demurring manner.

He cringed as Rosalina glared at him. He had just now not only betrayed his friend's trust, but his sister's, as well.

"Is that true, Stanley?" she asked, her eyes widening in fear at the thought of the news "He's enlisted?"

"Oh, I'm so sorry, Rosalina," Stanley said. "I didn't mean to blurt it out... But I am just... well, you know, upset."

"So am I. Did you not think I wouldn't be? Hearing it from you and not from him?"

"Well, I guess I didn't think..."

"That's just it, Stanley, you don't think. At least not about me. It's all about you, isn't it?"

"No, no... Rosalina... Rosie... I..."

"Do you even care?"

"Care?"

"About others? About me?"

"Rosalina Bridgette," Dolly spoke up. "I think that's just about enough..."

"Sure, Momma. Speak up for your son and not your own daughter."

"Rosalina," Carlos said quietly. "That is not what your mother meant."

Rosalina turned away from her father and looked at Dolly. "Momma?"

"I was simply referring to your lack of respect for your brother who mistakenly spoke out of turn... Thusly causing you a bit of pain..."

"A bit of pain? A bit?! My fiancé is going off to war without so much as a by-your-leave. Without telling... And you think I am in just a 'bit' of pain? Oh, Momma. how could you?"

It was the most emotional outburst from Rosalina the family had seen in months.

"But, that is just the point," Stanley interjected. "I am in pain, too. I should be proud of Eddie... We all should. But I'm hurt by his actions." He turned to his sister, nodding as he accepted his own laden plate from his mother. "I am proud of him... I think. But I am more afraid for him. You may be losing your fiancé, but I might also lose my best friend." He cut a bit of meat and speared it with his fork. "What else could I do?"

"There you go again," Rosalina sobbed. "Thinking and talking about yourself...."

"Perhaps... Instead of arguing, could we just all pray for Edmond?" Dolly offered. "And others of our village that are going off to war."

"Yeah," Stanley muttered, chewing thoughtfully. "As if an act of God could... would even stop it. And, to be honest, I am not sure if even He cares..."

"That is blasphemy," Dolly said, putting her knife and fork on her plate with a noisier than usual clang. She folded her hands under her chin in agitation. *"Mo náire thú.* Shame, my son. You should know better, Stanley Francis," she began to expound. "It says in the Bible that... having made us in his own image... He defends us against all evils..."

"Yeah, right," Stanley muttered. *I gotta get outta here,* he thought. *I love my parents... even my sister... but I need my own space. My own time... For myself.*

The air-pressured horn sounded loudly through the open window, abruptly cutting short Dolly's lecture, shattering what little remained of the family's quiet solitude.

Rosalina was the first to react when the loud blasts sounded from the Gamewell Diaphone horn atop the tower of the Phoenix Iron Company's Pipe Mill. She jumped up from the table, tipping over her wine glass onto Dolly's favorite white Chantilly lace tablecloth. She raced through the kitchen onto the open back porch overlooking French Creek and the Borough proper below.

Dolly frowned, dabbing the quickly spreading dark red blotch with her damask napkin. She considered following Rosalina, but then decided to leave her daughter to her own devices.

"What's gotten into her?" Stanley smirked. "It's only a fire alarm."

"She's upset," Carlos countered, "And rightly so."

Stanley ignored the comment and counted the regulated blasts of the Claxon horn. "Two... one... That's Bridge and Gay," he announced. "Four stores and the Colonial Theatre... Two... four... Bridge and Main. A bank and the offices of ..."

"... *The Daily Republican,*" Carlos finished his son's sentence. "You think?"

Stanley stood up and asked for permission to leave the table.

"I don't know, Papi. Could be anyone of them," he said, as the fire horn continued to blast and the bell atop the firehouse tower started to ring. "Including your store. That's near the Colonial... Whatever it is, it's gotta be a big one. They're ringing more than three alarms."

"The store, Papi!" Rosalina shouted from the porch. "I can see it from here. I can see the flames. It's our store!"

Carlos quickly stood up and raced to join his daughter.

"*Dios mío*! Dear God in Heaven!" he said, covering his eyes with his hands. "It can't be..."

"I am afraid it might be," his son said behind him. Stanley placed a comforting hand on his father's back. "Maybe... I should go and see..."

"*Si, si*... Yes. That is a good idea," Carlos said. "Take the car."

"No, Papi. There'd be too much traffic and no place to park."

One of his few pride and joys purchased four years ago, the American Underslung touring car manufactured by the American Motor Co. out of Indianapolis, Indiana, Carlos had vowed that he, no one else in the family, would be the only one to drive it. He had fallen in love with the sleek white body and the plush red leather seats, reminding him of the soft, exotic leather he used to manufacture shoes. While he seldom drove it into town, preferring to walk to work on most fair-weather days, it proved to be a worthy way for the family to jaunt out over the countryside on Sunday afternoons.

When he offered it to Stanley to find out where the fire might be, it was, in Stanley's eyes, a rare moment of implicit trust. But Stanley was more concerned about his father's livelihood than his trust in his son.

"It's best I go on foot," he said. "It's not that far if I scoot through the woods down the hill and cross the iron trestle bridge over French Creek behind the foundry."

"Be careful, son," Carlos said, giving Stanley a brief, but heartfelt hug. "Be safe."

Stanley raced into the front hall and donned the light canvas jacket he normally wore to work on chillier spring and fall days.. As Stanley raced down the back steps and into the woods behind the house, he felt as if he was already a full-fledged member of Phoenix № 1. Even with a just few weeks of intense training under his belt, he was keenly anxious to see what actual, real-time firefighting was all about

Even if it meant watching the family store go up in flames.

Racing down the hill, he followed the old Lenape "Indian foot path he often used to walk to work at the foundry. He brushed away low branches of prickly pine, ash, and white sycamore trees that slapped across his face and chest as he ran. He sensed, as he drew closer to the fire raging on Bridge Street, that he was being called to a much higher purpose than his friends Edmond, Hans, Campbell, and Frank merely marching off to war. He was grateful that he had the hope of being exempt from the draft. But the imminent danger to Martinez's Footwear Shoppe precluded his thoughts.

The promising letter from Washington in the sock drawer of his dresser, in the heat of upcoming events, would soon be ignored and forgotten.

Lenny watched in awe as the flames licked up into the night sky over Phoenixville. It was the best fire, he knew, the village had ever seen. The biggest and the best.

Better than Puddlers Row fire, he smiled to himself. *Way better. Very. Fairly. Muchly better.*

"I teach Stanley not send police after me," he scoffed.

He was standing across the street, watching the firemen hooking hoses up to the fire hydrant two doors up from the shoe store. An empty badly stained burlap bag stenciled PERSEVERANCE KNITTING Mill dangled from his left hand. He clutched his small cigar box tightly against his chest with the other.

His face looked almost euphoric as he watched the fire, which had started on the roof, burned through to the third floor and then begin to spread to the second. Smoke spewed through open windows as the blaze migrated, threatening to engulf another building next door.

He didn't see Stanley running up the street, passing Duke and Harry standing quietly by. But Stanley saw him.

"What happened, Lenny?" Stanley asked, slightly out of breath, as he crossed Bridge Street. "You see what happened?"

Lenny shuffled his feet, swinging the burlap bag. "Yeah," he said, "kinda. Yeah, I see the whole thing. Someone, someone started it..."

"You see who it was?"

Lenny gulped, not sure if he was being caught in a lie.

"Nah. No one..."

"No one?"

"No one... ya'd know."

"Well, maybe I might. Can you describe him?" Stanley pressed. A new trainee-member of the company, he was anxious to prove his worth. *Why not find out who started Papi's store on fire?*

'Someone's in there!" Mendowski shouted, pointing to a third-floor window. "Move the ladder... Over here!"

Stanley watched as the Chief climbed up the extended ladder. He saw the figure of a man reach through the opened window, pleading silently for help, then disappear back into a plume of smoke.

"That's Jerry Marfit!" Stanley exclaimed. 'He's a steelworker... welds bridge fittings and columns together. He and his wife rent the apartment from my father," he tried to explain to Lenny.

But Lenny wasn't listening.

"Monkey up tree," he said, intently watching as Fire Chief Mendowski, followed by another fireman, scaled the ladder.

"What?" Stanley frowned.

"Aim a hose up here!" the Fire Chief yelled again, almost to the top of the ladder. When a heavy stream of water shot through the window, he covered his nose and mouth with a bandana and climbed through it.

"Monkey in fire," Lenny said repeatedly. "Monkey in fire... Monkey in fire."

Stanley wasn't sure what to say. Or if he should say anything. Lenny, he knew, was not a normal person. An anomaly in the village... And, right now, it seemed that he was in his own world. His own alternate reality, impenetrable and unfathomable by anyone but himself.

Yet, he had seen who had started the fire...

"Lenny," Stanley asked gently, continuing to watch the window, hoping the Fire Chief would reappear. "Can you describe who set the fire?"

"Huh?" He clutched the cigar box harder against his chest, covering it with the burlap bag. "Not me! Not me!"

"Whatcha got there, Lenny?" Stanley asked even more gently. He knew how Lenny could be easily spooked. He rubbed a hand over his left eye, his sight now slightly blurred from the damage to its outer white covering.

"Nothing."

"Okay.... Then.... You said you saw who set the fire... Who?"

"Not me!" Lenny shouted.

"Didn't say it was."

"Wasn't me! You did! You did! You did!"

"No, Lenny. Calm down. You know that's not true..."

But as he did many times before, Lenny turned away and left. Lumbering up the street. Desperately clutching the box and the bag.

Ten minutes later, Fire Chief Mendowski burst out of the building's front door, carrying the unconscious Jerry Marfit across his shoulders. He lowered the unconscious steelworker onto the sidewalk.

Helen Marie, Marfit's dark-haired buxom wife, started to race down the street. She had been shopping for a late supper at Kettleman's General Food Emporium. When she saw her husband prone on the sidewalk and flames spewing from their windows, she dropped her canvas shopping bag and dropped to her knees beside her prone husband.

"Is he dead?" she asked.

Mendowski put his head against Marfit's chest.

"Um, I don't hear... anything. He's overcome by the smoke... Inhaled too much," the Fire Chief said, coughing and sputtering. His voice muffled through the red bandana. He yanked it off. "Get the ambulance!" he shouted in a harsh rasp.

"I just went for groceries," Helen Marie sobbed, watching as her purchases spilled over the sidewalk, the curb, and onto the street. A few apples rolled in front of Duke who lost no time scarfing one up.

"He was too heavy to carry so I dragged him most of the way down by the feet," the Chief tried to clarify. "His head bumped on each step, all the way down the stairs. I think I might have killed him, if inhaling the smoke hasn't already done him in."

Stanley, who had raced back across the street when he saw Mendowski emerge from the building carrying Margit, stood quietly next to Helen Marie.

"Who did this?" she demanded? "Who killed my husband!?!" She cradled his head in her lap as the Fire Chief, without rhyme or reason, began thumping on this chest.

"What are you doing?" Stanley asked.

"Not sure. Read it somewhere..."

Jerry Marfit suddenly opened his eyes. He glared up at his wife. "Hey, woman," he demanded. "Where's my goddamn supper?"

When the fire had been finally put out – the top two floors had been destroyed, but the bottom two had been saved, including his father's shoe shop – Stanley stayed on to help Chief Mendowski and the other six firemen. Even with his nose still healing, Stanley managed to help roll up the hoses and put them back onto the combination wagon.

He made it a point to also gather up Helen Marie Marfit's split groceries, salvaging what he could and putting them into her canvas bag.

"I am so sorry," he said. "We... my father will find you a place to live... Until the damage is repaired..." Stanley handed her the half-filled bag of groceries. "Here," he sighed. "You might need these..."

"Thank you," she mumbled, walking alongside her husband, holding his hand as he was carried on a stretcher to the horse-drawn ambulance.

"You're a..." she tried to smile, trying to find the right words. "You're a good person, Stanley Martinez," she said, handing him the rest of the recovered apples. "The horses deserve them," she grinned, and then climbed up into the back of the ambulance to sit beside her husband on the short drive to the emergency room.

Stanley loaded her two grocery bags next to her, then turned to Chief Mendowski.

"That was a brave thing you did... Dragging him out like that..."

"All in the line of duty."

"You mean, in the line of fire," Stanley quipped.

"Something like that."

Nat White climbed up onto the bench seat of the combination wagon, taking the proffered apples from Stanley.

'They'll be welcomed treats after they're unharnessed groomed...."

"Do you need help?"

"No... You go back to your father," Nat said. "I am sure he's going to be upset... The top half of his building destroyed like that... like this." He nodded to the top of the burnt structure, then clucked at Duke and Harry and drove away.

A disheveled firefighter emerged from the small alley alongside the Martinez property and walked up to Stanley and Fire Chief Mendowski.

'I found this on what's left of the roof," he said, handing the Fire Chief what looked like the handle of a wooden torch. The top was burnt through, but the handle, covered in ashes and soot, was finely carved, as if it had been honed to accommodate the beefy hand of its carrier. A small tuft of cotton lint clung to the base. The Chief inspected it carefully.

"You think it could be the arsonist's?" Stanley inquired.

"Why do you ask that, Martinez? Think this was arson?"

"Don't know..." he muttered, recalling the disturbing conversation he had had across the street with Lenny Lochmann. "Just a hunch."

"Please elaborate," he suggested watching the young recruit thoughtfully. *Stanley knows something,* the Chief thought. *Something he's not telling me.* "Listen, Martinez, if you know something..."

"Lenny Lochmann was across the street. Watching the fire. Mesmerized." Stanley blurted out. "He said he saw someone start the fire, but couldn't tell me who, yelling, 'Not me! Not me.' He talked about a monkey up a tree... And, he was carrying a burlap bag labelled..." He tried to remember.

"Labelled?"

"Perseverance Knitting Mills."

"Perseverance Knitting Mills? On lower Bridge? Near the Battery C complex and training grounds?"

"Yes, I think so."

"You think?"

Stanley faltered, took a deep breath, then said, "Yes, I am sure. Perseverance Knitting Mills. And there were pieces of thread and cotton lint on Lenny's jacket."

That's hard evidence to share with Constable Tucker, the Fire Chief thought. "Excellent observations, Martinez," he said, smiling at Stanley. "Anything else?"

"No, sir. Thank you."

"No. Thank you."

Stanley smiled weakly then turned away, walking back to where the other firemen were sweeping up the sidewalk. He had a suspicion, but wasn't ready to share it with anyone. Until he was certain. Then he, too, would consult Constable Tucker.

But one thing he as sure of was that he was impressed with Fire Chief Mendowski's heroism.

Don't think I could dive into a burning building like that, he thought, still forever cautious about most things in life.

However, it was the action of Fire Chief Mendowski that spurred Stanley's excitement about joining the force. Solidifying his resolve. Broken nose or not, and despite his hesitation to dive into the fray to save lives at the cost of his own, he was eager to be a valued member of the fire company.

More importantly, he couldn't wait to tell not only his parents, but Rebecca, whom he was casually dating off and on and her brother, Edmond Hope.

The following Monday night, Edmond Hope marched into the Martinez living room, bedecked in matching brownish tan military woolen tunic, jodhpurs, brown riding boots, and a wide-brimmed peaked hat. The red keystone-shaped insignia of the 28th "Keystone" Division, into which the Battery C Artillery unit – just recently Federalized – had been absorbed, was neatly sewn onto his left sleeve.

His aim, he later admitted – no pun intended – was not so much to show off his new uniform, but to impress Rosalina. He had been in love with her ever since she had started, well... *maturing*. And he had every intention of marrying her. Just not yet, as he had told Stanley. However, conquering and commanding her affections had been his most daring – and dangerous – challenge he had ever faced so far.

And now, he was about to partake in the ravages of war. In his mind, if that wouldn't impress her, nothing would.

"We got horses to pull the cannons, and blacksmiths, and just about anything else a horse-powered military needs," he exclaimed to the Martinez family. "Even fireman!" He slowly turned so that Stanley, his sister, and his parents could get the full effect of his new uniform. Then he struck a heroic pose and asked, "Well, do you like it? Are I not the handsome soldier?"

"More like the handsome fool," Stanley quipped. But, in truth, he wasn't kidding. Uniforms to him were just another sign of unnecessary militarization and controlling authority. He was beyond relief that he, himself, had been possibly deferred. Yet, the uniform of another kind of army – the company of the local fire department, proudly hung in his closet upstairs.

"Stanley!" his mother admonished. "Mind your manners. Edmond is offering his life for his country…"

"For our freedoms," his father continued. "Show some respect."

"And what about respect for my own life?" Stanley glowered. "Don't I get some credit for not laying it on the line for… for some… asshole dead prince overseas?"

"Hey, buddy," Edmond smiled, trying to defuse what would surely become yet another dispute. "We all have our opinions and stuff… But, well, this is what I want to, I have to do. You know?"

He reached for Rosalina's hand. She slipped it into his bent elbow. But she didn't look at him as admiringly and adoringly as he had wished.

"What's the matter, Rosie?" he asked.

"You could have told me," she sulked. "Instead of me hearing it first from Stan."

Edmond glared angrily at his friend. "I… I wanted to tell her."

"It just slipped out. Sorry."

Rosalina began to weep. "Stanley says you're going to be… going to be…"

"No, no, my sweet," Edmond whispered in her ear, still frowning. "It, I will be alright."

"You promise?"

"Just a little skirmish," he said. "Nothing to worry about. I promise." He turned to Stanley. "You know... right? While I have to do this... I'll be okay."

"No, I don't know. And you don't have to do anything you don't want to do. It wasn't really your choice, Eddie. They forced it on you."

"No. Remember, Stanley, I signed up. Volunteered."

"And we're proud of you for it," Carlos grinned, patting Edmond on the back. "You're already a hero. Fighting for our country and all..."

"Ah, Mr. Martinez. I am not over there yet, you know...." Edmond seemed to blush under his kepi hat. "But when I do go... I'll..."

"Probably be killed in the first salvo," Stanley whispered, remembering reading the recent "Local Casualties" listings in *The Daily Republican*. "Like Campbell. That is NOT what best buddies do! You are a flaming... idjit!"

Rosalina began to sob again. She turned her face away from her brother and buried it in the shoulder of Edmond's woolen tunic.

"Oh, for God's sake," Stanley said under his breath.

"Well, you could come with me and defend our country against the Archies. Or, as they call them in France, the Boches," Edmond said. "It isn't too late."

"What do you say, son?" Carlos asked. "Join Battery C? Along with Edmond?"

"I've probably been already deferred," Stanley stated, turning his back away and walking out of the room without providing any further explanation. "And even if I wasn't... I wouldn't," he scowled. "Not on your life. Certainly not on mine."

In the first week of August, the third of what would become a series of considerably sizable fires broke out just outside Phoenixville proper.

Both Fire Chief Mendowski and Constable Luke Tucker were beginning to believe that a serial arsonist was on the loose. Especially since the latest conflagration – the largest house fire in the Borough's recent history.

On Sunday afternoon, Paul and Mary Reeves were hosting an afternoon summer lawn party followed by dinner and dancing in the opulent second-floor ballroom of their estate.

Located off Nutt's Avenue on Main Street in the southern perimeter of Phoenixville proper, it was known as The Knoll House. Originally build in 1814 by Louis Wernwag, founder and manager of the Phoenix Nail Works, for the families of Benjamin and Cadawalder Morris, it was a model of Georgian-style perfection. Built entirely of stone locally quarried on the Rhoades Estate, it was the envy of the town, sporting massive three-foot thick walls; hand-carved mahogany and oak molding, mantels and staircases; and twenty-eight spacious rooms just recently updated and remodeled by the Reeves.

The Sunday elaborate festivities had been planned to celebrate completion of the renovations.

Disaster struck half-way through the evening meal.

Stanley was on call when the call came in. He had been, as usual, helping Nat Turner groom the horses, idly chatting about the latest developments oversees.

The Kerensky Offensive, the last Russian initiative in the war had failed and Alexander Kerensky became the new Minister-President of the Russian Provisional Government. German troops continued to pour into France and portions of the 28th Division, of which Edmond was supposedly to be a part, had already been shipped to Belgium.

"Things are heating up for our men... Any word from your buddy?" Nat asked, vigorously brushing Duke's flank while Stanley worked on his withers.

"Eddie? He's in training in Camp Hancock in Georgia," Stanley declared. "The whole artillery unit was shipped down a few days ago..."

He remembered Rosalina telling him after waving her boyfriend off to war how upset he was not being sent directly to the front lines. Stanley had shrugged and commented, "At least, for a few more months, he'll be safe."

"Seems to me, they've been trained enough," Nat commented. "Time to see some action..."

The fire bell suddenly rang a few seconds before the Diaphone atop the Pipe Mill sounded.

Nat unhooked Duke from the crossties and nodded as the large Percheron, his ears perked up as the sound of the alarm, automatically went to stand in front of the steam pumper. Harry, the smarter of the two horses, immediately unlatched his stall door and stood by his side. As Nat lowered their suspended harnesses from the ceiling, Stanley and two other "newbies" lit and stoked the fire underneath the boiler already filled with water.

This would be their first real fire after being sworn in as official, full-fledged members of the company. They were more excited than scared, even when, during training, Chief Mendowski had cautioned them about being "overly eager".

"Being too eager could easily get you killed," he had warned. "You lose focus and perspective. You've got to remain calm under any and all circumstances."

"Two... seven!" the Chief exclaimed, bolting out of his office. He grabbed one side of the hose wagon and, along with five other firefighters, began pulling it out of the firehouse. "This is going to be a long haul," he grunted. "Two-seven is Nutt's Avenue and Main Street."

"You come with me, son," Nat beckoned to Stanley.

Perched high on the bench seat alongside the driver, Stanley buttoned up his dark tan canvas tunic, then braced himself for the swift and perilous ride through the streets of Phoenixville.

Ten minutes earlier, Mark McGrady was returning from a jaunt with his horse through Valley Forge Memorial Park, trotting along the edge of Nutt's Avenue when the slender bay suddenly whinnied in alarm and then shied.

"What's the matter, Camille, ol' girl? It's okay... We've got to get home before the missus sets dinner on the table." He tried to urge the mare on, but she refused; instead shaking her head and sidestepping away from the road onto the front yard of a grey clapboard house. It was then that Mark saw the smoke billowing up from behind the copse of giant oaks.

"That's The Knoll House," he exclaimed. "C'mon, Camille, we've got to... do something!" He whipped the horse around and spurred her into a gallop. The nearest Gamewell manual call box, he knew, was on the corner of Main Street. Number 27, just a mile or so away.

He alit, pulled the lever, and then led Camille a half-block down the street, rubbing her neck to calm her down. When he heard the Claxon horn blare in the distance, he knew the fire company was on its way.

They would surely be barreling up Main Street. It would be the shortest and straightest route from the firehouse just a half-block away on Church Street.

Someone, he knew, would have to direct them to the exact site of the fire. It might as well be him.

Supper, he rationalized, will just have to wait.

The woman on Paul Reeves' right at the dining table was Estelle Griffin Higgins, a supposed grandniece of John Griffen, the inventor of the Griffen Gun. Manufactured by the Phoenix Iron Company, the three-inch bore cannon had had helped turn the tide of the Civil War. However, her greater claim to fame, besides having Griffen as her great uncle, was her extensive travels around the world. And her insatiable desire to be seen with and known by the upper echelons of local, national, as well as international society.

So far, she had traveled to Egypt, South Africa, China, and East India. Riding camels, hob-knobbing with pashas, shahs, emperors, and kings. Writing about them in dark blue felt-covered diaries that bespoke more of snobbery than history; more shallow social snippets than in-depth astute observations.

Most recently, she had sojourned in England, then Paris where she had witnessed the devastating outbreak of what people where now calling "The Great War". Upon her return stateside, without anywhere to stay in her home town of Phoenixville, she had wheedled her way into an invitation from the reluctant Mary Reeves to stay "for a while" at The Knoll.

"So, tell us all, Estelle," Paul urged, trying to be polite to whom he considered an unwelcomed, sometimes ungrateful guest. "What was it really like? A Yank living on French soil with Kaiser Wilhelm's troops poised at the door?" He took a sip of claret, awaiting what would probably be a vapid, airy response.

Estelle delicately dabbed her thin lips with a light-blue linen napkin. Then, as she was about to reply, she flipped her head to one side.

"Oh, my, my, my," she sniffed. "Is that smoke?" She sniffed again. "Yes, it is smoke. How disgustingly odd." She turned haughtily to her hostess. "What is burning in the kitchen, Mary?"

"All the food has been prepared on a grill outside," Paul's wife replied. "It's all the rage in the south, I understand..."

"Well, it is delicious," Estelle nodded, pushing the gently seared sirloin steak to one side of her plate. She smiled, then sniffed again. "Even if it is a bit too smoky."

Mary sniffed, too, then looked up.

Thick billows of grey smoke drifted down the circular staircase leading up to the third floor and, beyond, the attic. Small flickers of flame darted down from the ceiling.

"Paul!" she screamed, jumping up from the table. "Our lovely home is on fire!"

"Don't be silly, dear," he said dismissively. "It's just smoke from the smoldering coals outside." But when he, too, finally looked up to where Mary was pointing, he started to shout.

"Get out!" he jumped up, yelling at the top of his lungs. "Everyone! Get out! Now!"

Mark hailed Nat and Stanley as Duke and Harry galloped down Main Street. Nat slowed the horses down long enough to ask "Where?"

"The Knoll House!" the Irishman shouted. "Looks like a big one." He pointed to the clouds of rapidly darkening smoke, trying to keep Camille in check. On the very few times that the horses had met, his bay mare, he knew, had had a "thing" for Harry, the handsome Percheron.

"Thanks, Mr. McGrady!" Stanley shouted, waving his hand high about his head. "You did a good thing!"

But Mark didn't hear. Instead, he was concerned about the welfare of his still skittish horse, who was now trying to shy away from the smell of acrid smoke.

"Easy, girl," he chided, watching as Nat whipped Duke and Harry back up to speed and wheeled around the corner across Nutt's Avenue, back onto Main and then up a few yards up to take a sharp left onto the long entrance to the large estate house. Six more firemen followed jogging quickly as they hand-hauled the hose wagon. A few others arrived in their own cars or on foot, having left their place of work when the alarm sounded.

Camille shuttered and neighed heavily, as if to sigh. Mark laughed, patted her neck again, then mounted his horse and trotted away.

His dinner, probably now cold by now, was waiting for him.

"Whoever called in the alarm..." Mary Reeves said, wrapped in a woolen blanket and encased in her husband's arms. "We must reward him. Or her..." They were both watching, along with their many guests scattered across the lawn, as the top two floors of their beloved house and home burned away.

Stanley, clad in his baggy canvas pants, tunic, and red peaked fireman's hat, helped two other members of the company steadfastly hold the leather hose as the steam pumper huffed and chugged, spewing streams of water onto the roof of the large mansion. The hose was hooked into the fire hydrant Paul Reeves had installed as a precaution in the back garden near the stone well during the renovations. He never thought, however, that it would ever be needed. But that was his way. Always thinking about what might be and what might be required.

Reeves watched carefully as Fire Chief Mendowski and his men swung two nozzles spewing water back and forth, up and across the roof, dousing as much of the fire as they could.

"We can't go into the house," the Fire Chief explained, "until we staunch the blaze on the roof. Keep on drenching, boys!" he commanded, watching with dismay as the sun began to set along the edge of The Knoll's near fields. "Soon we won't be able to see what we're doing," he sighed.

"Someone's in there!" Stanley suddenly yelled, pointing up to the second floor. "Look! It's a woman!"

The crowd of guests, standing as close as they could to the action before being shooed back by Nat White and the Fire Chief, inched forward. Estelle Griffen Higgins, puffed up with anxiety and a desire to be at the forefront of the action, marched past Duke and Harry standing placidly by and, commanding everyone's attention, attempted to ascend the front stairs of the house.

"Emily!" she screamed. "Emily! Emily! Emily!"

"What the hell is she doing?" Paul asked Mary. "And who is Emily? I don't recall seeing her at dinner."

"Emily..." she hesitated, trying to recall. "Oh," she finally said, drawing the blanket up to her chin. "A houseguest. A young friend of Estelle's." She brought her back from England... maybe France. I don't know. I do believe... some sort of refugee from the war... Parents lost in the battle of the Somme, perhaps?"

"All well and good. But... Why is she in trapped by a fire in our house?"

"I do not know, dear," Mary replied. "Estelle ask me to allow her to stay until she recovered from the trauma of war... and they both found a 'suitable place' to live. Estelle, as you know, is currently without accommodations elsewhere and... well..."

"... and, well, you said 'yes'. Such altruism, my dear," he smiled, hugging her closer. Still in all, he was uncomfortable housing two homeless women, however large and accommodating The Knoll House may be. He didn't wish to set a precedent for expectations from Phoenixville's most notorious freeloader and gossiper. However well-heeled and well-travelled she claimed to be.

Suddenly, Stanley bolted away from manning the fire under the steam pumper and sprinted toward the front door. Atop the steps, he paused, wrapped a wet bandana cowboy-style across his face, then, without warning or forethought, burst through the door and disappeared.

Got to save her. Got to save her, he repeated over and over again as he tried to wave away the increasingly acrid swarms of smoke now cascading down the massive center circular stairway. He raced up the stairs, determine to save, if he could, the "damsel in distress." Straight out of the Black Bart adventure penny-dreadfuls he and Edmond used to read together as children.

As he rushed up the staircase and then down the burning carpeting hallway to the room where he calculated the woman to be, he did not take into account that it was the very first time in his life that he took a dangerous risk without considering the consequences.

He didn't realize he was about to become a hero.

It would be his first moment of greater glory.

"That damned young fool," Fire Chief Mendowski swore under his breath, watching as Stanley dropped his part of the narrow hose and entered the building. "He'll get himself killed by acting so rashly."

He shouted to the men tending to pumper hose. "More water! God damn! Two hoses are not enough. We need three!" He made a quick mental note to ask the Borough Council for more funds to purchase additional 50-foot lengths of 2½" leather hose so that large conflagrations like this one could be adequately and more efficiently fought. They had already approved the purchase of the gas-powered Brockway Combination Chemical and Hose Car, but it was slated to be delivered early next year. Too late, in his mind.

An extra hose line would have come in handy just about now. Especially in aiding and saving a, albeit new, member of his own crew. *More equipment, more modern equipment,* he thought, glancing over at Duke and Harry, patiently and bravely standing in front of the steam pumper, *are desperately needed if we are to continue to save the lives of Phoenixville residents.* Still, the horse-drawn American LaFrance "Metropolitan" Steamer was what they had. And it would have to suffice to save the day.

Mendowski took a moment to appreciate the apparatus with its large black boiler, brightly painted wheels, and the brass, copper, and nickel parts that Stanley and Billy Szabo, an accountant at Phoenix Bank and Trust and a ten-years veteran volunteer of the company, faithfully shined to keep them brightly gleaming.

Purchased in in the fall of 1906 for $4,000, the steamer was the first self-powered fire-fighting pumper in the Borough. Not even the newly formed Friendship or West End Fire companies had one. Replacing the 100-year old hand pumper, the LaFrance could impel 600 gallons of water per minute, capable of extinguishing just about any fire his crew would be called upon to fight. The only thing wrong with the pumper was the time it took to fire up a head of steam. Five to seven minutes from the moment an alarm sounded was too long to ignite the chips of wood and shards of paper pre-stacked in the fire box under the boiler so that the contained fire could burn, turning the water into the steam needed to power the pumper. That had recently become Stanley Martinez's job. Preparing the kindling, stacking the wood, stoking the fire on the way as the company responded to an alarm. And, lately, all too often lately, Duke and Harry had charged through Phoenixville on the way to a raging blaze with great tufts of smoke billowing behind their wagon as the boiler heated up. But, as Stanley had frequently observed, "the delay is nothing compared to being able to shoot lots of water for a long period of time. I can just imagine what it was like when the guys got exhausted from all that hand pumping."

Mendowski thought all of this in less time than it took to hook up the 2½" hose to the steamer and commandeer two more men to help handle the long brass nozzle. If not firmly controlled as it spewed pressurized water, it could easily wildly whip around like an angry brown hard-headed cobra spitting out hot venom.

Ignoring the rest of the Reeves' guests mingling in small groups on the front lawn watching the fire and the firemen fight it, Estelle continued to impatiently stare at the second-floor window.

"C'mon, Emily," she whispered under her breath. "We've not come this long way through the ravages of war for it to end like this." She shaded her eyes against the sparks of fire and fading sunlight reflected in the spumes of water splattering against the walls and roof of The Knoll House. "C'mon, Emily. Where are you?"

She gave no thought to the young firefighter who had set aside his own safety and had rushed into the burning building to save her orphaned friend.

Less than three minutes later, Stanley Mendez Martinez, covered in soot and sweating, as he put it later, "like a screaming banshee announcing the new dearly departed", emerged through the battered-down front door of The Knoll House, carrying the frail, limp body of Emily Harris in his arms. With each step, he silently prayed she would make it.

"She's alive, barely, I think," he gasped, removing the now dried bandana from his nose and mouth. "She was leaning out the open window, gasping for air. I... I..."

Estelle Griffen Higgins rushed to the side of her young friend, nearly shoving Stanley aside.

"Emily. Emily," she whispered, clutching her limp hand. "Thank God." She looked up and, as an afterthought, smiled a gentle, yet haughty "Thank you" to Stanley. "You saved her life, brave boy," she said condescendingly. As if Stanley's putting his own life in jeopardy was, in her limited perspective, to be expected.

Stanley smiled shyly, nodded, "You're welcome," and then bent over, his hands on his knees, coming to grips with what he had just done. He had walked into the flames of near death, almost unselfishly sacrificing his life for someone else.

Not what he had expected to do. Ever.

But he had.

And a young woman will continue to live her life because he had risked his own.

Stanley shuttered at the thought of what might have, could have happened. He didn't hear nor see the Chief walk up beside him.

"Running into open flames like that..." Mendowski said. 'Could have cost you..."

Stanley looked up.

"I know, sir," he heard himself say. "But something inside of me... I couldn't let her burn to death..."

"No need, son, to say anything more." Chief Mendowski said, patting Stanley on the back. "You... You did a brave thing. Saving this woman..." He looked at Emily lying prone on the woolen blanket his crew had provided. It would be a while before the Phoenixville Hospital dispatched their ambulance to the site. At least she was alive and, with any luck, would remain so. "Brave lad. Good job."

"Nothing that you wouldn't have done, sir," He paused. "At the fire at my father's store, you saved Marfit..."

"But that was... different."

"No, sir. It was not. As you said, it's all in the line of duty."

Mendowski smiled, touched by the boy's sincerity and bravery. Despite being his shortest recruit, young Martinez was going to be a long-term keeper. A valued and respected member of Phoenix Nº 1.

Except for the few seconds basking in the Chief's praise, Stanley did not feel at all like a hero. He was beginning to realize that fighting a fire was just as important and just as dangerous, if not more so, as fighting a war.

When the fire was finally controlled and then put out, Chief Mendowski and Nat White, accompanied by a more somber Stanley Martinez and an exhausted Billy Szabo, meticulously walked around the perimeter of the almost destroyed Knoll House.

Their search went well into the night, aided by kerosene lanterns supplied by Paul Reeves.

"They were once old man Wheatley's, I think," he explained. "I found them in the barn before we finally tore it down. He was a miner, you know."

"So I've heard," Mendowski smiled, passing the lanterns around. "Also, a famed paleontologist..."

"My friend's great grandfather," Stanley added, taking one of the ancient lamps. But he refrained from adding what he knew what had befallen Campbell. The first causality of the war from Phoenixville, Stanley was reluctant to mention his buddy's ignoble fate. And he wasn't sure if anybody else in the village, besides his immediate family and closest friends were aware of it. Mrs. Wheatley had made it a point to tell the news to Dolores Martinez who then tearfully relayed it to her son. Lest he read about one of his best friends in the paper.

"Wheatley would have been quite upset to see what has happened to his beloved home," Reeves said. "As I and Mary are..."

"Rest assured we will figure out what happened," Mendowski said. 'You have a place to stay?"

"The Pickering's. The farm next to ours. They've plenty of room for my family as well as our overnight guests."

Mendowski nodded, squeezed Reeve's shoulder, then, beckoning to his search crew, led the way around to the back of the house.

Slabs of hot tile, charred wood, and smoldering bricks littered the ground. Carefully avoiding them, he looked up.

The east section of the second and third floors had been badly damaged by flames. The whole roof had been destroyed and what remained of the west wing was covered in ashes and soot. *No doubt the Reeves would once again restored the house to pristine condition,* he thought. As he promised Paul Reeves, Mendowski was adamant about determining the cause of the needless fire.

They meticulously searched the area and then he, Nat, and Billy walked into the large house through the kitchen and entered the front parlor. Except for minor smoke and water damage, the first floor had not been touched by the fire.

"Nothing to see here," the Chief commented after sifting through a pile of blackened rubble. "I can't fathom how the fire started."

Stanley, however, remained outside. Holding his lantern high, he rummaged through the rubble, kicking some of the smaller tiles and bricks away. Underneath two of them, he picked up what looked like a flour sack. Then, looking around some more, he edged his way toward the hedgerow that separated the kitchen garden from the back lawn.

A long, tapered piece of wood was hidden under the lower boughs of one of the low, squat yews. Where it lay, Stanley surmised, it couldn't have fallen off the house. Stanley picked it up. Its heft and light weight felt familiar in his hands. *It's a sanded down baseball bat,* he realized. *How the hell did it get here?* He hailed the Fire Chief coming out of the house.

"I just found this under a bush. It's an old baseball bat, but... Could it also be a torch, Sir?" Stanley asked, holding up the tapir. "See how it's blunt and charred on one end and narrow at the other..."

"It's still warm," the Fire Chief noted. "What else you got?"

"Looks like a burlap bag, also partially burned." He held it up for Mendowski to see. PERSEVERANCE KNITTING MILL stenciled on both the front and the back was nearly obscured.

"Could someone who worked there... have caused the fire, Sir?" He refrained from saying what he thought.

Lenny Lochmann was carrying a bag just like it the night of the fire atop Stanley's father's shop. He wondered if Lenny had been here, too, on The Knoll House property, with a burlap bag from work. *But, then, lots of people work there,* he frowned. *Anybody could have left the bag. But why? And why would Lenny be here, on the Reeves' prestigious estate?*

"Thanks, Stanley. Good work," Mendowski said taking the shaft and bag. He walked back to where Nat was adjusting the harnesses on Duke and Harry and stowed Stanley's finds under the wagon seat. "We'll figure this out later," he said, then instructed Stanley to collect the lanterns and put them on the front porch.

Sitting next to Nat on the driver's bench, he beckoned him to move Duke and Harry forward. It had been a long day and an even longer night. Fire Chief Mendowski was ready to record the fire into the company's log book and then wend his way home.

As he wrote up the details, he thought here were too many similarities between this fire and the ones preceding it. For one, the burlap bags from the mill. And, for two, the sanded-down baseball bats possibly used as torches.

The Fire Chief pinched and rubbed the bridge of his Roman nose. Exhausted by fighting fires back-to-back, he was beginning to feel his age.

Someone has to be behind them, he reasoned. *But who? And why?*

He decided he would follow-up with Constable Luke Tucker first thing in the morning. Perhaps Luke would have some ideas. Perhaps also a way to come up with some answers.

Stanley lingered on the estate, knowing he'd have to walk the long way back to the station to help clean, oil, and hang the leather hoses in the drying tower. After they were cleaned, the fifty-foot long hoses were folded in half and hoisted up the twenty-five-foot spire by rope and left to dry. Then they were rolled and packed back onto the combination wagon hose cart. He was also expected to assist Nat grooming the horses, cleaning tack, and then laying the makings of a new fire under the steamer's boiler.

It was going to be a long while before he would even be able to think about going home.

He was half-way down the dirt entranceway of The Knoll House, walking quickly toward the wrought iron gates that fronted Main Street, when he saw the tire tracks, lit by the silvery moon.

They were in tandem, one tire following another. Obviously made by a two-wheeled vehicle, not a four-wheeled car or truck. Whatever it was definitely had wide-nubby tires. He thought the tracks might have been made by a bicycle, but they looked to be too deep for a light Schwinn like the one in his father's garage that often pedaled to work. They had to have been made by a heavier vehicle.

Stanley wasn't sure, but he thought he had seen the tracks somewhere else before. Frowning, he continued his long, weary walk back to the firehouse.

After the fire had ignited and started to consume The Knoll House roof, Lenny scuttled back into a wide watch of shrubs bordering the garden. He watched as Duke and Harry galloped by, pulling the large steam pumper. He angrily clenched his fists when he saw Stanley sitting proudly on the seat beside the driver.

How does he do that? Not me? he asked, gritting his teeth. *I want to be brave fireman. Not him.* Lenny wanted to scream out his anger, but knew if he made a sound, any sound, he would be discovered. Instead, he bit the inside of his cheek until it bled. Spitting out blood, he wished, *I hope Stanley burns to crisp.*

After the chemical pumper and hose wagon with six more firemen had passed, Lenny scurried into a copse of tall oak trees and hid behind one, patiently watching as the mansion burned and the fire department tried to squelch the fire.

When the fire had finally been contained, and he was satisfied sufficient damage had been done, Lenny shuffled, as best he could, across a front field to the woods behind the house where he had hidden his shiny Smith Motor Wheel motorized bicycle. He had bought the Briggs & Stratton bike, with its wide, nubby tires, a month ago from the Marcelino's. Neighbors on Scape Level, their first-born son, Tony, had just purchased the Smith Motor Wheel before being shipped off to and killed in the war. He never even had a chance to ride it. Lenny paid $125 for the bike, Money he had carefully saved out of his earnings working as a janitor at PERSEVERANCE KNITTING MILL and kept hidden from his father in his wooden cigar box.

Halfway across and down a wide stretch of a grassy knoll alongside Gay Street, Lenny remembered the bag he had dropped and the torch he had hidden in the bushes near the garden. He could have putt-putted his way back to the burnt house and retrieved them, but he didn't. He was too anxious and too much in a hurry to get back home before his father realized he was gone.

"I steal more bats," he laughed, revving the engine and speeding away. "And more bags

As Stanley trudged down the long, narrow lane leading from the burnt-out estate home, a pair of narrow car headlights seared through the descending darkness. The vehicle was barreling down on him, a bit too fast for his liking. He quickly stepped aside just in time to watch it pass by, stop, then back up. The car stopped in front of him.

"Been to the dinner party?" a deep velvety alto voice inquired from the driver's seat of the canary yellow 1916 Oakland Model 38 Speedster two-seater. "Or on a Sunday night stroll and just happen to be trespassing?"

"No! I am a firefighter."

"Likely story." The low-pitched laughter pierced his soul. He was proud of his new avocation, just as he was also proud of his professionl as a master pattern maker. He brushed off the sooty residue from his coat, and peered closer at the driver of the fancy car.

The woman's dark eyes brazening stared into his steel-blue ones. Topped by a wide-brimmed straw hat tilted jauntily to one side, her long, shiny ebon hair was curled into a tight chignon at the nape of her long, tanned neck.

"It's true," he muttered, taken aback, yet attracted, by her stunning looks and haughty demeanor. "The Knoll had been set ablaze by an arsonist. At least, that's what the Fire Chief thinks..." He waivered at her look of incredulity.

'The Knoll? On fire? Surely you jest," she laughed again. "My aunt's friends just rebuilt and fortified the place... It's air-tight, impenetrable. Besides, who would want to..." She stopped mid-question, seeing the truth and sadness in the young man's eyes. "Wait, is it... Is it?"

"Whole roof gone. Most of the third and part of the second floors... Also gone." He paused. "Sorry, but it took a good three hours to put it out. Smoke and water damage everywhere..."

"And the owner's? Their guests?"

"They Reeves are safe. The guests, too. Emily, though, was trapped..."

"Emily? Oh, no... Not dear Emily!" Although the words, Stanley thought, were meant to be ones of concern, he did not detect a note of softness or sympathy in her voice.

"I pulled her out of the burning building."

"Such a brave... fireman," she laughed again. "So, no one hurt or, lost. That is good."

"But the house is badly damaged."

"Pity." She said without expression. "And you are?'

"Stanley Mendez Martinez," he half bowed, regretting that he had deferred to whom he assumed was one of the Reeves' three daughters, but turned out to be the niece of a guest.

"The shoemaker's son?" she snorted.

"Yes. Why? Is that, um, bad?" Weariness of the evening fighting the fire was quickly draining his energy. He was anxious to get back to the station and then home to a hot bath and the cool sheets of his small bed. "How do you know?"

"I visit town a lot... when my aunt is here. When I do, I have your father custom-make my shoes. Better than the boutiques in New York. Huh. It never dawned on me he had a family..."

"My mother, myself, and my sister, Rosalina." He paused. "Look, the house is uninhabitable... Your aunt and the other guests are staying with the Pickerings next door." Stanley waved as if to both indicate the neighbors and shoo this brazen, yet very attractive woman away.

"I know where they live. But, where do you?"

"Vanderslice Street."

"Huh, a Northside boy." She revved up the four-cylinder thirty-nine horsepower engine. His neighborhood, coupled with this mixed Latino and Celtic good looks, intrigued her "Wanna lift?"

Stanley carefully considered the offer. "I, um, have to go back to the fire station. Horses to groom, hoses to clean and all that..."

"That's on our way," she smiled coyly. The North End was, they both knew, in the opposite direction of the Pickering Farm. "Name's Samantha," she said, extending her hand. "Samantha Higgins Rouleaux. Hop in."

When he hesitated again, she said, "Suit yourself, but it's faster than walking. And you've a long to shuffle across town..." She waited. And then just she was about to put the car back into gear, Stanley hastened around the front of the roadster and got in.

He felt awkward riding in a car driven by a woman. Especially a woman he did not know. He also felt guilty. After all, Stanley had been dating Rebecca, Edmond's sister for the last two years. But their relationship was sketchy. On again, off again. More off than on when she had accepted a date with Campbell Wheatley.

But why should I feel guilty? he asked himself as they tooled northward along Starr Street. *It's just a ride. Not as if we're dating or anything...* He looked sideways at Samantha's strikingly handsome, good looks. *But, then again, why not?*

"Say, Miss Rouleaux... I was wondering..."

"Samantha. Sam, for short," she laughed, making a quick, careening wide left turn onto Church Street. "Even though I am tall..." She glanced at the blank look on his face. "A pun, Stan. May I call you Stan? A pun, see? Tall gal? Short name."

"Um, sure," he nodded. He knew all about puns, having suffered through the many Edmond inflicted upon him over the course of their friendship. Not that he didn't have a sense of humor, but puns, to him, as the saying went, were the lowest form.

Suddenly, he missed his best friend with an ache in his heart he had only felt when the aged family poodle had died. *At least Edmond will be coming home,* he reasoned, trying to shake off the feeling.

"Hey, Stan... No, No, not Stan. I think I will call you 'fireman' Fireman, we're here." She shifted the Oakland Model 38 into Neutral, then pulled up the handle of the emergency brake under the left side of the dashboard. She turned to him. "What is it you want to ask me?"

"Um, I'd like to thank you for the ride, um, Sam. Could I, er, I mean, could I..." *Damn it! Why am I so intimidated by this woman? She's just a long-legged lass with a fancy car and just happens to be related to a guest of the wealthy owners of a large mansion...* Which, he reminded himself, had just been almost totally destroyed.

"Listen... Um, how long are you visiting... In town for?"

"Oh, I don't know. Depends. Aunt Estelle and I, well... we're no place else to go at the moment. The end of the summer... mid-September or so, if we can't find a decent place to stay. And, if there's nothing else to keep us... me here." She smiled broadly. "Why?"

"Well, listen, The Columbia Hotel..."

"I know of it. Eaten there often..."

He was going to ask her out just for drinks, but, on an impulse, he blurted out, "I'd be honored if you would join me

114

for dinner tomorrow night. Say, around seven?" Just like his father had asked his mother a little more than twenty-two years ago.

"Great, fireman," she smiled again. "I'll pick you up at…"

"No, I will pick *you* up," he insisted with such command in his baritone voice that she snapped her head back and regarded him in a new light. *Huh,* she thought. *He isn't just another tradesman, is he?* Like the more than several she had "picked up" in the past. *No, this boy… this man is different. More defiant. I like that. I like that a whole lot.*

"Seven o'clock at the…" he was saying. "No, it's not habitable. Where will you be staying?"

"I haven't decided. Probably Pickering Farm…"

"Fine, then," Stanley said, pushing the passenger door open. "I'll see you…"

"No, on second thought, I'll meet you there. My uncle's firm has a standing reservation account at the Columbia. I'll just stay there."

That slightly blew the wind out of his sails. Stanley would have loved to have picked her up in his father's American Underslung touring car with its sleek white body and the plush red leather seats. In his mind, it was more elegant, more stylish then her low-slung Sportster. *Why,* he asked himself, *am I trying to 'one-up' this woman?* In any case, it was a date. He wouldn't press his case. Half standing out of the two-seater, he turned toward her.

"Fine, Sam. I'll meet you there… In the French Country Room…"

"Shall I make reservations while I'm…"

"No!" he fairly snapped. "I'll do that. After all, I asked you – as is most proper – not you… me."

They both glared at one another until she burst out laughing.

"One point for you, fireman! All right. I'll wait for you in the...
No, I'll wait in my room until you call for me from the lobby.
How's that?"

"That'll be just fine."

He finally got out of the car and closed the curved door
trimmed in brown leather.

"Don't be late. Fireman!"

Without another word, he strolled nonchalantly through the
firehouse double doors.

SEPTEMBER 1917

Campbell Wheatley was the first from Phoenixville to be killed in action, *The Daily Republican* reported. And Frank LaBronsky, it also stated, had been sent to Baltimore, then deployed on a troop ship to God knows where.

And now it had been three months since Edmond had said goodbye and was posted to Camp Hancock in the deep south. Stanley had watched and politely waved from the platform of the Philadelphia and Reading Railroad Station at the tip of Bridge Street as he watched the men of Battery C – Edmund Hope and Hans Gruber among them – load supplies, horses, and caissons into freight cars, then board the two Pullman cars set aside for the troops.

It was the beginning of September and the imposing letter ominously postmarked WASHINGTON, D.C. was still unopened under a pair of Argyle socks in a drawer of the pale Maplewood dresser in his small room. He was still not sure that he – broken nose and impaired eyesight not withstanding – was really deferred.

He was, in fact, afraid to find out.

It wasn't necessary, he reasoned, trying to allay his fears, *to read its contents*. He already knew what it might say. Yet, in what he knew was defiance of the law, he continued to refuse to acknowledge what could easily be its urgent request. *Let them come and get me,* he thought. *I'd rather rot in a dank jail or be shot in cold blood than die ingloriously – like Campbell – in vain on a field steeped in mud.*

Edmund Hope and Hans Gruber were not happy with their situation. They had arrived at Camp Hancock just a week ago and after only a morning to "get settled in". They and the rest of the other one-hundred and fifty members of the Battery C National Guard unit were in intensive training. The unit had been Federalized as part of the Keystone Division, commanded by Captain Samuel Whitaker, the nephew of former Pennsylvania Governor Samuel Whitaker Pennypacker.

Edmund was glad that Captain Whitaker was with them and had not opted to say behind. He was a fair, honest, however strict, experienced officer who led his men very much like a knowledgeable baseball team manager. With an iron fist in a padded leather glove. But his authority over his unit had been immediately suborned by the Camp's adjutant who promptly informed him that his troops would be trained by French artillery officers who had been wounded in the early stages of The Great War.

Outspoken, the newly promoted Corporal Hope, trailed by the taciturn Private Gruber, accosted Captain Whitaker on his way to the mess hall.

"What gives?" Edmund demanded. "I thought you would command us as we trained."

"Seems not, Hope. Apparently, the French, who have seen the ravages of war first-hand are better able, more knowledgeable to show you, us the ropes."

"But you fought in Cuba…"

"A different kind of warfare, I am told. And, we're to use French artillery pieces." He paused. Normally a stoic man who barely acknowledged his feelings let alone express them, he sighed heavily and frowned. "And… we are to use their horses, too."

"Not ours?"

"Not ours. They're to be shipped back home tomorrow, along with the bulk of the artillery cannons we brought with us."

Edmund hung his head at hearing the news. He had become quite fond of Crimson, the dark bay gelding with the soft whinny whom he had been grooming and working with since his induction three — or was it already four? — months ago. He wondered who would take care of him and remember his nightly snack of three carrots.

"The rest of our unit, the twenty-five men we left home in Phoenixville will tend to them."

Edmund shook his head. He was not too keen on being trained by a bunch of foreigners whose language he did not understand, whose weaponry was totally unfamiliar to him, and whose horses, he surmised, were, like the French, surly and, from what he had heard, unkempt.

"Buck up, sons. Have a little, er, hope, Hope," the Captain tried to smile. "Remember, we are here to learn to fight on foreign soil for a larger cause then just our American principles."

"However," Hans whispered as he responded in broken English. "That's the point."

Edmund nodded. "Looks like we're stuck here. But, I wonder... For how long?"

Rosalina received her second letter from Edmond, unfairly criticizing the fetid conditions at Camp Hancock. Which *The Daily Republican* reported as "the most favorable". She shared the letter with her brother, who only shrugged.

"At least, as I said, he's still safe. Even if he is playing with the selfish Frenchie guns."

Stanley's sister winced at the bigoted slur. She hadn't known nor imagined her brother to be so biased. But since the war had begun, she noticed how he was, ever so subtly, changing.

'Stan-Stan," she pouted, calling him by the name she used for him when she was just a toddler. "Don't be such a... Such a..."

"Such a what? Don't be so aghast. You know how I feel about the war. Fighting someone else's battles..."

119

"But this is about protecting our freedoms Our rights. As Americans."

"Since when have you become such a liberal?"

"Stan-Stan! It's not about politics... It's about right and wrong. Good versus evil..."

"Not on my watch," Stanley said. "And stop calling me Stan-Stan! How old are you?"

"Eighteen."

"Then... then... Good God, Rosalina. Grow up!"

Edmond was seething, but he remained silent during the next few weeks of training. Although he inwardly railed against the French officers who tried to retrain him and his comrades in broken English and often with defective and damaged artillery equipment, he dutifully followed Captain Whitaker's orders issued just last evening.

"Just obey, men. Get through this. We'll wreak our own havoc once we get over there..."

Sung by George M. Cohen, both its composer and lyricist, *Over There* was played non-stop on Victorphones located throughout the camp. It was played over and over and over again in the mess tent by a member of another unit, a famed pianist. And it was sung over and over again by every small cadre of troops marching around the parade grounds.

"Over there... over there... and we won't come back 'til it's over, over there...." The refrain echoed in Edmond's head over and over and over again.

We could win this war, he thought belligerently. *If only we had the chance to finally be "over there".*

Edmond reluctantly had to finally agree with the Captain. He shrugged, smiled outwardly, and begrudgingly went about doing what he had to do.

That night he penned a letter to his best friend, hoping that at least Stanley would, hopefully, understand.

The fourth fire broke out on Wednesday afternoon, right after most of the workers at the foundry had returned from their half-hour lunch break.

Stanley's shop was close to the pipe fitting building; the blasts from the Diaphone Claxon horn atop it were deafening. He didn't stop to count them. Instead, he raced back out the door and ran all the way to the firehouse.

He was joined by other volunteers who also left their own jobs and places of business. Doc Kimshaw, the pharmacist, literally barreled into him as they reached the east corner of Main and Church at the same time. Stanley sprinted ahead of the older man and arrived at the firehouse just as Nat was trotting Duke and Harry out of the large red double doors.

"Hop on back and tend to the fire!" he shouted.

"Where?!" Stanley shouted back, struggling to get a firm hand-hold on one of the steam pumper's back rails alongside Billy Szabo. As the wagon passed him, Doc also managed to hop on board.

"Other side of Nutt's... behind the cemetery," Billy yelled, hanging on tight as Nat urged the two Percherons into a steady canter down Church Street, crossing Main and Gay on their way to Bridge and then left onto Nutt's Avenue. Five other firefighters on the chemical and hose wagon followed.

Stanley, taking over the task of stoking the fire under the boiler, surmised they were headed to Gregg Altemose's large manor house and stables behind Morris Cemetery. As he tended to the burning coals in the hopper, he hoped that it was just a swath of brush on fire and not any of the buildings.

His suspicions proved incorrect, however, as they raced down the narrow lane bordering the cemetery.

One of the barn roofs had already collapsed. Frightened squeals of Altemose's prized thoroughbreds trapped in the burning barn pierced Stanley's ears. Harry, startled by the bellows, lurched sideways, nearly up-ending the steam pumper. It took Nat's firm hands and soft, assuring whinnies from the steady, more experienced Duke to calm him down.

Stable hands were already darting in and out of the barn, trying to rescue the horses.

"How many?" Stanley asked one of them leading a sleek bay mare toward a far paddock area. A foal, no more than a week or so old, followed at her side.

"Four more. But... it's too hot in there."

Stanley started to sprint toward the burning barn, but was stopped by Fire Chief Mendowski, jumping out of Constable Luke Tucker's dark blue and crimson police car.

"I got this!" he shouted, grabbing his canvas tunic and fire hat from the back seat of the 1910 Torpedo limousine. "You stay back!" As the Chief raced past Stanley, the young firefighter paused and waved at the policeman.

"No, wait!' he shouted after the Chief. Adamantly refusing to follow orders, he wrapped a red bandana around his lower face, and followed Mendowski into the blazing barn, now totally engulfed in black, acrid-smelling smoke.

Tucker parked his car on the other side of the pumper and ambled over to the two horses standing placidly in their harnesses. He had been meeting with Mendowski to discuss the recent outbreak of conflagrations in the Borough when the alarm went off and had instantly offered to drive him. Now was his chance to witness the company fighting what could easily be a fire set by the serial arsonist. Being on site meant he could find fresh evidence first hand.

And maybe, finally, solve his second major case.

As he gently stroked Harry's white muzzle, he looked back at his car, recalling that the German-built open-air limousine had been purchased seven years ago with funds from the sale of a necklace stolen during a senseless murder at the Columbia Hotel. The perpetrator, suspected to be a local "lady of the evening", had never been caught, but the emerald and garnet necklace had been recovered and eventually sold. Part of the proceeds not only bought the police car, but also went toward the purchase of a motorized paddy wagon. Its custom-built boxy cabin designed to hold detainees was built on a Ford Model T chassis. Tucker still missed his trusty steed, Ellington, but had to admit that having the motorcar and the new paddy wagon was indeed much more efficient and easier to maintain.

Dismayed that his friend, Dave Mendowski, had once again been so quick to dive into a burning building and had not yet reappeared, Tucker anxiously watched as Nat, Kimshaw, Szabo and the other brave Borough firefighters worked furiously, aiming the hoses at the burning sides of the barn. *Dave,* he mused staring into the billowing smoke, *is certainly dedicated to saving lives whatever the cost.* Although a few years older than the Fire Chief, the rugged policeman considered him a hero.

Inside the barn, Mendowski found himself in the middle of a pocket of hot, dry clear air surrounded by a wall of smoke and burning timbers. He could barely see to ascertain the location of the four screaming horses. He had only a few minutes before the fire consumed him or he was baked alive in his leather-lined metal helmet and wool-lined canvas tunic.

He briefly paused, debating which horse he should attempt to rescue first. All, he knew, were valuable steeds and the loss of even one of them would financially set Altemose's equine and racing business back several years. Not to mention the loss of life of the stately sentient beings.

"I'll take the two in the far stalls!" Stanley called as he hastened past the Chief, his voice muffled by the moist scarf over his face.

Mendowski didn't take the time to argue with the brave lad who had, once again, disobeyed his direct order. Instead he grabbed empty burlap seed bags piled on one side of the wide aisle and threw two to Stanley.

The skittish horses, thank goodness, were wearing leather halters. Stanley said a silent prayer, knowing that this would make it easier to catch the horses, cowering and squealing in the back of their stalls.

"Easy, easy," he said to the dark chestnut on his right. Not really knowing what he was doing, Stanley quickly – and instinctively – whipped one of the bags over the horse's eyes and secured it under the straps of the halter. He then led the now somewhat calmer gelding out into the aisle.

He looked over to the smaller, obviously older, grey thoroughbred, trying to figure out how he was going to handle two scared horses at the same time.

Nat, when he saw the Chief and then Stanley bolt into the barn, made sure the pathway to and from it were completely doused. Thank goodness, the door was slid open. Grabbing the back of the nozzle of one of the three hoses spewing water, he directed the fireman holding it to spray high up into the barn.

Expertly leading his two horses into a billow of smoke, Mendowski was relieved to feel a shower of water wash over his face and the shoulders of his already stifling tunic. Close to the entrance, Nat dashed in and grabbed the halter of one of the thoroughbreds and led it and Chief Mendowski, grasping the halter of the other horse, out to safety.

"Where's Stanley?" Nat asked, handing his charge over to one of Altemose's stable hands.

"Back of the barn... two more horses..." Mendowski wheezed. He had failed to cover his month with a wet cloth and had inhaled a bit too much smoke. His lungs ached from the effort to breathe in cool air. He surrendered the light bay with a crooked white stripe on his forehead and turned back toward the barn.

"Stanley... I have to go back in..."

"Watch out!" Stanley screamed from behind two horses charging ahead of him out of the barn, now completely saturated with water. Its burning frame now reduced to smoldering wood slats and rafters.

Nat, the Chief, and three other firefighters scrambled away as the chestnut and grey, still with burlap covering their eyes, blindly barreled out of the barn. They nearly collided with the pumper wagon before Duke and Harry whinnied, snorted, and snickered as if to say, "It's okay. You can stop now."

"Ellington!" Constable Tucker exclaimed, both surprised and pleased to once again see the horse he had so fondly, years ago, dubbed his "partner-in-crime". He gripped the dappled grey's halter, gently stroked his muzzle to calm him down, then led him toward one of the large paddocks. He gently removed the bag, opened the gate, rubbed his hands along the horse's sleek neck, then released him. He watched as Ellington bucked and galloped across the enclosed field to the other side.

"Didn't know you were still here," he sighed out loud. "I thought you were sold... retired..." He didn't see Greg Altemose walk over to stand by his side.

"Yes, but the new owner left to serve in the militia a few months ago," Greg Altemose said, crossing his lanky, sinewy arms over the top of the split-rail fence. "He asked that we take him back and sell him... Apparently, Ellington, while treated quite well by the young preacher, wasn't too thrilled with living in New York. Too much noise... No place to run around..."

"Why didn't you... Let me know?"

"Was going to, but then, we entered the war and I've been busy supplying horses for Battery C as well as other units of our Expeditionary forces."

"So, he's for... sale?"

"Yeah, but... He's going on sixteen now. A bit too old to interest..."

"I'll take him," Tucker blurted out, without even thinking of asking about the price.

The horse breeder and trainer smiled. "How much you got in that wallet I see bulging in your jacket?" he kindly asked.

"What? Oh... um, about ten, twenty dollars, I think."

"Ten it is!" Altemose laughed, slapping the police Chief on the back. "Sold to the highest bidder!"

"Can he stay here? The station stables have been converted to garages." Tucker nodded toward the Tornado. "Cars, you know..."

"Board and exercising... Five dollars a month. That suit you?"

"Yes, very much. Thank you, Greg."

"My pleasure. It's the least I can do for our men in blue." He shook the Constable's hand, then sauntered away to chat with Chief Mendowski.

Luck Tucker watched his now new, old horse for a while. Then, remembering the real reason for his presence at yet another area fire, walked back toward the destroyed barn to join Altemose and Mendowski.

Stanley was helping to re-roll and pack the hoses onto the hand-pulled wagon when he noticed a glint of metal on the ground on one side of the barn. Thinking it was a stray piece of firefighting equipment, he walked over to pick it up. The slender, rectangular tin box was about the size of a deck of playing cards. Small enough to fit into a pocket. A strip of sandpaper was glued to one of the longer sides, the center of it worn down as if being struck often. An insignia shaped like an eagle with wide-spread wings was crudely etched on one side with the words, *MEIN LAND FÜR IMMER* under it.

Stanley shook the box, wondering what was causing the rattling sound inside. He turned the box over and over in his hand, trying to figure out how to open it.

"What's that you got there, son?" Doc Kimshaw asked, wiping sweat from his furrowed brow. His bushy eyebrows, tending to grey, were raised in eager anticipation.

"Not sure, Doc. But it rattles, see?" Stanley shook the box again.

"Here, let me." Stanley placed the box into his outstretched palm. The pharmacist flipped the box onto its side, held it between two fingers and then pushed one end of the box until the other end slid out from under the insignia. He smiled.

"I've seen these lots of times in my line of work," he explained. "This is a pill box. Used to, of course, carry pills and medicines. Looks like, though, it's been converted into a metal matchbox. Well used, from what I can see." He handed the box back.

Stanley, marveling at the ingenuity of design, opened and closed the box again and again, counting ten kitchen matches inside.

"Wonder what the insignia means... "

"It's German. 'My country forever'."

"I wonder who it belongs to."

"Oh, there are lots of Germans here in Phoenixville," Kimshaw stated. "Could be anybody's... It's yours now. Finders keepers..." He paused. "Nat's calling to us. Time to head back to the station and get those damn hoses cleaned and hung out to dry."

Stanley pocketed the matchbox and jumped back onto the pumper wagon just as Nat was slowly guiding Duke and Harry back down the lane. He would worry later about who the owner might be and why it was left at the site of the fire. There was, for now, volunteer fireman chores to attend to.

Fire Chief Mendowski and Constable Tucker lingered behind with Greg Altemose after the Phoenix № 1 firefighting crew had left. The trio were walking around the barn searching for clues of the cause of the fire.

Altemose was frowning, saddened that his largest barn had been destroyed, but grateful that all his horses, including Ellington, had been saved.

"Know anybody might want to, um seek revenge?" Tucker asked Altemose.

"Me? Revenge. No, I don't think so. I am as honest as they come. You know me better than that, officer... Er, Luke."

"Yeah, I do," Tucker grinned amiably. "That's why I asked." He knew full well that the notorious horse breeder also helped to manage the 19-acre Phoenix Driving Park – nestled in a corner between South Whitehorse Road and East Pothouse just outside the far southeastern corner of town – was also a closeted bookie and gambler who had been accused several times of "fixing" the sulky races. Especially when his own horses were in the running.

"A gambling debt gone awry, perhaps?' he pressed. "A dissatisfied jockey or... hum, a horse owner promised a 'thoroughbred' and was sold a bill of potential glue..."

"Luke!" Altemose protested. "I know of no such..."

"Let's change the line of questioning," Chief Mendowski interjected. "Greg here is not on trial. So, let's find the real culprit. If there is one."

Tucker sighed. He flipped open his worn small notebook and licked the tip of a pencil nub.

"Whom do you think would perpetrate such a heinous crime – if, indeed it was one – against you or any members of your family?" he inquired in his best, most professional voice.

"Don't know. Could it have been a prank?"

"I doubt it," Mendowski frowned. "But, consider this. A German spy. One was spotted near Battery C when that burned."

Greg Altemose looked at him incredulously.

"But when we questioned the Captain," the constable reminded the Fire Chief, "he didn't mention the word 'spy'. Just that someone was lurking about."

"You're right, Luke. But he did say... German."

"That's correct. German, with coppery-blond hair. Sentry said later he thought the fella was younger, though..."

"Yes, but, consider Greg has been supplying horses to the military. For free, I might add. For the war effort...."

The horse breeder nodded. "Yes, but please don't let that get around. I don't want..."

"Everybody in town knows," Tucker smiled. "You can't keep a secret worth a damn in Phoenixville. The moment you sneeze or cough on the Northside, someone on Fourth Avenue has already called the ambulance."

"Suppose the Germans might have gotten wind of Greg's patriotic generosity ..." Mendowski suggested.

"Worth considering, Dave," Tucker said. He made a few notes, then flipped the pad closed and put it and the pencil stub back into pocket of his blue policeman's jacket. "Let's just search some more and see what we can find..."

It was the Fire Chief who pointed out the two sets of wide nubby tire tracks in the dirt behind the barn. One led toward the building; the other away, across a field toward Morris Cemetery.

"Stanley Martinez said he saw tracks like these on The Knoll House property the evening of the fire there."

"Think they're related?" Altemose asked.

"Could be. Luke, what do you make of it?"

The constable drew out his notebook and pencil again and once again scribbled a few notes. Then he drew a rough sketch of the tracks.

"Could be something. Could be nothing," he thought aloud, wrote, and then frowned. "Then again, I don't think their appearance in both places is coincidental."

All Frank LaBronsky ever wanted was to be a good sailor. Growing up, he had listened attentively to his father's stories of crossing the Atlantic Ocean as a young boy sailing to American with his parents. Across the wide, blue expanse of high rolling waves, trailed by leaping flying fish and cavorting dolphins.

He relished the rare weekends during the summer when his own parents took him by train to Philadelphia and then by a second train to Cape May, New Jersey, where he was allowed – for hours on end – to swim in the pounding surf and sail the small ketch his father had rented for his son's enjoyment. He had become good at gauging wind speed and direction, carefully guiding the small boat parallel to the shoreline, promising his mother he won't stray further out onto the seas, away from her sight.

But he knew, someday, he would do just that. Venture well away into the wild blue yonder, out onto the open sea like the mariners and explorers of old. And now, he would be like them joining the brave sailors now manning destroyers and cruise ships along the coasts of England and France. Defending their shores against invasion by the Kaiser's armed forces.

It was, he knew, his dream and his destiny.

So, when Woodrow Wilson, with the assent of Congress, finally declared war against the Central Powers and then sign the Selective Service Act, Frank was eagerly anxious to register with his buddies on June 5th. Then, not waiting to be called up, a week later he took the train to Naval Headquarters in Washington, D.C. and volunteered.

Even as tall and slender as he was and prone to what the doctors called a mild case of asthma, he easily passed the physical and was instantly accepted. He took an oath of allegiance, slipped his Navy identification card into a pocket of his wallet and returned home to Phoenixville to pack. He had had less than a week to report to the naval base just outside Annapolis where he was assured he would be trained as a seaman and then shipped overseas.

Frank was gravely disappointed when he was told, once he reported for duty, that, rather than being a gunner aboard a destroyer or battle ship, he'd best be suited to be a Navy fighter pilot. Which meant he'd be taught how to fly motorized vehicles constructed with nothing more than thin strips of wood, linen cloth, and wires. When the instructor, a supposed veteran flier told the class the average amount of time for fatalities was far less than sixty hours of flight time, Frank turned pale white and vomited onto the floor beside his desk.

He was escorted to the training camp's commissary where he was treated for "indigestion" and then released. He didn't have the heart to tell the camp physician that he was deathly afraid of heights. Learning to fly was the last thing he ever wanted to do. He wanted to be a sailor, for God's sake. On the high seas, not up high in the air.

On the morning of September 5, 1914, Frank LaBronsky found himself on deck of the USS DOVER, enjoying the crisp sea breezes and the gentle stings of salt air on his cheeks. The troop ship, along with a flotilla of three others accompanied by various Naval destroyers and cruisers, was completing the final leg of its journey to Queensland, Ireland where an American base had been established for the training and deployment of both British and United States Naval forces.

He looked out over the white-capped swells, lit a Camel cigarette, and leaned forward on the wooden railing. Staring hard into the horizon, he wanted to be the first on board to catch a glimpse of the Irish coast. He was also concerned about his impending fate, trying to figure out if there was any way he could get out of becoming a fighter pilot. The thought of bouncing up and down, in and out of clouds with nothing to tether him to the ground made Frank more than nauseous. Beads of nervous sweat broke out on his brow and beneath the dark blue woolen cloth of his Navy jumper.

Lost in thought, Frank squinted, inexperienced with such things, not sure that he was seeing.

What looked like the tip of a periscope was bobbing between the gently rolling ocean swells. about a hundred or so yards off the bow of the USS DOVER. He wasn't positively sure what it was. Maybe the fin of a shark enjoying the morning sun on its back. It didn't register until much later that it could have been one of the infamous German U-Boats that plied along the English and French shorelines.

Frank quickly dismissed the thought and strolled forward to join a small group of his new Navy buddies who had also come up on deck to enjoy a smoke. They reminded him of his friends back home. Stanley, Hans, Edmond, and Campbell. He wondered where they were, what they were doing.

Especially Stanley. He worried that he still refused to register for the draft. His parents had written that Stanley had joined the local fire department and wondered if that would grant him a deferment. Frank thought about Hans Gruber who, he had heard, even after their fight in the bar, had so willingly followed Edmond into the company of Battery C. And was Campbell still up to his old tricks on the baseball diamond in Reeves Park? Or did he, too, march off to war?

Frank even recalled his brief encounters with Lenny Lochmann and the Saturday afternoon when "the big lummox" punched Edmond in the gut, threw a baseball sullied with dog feces at Stanley, then broke Stanley's nose. And how all four of Stanley's friends marched the next afternoon into Constable Tucker's office to report the incident. Was dummy Lenny ever charged with a crime?

He sighed as he flicked the butt of his Camel over the railing into the ocean. He wished he was back at work at the Phoenix Iron Company as a master puddler overseeing the firing of one of the massive furnaces that turned pig iron into steel. He wished he could play one more baseball game with the guys back home, catching fly balls in the outfield before being forced to fly into the face of war.

Frank suddenly felt his stomach turn into knots and bent over the railing to vomit. That's when he saw the wake of foam speeding toward the ship.

It was the last thing he saw before he and his shipmates were blasted overboard into the ocean.

With the invention in 1850 of *Unterseeboots*, -- quickly anglicized as U-Boats – Germany had ushered in the Age of Unrestricted Warfare on and under the high seas. In 1912 the U-19 class of submarines was introduced with the first diesel engine ever installed in a German navy boat. Then came the U-21. With its self-propelled torpedo, it the most popular and the most the deadliest, gaining a reputation as the most dangerous weapon in the German Navy's arsenal, having already destroyed three British warships in less than an hour.

It had quickly become, to say the least, the bane of American troop ships that crossed the Atlantic Ocean and sailed over the Celtic Sea and up the English Channel.

And it was the very same deadly U-21 that had blasted Frank Lebowski's ship out of the water.

Frank managed to swim up to the surface, but the miasma of blood around him clouded his vision. He heard screams for help in the distance and instantly knew what had happened. Their ship had been torpedoed and many of the troops aboard as well as crew members had been wounded and pitched into the cold waters of the Celtic Sea.

He could see, but not feel the sunlight streaming through the swells. Nor could he feel his right leg. Gasping for breath, Frank tried to tip his head up, but with sensation in just one leg, had a difficult time treading water long enough to keep himself afloat. He dipped under the swells, then bobbed up again.

The third time breaking the surface he was able to paddle around, looking for other shipmates, watching in horror as the bow of the ship dipped and the stern up-ended. The USS DOVER then slowly and effortlessly slid into the sea.

His arms flailing in the water, Frank again began gasping for air. He tried to figure out an escape. After a few minutes, he espied a ridge of shoreline in the distance. He wasn't sure if it was France or England. Regardless, it was a shore of safety.

But, could he make it that far?

Forcing his wounded right leg to move, Frank managed a powerful scissor kick that propelled him into a breast-stroke. Swimming slowly to conserve what little energy he had, he headed toward the horizon, struggling not to slip again under the surface.

But, even If I did make it, he thought as he slowly swam in the icy waters of the Irish sea toward safety, *I wouldn't have to face flying. So high. So high... Up in the sky.*

It was his last thought as he slowly, mindlessly stroked his way toward Dover.

Since the first day President Wilson had declared war on Germany back in April, Stanley had assiduously read all the accounts from the European front in *The Daily Republican*. Its news articles and published letters home from the front were filled with gory details of men being blasted open by shells and suffocating from plumes of mustard gas. He shuttered to think that that would happen to Edmond and the rest of the Phoenixville men who had so willingly went off to fight.

With most, if not all, of his close friends now in training or overseas, and Campbell Wheatley dead on a bloody battlefield, Stanley felt very much alone.

.

Yet, a part of him, a very small part, had felt guilty about not registering in the first place. When he finally did, he knew in his heart that he wanted no part of the merciless killing; the senseless slaughter; the needless waste of life and limb. And, to make matters worse, he felt guilty about remaining in the fire company, without knowing for absolute certainty his Selectee Service status. He had even lied twice to Dave Mendowski about being deferred. And Stanley felt guilty about that, too.

To keep his mind off his loneliness, Stanley spent his evenings reading his precious books and dreaming of better days ahead when the war would be finally over and his friends were safely back home. He spent his days, concentrating on being a good fireman and doing his job at the foundry, perfecting his skills at pattern making. The longer he read and the harder he worked, the more his anxieties were dispelled and quieted.

His diligence began to pay off. Not only at the steel company but he was becoming a well-respected member of Phoenix Hose, Hook & Ladder Co., No. 1.

In just the last two months, he had saved a young maiden in distress, rescued two very frightened horses, and had become an expert at lighting steamer fires, cleaning leather hoses, and grooming Duke and Harry.

Recalling what could have been the disastrous fate of the chestnut mare and the much older grey gelding out at Altemose's Stables, he fed the fire horses extra apples and sugar cubes snuck from his mother's precious china tea set. He spent more time than necessary currying their already sleek coats. He even made it a point to occasionally accompany Nat when the fire horses pulled the large sprinkler wagon up and down the majority of the not-yet paved Borough streets.

Begun in March, 1903 with the purchase of a Studebaker sprinkler wagon, the sprinkling service was a fund-raising project for the fire company. Borough residents paid a monthly subscription fee to have the dirt streets in front of their houses wetted down, thus tamping down dust raised by passing horse and carriages that left a layer of dirt both inside and outside the homes.

Nat, as the driver, was one member of the three-man "sprinkler committee" and often recruited Stanley to help with the care of the sprinkler wagon, collecting sprinkler receipts, and, of course, helping with Duke and Harry.

"They've taken quite a shine to you," Nat had commented one Saturday afternoon as he guided Duke and Harry at a leisurely pace down Bridge Street. Stanley watched as drifts of water were sprayed side-to-side, sidewalk to sidewalk. "Especially after the Altemose fire. You were quite the hero..."

"Yeah, well... the flames... the fire...."

"Hotter than what you would have faced if you had been drafted?" Nathan White knew of his young protégé's reluctance and then dreaded acquiescence to register and his subsequent fear of being sent overseas. He acknowledged, but did not agree with his reasoning and rationale.

Hell, if I were younger, I'd be training with Battery C right now down in Camp Hancock, he mused, *readying myself and a few horses to go off to war. This guy should be grateful he's just fighting local fires and not enemy fire in a war.*

But who was to say that the recent fires occurring all over the fair, patriotic Borough of Phoenixville were not being set by just that? The enemy. Nat was convinced the arsonist was a spy and had adamantly expressed his opinion to Fire Chief Mendowski and Constable Tucker.

"Just doing my duty," Stanley said dismissively. He frowned at the determined look on Mr. White's face as he deftly steered the horses left onto Gay.

"Nat... I, um..."

"Yeah, hero boy. Out with it," he smiled.

Stanley reaching into his pants pocket and pulled out the tin box.

"I found this at Altemose's. Right after the fire when we were rolling up the hoses. It was by the doors... or what was left of the barn doors."

"Curious and curiouser..." Nat commented, quoting a character from one of his more favorite novels. He frowned at the etched letters and then asked Stanley to turn the box over. "What's inside?"

"Matches. Small kitchen matches." Stanley showed the driver how the box was opened to display twelve slender small Sulphur-tipped sticks inside.

"You think the person who started the fire.... left that?"

"I'm no detective, but I think so."

"And I think you need to give it to Dave. He'll know what to do..."

"But the eagle, if that's what it is."

"It's a German insignia, for sure. That much I know. I read up on the Franco-Prussian Was. 1870 or so, I think. Anyway, that looks like one of the emblems... of German-Austrian Army."

"And the words? Doc says they mean 'My country forever', but he wasn't sure."

"I have no idea," Nat sighed, nodding at the box. But if the box and its ominous insignia was, in fact, of German origin, then that would confirm his own suspicions of an enemy arsonist – most assuredly the spy – setting the fires. At least the one at the stables.

Stanley sighed, then pocketed the box again. Without any proof that his own suspicions might be correct, he immediately thought of Lenny Lochmann. Then, as the horses pulled the sprinkler wagon passed the Phoenixville High School on Nutt's Avenue, he remembered one morning before class – it seemed such a long time ago –when Lenny had smirked and pulled out a tin box from his jacket pocket and tried to explain it was his grandfather's from "the Russian war." Classmates had laughed at him, claiming the United States was not at war with Russia.

When was that? Sixth, seventh grade. I don't remember, but I do remember... Stanley vaguely recalled, *I remember! The emblem Mr. Ertell showed us in history class. A red and gold bird with the outstretched wings!*

When they returned to the firehouse, Stanley quickly jumped down from the wagon and purposefully barged into Fire Chief Mendowski's office without knocking.

"I think you ought to know about this," he stated, carefully placing the tin box onto the desk. "I found it the afternoon of the barn burning at Altemose's. I think it belongs to..." he blurted out, "to Lenny Lochmann."

"You sure?" the Chief asked, as he picked up and fingered the small container.

"No, not positively. But... He used to flaunt it about during recess at school."

"Well, if it is his, that would mean Lenny was at the scene..."

"And started the fire."

"Strong accusation, son. You willing to back that up?"

"That, sir, with all due respect, is for the police to decide."

Mendowski was taken aback. He did not expect Martinez, given his predilection – despite his recent heroism saving human as well as equine sentient lives – to be so forthright. He paused, leaned back in his rickety Windsor-backed office chair, and smiled.

"Okay, son," he said. "I'll give this to Constable Tucker and tell him what you said. Thank you."

"No problem, sir. Just, um, just doing my duty."

"It's too smudged," Detective Hoolmes said, inspecting the box under a magnifying glass. "There's no way to 'lift' and identify any fingerprints. Too old; too many handlers."

"Stanley remembers Lenny Lochmann flashing it around in school," Chief David Mendowski tried to explain. "Think there is anything to that?"

"Too circumstantial," Tucker frowned. "Not admissible in court, let alone warrant an arrest."

"But... the tire tracks at The Knoll. The big lummox tooling around on a motor bike With nubby tires? That means something..."

"You're a firefighter," Tucker snapped. "Not a crime investigator."

"But, Luke..."

"Sorry, Dave. But I'm just as upset and frustrated as you are with all these crimes... These fires around town. I want to find the arsonist, just as much as you do."

"So, you think there is an arsonist."

"I, er, um.... Well, yes... We haven't had these many fires in the Borough since... Since, well, since the fire department started in... in...."

"Eighteen seventy-four. February twenty-seventh, to be exact. Borough Council adopted a resolution to organize a fire company."

"Yes, well..."

"The organizational meeting of the new fire company was held on March third."

"Thanks for the history lesson, Dave..."

"And, Luke, there were many fires before that... But not recorded as accurately as they are now."

"Okay, okay, Dave. You've made your point."

"So, you'll at least look into it? Question Lenny?"

Constable Luke Tucker sighed. He dreaded the thought of once again accosting Lenny and his father, Herman Lochmann. *He was,* he thought to himself, *a mean son-of-a....* he refused to complete the sentence with the derogatory epitaph, even in the privacy of his own mind. But he believed it to be true.

Nevertheless, he had a duty as a police officer and as a valued and respected member of the community to perform, to the best of his ability, that duty which the Borough Council and the residents had entrusted to him.

"Yes. I'll look into it," he said.

It had been a month since the major fire at Altemose's stables when Stanley found the matchbox. Both Hoolmes and Tucker finally decided that while it might be evidence, it was "cold" evidence, despite Dave Mendowski's claim that Stanley had once seen it in the possession of Lenny Lochmann.

When the Fire Chief left, Tucker pondered the dilemma. After consulting with Detective Hoolmes, he was convinced the lack of fingerprints would lead to a dead end. Deciding ownership of the matchbox would be a useless path to pursue, he put it into the top drawer of his desk and forgot about it.

Despite his promise to Dave Mendowski that he'd investigate.

I can't waste my time... the taxpayers' money... on a wild goose chase.

Lenny had been scouring his room every night for weeks looking for his prized matchbox. It had been given to him as a toy by his mother the year before she had died.

"Here, son..." she had said. 'It was my father's pill box. He carried it with him during the Franco-Prussian War – 1870-71."

Lenny couldn't grasp the import of what his mother had told him, but he was attracted – and now attached – to the shiny box with the crudely colored bird and the funny etched letters. Besides, when his mother showed him how to open and close it, he was ecstatic.

He could hide things, small things in it.

Away from his father.

He cherished the tin box, often wiping it to keep its dull sheen clean. Keeping it safe in his cedar cigar box, putting it into his pocket only when he had, as he had been explaining lately to his father, to "run some errands".

He remembered taking it out the morning of the last fire and putting it into the right front pocket of his work pants. He remembered, once at the stables, taking a match out of it and striking it on its side, lighting a bundle of brittle dry straw just inside the barn doors.

And after that? He wasn't sure.

He couldn't remember.

In the excitement of watching the fire catch quicker than he had anticipated, and having to step away before he was overcome by the flames and billowing smoke, he wasn't sure if he had slipped it back into his pocket or... or...

Could he have dropped it?

Lenny stewed over his mistake for days until he finally decided he had to go back and search for his cherished tin box. As he guided his motor wheel down Nutt's Avenue and onto Cemetery Lane toward the horse farm, he realized it might be too late. *What if after all that time someone found it? And someone recognized it?*

Although Lenny had been, ever since his mother gave it to him, careful not to show it to anybody. Except, perhaps, a few times at school, showing off, to Stanley and Edmond Hope.

Trying to impress them. Trying to gain their friendship.

As hard as he tried, he just couldn't remember.

In his simple mind, he rationalized, *Stanley too busy fighting fire. Edmond no longer here.* So, Lenny pressed on, skidding the Smith Motor Wheel to a rumbling halt near what was once the site of one of Altemose's stately barns. He looked around, hoping no one could see him.

Three grey bulky box-shaped wagons were parked in a field at the end of the lane and three mangy-looking standardbreds were standing in a nearby paddock munching hay.

Lenny revved the engine just for the sadistic joy of startling them. One snorted and the other two merely looked up to see who was disturbing their peace. Lenny sneered, revved the engine up once more, then turned it off. He ambled to where he recalled the doors once were and stepped to one side.

Greg Altemose had wasted no time in rebuilding what had been, he had surmised, purposefully destroyed. A laid-back ride to the small farming community of Paradise in Lancaster County secured him the services of Stoltzfus and Sons, who, within just a few weeks, had started the reconstruction.

Three Amish men, clad in blue work shirts and black cotton pants held up by leather suspenders attached by hand-hewn wooden buttons, were busy erecting a newly-framed side wall. Two more young boys were raking up debris. Ashes; bits of cold burnt wood; charred door handles; frayed, blackened pieces of harness and tack.

The boys smiled and waved at Lenny, but he ignored them and began searching in front of the barn site. He kicked up a few tufts of dirt and scraped the ground with the toes of his hobnailed boots, alternating as he slowly walked around, head bowed, his beefy shoulders slumped.

"Something ya looking for?" one of the workers asked, stashing a hammer into a leather took belt slung low on his waist.

"No," Lenny said. "Just, um..."

"*Vas is letz*? Something wrong?"

"Yeah. I lost... I lost...." Lenny was reluctant to describe the tin pill, now matchbox. But the older man, with a long bushy black beard flecked with grey and a wide-brimmed stained straw hat, didn't know him. And, obviously, did not know about the box.

So, he described it to him.

"My mother gave me. Only thing left of her."

"Heirlooms gone not?

"My father burned all."

"Sad." The Amish man reached out to pat his shoulder, but Lenny shirked away. He hated to be touched by anyone. Even his father. Especially by a stranger. "So sorry. But, we will look out for it, surely. Your name, what is?"

"Lenny... Lochmann."

"Ah, Lenny. If we find it... I will, um... You live... where?"

"Scape Level. Other side town." But just as soon as he said it, Lenny regretted given away even the smallest bit of information. He turned away, angry at himself, then marched back to his motorized bike without even saying "thank you".

Lenny rode the Smith Motor Wheel, with its deep nubby tires back up Cemetery Lane as fast as he could. He did not look back and thus did not see the Amish man staring at the tire tracks left by his motorized bike in the soft dirt and then hasten toward Greg Altemose's manor house.

The father of five sons and the grandfather, so far, of four lanky boys and two dark-eyed girls, Jacob Stoltzfus was not a fool. On the contrary, he was a very wise and astute elder; an esteemed leader of the Paradise Amish community. He knew a conniving simpleton when he saw one.

Lenny Lochmann, if that was his real name, was up to something. *Not gut*, he thought, ambling toward Altemose's house. Mr. Greg had said that the barn he was rebuilding had been burnt down and the large, lumbering young man had admitted he had lost a box of matches on the property.

Jacob was an honest, loyal man. So, he told the horse breeder and trainer exactly what had transpired. Including the strange looking tracks crisscrossing the dirt in front of the construction site.

"Truth there is," he smiled when Altemose shook his hand in thanks.

"You did the right thing, Mr. Stoltzfus, telling me about Lenny. He's a reputation for being a bit of a... How shall I say it? The town..."

"... simpleton?"

"Yes, I guess... but, even more so... A trouble-maker."

"In our community have we those," Jacob smiled again. "Back to work I now go. Barns, such as yours, do not themselves build."

"Do me a favor?" Altemose asked before Jacob Stoltzfus left. "Describe once again the motor bike Lenny was driving." When he had memorized what the Amish man told him, he added, "And, please, whatever you do, please do not disturb the tracks. Nor let your workers do so.... They might be, um, evidence."

Stoltzfus nodded, put his straw hat back on, strolled out of the mansion, and instantly went back to work.

Greg Altemose, a determined man of action, once again wasted no time. He walked into the front foyer where the telephone box had been mounted on the wall near the hand-carved oak circular staircase. He picked up the receiver, turned the crank four times, and asked the operator located in a small brick building on Gay two blocks up from Bridge to "please connect me with the police".

Constable Luke Tucker tried to listen patiently as Greg Altemose told him about how the Amish man rebuilding his barn had described a tin box and the ruts in the dirt made by Lenny Lochmann's motorized bicycle. The telephone connection was rife with static; the local, newly-formed communications company had yet to master the new art of properly installing electrical wiring. Greg's otherwise deep baritone voice came across as garbled high-pitched whining.

But he had heard enough to convince him he now had a suspect.

"Hold on," the police officer finally was able to communicate. "I'll be there in a half hour." He had planned on going to the stables that afternoon anyway to take Ellington for a leisurely ride along the banks of Pickering Creek bordering the far end of Altemose's grazing fields. He'd check out the tracks, chat with Greg as well as the barn builder whom Altemose had identified as "Jacob".

Then he'd share whatever he deemed usable findings back with Fire Chief Mendowski. Between the two of them, they could probably figure out exactly what – and who – had started the barn fire that nearly destroyed four good horses. Including his own.

But there might not be any figuring necessary, Luke Tucker thought to himself. *I think I know who... And he isn't any German spy*

Altemose again relayed what Stoltzfus had told him about Lenny and the pill box converted into a matchbox. Tucker took careful notes on his small trusty notepad.

"Thanks, Greg. Most helpful," he said. "But, um, while I'm here, I thought I'd take Ellington out for a hack. You know, to clear my head. Do a bit of thinking."

"Sure, Luke. My stables are your stables. Be my guest."

Three hours later, refreshed by his brisk ride along the stream and through the woods, Constable Luke Tucker strolled into the police department offices. He instantly retrieved the tin matchbox from his desk drawer and carefully placed it upon the desk of Detective Hoolmes.

"I know we agreed before that this wasn't worth anything... But... I have a hunch. See what else, anything else you can make of this."

Hoolmes nodded, uncertain if he could even find anything more about the small box of any evidential use. He had already, after Fire Chief Mendowski had first handed it to him, dismissed the smudges as worthless. But, he told himself inwardly, *In the interest of crime investigation, and because Luke asked me… I'll try once more.*

Detective Hoolmes did a few more preliminary tests. Tten, with unqualified authority stated to Constable Tucker that "the tin, as I said before, is so smeared, there is no way to 'lift' and identify fingerprints… But I did find something of interest."

"Not fingerprints?" Constable Tucker queried.

"No, not fingerprints. Thread."

"Thread?"

"Yes, a thread. A shred of evidence." The young detective smiled at his own pun. But, seeing the frown on the Constable's face, returned the look with how own puckered frown. *Honestly,* he thought, *Luke has no sense of humor.* Hoolmes, on the other hand, was of the philosophy that detective work should have an element of fun. *After all, we're putting together pieces of puzzles.* He sighed, then hovered his magnifying glass, Sherlock Homes style, closely over the box. "Peer through it into the box itself," he commanded.

"Where am I looking?"

"Alongside the inner edge. There is the tiniest piece of thin thread."

"It's… um, red."

"Yes. And notice the tinier, ever so tinier white piece of…"

"What is that?"

"Lint."

"Lint?"

"Highly combustible, sir. I suspect that whomever started the fire, er, fires, worked in a place where he – or she – had access to not only thread, but lint."

"Hmmm… Like a mill?" The Perseverance Knitting Mill instantly came to mind." Hoolmes nodded. "Hmmm… Interesting. Good work, Hoolmes."

"Thank you, sir. Only doing my job."

Constable Tucker grunted, then concluded, "Lenny Lochmann, according to young Stanley Martinez and now Jacob Stoltzfus, once owned this box. I understand that he works at Perseverance Knitting Mill. Do you think he might be the one who... started the recent fires?"

"It certainly is a possibility, sir."

"And one very well worth looking into," Tucker smiled. He finally had the major case he was looking to solve. Ever since the murderous woman of ill-repute had slipped through his grasp and gotten away.

October 1917

As the war in Europe raged on, the small Borough of Phoenixville was caught in the throes of its own battles. There were food shortages – most of the country's fresh meat and vegetables, not to mention dairy products – were shipped overseas to support the American Expeditionary Forces and their allies. And this affected local groceries, like Eyrich's Meat Market, who turned to local farms for viands. Families who had even the smallest modicum of property planted Victory gardens to grow their own vegetables. *The Daily Republican* listed tomatoes, beets, turnips, and potatoes to grow and preserve for the upcoming winter months.

Over 265 young men, members of Battery C and Company D were now training in Camp Hancock just outside Atlanta, Georgia, to eventually be shipped overseas. Many more were culled from the Selective Service registrants, while several others, including a few women who joined the Red Cross to serve as nurses or to become Donut Girls, volunteered to serve.

At final count, 420 Phoenixville men, out of a population of just over 10,000, would eventually be fighting in the Great War. As a result, there was a slight, but noticeable deficiency in manpower. Young boys had to leave school, stepping in to fill the jobs their fathers had left behind. Wives and mothers took over their husbands' and sons' daily tasks and some of them took work outside the home. Including piece work sewing at the Perseverance Mill.

What had once before the war been a sleepy industrial town nestled in the foothills of the Appalachian Mountains, was now rapidly transforming into a bustling community. It was, like hundreds of small towns across America, trying to maintain an optimal standard of living along with a sense of normalcy in a time of international crisis and chaos. All the while, as the popular British song of the day declaimed, they were "Keeping the Home Fires Burning".

Families worried for the safety of their male members who had gone off to fight. Newspaper accounts were dire, at best, filled with graphic accounts of battles fought over muddy terrain, the metallic stench of blood in the air.

Would any of them even come back alive?

Rosalina, for one, was fearful for her fiancé, Edmond Hope. He had just relayed in a letter that he was, hopefully, about to finish training and would shortly be transported to New York. From there he'd sail to Southampton, England and then across the English Channel to engage in battle.

My Dearest Rosie, Edmond's most recent letter began. *I am not allowed to write much about the actual training. For fear, I guess, of inadvertently relaying French artillery secrets to the Germans. Not that I would ever suspect you of being a German spy. I jest, my dear.*

Truth to tell, there really aren't any great secrets to tell. The artillery we are using in training are antiquated. The horses – ours, as you know, were sent back home – are cumbersome Belgian draft horses. Oh, they're strong enough, but they are not at all suitable for agilely navigating what we are being told is rough and muddy Belgian terrain.

Gritty sand is all over our campgrounds and in the very air we breathe. It gets into our hair, our eyes, and seeps through the weak seams of what are supposed to be sturdy boots, lodging between our toes. Your father would be appalled to hear we are shod in cheap boots – although I am sure he, as well as you, will enjoy my little "bon mot".

Nearly every night for dinner they serve us overcooked ham, bad lima beans, boiled sometimes mealy potatoes, and slightly stale bread. Coffee, of course, but even that is weak and boiled, not even perked, as you know how much I like that.

As you can tell, I am distraught at our conditions and becoming more so every day that we have to spend in this hell hole. It's is filthy hot. Extremely filthy hot. Even through summer has been over for two months. I hope you are enjoying the changing of the leaves and the cool evening breezes. Please send a zephyr or two my way, won't you, my dear?

Edmond went on to write about his conversations with Captain Whitaker and his feeble attempts at cajoling and consoling his troops.

The more we complain, the more ineffectual he becomes in improving anything. And the French officers are insufferable. They turn blind eyes and deaf ears to our plight. I am nearly at my wit's end... and there is no end in sight.

The only thing that keeps me going is knowing that someday, in the near future, I hope, we'll be shipped to Europe to fight... and, of course, my constant thoughts of you, my darling...

Whom I hope to marry when I return home May I presume your answer is still yes?

He rambled on a bit more, then closed with *I love you. Yours affectionately, Eddie,* followed a string of X's and O's.

"Yes, dear Edmond," Rosalina smiled. "Of course, I will till marry you. Yes, silly man."

Rosalina carefully refolded the letter and put it between the pages of the book she was reading.

"News from our brave boy?" Stanley asked, non-clamantly strolling into the small library off the parlor. Every wall lined with floor-to ceiling shelves, it sported a wide variety of both fiction and non-fiction, including all the latest bestsellers and leather-bound reprints of the world's classic literature. Most of the volumes were garnered second-hand from used book stores, yard sales, and the discard stack of the local library. *But still,* Stanley thought, *it is an impressive collection.*

Growing up, he and his sister spent countless hours on rainy and snowy afternoons reading together, often aloud to one another. One of the last things they still shared as they both moved into adulthood.

"Here to get a book, Stan-Stan?"

"Sure thing," he said, tossing a tattered copy of *Ivanhoe* onto the pier table behind the maroon camel-back couch where Rosalina was sitting. "With all this war talk, I am a bit scotched on reading any more adventure stories." He sat down beside her. "What are you reading?"

"*Elsie at Nantucket,*" Rosalina responded cautiously. She was not as erudite as her brother and often her reading tastes tended to be more light and frivolous.

"Ah, Martha Finley. Wasn't she a local religious fanatic? Espousing Christian ethics and values in her writing? I thought you grew out of that a long time ago."

"We are still Catholic, Stanley. At least I still am," referring to his lapsed attendance at Mass at St. Mary's. "I find the Elsie stories comforting and... and.." she searched for the right word. "Uplifting."

"Harrumph. Women's literature. Not fit for a man..."

"Edmond shares my love of Martha Finley. And he is just as masculine as you are, Stanley. If not more."

"Edmond? Didn't he ever tell you about the raucous penny-dreadfuls we used to buy at Kettleman's? Swashbuckling adventures, they were. Black Bart's revenging raids... Rescuing beautiful and beguiling damsels in distress... Slaying dragons with bare hands. Arrrgh! No wonder he's so gung-ho on going to war."

"He is brave... and honorable. And I love him." She paused. "And, I am going to marry him."

Stanley looked into his sister's eyes and saw meek defiance tinged with fear. He backed down.

"Okay, you win," he said. "Edmond is a good guy. After all, he is my best friend. He'll make you a good husband."

His sister tried to smile, then burst into tears.

"I am so... concerned for him. That he will not come back. Or come back... wounded."

"Ah, c'mon, little Rosie," Stanley whispered, a bit choked up himself. He wrapped his arms around her and kissed her forehead. "Listen, Edmond is big and strong and bright and... Well, he knows how to take care of himself. Just wait and see, he'll come through all that brutal, needless nonsense and will come home safely as a hero."

"You think so?"

"I know so."

They sat quietly together for a while; a rare moment of closeness between them. Rosalina sobbed quietly against Stanley's shoulder as he gently rubbed her back. Then, when she stopped and wiped the tears from her eyes, he took a creased white envelope out of his pants pocket.

"Here, I got us something."

"What is it?"

"Several Victory Liberty war bonds..."

"But you hate the war. You promised not to support it..."

"Yeah, but if I, we can make money off it..."

"How many?"

"I've had money taken out of my pay every week since the war started. So, after a few months, voila! War bonds. Five or six, I think. So far."

Rosaline couldn't believe her ears, nor eyes. She grasped the envelope in her hands.

"Momma and Papi will ever be so pleased!"

"Well, they're not for them…"

"What?"

"They're for us. For you. For when you and Edmond get married… Or for when you decide to go to college. I opted not to, but… No reason you can't…"

Before she had promised to marry Edmond, his sister had expressed an interest in matriculating at Bryn Mawr College on the Main Line. She wanted to become a social worker and champion the rights of women and children. But the college was a bit more expensive than their parents could afford and, well, the Great War had started. And then, what had begun as a mutually innocent childhood crush on her brother's best friend had turned into a robust romance.

"Stan-Stan, I can't. But, what about you?"

"Oh, once they all mature, I'll take a bit out for myself. Don't you worry." He was sure what he would use the extra money for, but, for the moment, wasn't ready yet to reveal his plans. He stood up, stuffed the bonds into his back pocket and offered his hand to his sister.

"Well, now there, my dear sister Rosalina. Aren't you going to help me select my next read?"

Before he joined Dr. Harrop's medical practice behind the Phoenixville Hospital on Gay Street, Dr. Galen Hall had played wide receiver for the Phoenix Athletic Association. The renowned football team, undefeated for several years, was victorious against several other teams in the tri-state area of Pennsylvania, New York, and New Jersey. The PAA had twice held the "national" championship title.

Hall was proud of being a member of the renowned team as well as his record. He had scored more touchdowns than he could remember and had hoped to continue his sports career as a professional. But his mother, a member of the local Red Cross, had persuaded Galen, whom she had named after an ancient Greek physician, that he had a "higher calling as a doctor".

At Penn State, he traded his prowess on the gridiron for diagnostic and surgical skills, earning his Summa Cum Laude Ph.D. in medicine. Yet, his penchant for sports never left him. He still had his leather-padded uniform with the red "U" on the front hanging in the hall closet of his cape cod on Fourth Avenue. Right above his trusty wooden tennis racket that leaned jauntily against the inner wall.

He often wielded the well-worn racket on the newly built-clay courts two blocks up from his house to defeat not only the much older Dr. Harrop, but his contemporaries. Including Samuel Whitaker, who was now commander of the Battery C Artillery Unit and Joe O'Donnell, now Captain of Company D.

Harrop's general practice and reputation had been growing steadily ever since the inception of the new hospital in 1900 on Nutt's Avenue. A native of Phoenixville, Hall immediately returned home right after graduation. The day after his arrival, he marched into the older physician's office and asked for a job. He was hired on the spot and saw his first patient that very afternoon. Ever since, he maintained the status of being one of the finest, most caring doctors in the fair Borough.

Now in his early forties, Hall was a tad under five-foot seven, with pre-mature salt-and-pepper light brown hair, kindly pale blue eyes, and a soft baritone voice that he effectively used to calm even the most frightened of his patients. Especially the older females, whom Corrine, his Irish-born wife of ten years, often teasingly accused him of seducing. It wasn't true, of course. She knew full-well how much he loved her; and she, him.

When war broke out in Europe in 1914, Hall was one of the first in the community to promote the entry of the United States into the escalating conflict. At first, he was opposed by most of his friends and relatives, but he persisted anyway. In early 1915, he offered his services as a military physician to the Company D National Guard Unit.

O'Donnell was delighted his tennis buddy wanted to join the unit. He needed a dedicated, able-bodied medic and Doctor Hall neatly fit the bill. His decision to join Company D, however, deeply distressed Corrine. It meant, now that America had finally entered the war, he would be a participant. The writing, she was sure, was boldly written in red ink on the wall. As well as in her aching heart.

Galen, however, was not among those of Company D who were sent to Camp Hancock for training back in August. Instead, he was permitted to take care of his patients in Phoenixville until the 28th Division was finally shipped overseas. The rationale was that most medical personnel would be behind the lines, not directly in the line of fire and, thus, not required to undergo any formal military training.

So, Dr. Hall stayed behind to serve his fellow residents of the Borough instead of going off to serve his country. Which pleased his wife. But she still dreaded the day he would eventually be called away.

Which was why Galen Hall, Ph.D. was in the surgery center of the brick Harrop Medical Center building when, of all people, Dolores Martinez walked in and declared she had a wounded Lenny Lochmann in the back seat of her car.

Lenny hated to read. He preferred pictures and charts and bulleted lists of unrelated, absurd, and arcane facts. If he had to tackle anything that looked longer than 140 – his "magic" number – characters, he would scribble over or rip out the rest. He actually preferred to be read to. This had exasperated his teachers at school and angered his father, who dubbed him *dummy, dummy Dummkopf.*

155

But it did not frustrate or annoy his mother, who loved her son more, it seemed, than her cruel and demanding husband.

"Forget about it, Helga," Hermann would tell her as she poured over pages of *The Child's World Primer,* pointing at the words as she read out loud to their son. "He can't get anything through his thick skull, even if you try pounding it in," he sneered, slapping Lenny up one side of his head. "Can't you? Son?"

But no matter how hard he tried to please her – and, ironically more so, his father – Lenny had no aptitude nor capability of comprehension much beyond the second-grade level. His mother finally realized this, but continued trying to teach her beloved son anyway. And, despite her efforts and Lenny's attempts to please both parents, Hermann continued to berate and beat his son.

"Hermann! How can he learn if you constantly hit him and treat him like that? *Wie ein...* Like an Idiot?"

"Because he is one!" Lenny's father shouted, hit Lenny again, and then stormed out of the room.

Lenny never forgot that incident nor many others like it.

After his mother had died, his father burned all the books she had tried to interest Lenny in. Including the primers and the picture books Lenny seemed to like, as well as Estelle's own collection of English and German authors. Jane Austin, Emily Bronte, Mark Twain, Proust, and Theodor Storm, whom his wife particularly enjoyed, were burned together in a collective miasma of flames and fiery words turned into ashes. A burn pit in the back yard was then filled with librettos of operas by Wagner, Mozart, Étienne Méhul, George Frederic Handel, and the operettas of Gilbert and Sullivan, whose music she adored... They, too, went up in plumes of smoke.

Hermann Lochmann, an avid reader himself, locked up his own collection in a large armoire ensconced in his bedroom. He had forbidden Lenny to enter, let alone try to touch the books.

Locking them up, of course, was unnecessary. His son was immune to anything literary.

Lenny would often cry himself to sleep at night, listening in his mind's ear his mother's contralto voice singing "When I Was a Lad" from *HMS Pinafore*. He would hum softly to himself, repeating the last few lines of the first verse over and over like a lullaby as he wept. He did not understand many of the lyrics; only that his mother had repeatedly sung them to him.

> *I polished up the handle of the big front door*
> *So carefully, that...*
> *Now I am the ruler of the Queen's Navy!*

Lenny knew, though, what being a ruler meant. He longed to be something big and important. Something, someone more than he was now or could ever hope to be.

Imagine, being ruler, he would sob. *If only Mama not died. If father loved me... If ... if... if..* he would wish, finally falling into a light, fitful slumber.

Stanley and Edmond read, he had been lately thinking angrily when he woke up in the first dawning hours of the morning. Drenched in cold sweat from his last terrifying nightmare, Lenny clutched the thread-bare woolen blanket to his chest. He remembered... He had watched Stanley and Edmond leaving the library many times carrying books, avidly discussing their anticipated reads. They shared the titles they had checked out. *The Wonderful Wizard of Oz, The Call of the Wild, Riders of the Purple Sage...* These were strange, foreign words to Lenny. *What did they mean. Why I not know?*

Lenny swung the sanded bat loosely by his side as he walked up Bridge Street. He had parked his Smith Motor Wheel in the small lot alongside the Perseverance Knitting Mill where he had, earlier that morning, clocked into work. He smiled crookedly at the weavers and sewers on the second floor already toiling away as they manufactured children's underwear, women's pajamas, and men's coarse denim shirts and trousers.

He continued to smile as he swept up residual lint and loose threads and stuffed them into a burlap bag. When it was full, he retrieved the bat hidden in his cloakroom locker, and snuck out the back door of the clothing factory.

In his pockets were a small box of matches he had swiped from atop his father's desk – he never did find his cherished tin pill/match box – a small whisky flask filled with kerosene, and a tattered copy of *Codes und Verschlüsselungen*.

He didn't understand the last word of the title of the book; his father never bothered to teach him the language of his native land. But he suspected it might have something to do with Hermann's own occasional forays into the dark of night. But Lenny didn't care. He was on his own, more important foray into the light of day.

No one seemed to be around as Lenny walked down the narrow alley beside the book and music store, whimsically called *Price's Notes and Books*. When he reached the back of the building, he crouched behind two large trash bins, took out the matches and flask, carefully wrapped wads of lint and thread around the blunt thick tip of the bat, and doused it with the kerosene. He set the torch on fire. With a grunt and a practiced aim, he tossed it onto the second story roof of the store he so despised for selling things he didn't understand. For selling them to the young men in town who, for unknown reasons, refused to be his friends.

Christopher Price immediately recognized the hulking frame of Lenny Lochmann as he snuck past his store's showroom window. He was arranging a new display of books when he glanced up and watched as the young man, carrying a baseball bat and nervously fingering the front pocket of his loose-fitting grey slacks, entered the alley.

Price glowered. The bookstore owner, like everyone in the Borough, newcomers as well as native-born residents, knew that wherever Lenny Lochmann went trouble followed. It did not take any internal persuasion to prompt the literary and music aficionado to race to his office in the back of the store and ring up the police.

"Better request the services of the fire department, too," he commanded. "I have... I have this feeling."

No sooner had Lenny tossed his torch and a few licks of flame appeared on the roof when the Diaphone Claxon horn atop the pipe-fitting building started to sound. Two-five. Bridge and Main. Over and over again. Then came the faint clanging of the large bell atop the fire company's hose drying tower. And then, shortly afterward, the sound of horse hooves thundering down the street.

Lenny stopped dead in his tracks. *How did anybody know...?*

He did not hesitate. He gathered up the burlap bag, the box of matches, and began to run. He hoped that the torch would burn up on the roof once the flames started to spread. In his haste, he forgot to pick up the half-empty flask of kerosene where it lay half-hidden alongside one of the wooden-slatted trash bins. He didn't remember it until he was halfway to Perseverance Knitting Mill.

But he could not go back and retrieve it.

When he did stop and look back, hoping to see books burning, Constable Luke Tucker's red and white Tornado was parked in front of Price's store. The horse-drawn LaFrance wagon, with Stanley stoking the steam pumper fire, had pulled into the back alley.

Lenny watched as Stanley and two other firemen quickly jumped down and unwound the hose as three others of the company extended the hook ladder up to the store's rooftop. With the nozzle of the nose slung over his shoulders, Stanley mounted the ladder. As he climbed, Doc Kimshaw attached the other end of the pumper hose to the fire hydrant across Price Street, then cranked up the pumper.

I should be doing that, Lenny hissed. *I be fireman. The best fireman. The very best.*

Stanley was joined at the top of the ladder by Billy Szabo, who turned on the valve. The two of them then aimed the brass nozzle at the flames licking up from the tarpaper. It took the strength and agility of both to handle the pulsating hose and stay on the ladder. Stanley wrapped one leg around a steel railing and hooked his other foot beneath a rung.

"Sweep across!" Chief Mendowski called up from below. "That's it! Slowly sweep!"

Carlos Martinez stepped outside his shoe story to see what all the commotion was about. He walked a half block toward Price's shop when he was stopped by a police officer ushering people to the other side of the street. He looked up at the burning building and was stunned to see his son scale the ladder toward the roof fire.

"Stanley!" he yelled, a lump in his throat, his heart beating twice its normal rate.

"Walk away, please," the officer waved at him. "Nothing to see here."

Stanley's father shook his head and walked back to the entrance of his own store, but not before he saw his only son disappear into a thick column of white smoke.

It took less than ten minutes to contain what turned out to be a small fire. Billy shut off the nozzle, then signaled to turn off the pumper. Behind Stanley on the ladder, he shouldered the hose and climbed down. Stanley, however, stepped out onto the smoldering, now drenched roof. Smoke and steam occluded his rubber boots as he walked around.

"Martinez!" he heard the Chief yell. "What the hell are you still doing up there? C'mon down!" Stanley walked to the edge and shouted, "Clues, sir! Looking for clues."

"That's my job, son!" Constable Tucker yelled.

"Then come on up here!" Stanley chuckled. He knew full-well from the stories his father told over Sunday dinner about the residents of Phoenixville he had shod over the years, that the police officer had more than a slight fear of heights.

"No, no. That's okay, Stanley! I'm fine down here. Just be careful and... and let me know if you find anything."

Stanley saluted and then went back to his search. He did not see the half-burnt Louisville Slugger smoldering against an abutment. Sure that there was nothing out of the ordinary on the roof except for burnt tarpaper, ashes, and puddles of still-steaming water, he scrambled down the ladder. When he reached the bottom, he jumped off a bit too quickly, lost his balance and, stumbling back, and fell against one of the trash bins.

His slick wet boot slipped, accidently kicking a small leather-clad vial.

"What the...?" he mumbled, stooping to pick the object up. At first, he thought it was a piece of trash, but when he realized that a book store wouldn't carry such an item, he unscrewed the top and sniffed the contents. "Kerosene," he stated in disgust, then screwed the lid back on and put the flask into a side pocket of his fireman's canvas tunic.

Another item for Fire Chief Mendowski and Constable Turner to consider, he thought. He was just as anxious as they were to solve the on-going mystery of the inscrutable fires lit around town. Like them, he was sure they were set by an arsonist. And, like them, his was just as anxious to know by whom.

Although he was almost positive it was Lenny.

But, why?

Lenny spent the rest of the day sweeping floors and stuffing bags with clouds of lint and tangled balls of loose threads. When the bell rang signaling the end of the work day, he whipped off his denim apron, picked up the filled bags, and lumbered out the factory doors to where he had parked his motorized bike. He threw the bags, save the smallest one, into the incinerator in the back of the mill.

In his haste to get home, Lenny decided to take another route back to Scape Level. Rather than putt-putt his way up Bridge Street and then onto Main, he decided to cross the Gay Street Bridge and follow High Street west along Freemont. He did not see the thinly-spread oil slick on the north end of the bridge until it was too late. The Smith Motor Wheel, racing along at top speed, skittered across the road, careened onto its side and slammed Lenny Lochmann's hulking body into the concrete.

The Motor Wheel was fine, just barely scratched and dented, but its rider not only felt but heard the crunch of bone against hard wood before he passed out.

The driver, on her way back from meeting with the Hospital's Women's Auxiliary, saw Lenny's bike tip over and nearly careen off the bridge into a Phoenix Iron Company yard. She instantly slowed down and edged the family's American Underslung touring car along the curb.

Dolores Martinez had managed to upright the Motor Wheel, roll it to the sidewalk, and lean it against a railing. She then roused Lenny, somehow got him onto the back seat of the car, and drove straight to the Harrop Medical Center.

Dr. Hall, she was pleased to see, was still there, just finishing up attending to another patient.

Galen smiled when he saw Dolores enter the outer office. His smile turned into a frown when he saw she was obviously in distress.

"What's wrong? Are you hurt? In pain?" He reached for her arm.

"No, no... Not me. Lenny Lochmann has had an accident. He's in the back of the car," she sighed. "I somehow got him in, but need help getting him out."

The doctor, quickly dismissing his current patient, escorted her out of the building toward the Underslung; its engine still running. And although Lenny was bigger than he, Doctor Galen Hall managed to wake him up again and half guide, half carry him into the building and into an empty examining room. Dolores followed, concerned about the young man who, while being the Borough bully, was obviously seriously injured.

"You could have taken him to the hospital, Dolores."

"Yes, but..." She had no excuse. The Harrop Medical Center had been in business long before the new hospital had been established. Even with proper funding from the Ladies Auxiliary, of which she as a member, for the purchase of the latest "state-of-the-art" medical equipment and supplies, it would take a while before most of the residents of the community would have total faith and trust in its staff.

She, however, was one not of them. But all her life she had thought of Harrop's Medical Center as Phoenixville's primary care facility. And her first thought was to take Lenny there, not to the emergency room. *Old habits,* she shook her head, *never die.*

"I didn't think," she stammered. "The, my first thought was... of you."

"Of course," Galen smiled again. He knew what she was trying to say, but didn't respond. They had grown up together during the Borough's burgeoning era of industrial growth and prosperity. A more peaceful time, he reflected, when he had become enamored of the fair-haired Irish lass from the North Side. Their eyes locked for a brief moment before he looked away.

"Best we alert his father. I would, but... He needs immediate attention." He turned to his receptionist. "Could you please call..."

"I don't think they have a phone," Dolores said. Then, without hesitation, "I'll drive up there straightway."

Dolores, flustered and a bit red-faced, sped to Scape Level to retrieve Hermann Lochmann.

"Your son is badly injured and he needs you. Now!" she had commanded when Hermann Lochmann annoyingly opened the door. "Come with me," she ordered and then drove Lenny's father to the clinic. She hastily dropped him off and then raced home to see if there was any news of her own son.

"Him and his damn bike," Hermann hissed in broken English when he saw his injured son. "I told him not to buy it... *Dummy, dummy Dummkopf.*"

"That is not the issue here," the doctor said, concerned about the scurrilous labels the German was attributing to his son. He looked at the X-rays in the small examining room. "What is at issue here is that the radius is definitely snapped."

Lenny moaned, lying on the table, his father growling softly in a white metal chair beside him.

"Luckily in just one place. But it's a bad break." Dr. Hall observed. "Hmm... How, how did this happen?"

"I slipped," Lenny mumbled, cradling his broken arm, moaning in a semi-fetal position on the examining table. "Cycle slipped."

"Well, you were lucky. It could have been worse. Well, we'll set the bone and treat you for a possible concussion. That means no riding or working for a while until your arm starts to heal." He paused and assessed Lenny's blank look. Despite being sure if the young man completely understood what he was saying, he continued his instructions.

"You are to remain at home, with the arm, once we set it, raised on a pillow. And you, Mr. Lochmann, will see to it that he gets proper... and considerate care."

Hermann scowled, turning away from both the doctor and Lenny. He had no intention of pampering his idiotic son, broken arm or not. *That dowdy Italian Mrs. Marcelino can take care of him,* he smirked to himself. *She dotes on him, anyway. Selling him that troublesome bike..."*

"How long?" Lenny managed to ask, searching for some sort of comfort and concern from his father.

"At least two, three weeks until the bones start to knit".

"Time... I need time... to do..." He drifted off again in yet another blank stare.

"To do what, Lenny?" Dr. Galen Hall asked, starting to mix plaster-of-Paris to set Lenny's arm.

But Lenny was again lost in his own dream world, wondering how he was, with a broken arm, going to sand down the two baseball bats he had stolen from Meadows' shop on Main and complete all the errands he had planned.

Frank LaBronsky's parents were elated when the British Government announced the Balfour Declaration, giving its support to a Jewish "national home" in Palestine. It would probably take decades before it came to fruition, but Sarah LaBronsky née Sevkowski was ecstatic. She might never live to see the day when such a thing would really happen, but she and her parents had narrowly escaped one of the many anti-Semitic pogroms in Eastern Russia during the latter part of the last century. They had managed to secured passage in steerage on a rusting Slavonic merchant ship on its way to the United States. Had there been a Jewish homeland, the family would have gone there instead.

But, somehow, after a difficult time getting through the custom requirements at Ellis Island, they finally made their way to Phoenixville, PA, where Sarah, a few years later, had fallen in love with and married Harold LaBronsky.

Harold wasn't Jewish nor of Russian extraction like his wife. His parents, in fact, were from the eastern shore of Poland and he had been raised in the Protestant tradition. Despite their differences in background and religious beliefs, he was instantly smitten with Sarah's wide-spaced dark chocolate eyes, kinked black hair, and faint foreign accent. Her robust sturdy but feminine build added to his mixture of desire and unabashedly total devotion. Once a member of the Central Lutheran Church on the corner of South Main and Church, he instantly converted for her sake and joined the B'nai Jacob congregation that worshipped in the converted residence on South Main across from the Company D Armory.

He, too, for the sake of his wife, was glad about the Balfour decision and was worried its implementation would have a few setbacks. But he was more concerned about his son who was, the last he had heard, somewhere in the south of England, having survived the sinking of his troop ship by a German U-Boat in the North Sea and had bravely rescued five of his shipmates.

Harry flipped open the pages of *The Daily Republican* and, after first reading the sports section – the Union Club had once again won yet another game – turned to the comics, his favorite section, and then scanned the headlines about the Great War.

SUPREME WAR COUNCIL CONVENED BY ALLIES IN VERSAILLES
BOLSHEVIKS REVOLT AND SEIZE POWER
NEW COMMANDER-IN-CHIEF OF THE ITALIAN ARMY
BATTLE OF PASSCHENDAELE ENDS

"My God," he muttered. "When will this all be over?" He hoped Frank wasn't involved in the last battle at Ypres, although the paper did say that American fighter planes may not have been involved. "Thank goodness," he muttered again, then looked up as his wife strolled into the parlor with the mail.

"A letter... Finally, a letter from Frank," she smiled.

"What does it say?" He reached up to take it from her.

"No, no! Wait, let me open it..."

Dear Mom and Dad, the short letter began. *I am safe for now.*

Sarah breathed a sigh of relief.

"Go on," Harry urged.

As you know, I survived the shipwreck. I don't know how I did, but thanks, Dad, for teaching me to be a strong swimmer and basic life-saving skills. Because of you, and, as you know, I managed to save five guys in my unit. We were then transported to [censored] where we are now.

Our commanding officer was kind of thrilled with what I did and asked if there was anything else he could do, besides seeing to it I get the Medal of Honor. I told him point blank I was afraid of heights and really didn't want to be a fighter pilot. I was pretty adamant and finally he said firefighters were needed aboard ships. I'll be serving on the seas, not over the seas. After training, I'll be going to [censored] to join the crew of the [censored]. It's a whole lot safer than flying a flimsy kite made of thin wood and brittle wires.

When you see him, tell that laggard Stanley Martinez that if ever I survive this war, I'll be home soon joining him at Phoenix № 1. Got to go now and grab some dinner in the mess. Nothing like your Friday night roast chicken, Mom, but substantial enough.

My love to you both. Give old slobbering Shasha a belly-rub and an extra biscuit for me.

Affectionally, your son, Frank.

"Safe for now," Sarah sighed again. "The letter is dated two weeks ago... Where is he now? Today?"

"Probably already fighting fires somewhere on a destroyer," her husband stated softly. He waited for Sarah to dry her tears. "Listen, let's not waste our energy worrying until... Until we hear something for sure. Let's just be grateful for the letter and the life of our son. *Loyb di har.*"

"Yes. Praise the Lord," Sarah repeated, dabbing her eyes. She leaned over her kindly, wise husband and kissed his forehead.

"Sometimes," she whispered lovingly, "in moments like this I am convinced you, the convert, are more Jewish than me."

Harry LaBronsky harrumphed and continued reading the paper.

In the first battle of the Plave, the Austro-Hungarian and German troops attempted to cross the river but were thwarted by the combined French, British, and American Forces. The battle of Mughar Ridge began as the Austro-Hungarian offensive during the first battle of Monte Grappa was halted.

The last item he read before dozing off in his plaid upholstered arm chair was that Georges Clemenceau replaced Paul Painlevé as France's Prime Minister.

While Lenny Lochmann languished on the frayed couch in the front parlor, Mrs. Marcelino bustled around the Lochmann's filthy kitchen, attempting to make her soothing Italian wedding soup. She had shooed Hermann out of her way, telling him she "would take care of dear Lenny without your help".

"That's fine with me. Perfectly fine," his father grumbled, slamming the kitchen door behind him as he stormed into the back yard. "You do it. I don't have the stomach for it. Or him."

Lenny heard his father and vowed, once again, since he couldn't please him, that he would get even. With him, with Stanley, and with the rest of the community that he felt, he knew, was against him.

Fire Chief Mendowski, Constable Tucker, and Detective Holmes met in Tucker's office. Tucker fidgeted with a typewritten list of those in the Phoenixville area who had been identified as "confirmed residents with ties to Germany".

"Hermann Lochmann on the list?"

"No, Dave. But I have a suspicion that he ought to be."

"Ahem," Detective Hoolmes cleared his throat. "But maybe we ought to pay him a visit and find out why... he hasn't registered."

"Maybe he has no cause to..." the Chief shook his head. "Just because he's German doesn't mean he is..."

"And it doesn't mean he isn't, either. I heard that enemy spies don't bother to register and..."

"You think Hermann's a spy?" Dave Mendowski asked incredulously. He smiled, despite the rumors in the past few months to the contrary, at the absurdity of having a German espionage agent living in their midst.

"He's a sympathizer... Not letting his son join the military."

"Oh, c'mon, Simon. Hermann Lochmann is no more a spy than, then..."

"Then his son setting all the fires around town?"

"That is not what I was going to say..." The Fire Chief stood up to leave. "Besides, he didn't stop his son from enlisting. Lenny was deemed 'unfit for service'." He paused, then nodded at the Constable. "We'll talk about this later, Luke," he said and left.

Chief Mendowski had other pressing business at the firehouse to attend to.

But he couldn't shake from his mind the thought that someone living up at Scape Level might actually be in collusion with the Central Powers.

November 1917

The Third Battle of Ypres, also known as the Battle of Passchendaele finally ended on November 10, 1917. But not before several local men, including Campbell Wheatley, had lost their lives. It would be remembered as a bloody massacre of the war. But the even bloodier campaigns in the Argonne Forest and the Battle of the Somme had yet to come.

Still mired in the heat, mud, and mosquitoes of Atlanta, Georgia, Edmond Hope and Hans Gruber continued to train in Camp Hancock under the tutelage of French artillery officers.

Edmond had grown tired of the constant diet of boiled ham, cabbage, weak coffee, with stale bread and butter for dessert. He longed for his mother's home-cooking, recalling the aroma of a rack of lamb or a wine-soaked pot-roast wafting through the large Victorian on Second Avenue. He even missed the family's old basset hound, FrankieBernard, who left a slimy trail of drool as he faithfully followed Edmond everywhere around the house.

And, despite his now monotonous complaints to Captain Whitaker and his artillery sergeant, there was nothing much else for Edmond to do except grin and bear it. And endure the incessant repetitious training.

On occasion, his mother or sister would send "care packages" for himself and to distribute to his Battery C buddies. Baked cookies that had grown stale by the time they were delivered; old copies of *The Daily Republican* – to "share the news from the home front" – hand-knitted woolen socks and sweaters; crocheted mittens... He didn't have the heart to write back that down south, even in November, the temperature never dipped below eighty-degrees. But then, he had learned it was already a searingly cold winter in France. He would need the warm clothing if... when he finally got there. He sighed, sharing the latest packet from Rebecca with Hans.

"Stow them in your foot-locker," the stocky lad shrugged. "Mittens be handy in France." Edmond did a double-take at Hans' pun. How could he ever have been mad at him? More optimistic than he was, it was obvious Hans' normally shy and reticent buddy welcomed the kindnesses shown by others. It meant that although they were stuck in the morass of training camp, they were not forgotten.

Each time he saw her, Stanley was more disgruntled with Samantha than he was pleased. Or even happy. Regardless what he suggested or planned for their "get-togethers" – she refused to call them "dates" – she always took the upper-hand and overruled it. Whenever he asked her out for dinner, she changed the time and made the reservations. When he suggested a hike through Valley Forge State Park, she planned their route. When Stanley proposed seeing a movie every Thursday evening at the Colonial Theatre for Red Cross Benefit Night, Samantha pooh-poohed the idea, telling him, "I'll decide what flicker we'll see."

The straw that cracked the proverbial camel's back was the late Saturday afternoon when she strolled unannounced into the firehouse while he was on call. With a long multi-colored silk scarf causally wrapped around her neck, thrown over her shoulders, and trailing down her back she marched into the Captain's office and demanded that he give Stanley the evening off.

"I've planned dinner in town..." she started.

"B-but, sir..." Stanley stammered behind her. "I didn't know..."

"It's okay, Martinez." He held up his hand and stared at the tall, lanky woman, dressed in the latest mid-calf length fashionable shirtwaist standing with her arms akimbo, glaring at him. 'Sorry, but Stan is on duty and can't be called away."

"But, it's an emergency."

"Since when is eating dinner an emergency?" Stanley ventured.

"We have things to talk about."

"They'll have to wait," Mendowski said sternly. "Just because your aunt's a guest of one of the wealthiest..." He didn't complete the sentence. Instead, he said, "You can't come barging in here like you own the place and... And... Demand...."

"Who? Me? Demand?!" she exclaimed, haughty fire in her eyes. "Well, I never!" Samantha Higgins Rouleaux turned smartly on her hour-glass shaped heels – custom-made by Carlos Martinez – and stormed out the door.

"And you won't. Ever!" Stanley said and then burst out laughing.

"Quite a scene," the Chief joined in, his deep baritone chortle ringing throughout the firehouse. "That lady you have there... Certainly a handful."

"Not anymore," Stanley stated, vowing to break it off with Samantha Higgins Rouleaux once and for all.

That night, from the privacy of the office of his father's closed store, Stanley called Samantha.

"This isn't working," he said. "I don't think we should see each other. Anymore."

With words Stanley was sure not even a longshoreman would use, she vehemently objected, berating him for humiliating her earlier that evening at the firehouse. When he refuted her claim -- "I did no such thing!" – she began ranting about what he was going to do with the rest of his life. All her suggestions, commands, and unreasonable demands were unacceptable to Stanley.

He was not going to move to New York and be her lackey. He was not going to work for her father in an investment house. And no, he was NOT going to dress up in hand-made Edwardian three-piece suits and a bowler hat nor a tuxedo and top hat simply to escort her to fancy dress balls or to the opera. He had other, more important things to do.

Like fighting fires. And saving lives.

For the next hour, Samantha continued to rant and rave. How dare he cut her off from his life? It was hers, too. Now theirs. He was being selfish, after all she did for him. Which, Stanley stated, was "absolutely nothing." The conversation when on, back and forth, until the small hours of the morning. Stanley, in a moment of weakness, backed down from his decision to break off all ties with Samantha.

"I'll see you occasionally. But only occasionally. On my terms."

She softened her tone, but just a tad. The last thing he did before they hung was to promise to call her. But he knew that in the ensuring months, he never would.

A week later, he happened to espy Rebecca Hope coming out of Eyrich's Market, a packet of meat wrapped in brown paper neatly tucked under her slender arm. As he followed her past the butcher's window advertising "locally grown" round steak at 35¢ a pound and homemade half smokes at 24¢, an idea formed in Stanley's mind. Perhaps it was time to pay a visit to Edmond's parents. After all, he had practically grown up in their large Victorian. As Edmond had in his parent's home on Vanderslice.

They sat primly side by side on the maroon horsehair settee in the front parlor. FrankieBernard snored at their feet.

When he asked, Rebecca was, at first, lukewarm to Stanley's suggestion that they "take in a show" at the Colonial Theatre.

"The film is *Reliable Harry* starring Madame Olga Petroud," he stated, noting that it was to be shown again after being such a hit in June.

"Well, I guess," she finally acquiesced. She was still reeling from the loss of Campbell, whom she thought was the greatest love of her young life. But she had always been fond of Stanley Martinez, with his dark, somewhat sultry good looks, and winning smile. Not to mention his subtle though adamant sense of honor.

"Can you believe her looks?" Stanley asked after the movie as he drove Rebecca home in his father's Underslung touring car through town. "She's French, right? Those wispy clothes, the fluttering eyelashes... So, um, fake."

Rebecca only nodded, not sure how to answer his comments on French fashion. Not quite into haute couture, Rebecca did, on occasion accompany her mother to Seacrist's Stationary on the corner of Bridge and Main to pick up the latest copies of *La Mode* and *The Delineator*. The magazines, according to the local seamstresses, were *the* authorities on what – or what not – to wear.

But Rebecca had to admit that Stanley was right. Madame Petroud's costumes were *outré*. Over the top. Because of the war, women's clothes had become simpler and easier to care for. Straight, though flowing lines. Looser, with narrow pleats. And the colors were more muted light greys, greens, and pastels. Yet, just last month, the cover of the April issue of *The Delineator* featured a blue and white ankle-length silk and light cotton apron-shift, with bell sleeves, ample pockets, and flocking across the top of the bodice. It was flimsy. But not quite as flimsy as the dresses Madame Petroud wore in the movie.

Maybe Stanley won't like it, Rebecca thought. Regardless, she had planned on wearing it the next time she and Stanley stepped out. If they again stepped out. But now, with his comments, she wasn't so sure about the dress. Instead, thinking of an alternative ensemble, she placed her hand on his arm and simply smiled.

Best not to say anything more, she chided herself. *Let him... Stanley take the conversational lead.*

Stanley had learned in the past that, like her brother, Edmond's sister, unlike his own, was an articulate and opinionated young woman who often spoke out whenever and whenever she felt the need. Now he was concerned about her sudden recent predilection for silence. He attributed it to the somber loss of Campbell Wheatley. A loss not only she, but himself and other residents in town deeply felt.

He patted her hand, now snug in his elbow. "How about a cocoa and cookies at The Columbia?" he suggested, although he would have preferred a brandy. "It's not too late, and the weather is a bit nippy..."

"That would be wonderful... and welcoming," she smiled. "You could tell me again how patterns are made and used in the manufacturing of bridges."

Stanley smiled back, maneuvering the Undereslung into a parking spot in front of the hotel. He knew at that moment he was going to married Rebecca Elizabeth Hope.

The only problem he had was what to do with Samantha Higgins Rouleaux.

Lenny was more cautious this time, leaving nothing behind except for the nubby tire tracks in the melting snow. The fire, he recalled later, was the easiest to ignite and the fastest to burn. The materials he needed were already in place. He just had to access the row of furnaces in the open hearth building behind the Phoenix Iron Company foundry building. And even that should be easy.

The older night watchman, he had assessed a week earlier, made his rounds on the odd hour. All Lenny had to do was slip into the yard at quarter to five on his way to work, wait for the guard to leave, sneak into the building, set the fire, and then slip back out into the darkness.

Simple. Nothing go wrong.

When Stanley reported for work in the pattern shop early the next morning, smoke was billowing upward from behind the foundry. He didn't need to second-guess that it was one of the puddling furnaces. Only master puddlers and their rabble boys had the knowledge and skills to light and control the blast furnace used to melt and purify the iron and then form it into "puddles" for shaping. The fire couldn't have been set by any of them, he knew. He recalled the many times he had watched Edmond, a master puddler in his own right, set the kindling in a stack of firewood, and then shovel slag embers under the grate, readying it to be lit the next day.

Stanley watched from one side of the open-hearth area as the company's own fire brigade doused the base of the smoldering blaze with sand. Phoenix № 1 had not been called. There was no need; the fire was more smoke than flame. The iron company had, in the past, adamantly refused to request the services of local firefighters unless a foundry fire got out of hand, which, this time, didn't seem likely. As he and his foreman watched, Stanley had to admit that the men from the brigade seemed to know what they were doing. But that whoever set the fire didn't.

"Not that anyone was careless, Martinez," his boss continued, shaking his head. "It's common practice for a puddler to lay the fire before leaving, but the furnace couldn't have fired itself up."

Stanley frowned. He edged closer. A huge crack split the side of Number Three, Edmond's furnace. Sparks from the dying internal fire spewed out into the early morning air; a few flames still flickered through smaller cracks.

His foreman was right. After it was lit, the fire had not been properly stoked and tended to. And unless it had not been spotted, contained, and put out, the furnace could have easily blown up, taking part of the building and foundry employees with it. Including himself.

What a horrible thought, he mused. *To be consumed by a fire."* He shuttered, sensing a twinge of déjà vu. As if, his mother would say, someone had walked across his grave.

In any case, the furnace was now totally unusable. And the foundry open hearth building for now, was not a safe place for any of the puddlers to work.

Stanley slowly walked toward the foundry entrance. The two or three inches of snow, which had started to melt the night before, had started to freeze in the cold morning air. He stopped. There, in front of him, partly frozen in the snow, was a single line of tracks. Made by nubby tires. Stanley was positive this time.

He knew who and what had made them.

Frank LaBronsky thought it kind of silly that he was training on dry land to be a firefighter on the ocean. Cork, Ireland was several miles inland from the Irish Sea, at the western tip of the River Lee that formed part of Loch Moran. He and one-hundred other United States Naval trainees had travelled by large troop tenders from a ship moored two leagues out from Roches Point.

A few of the others, like him, thought it silly, too. But the base was large enough to easily accommodate a few thousand men. And the panoramic countryside surrounding the city of Cork was lush green. In many ways, the whole area reminded him of the rolling hills back home that surrounded the small Borough of Phoenixville, where, like Cork, the locals were friendly and caring – almost to a fault – of each another.

"I think I'm going to like it here," he commented to himself, getting readying for his first drill as a neophyte fireman. "So much safer than flying rickety bi-planes."

Fire Chief David Mendowski and Constable Luke Tucker were not surprised when Stanley told them about the tire tracks in the snow.

"The same at The Knoll. The same in other places Lenny has been," he said. "And he rides that bike all over town. Even in foul weather There's no mistaking the staccato sound... and the tracks..."

"Seems to me we might have a case, Dave."

"Hmmm, I am leaning on the side of caution, Luke. What have we got, really?"

Detective Simon Hoolmes strolled into the office, brandishing part of a charred torch.

"You, we've got this," he stated, laying it in front of the Fire Chief. "A sack labelled Perseverance Knitting Mill obviously used to carry flammable lint and cotton." He paused. "Maybe someone should go out to the mill and ask a few questions..."

The Fire Chief shook his head. He wasn't an experienced policeman like Luke or Simon, but he did know the law.

"I still think it's just circumstantial evidence."

"That's for a judge and jury to decide, David," the Detective said. 'No, um, offense." He grinned at yet another of his trite puns.

"None taken. But..."

"Well, it's worth a shot," Tucker shrugged. "Simon and I will head out there first thing in the morning... Poke around a bit and see who does have access to the bags... And what they're used for."

For some strange reason, he enjoyed sweeping up the stray bits and pieces of lint, thread, and cotton bits dropped by the mill workers as they sewed men and children's underwear and pajamas. When a sufficient pile was swept up, he took great pleasure in stuffing the remnants into the large burlap sacks. And, at the end of the day, cart the many sacks outside to empty them into the incinerator. When he learned that pieces of cloth and bits of lint and thread were highly flammable, he was ecstatic. He could put into action the big plans he had formulated for revenge.

Lanny, his left arm now in a light cast, was allowed to work part time as long as he "took it easy". He had looked blankly at Dr. Galen Hall and wondered what *dat meant.* He was languidly, yet happily, pushing a wide broom down one of the aisles between rooms of the large Singer sewing when he espied the two local policemen follow a mill foreman into the work area. He instantly recognized the "bad man" who had threatened him and his father two days after he had supposedly broken Stanley's nose.

Why he here?

Frightened, he ducked through a door in the back wall leading down to a cordoned-off stairwell. He left the door, normally kept locked during working hours, slightly ajar, hoping to listen in on the conversation.

"Yeah, we use those bags for any number of purposes," Nick Letterman was explaining in a thick Eastern European accent. He was a short, dark stocky stub of a man with an equally short, fat unlit cigar stub squeezed between thin, tight lips. He had an annoying habit of taking it out and spitting tobacco juice onto Lenny's cleanly swept floor. Leering all the while at "the lumbering ox of a janitor". It was obvious both men loathed one another, but both had a job to do and, although he hated "Nasty Nick", Lenny tolerated his abuses, much like he did those of his father.

"Such as?" Constable Tucker asked. He, too, had an instant dislike for the almost gnome-like character who clumsily pranced around the shop floor idly fondling the shoulders of the women workers and pushing the men aside as he self-importantly conducted the impromptu tour.

"Well, we use them downstairs for delivering orders. Pack the shirts and trousers... the jammies and underwear into them, a tag attached with the customer's address... For storage, sometimes. And, well, also, up here... the janitor collects his sweepings in them."

"Sweepings?"

"Yah. Bits of thread and cloth. At the end of the day, he empties them into the incinerator... I think."

"So that would be, um..." The Constable pretended to consult his small notebook. "... a one Lenny Lochmann?" *As if I didn't already know.*

"Yeah, that's the *one*. The ox... the supposed janitor..."

Detective Hoolmes leaned into Tucker's ear. "So, Lenny has access to the bags and the combustible lint..." he whispered.

"I understand that, Simon," the Constable whispered back. 'Now, hush. Let me ask the questions first. Then you can..."

"So, collecting lint and scrapes. Is what Lenny Lochmann does? What else?" Hoolmes piped up.

Letterman spat out a wad of tobacco juice scornfully onto the floor, then sneered at the young Detective. "Rethreads the machines, replaces the needles when they break. Locks the doors... Unlocks them."

Hoolmes frowned in thought, as did the Constable. He returned to the usage of the bags.

"So, that means, once shipped... and delivered, anybody has access to the bags? They are not, um, sent back?"

"*Nyet*.. er, Nah. Anybody can make use of them when we're done..." He jutted out his lower lip. "They're welcome to them..."

"So, at the end of the day... Does Lenny bring the sacks back into the building once they are emptied into the incinerator?"

'No, yes. I don't know. I suppose." He spat out more cigar phlegm. "I think... Um, I think he just throws the bags into the furnace. But we've so many of them... If he does take one or two, empty or not, it really doesn't matter," he shrugged, making a mental note to see if the janitor was, in fact, stealing from the company. Even if the stolen goods were supposed to be burned.

"So," the Constable continued the line of questioning, with a quick "I've got this..." aside to the Detective. "So... the bottom line is that once used, anyone has free rein to reuse the bags. Including Lenny? Am I right." He jotted a few notes onto a blank page of his pad while waiting for the answer.

"*Da.* I guess. So what? *I chto? Kakaya raznitsa?*"

"Well, see, Mr. Letterman, that's just the point. I, we *do* care..."

The shop foreman reeled back in surprised. *This Constable knows the language?*

"Just one more question, if I might?"

"Yeah, make it quite." It was evident the little man was highly annoyed at the probing questions and the intrusion on his shop floor.

"Are you Russian?"

"*Kakoye eto imeyet znacheniye, yesli ya?* Does it really matter?"

"No, it does not. Not really. Just wanted to make sure..." He turned to the Detective. "Come on, Simon. We have other business elsewhere." He shot a quick insincere "Thank you" to Nick Letterman and hastened out of the mill.

On their way across the empty lot next to the mill building to the shiny police car, Detective Hoolmes pointed out the wide tires on Lenny's Smith Motor Wheel that was parked by a side entrance to the mill.

"Look at the tires, Luke. Just like the tracks..."

"Nubby. And we don't have the time or equipment to take a picture."

"No, but I can draw fairly well... And..." He whipped out a folded sheet of parchment paper and a charcoal pencil from his inside coat pocket.

"What the...?"

"Watch and learn, sir... An old hobby of mine..."

Detective Simon Hoolmes expertly overlaid the top portion of the front tire of the Motor Wheel and, holding the paper securely, began rubbing the flat side of the pencil point against it. Within minutes, the nubby tire pattern had been duplicated in detail onto the paper.

"Well I'll be... Just as if you took a picture..."

"Brass rubbings, Luke. I did them as a kid in local cemeteries. Gravestones and images and all that... My mother taught me..."

"If they match the tracks Stanley Martinez saw... If he recognized them... Can we use them as evidence?"

"I don't see why not. Luke," the Detective grinned. "I think we've moved beyond the realm of circumstantial and into building a case..."

"Against Lenny Lochmann."

"Exactly."

"Well done, Hoolmes!"

"Elementary, my dear..."

"Don't you dare!"

Later that afternoon, the foreman accosted Lenny on his way to the employee locker room to retrieve his plaid flannel jacket and worn leather backpack.

"Why are *politsiya* asking questions about you?"

"I don't know," Lenny lied.

"Ha!" He spat yet another wad of dark brown tobacco juice at Lenny's feet. "You cause trouble around here. I don't like that. *Mne eto ne nravitsya.* Not one bit. It happens again? *Ty uvolen.* Fired. Got it?"

"Yes, sir," Lenny mumbled.

"*Da*, dumb ox. *Nemoy.* Now we understand one another."

Lenny bristled at the words "dumb". Just like his father used. It was entirely different sounding in Russian than in German, but he understood its meaning just the same.

Not nemoy. Not dumpkopf, he chanted as he hastened down the stairs. *Not nemoy. Not dumpkopf.*

He was in a hurry to empty the several sacks he had filled during the day into the incinerator. All four of them, except for one.

Tying it to the back of his Smith motorized bike, he fired up the engine and sped off the mill property onto lower Bridge Street.

He was anxious to get back to Scape Level and the privacy of his own third-floor room.

Where he would make more plans.

Many more plans.

More than he or anyone else would think he ever would have.

Not nemoy. Not dumpkopf. Not nemoy. Not dumpkopf.

I smart!

Lenny Lochmann laughed manically as he rode at breakneck speed through Phoenixville toward the Main Street Bridge.

DECEMBER 1917

On December 7th, the United State declared war on Austria-Hungary, which meant that more troops were to be deployed and spread across an even larger front than the one spanning France and Belgium. English forces invaded the city of Jerusalem and Russia, in the throes of its own revolution, signed a preliminary armistice with Germany.

In Camp Hancock, Edmond had hoped for a promised, long-awaited two-week pass to visit his family for the holidays. But with the latest declaration of Congress that resulted in the expansion of the war westward, all requests for leave were denied.

"Not fair," he grumbled to Hans as they walked to the mess tent for yet another tepid supper of boiled ham and cabbage. "We're not even over there. We're here. Doing nothing."

In a moment of insight, Hans tersely suggested that perhaps "they" were waiting for the order to "ship us out to Europe" and wanted all the artillery troops ready and available. Edmond, somewhat mollified, shrugged. He might be able to stomach over-cooked meat and rubbery cabbage, but he was finding it harder and harder to swallow what he thought were unreasonable and arbitrary decisions by high-ranking officials. Whom, he was beginning to realize, did not know what they were doing.

And, unfortunately, he knew that after his last chat with Captain Whitaker, any further complaining would only fall upon deaf ears.

The next morning, during roll call, he received a letter from Stanley relating the latest news from home: The continued setting of fires by a still-unknown arson, even though the Fire Chief and Constable suspected Lenny Lochmann; the continuing Thursday night Red Cross benefit concerts at the Colonial Theatre; the permanent presence of two recruiting officers – one for the Army, the other for the Navy – at the post office; and the on-going "knit to do your bit" campaign now chaired by his mother who, along with his sister, had just, in the last few months, learned to knit.

Expect a few mismatched socks and a ragged sweater, Stanley wrote, unaware that a care package from Edmond's mother and sister had already been sent. His comment was more in the way of teasing than information. *I watched Rosalina knitting the other night. Not a pretty sight. But at least she tries. And I think she does it all for you. Lucky guy!*

On a more personal note, he related his qualms in shaky handwriting – half cursive, half printed – about continuing to "keep up" with Samantha Higgins Rouleaux.

I asked your sister out again, Edmond. We had a fun time at the movies, but I am reluctant to ask her out again... Samantha still demands chunks of my time, despite my constantly telling her I am no longer interested. It is, she is, to be honest, sapping my energy. She still shows up at the firehouse while I'm on call demanding I take her to lunch or dinner. Of course, I refuse – and the Chief, thankfully, ushers her out – but then she whizzes by the shop just as I leave work and tells me she's driving me home... Even when I have my rusty but still trusty old bike... I am at my wit's end. And, I tell ya, my friend, it's getting so that...Well, I am not sure what to do...

"You're in deep trouble, my friend," Edmond chuckled to himself. He had heard that Estelle Griffen Higgins' niece was fast and furiously loose with a few of the young men in town.

When she was in town. And not gadding about in New York City, where she most probably was even more fast and more furious. He was about to take a few minutes to jot down several lines of advice and encouragement when the bugle sounded to begin yet another redundantly tedious training drill. The return letter to his dearest and best friend would have to wait to be written until later that evening.

Earlier in the month, Constable Tucker reported in a private Borough Council session, much to the members' dismay, that he had spotted the "alleged German 'spy'" loitering along South Main Street.

"I feel it my duty to bring this to your attention rather than keeping it within the confidential bounds of law enforcement," he pronounced, Detective Simon Hoolmes at his side. He described the "so-called intruder" as having coppery blond hair and wearing a non-descript frayed flannel jacket.

"He looked vaguely familiar, but not a resident that I know of. For sure... Although I do have my suspicions."

Burgess Mosteller asked for more information, gravely concerned that the rumors of a real spy could actually be true. The safety of the community would be at stake, if they were. If not, he would be gravely concerned about Luke Tucker's continuing credibility as the village Constable.

"Are you sure it was a... spy?"

"I'd say more of a loiterer, but he fit the description of the man reported last spring skulking along the wall of the Battery C Armory in *The Daily Republican*."

Another council member scoffed and snorted. "That rag," he whispered under his breath. "They'd print anything so that papers are sold..."

"I heard that and I beg to differ," J.O.K. Robarts chided, banging a fist on the long conference table. The editor and one of the publishers – H. H. Gilkyson was the other – bristled at the low-handed and low-voiced slur. "We do the best we can to report the news as accurately and as fairly as we possibly can!"

"You can't even get the war facts straight..." the dissenting Burgess began.

"Enough!" Burgess Mosteller barked, rapping his small gavel on the table. "This is not a discussion about the quality or lack thereof of our local journalist endeavors. It is about the safety and welfare of our community."

"I'll take this up with you later, Sinclair," Robarts feigned a smile.

Mosteller grunted then turned back to the two policemen standing in front of the six councilmen. "Now, Tucker, if you would please elaborate about your sighting of the... er, the spy?"

"I am not saying it was a spy. Just that he fit the description. However, he was acting a bit suspicious."

"Much like a spy would do," Detective Hoolmes interjected. "I read that..." He stopped talking when Luke Tucker nudged him with his elbow.

"When he saw me — at least I think he saw me," the Constable continued, "he was snooping around Meadows' Toy store, peering in the window. Like he was looking for something..."

"Probably just window-shopping for presents for his kids," Robarts smiled. He didn't believe in the espionage rumors, even though they had been reported in his own newspaper. The real spy, he explained, "was a German from Wisconsin — or was it Minnesota? Wyoming? Who had already been caught feeding information about American troop movements in and out of military training camps. Nothing to do with Phoenixville at all."

"Yeah, well what about the one seen lurking around the Armory?" Owen Sinclair shouted. "Unless, of course, you didn't consider him a spy, either... But you wrote about it anyway."

Mosteller banged his gavel down once again.

"Sinclair, if you don't contain yourself..."

"Yeah? And then what?" Owen slumped down in his seat, glaring at both the Burgess and the newspaper editor. "Fake reporting, that's what it is. Not true at all..." he muttered. "Fake news."

Constable Tucker waited until the chairman nodded for him to continue.

"He was more than window-shopping," he said. "He walked down the narrow empty lot between the store and the bank, stopping every few feet... Looking up at the roofs, looking down at the ground..."

"Looking for what?" Sinclair asked, a bit more subdued. He had known Luke Tucker for a long time and trusted his judgement More so than that, perhaps, the other council members. Maybe this whole spy thing could be true. Then, he thought, *Nah. He's just spoofing us. Or, is he?*

"I don't know, Owen. I didn't get a chance to ask him. When I approached, he disappeared behind the back and apparently ran behind Sacred Heart."

"Why didn't you follow him?" Robarts asked.

'I didn't see the point. He didn't do anything wrong, really, except loiter a bit..."

"But running from you presumes he's guilty of something. Could he be the arsonist setting all the fires around town?" Like Burgess Mosteller, his primary concern on Council was the preservation of community safety. After accurate and fair reporting of the news, of course.

"Maybe. But, but if he is, I am certain he'll turn up someplace else. Sometime. Soon. Then we'll get him." He refrained from suggesting the fleeting "spy" might be

PHOENIX HOSE, HOOK & LADDER

Hermann or Lenny Lochmann. He had looked so much like them.

It must be the father, he thought. *The man was moving too fast to be lumbering Lenny. Besides, One of Lenny's arm was in a cast and neither of this man's arms were.*

While not completely satisfied with Constable Tucker's report, the Borough Council voted to end the closed session. They thanked him for his time and efforts and then admonished Tucker to be "more vigilant in the future" and to report back if there were any more sightings.

The next day, the supposed "spy" was once again spotted on Main and Hall in front of Company D's headquarters. Once again frustrated that he couldn't be caught – one of the younger junior officers had given chase – Constable Tucker called an impromptu departmental meeting and ordered members of the small force to "be on the lookout for a hulking man with coppery-blond hair dressed in stained brown trousers and a frayed flannel jacket.

"Concentrate on the length of South Main, from Bridge all the way up to Nutt's," he continued. "That's seems to be where he's lurking the most."

Two days later, just before dawn, Detective Simon Hoolmes was driving his own little less than spiffy car down Main Street on his way to work. Slowing down as he approached the intersection of Third Avenue – where children had been known to dash across the street without looking both ways – he saw smoke rising from the front of the pavilion shell in Reeves Park. Curious, Hoolmes made a right onto Second Avenue and parked his brand-new Model T Roadster parallel to the side of the shell.

He cautiously approached, frowning at the sight of a husky man huddled in a thin blanket sleeping on the shell's cold concrete stage. On the edge, he was as close as he could be to the fire set on the ground. Hoolmes noticed it was set with coal and two old baseball bats. A cursory glance told him the man fit the description of the alleged "spy". The detective rousted the man up and, with a brief explanation of "sleeping in a public place" being a misdemeanor, arrested him and drove him to the police station.

"He's not Lenny or Hermann Lochmann, that's for sure," Tucker stated. "His features... too sharp and well-defined."

"Yes," Hoolmes started to agree. "But, with the coppery-blond hair and the tattered clothes, there is a strong family resemblance."

"Who are you?" the Constable asked the apparent vagrant. Was he... the "alleged spy"?

"Otto," the man said in broken English with a thick German accent. "*Mein Name ist Otto*. I look for long-lost cousin. For Christmas... But I do not know his address."

"Who is your cousin, Otto? The last name?"

"Schlemmer. Otto Schlemmer."

"No, no. your cousin's last name. Perhaps we can help you find him."

"Ludinksky, Lewinsky... Lowman. Louch... Something like that. Starts with an L."

"Could it be Lochmann?" the Constable offered. The family resemblance could not have suggested otherwise.

"*Ja, Ja, Das ist es*. Lochmann. Hermann Lochmann. He is, was my mother's *neffe*... nephew."

"Was?"

"*Ja*. Mamma died last year." He sniffed, still in grief. "I was a *Klempner*... a plumber. I took care of her until the end..."

"So, what brings you here?" The Constable looked at the man's disheveled state and surmised he must now be homeless. *The last thing we need here in Phoenixville,* he thought, *with all the rumors flying around, is a German vagrant prowling around town. Or yet another homeless person.* "Aren't you still a... plumber?"

"*Ja*, I did. I was. But then Germans in America had to register and then I lost my job. And the landlady... she threw me out of our apartment." He paused, looking forlornly down on rough, calloused hands caked in dirt.

"I... That is why I come looking for Hermann. He is my only relative. Who could help me, *ja*?"

The Constable chuckled at the thought that Hermann Lochmann would the common decency to help a distance relative. *He can't even take care of his own son, let alone himself.* He considered the options and decided to drive Otto to his cousin himself just to see Lochmann's reactions.

"He lives up at a place called Scape Level with his son, Lenny. I could take you there..."

Detective Hoolmes suddenly had a hacking coughing spell. Tucker knew he was faking. Simon had never been sick a day in his life. At least not since he joined the force ten years ago.

"Yes, Hoolmes? What is it?"

"I found these, sir. In the fire." He pointed to the two charred baseball bats on the edge of his desk. "Look like Louisville sluggers to me, sir. And they are sanded down."

Otto frowned in dismay. "I find them in the park..."

"I doubt that, Mr. Schlemmer," Hoolmes said.

"... the varnish burns badly, so I scrape some of it off..."

"A likely story," the Detective said accusingly. "Caught you red-handed with them, I did." He smirked at yet another one of his witticisms.

Tucker knew what Hoolmes was thinking. They had worked so close together on cases – albeit small ones, except for the Columbia Hotel murder – that each could read the other's mind. *Simon thinks this is the arsonist who's been setting the fires.* He frowned, then asked. "How long have you been in the area, Otto?"

"One, two weeks, I think."

"And before that?"

"*Wandern*. I go from town to town, looking for work. But no one hires me. I am good *Klempner*. *Das beste...*"

"Okay, Otto. You wait here. We'll be right back." Constable Tucker beckoned the Detective into the other room, out of earshot.

"You heard him. He hasn't been in the area long enough to set any if not all of the fires, Simon."

"He's lying. What about the burned bats?"

"He could have found them in Reeves Park, as he says. Kids are careless and leave all sorts of things laying around there. Even baseball bats."

"Why are you making excuses for him, Luke?"

"I'm not... But look at him. The guy's obviously down and out and he just doesn't seem like the criminal type." Tucker mentally reviewed the evidence they had about the local conflagrations.

"You searched his meager possessions, right?"

Hoolmes nodded.

"No bags from a local mill?"

"No."

"No traces of lint, loose threads, or scarps of cloth?"

"No."

"No small vials of kerosene?"

"No, but he had matches."

"To light his fires. Which he slept by..."

"Yes, but..." Hoolmes sounded frustrated. He, just as much as anybody else, wanted to catch the supposed arsonist. And if he happened to be what everyone in the Borough was beginning to think was a resident German spy... Well, then, he would more than happy to be the skilled investigator to do just that.

"Look, Simon," Constable Tucker said. "If it would make you feel any better, I'll hold him for a night or two."

"Charge him with arson!"

"No, we don't have the evidence. But I can charge him with vagrancy and starting fires without a permit on public grounds."

Hoolmes sighed. "Well, that should give me, us enough time to find the goods to keep him detained for longer."

"I doubt we will. The man looks innocent. He just needs a bath, a shave, and a change of clean clothes."

The next morning, while Otto Schlemmer was gratefully safe, clean, and warm in one of the three holding cells in the small prison behind Borough Hall, his second cousin once removed was motoring his way back from his last appointment with Dr. Hall. His arm had "sufficiently healed" to have the cumbersome cask taken off. His arm was now cradled in a white cloth sling tied around his thick neck.

Lenny Lochmann also had permission to return to work full time, which was where he was headed. To report back to Nick Letterman, his foreman at the Perseverance Mill, to sweep up tufts of lint, bits of thread, and small scraps of cotton cloth. He would stuff them into yet another burlap bag and then refill the glass vial in his jacket pocket he had palmed from the examining room while awaiting the doctor to come in. He would, that very afternoon, fill it with oil used to grease the sewing machines.

Everything has to be ready. Had to be just right.

Because Lenny had yet another errand to run that evening.

Right after work.

This one was going to be the biggest and best one of all.

Just watch. he said to himself. *Believe me. Wait and see.*

Inspired by the flyers posted all over town with the red, white, and blue cartoon of a woman exhorting "Socks Needed! Do your bit! Knit!" Dolores and Rosaline Martinez now spent their free time together each evening doing just that. Knitting.

As did other Phoenixville mothers and daughters, as well as housewives, crafting woolen sweaters, socks, scarves and mittens for their local brave men now serving overseas.

Dolores, now a valued member of Phoenix Nº 1 Women's Auxiliary, spent long Thursday afternoons in the second-floor of the fire station sorting out, packing, and labelling the latest batch of donations. She and two other volunteers then loaded the packages into the back seat of the family's touring car. She would bring them bright and early the next morning to the post office for delivery to the APO depot in Washington, D.C. Where they went after that, she would never know. Troop movements and locations were, rightly so, a darkly held secret. But she was assured by the postmaster that they would be delivered in time for Christmas.

That night, immediately after cleaning up the supper dishes, Dolores and her daughter set themselves back to work plying their needles, sitting cozily close together by the blazing fire Carlos had built before returning to Martinez's Shoe Shoppe. It was busier than usual this holiday season. Shoes and sturdy boots, for some reason, were the favored presents to wrap and place under Phoenixville Christmas trees. And Carlos, of course, was the favorite local provider of the footwear presents. Besides, as he insisted as he kissed his wife as he was leaving, "I have my own 'elfish' things to take care of." She smiled, knowing he had a few surprises planned for not only herself, but their two cherished children as well.

Sitting by the fire knitting yet another pair of thick wool socks, Dolores sighed, knowing full well that her husband would, once again, be getting home very late. She was looking forward to a Christmas when they could enjoy a least a few quiet days together as a family without the hustle and bustle of seeing to customers' needs. Nor, she hoped, worrying about the war raging thousands of miles away. Yet, here she was, knitting socks, scarves, and two-fingered mittens for whom she called "the lost boys" overseas.

She sighed again, dismayed that right after supper was over Stanley had disappeared upstairs, ensconced in the enclave of his own bedroom.

"I worry for your brother," she said, casting off the top of a dull grey woolen sock. She promptly set about casting matching wool on her thin needles to start its mate.

"He's probably reading yet another of his horrid adventure novels," Rosalina said. "Honestly, Mother... He may be twenty-one, but sometimes he acts like a ten-year-old. Dang," she said. "That's the third stitch I've dropped tonight. I am so tired of knitting brown socks... I long to make a sweater for myself. I found this pattern in *La Mode*..."

Suddenly, the Claxon horn began blaring. Dolores, unladylike, cussed in Gaelic -- *Shit. In ainm Dhia.*

"Ma!" Rosalina exclaimed, then threw down her knitting and bolted through the door onto the wide, wooden back porch. She leaned over the railing, trying to catch a glimpse of smoke and flames.

"It looks like the Foundry!" she shouted back to her mother.

"Stanley!' Dolores yelled as her son bounded down the stairs, two at a time, grabbing his coat hanging on a hook in the hallway as he bounded out the door.

"I'm on it!" he called back. "And I'm taking the bike!" Even with the light falling snow, he figured he'd make better time getting to the fire station on his old Schwinn Racer than having to run down the embankment on foot.

Lenny had just recently overheard one of the older sewing ladies tell the story about the worker who, way back when, had thrown water onto the smoldering puddles of coal oil in a pit in one of the foundry buildings. The volatile mixture had caused the building to go up in flames. In his warped mind, he had known it was where Stanley now worked as a pattern maker. The perfect place to execute the next part of his plan. It would be his next target.

He repeated his "Best ever! Biggest! Best ever!" mantra as he silenced his Smith Motor Wheel and coasted to a halt in the back of the Foundry building. *I ready*, he smirked as he brazenly strolled through the door he knew would be open. No one bothered to stop him. The iron works now was in operation day and night, manufacturing military equipment for the war effort. All sorts of workers came and went at will without notice. For just this once, he would be one of them.

A sawed-off sanded baseball bat in his hand, Lenny smiled and nodded as he made his way, unrecognized but not questioned, to the pattern shop. The stolen glass vial filled with machine oil along with a pack of matches were in his pocket.

Biggest! Best ever! He repeated over and over again. *Biggest! Best ever!*

As he suspected, puddles of coal oil were pooled in a shallow pit. Wood chips and shavings were scatter around it. *Easy,* he sneered. Emboldened, he kicked some of the wood scraps into the pit and emptied the vial of machine oil onto the scraps. He knew, from past experience, it would be an unstable mixture. He lit a wooden match and tossed it in. The oil and wood chips instantly caught. A hot, noxious fire quickly spread outward to the walls of the pit and then rose upward into the pattern shop.

Lenny watched as the flames rose up higher and higher into the open air. Then, for good measure, pretending he was trying to put it out, he grabbed a bucket of water that stood alongside the pit and dumped it onto the roaring fire.

He understood the theories of pyrogenics even if he didn't know the word or its meaning. Water and flaming oil do not mix.

"That teach him," he whispered. "Blame Stanley. Stanley lose job. Good for him. Good for me."

The night-shift workers did not notice the fire until a half-hour later. Distracted by their own work, they were not alarmed by the smoke and the acrid smell of burning oil until it was almost too late. The fire, by that time, was spreading hot and fast – too hot to handle by the foundry's own fire brigade. They had almost no time left to escape the building. One worker raced to the fire alarm box outside the main entrance inconveniently mounted on a telephone pole fifty feet away. By that time the alarm sounded, the blaze was engulfing the main portion of the building. It would take a massive effort to contain it, let along put it out before the whole factory – and the livelihood of the majority of Phoenixville residents – was destroyed.

Lenny Lochmann exited the foundry right after the fire started and was safely motoring up Freemont Street toward home when the alarm souded.

"Damn it!" Fire Chief Mendowski cussed, as he raced into the foundry wielding the business end of the two-and-a-half-inch fire hose attached the to the steam pumper. He flashed back to when, as a young fireman by his father's side, he had fought the very same oil-coal fire in the very same place.

"You'd think they 'd learned by now."

Two hours later, the fire finally extinguished, Constable Tucker ventured into the fire house.

"Well, we thought we had caught our arsonist earlier today," he said. "But it seems he's still at large."

"What are you taking about?" the Fire Chief wearily asked.

"Hoolmes arrested a vagrant sleeping in the band shell in Reeves Park early this morning. He looks a lot like Hermann Lochmann, whom he claims is his second cousin."

"And you think he set all the fires?"

'Well, I thought he had. But how could he have set the foundry ablaze while sitting in a jail cell?"

"Good point."

"So, was it arson?"

"Too hot to be spontaneous combustion. And Stanley Martinez found this empty glass vial by the site." He pointed to the fluted bottle sitting on his desk. "Reeking of machine oil."

"Did he? Did you...?"

"No, he was wise enough not to pick it up. And I was careful not to smudge it carrying it back."

"You both are becoming regular sleuths," the Constable smiled weakly.

"Yes, well. Think you could find some fingerprints on it?"

"That is Hoolmes' area of expertise. I'll have him come right over with his kit and test it right here. Whatever you do, don't touch it."

The Chief smiled. "Now, Luke, why would I ever do a thing like that?"

An hour later, Detective Hoolmes announced that he had "lifted" three "very clear" prints from the vial. "A thumb and a forefinger and the middle finger just below it. As if the owner was pouring..."

"Okay. The next step?" Fire Chief Mendowski interrupted, impressed by the new process and Detective Hoolmes' investigative techniques.

"Well, for one, we try and find a match. Get the fingerprints of any known suspects..."

"You mean, Hermann and Lenny Lochmann?"

"Yes, for two."

"Well," Constable Tucker mused. "That's easier said than done."

Even though Simon Hoolmes was still not convinced that he was not responsible or the other fires, Otto Schlemmer was released the next day. Constable Tucker personally drove him up to Scape Level, politely introduced him to his cousin without saying anything else, then promptly drove away.

Hermann Lochmann had no other choice but to let Otto stay.

"There's got to be a way to get Lenny's fingerprints," Constable Tucker said, pondering the options in his office. "You're my ace fingerprint expert. How would you go about getting them without upsetting the apple care?"

"I say... Go directly to the source. Drive up to their home on Scape Level and demand..."

"You know Hermann Lochmann's quick-release temper. Couple that with his attitude toward us... Toward me... You should have seen the look on his face when I dropped Otto off. No, Simon, demanding won't work." He sighed. "Anything else you might wanna suggest?"

"Go visit the Lochmanns and be polite?"

"Now that's surely a novel approach. And well worth considering."

The next evening, Constable Luke Tucker and Detective Simon Hoolmes arrived on the front stoop of Hermann Lochmann's house. Each armed with an M1917 revolver, just in case there would be trouble, they both knocked on the door – still in disrepair.

Lenny's father, already angry at the intrusion, regardless of whomever it might be, answered the door. One hand was on the door handle, the other behind his back.

"*Mein Gott, du wieder*. What the hell do you want now?"

"We'd liked to, um, please chat with Lenny," the Constable smiled. "If you don't mind."

"Well, I do. How about that? Get the *Scheibe* off my property!"

"Now, Mr. Lochmann, is that any way to talk to your village Constable?" Detective Hoolmes asked, placing his right hand into the side pocket of his finely-tailored wool suit. He lightly clasped the handle of the small gun, ready to whip it out if necessary. But Hermann had other ideas. He casually moved his own hand from behind his back.

"I'll talk any way I want, *Polizist,*" he threatened shoving the muzzle of a German Luger PO8 semi-automatic pistol. against the Constable's chest. "Now go away! *Bhevor ich dich beide in smithereens blasé."*

Both policemen did not need a translation. Both understood that one false move and they'd be blasted in tiny pieces all the way back to downtown Phoenixville. Constable Tuck backed down the stone steps into the front yard.

"No need to get... upset... We just wanted..."

"I know what you wanted. To arrest my son. And me. We do nothing wrong. *Hör auf, uns zu belästigen.* Stop harassing us!"

"We should have worn our bullet-proof vests, Luke," Hoolmes whispered.

'Wouldn't have done any good, Simon," he whispered back. "Let's just slowly back up. Quietly. Okay?" As he gingerly walked toward the car, Hermann Lochmann slammed the door shut. A broken hinge fell off and clattered onto the stone steps.

"Geez, Luke. You'd think it would be easy to collect the fingerprints of an addle-brained oaf..."

"Well, it isn't. We'll just have to think of another way," the Constable said, leading the way back to the gleaming Torpedo limousine. "He wasn't bluffing. Did you notice? That semi-automatic was locked, loaded, and ready to blast me into oblivion."

Detective Hoolmes shuddered as he opened the passenger side door and got in.

"I hate to think what I'd do without you, Luke."

"Shut up, Simon," the Constable frowned. "It was a close call. Nothing more."

"But... I mean threatening a police officer's life? That's a punishable crime."

"In most cases, yes. In this one, no." He paused. "Let's not press the point any further. At least not for now."

Christmas was, as expected, a somber event in Phoenixville. The shadow of war, more than 3,700 miles away, eclipsed even the brightest red and green lights that lit up the windows and doors of shops and homes on Bridge, Main, and Gay Streets. Many of the residents valiantly tried to keep their spirits up. But with more than 400 men away either in training camps or overseas fighting, it was a daunting task at best.

Most of the gold and red stars on display that season were sewn on banners instead of decorating the boughs of indoor pine trees. Each signified a member of the household fighting for their lives and American freedoms. Sadly, some were crossed with black ribbons.

To aid in the war effort, a concerted attempt was made to exchange more practical than frivolous gifts.

The most popular presents were shoes and sturdy boots purchased, of course, from Carlos Martinez, who, in turn, custom-made a pair of shoes for each member of his own family. For Dolores, he fashioned a pair of tall Edwardian button-up boots with squat hourglass heels. The bottoms were made of the darkest and softest brown leather he could find. The tops were white canvas. For Rosalina, squarish, low-heeled slippers crafted from black suede graced with grosgrain ribbons. And, for Stanley, a pair of shiny black Oxford dress shoes to accompany his new firefighter's dress uniform.

"When you march in parades and attend public affairs," he had explained. His son accepted them with perfunctory gratitude. Stanley was expecting something more in the line of a new baseball mitt or a hand-carved ivory chess set like the one he saw in the window of Meadows' Toy and Sporting Goods Emporium. Doc Kimshaw and Nat White had begun teaching him to play during idle hours while on duty at the firehouse. He had become quite fond of, if not mildly adept at the game.

For his part, Stanley opted to give the whole family a Colombia Grafonda player, complete with a set of Colombia Double-Disc Records. He had found it on sale at T.C. Kramers and had instantly bought it. The player came with several records including two patriotic tunes: "SS Banner" and "America", written by Samuel Francis Smith and sung by Louis Gravure, a little-known French, but moderately talented baritone.

It was his mother's favorite and, much to his own pacifistic annoyance, she played it over and over again all that afternoon.

The brass and chrome fittings of the brand-new Brockway Combination Chemical and Hose Car gleamed under the overhead lamps. The new apparatus had the same capabilities as the old Holloway chemical and hose wagon, except that it was motorized, not horse-drawn.

As Nat had predicted, Duke's and Harry's days as fire horses had finally come to an end.

"What happened to them?" Stanley asked. Not at the station when the horses left, he felt remorse at not being able to say "good-bye".

"Some farmer in the western part of the state bought them. Harness and all..." Nat wiped a stubbly cheek with the heel of his hand. "Didn't get his name... Guess we'll never know. I was told the company could use the money, but the lousy two-hundred or so dollars we got for them..."

"Will you still be the paid driver?"

"I expect so. For a while. But holding a round wooden steering wheel instead of soft, leather reins... just doesn't feel the same."

Stanley nodded, then looked around the station with its new combination firetruck and the two racks with their neat arrays of helmets, boots, and jackets. Even with the large piece of equipment filling up the space once taken up by the two stalls and horses, the firehouse, without the Percherons, seemed quite empty. Even the horse-drawn sprinkler wagon was gone, sold to a Studebaker dealer.

No, he thought. *It's the end of an era... Nothing will ever be the same*

The American LaFrance steam pumper was the only remembrance left of Duke's and Harry's contribution for nearly two decades protecting the lives of Phoenixville residents. It was parked in a darkened corner, under a large canvas tarp, now kept in reserve for major fires. If and when needed, instead of Duke and Harry, it would be pulled by a motorized truck.

Hermann Lochmann had been secretly sipping whiskey ever since his wife had died. He told his son it was "for medicinal purposes. Don't touch it, *dummkopf.*" But that made Lenny all the more curious. When his father wasn't looking, Lenny took the occasional swig from the bottle of bootleg scotch under the kitchen sink. He liked the acrid taste and the warm feeling that waved through his body. Soon, he, too, was secretly imbibing.

One evening in early January, after Hermann had gone to bed, Lenny once again raided his father's stash and drank the last dreg of scotch. The next morning, in the haze of a mild hangover, he knew he had to replace what he had drunk before his father found the empty bottle.

So, he went to Kettleman's Food Emporium and was told that "grain alcohol was no longer being sold". The clerk was kind enough, explaining that there was a temporary prohibition on distilled spirits because of the war. Something about conserving grain reserves for the soldiers. But Lenny didn't quite understand what that meant. All he knew was that he had to find more scotch. For his father and for himself.

At Gateway Pharmacy, across from the new hospital and the high school on Nutt's Avenue, Frank Ecock, the owner, tried to tell him the same thing.

"Only wine," he gruffed. "For medicinal purposes."

"Give me it!" To Lenny, who wouldn't have understood the difference even if it was explained to him, all alcohol was the same; whether it be liquor, wine, or beer.

"I can't sell it to you without a note from your doctor," Ecock said, then ushered Lenny out the door. Which irritated Lenny to no end. A little more than just irate, he raced his Smith Motor Wheel on Fifth Avenue across town to South Main. Doc would have to sell him "medical whiskey".

Lenny Lochmann lumbered into the small pharmacy, idly swinging a baseball bat at his side. Doc Kimshaw was behind the counter filling prescriptions. *Oh, no,* he thought, *here comes trouble.*

"Yes? How may I help you?" Doc asked, leery of the bat and what crazy large Lenny might do with it.

"Some medical whiskey."

"Can't do that, son. Not without a note."

"No note," Lenny slurred. "I have bat." He thwacked the pine Louisville Slugger onto the marble countertop, cracking it and shattering the plate-glass display case underneath. The bat split into two. A pointed wooden shard flew across the counter, barely missing the pharmacist.

"What the hell?!" he yelled, slapping his forehead. "What the hell?!"

"I not mean..." Lenny said, staring at the bat he still gripped tightly; the end now a sharp, ragged point. After a few seconds, he began twirling it in the air, shouting "Liquor. I want liquor!"

Doc Kimshaw wiped his hand down his face and clutched his chin. He wasn't sure what to do to defuse the situation; to calm the beefy, obviously angry young man down. *Was he drunk?* The Doc prayed silently for a miracle and then said, "Look, Lenny... I can't, I can't do that. Not without a note from..."

"No note! Have bat! Need liquor!" Lenny continued to brandish the bat, shouting, "Liquor! Liquor! Liquor!" He didn't hear the soft bell jungle as the door to the pharmacy opened behind him.

"Hola! What's up, Doc?" Stanley Martinez asked cheerfully as he walked up to the counter. Lenny turned to face him, stopped shouting, and dropped the bat. He turned away, staring blankly at the cracked countertop. "Hey, Lenny, whatcha doing with a broken baseball bat at your feet. Hit a homer? You should have used ash instead of pine... Oh," he frowned, noticing the shattered display case. "What happened?"

"He came in here, wielding his bat, wanting me to sell him liquor," Doc sighed.

Stanley put a hand on Lenny's shoulder. "You know, Doc here can't do that, Lenny. You need a doctor's note. There's a prohibition going on..."

"My father..."

"What about him?"

"He hit head again. Hurts when he hits head," he said, gritting his teeth.

"Why would he do that, Lenny?" Stanley asked softly.

Lenny did not respond. He continued to stare at the countertop. *Want liquor,* he seethed to himself. *Why not liquor?*

Stanley kept his hand on Lenny's shoulder. He and his buddies had grown up with the sad shadow of this young man and his abusive father lurking on the sidelines of their lives. He knew how cruel Mr. Lochmann was to his son. But there wasn't anything that Stanley could do about it except to try to be kind and understanding. Evidenced by his still healing nose, he also knew that Lenny had been violent many times before and had, just now, been once again.

The poor guy needs help, he thought. *But I not sure... what or how."*

"I'm calling the police," Doc said, visibly shaken.

"No, don't."

"I could've been killed."

"Lenny wouldn't have done that."

"How do you know, Stanley? The look in his eyes..."

"... is gone now."

Doc glared at Lenny, still standing stock still, staring blankly at shelves crammed with bottles and vials. "Yeah, it's like the fire is lit, but there's just smoke and no flame."

Stanley chuckled, shaking his head. "Spoken like a true firefighter, Doc."

No one spoke for minute or so. Then, heaving a sigh, Lenny heaved a sigh, shook off Stanley's hand, and lumbered out the door. His shoulders drooping in defeat. Not knowing what else to do, or where else to go, he putt-putted his way home. *Maybe he not see scotch gone* raced through his mind as he sped across the High Street Bridge toward Scape Level. *Maybe not notice...*

But Hermann Lochmann did notice. The empty bottle lay on its side under the sink, a silent rebuke to his own clandestine drinking. He wasn't sure if he had finished the bottle before he had gone to bed or if, somehow, cousin Otto had helped himself to the last dregs. But that didn't seem possible. In his mind, Otto was a *Nüchterner aufrechter Mann...* a sober, "dry" person who had applauded President Wilson's pronouncement of the temporary ban on distilled alcohol. *Perhaps it was me,* he thought. *I can't remember.*

It never occurred to him that Lenny, like himself, had become a closet alcoholic and might have finished off what Hermann thought was his secret stash.

It didn't matter to Hermann, though. The Marcelinos three doors down had a few cases of smuggled Dewar's White Label as well as several bottles of Canadian Whisky in their basement. He'd just go and pay Larry, his new best friend, a visit.

An hour later, as he was hiding two bottles of scotch under the sink, he heard the familiar sputtering of Lenny's motorbike speeding up Canal Street. Begrudgingly, he thought about what to feed the dunce for dinner. Fixing himself a stiff drink would have to wait until later.

The Daily Republican printed the full text of President Woodrow Wilson's "Fourteen Points" speech given on January 8th to the United States Congress. In it, he outlined war aims and peace terms in the hopes that the Allies, as well as the Central Powers, would come to a "sane and reasonable agreement".

Stanley read it in its entirety with avid interest and shared his thoughts with this parents over Sunday dinner.

"He's calling for principles for peace negotiations to end the war, Papi. Isn't that a step in the right direction?"

"Well, I read that the President's points were generally welcomed by most people in Europe, but his idealism..." Carlos responded, carefully slicing into the roasted chicken breast on his plate.

"Ah, what do they know?"

"Stanley... Georges Clemenceau, David Lloyd George, and Vittorio Orlando... They are all *estimados líderes*... um, three notables of their countries. Of course, they would know something. *Muchas cosas*."

"Yes, but... "

"Stanley," Dolores Martinez said. 'You've expressed your opinion. Now let your father express his."

"I was only saying..."

"Stanley, *mi hijo. Mi muy querido hijo,* you have not been in a war. You have not been in government. You have no experience of the world other than making patterns to fabricate bridge trusses."

"That is totally unfair, Papi! I know how to fight fires!"

"Ah, yes. *Un bombero.* A fireman." He said it softly without a hint of scorn, but his son thought he detected a inflection of disappointment.

Stanley put his fork down quietly. He had finally had enough of his father belittling him and his chosen path in life. "Fighting fires is almost as bad as being in enemy fire..."

"Almost... Not quite."

'I saved Mrs. Marfit's husband from the burning apartment above your store... I carried a young girl out of the burning Knoll House... I rescued two, no, four horses... Don't those count for something, anything in your eyes?"

"*Si, si.* I am very proud of you, *mi hijo.* My son, my son. But..."

"But... What?!" Stanley stood up and slammed his chair against the wall. "When will... what I do, ever be enough for you? When will you ever accept who I am? And be proud of me? Me! Your own son?!"

"Stanley Francis!' his mother shouted. It was not like Dolly to raise her voice, nor her hand in anger. But this time she did so and slammed her hand on the table with a bit more force then she intended. Wine glasses shook; silverware rattled. "Show a little more respect for your father."

"I will, Momma..." he stated, startled by his mother's forceful tone. "When he," he pointed at Carlos," begins to show a bit more respect for me!"

At that moment, he decided it was time to finally move out on his own. How could he be a responsible adult in an environment where his father was still treating him – at twenty-one years of age – like a child?

Yes, it definitely is time for me to leave.

Since he was on call that night for **Phoenix Nº 1**, it seemed that it would be just as good a time as any to do just that.

Stanley marched out of the dining room and stormed up the stairs to his room.

The twin homes at 176 and 178 Prospect Street, just behind the firehouse, had been purchased in 1881 from John Detwiler, a Kimberton farmer. Both "homes", as Fire Chief David Mendowski often quipped, served as housing for the paid driver and his crew when on-call, enabling them to immediately respond should an alarm sound in the middle of the night.

Since this last argument with his father, Stanley decided that he might be better off living in one of the small houses from now on whenever his was assigned night shifts. *And*, he decided, I'll *request them more often*.

Doc Kimshaw was also on call that night. Since he lived in the apartment above the pharmacy, he was close enough to the station on Church Street to stay at home with his wife and daughter. His son, as indicated by the gold-star banner hanging from the second-story window, had been drafted into the military in mid-summer and was now somewhere in the north of France.

The Kimshaw family was just about to sit down to a late, cold supper when they heard the faint sputtering of a small engine, then a crash of glass breaking downstairs, followed by unintelligible shouts from the sidewalk in front of the store. Doc raced to the window and saw in the dim evening light a hulking figure trudge across the street and disappear into the Central Lutheran Church cemetery. A quick glance to the right revealed a shiny motorized bike turning left onto Church Street.

Both figures, he noticed, were wearing plaid jackets.

Kimshaw raced downstairs. Wisps of smoke and small flames licked in the now broken front window display case. He grabbed the large oaken fire bucket filled with sand and began spreading it onto the fire. Luckily it was a small blaze, easily controlled, and quickly put out. When the fire was extinguished, Kimshaw scattered the ashes and brushed up the shattered glass. As he did so, he uncovered the stub of a burnt torch.

"Son of a bitch," he muttered. "The Chief is not going to be happy when he sees this."

The torch apparently had been wrapped in cloth rags and soaked in kerosene; a faint scent of it lingered in the base of the shattered display case where the clever arrangement of various face creams, perfumes, and sundry toiletries had been destroyed. But, luckily, the charred sawed-off baseball bat that was fashioned into a make-shift torch, had not.

Late the next afternoon, after finishing an early shift at the iron works, Stanley returned to the house on Prospect. An hour later, bored with the book he was reading, he crossed the street and milled around the equipment room looking for something more exciting to do.

Since the arrival of the gas-powered combination truck, he was at a loss. With Duke and Harry no longer part of their team, there was no need to clean harness nor groom the stately, stalwart beasts. There was nothing left but cleaning hoses and polishing up the brass and chrome fittings of the inanimate Brockway. Somehow grooming an inert truck was just not the same as brushing down two lively horses who craned their necks to gently nip and nuzzle his shoulder.

Stanley milled around the station until he absentmindedly walked past the Chief's office.

"You're kinda edgy, Stanley. What's up?" Dave Mendowski asked, beckoning him into his office. Stanley glared at the partially burnt torch now on the Fire Chief's desk and asked where it had come from. When the Chief explained about the small fire at Kimshaw's the evening before, he shook his head in dismay.

"Sir," he hesitated, then said, "I had a good look at Lenny Lochmann's motorbike yesterday when he was at Kimshaw's Pharmacy and..."

"Wait, both you and Lenny, were at Kimshaw's? Doc didn't mention that when he dropped this off."

"Yes sir. I had to refill my prescription for eye drops. You know, from Dr. Hall, for my left eye...."

"Was he angry at all?"

"Who? Doc? He was scared..."

JUNE J. MCINERNEY

"I meant Lenny. Was he angry?"

"He sure seemed that way. He had a broken bat in his hand when I walked in. Looked like he was threatening Doc... And there was a crack in one of the display cases. Glass all over the floor."

"And you or Doc didn't think to call Constable Tucker?"

"Well, Doc wanted to, But I managed to calm Lenny down somewhat, and when he left I didn't think that..."

"He apparently returned and tried to burn the store down." The Fire Chief paused. "What about his tires? You got a good look at them?"

"Yes, and for what it's worth, they were definitely nubby." Stanley paused in thought. "Wait, you said he tried to start a fire? You think it was Lenny?"

"I don't think. I know."

A week later, the Gateway Pharmacy went up in flames. Built in 1910 by Frank Ecock when he had sold The Columbia Hotel to Thomas Gavin, it was, unlike Kimshaw's small store across town, a large marvel of modern pharmaceuticals.

Two stories. I do this, the figure clad in a frayed plaid woolen jacket and a bright red tattered scarf thought. His acumen was bolstered by a few gulps taken earlier from the bottle of whisky hidden under the kitchen sink at home. He heaved the lit torch up into the air, hoping his aim was still true.

After flipping a few times, it landed onto the tar-papered roof. When he was sure the fire had caught, the large, heavy-set man leaned his forehead and hands against the plate glass window for a few moments to catch his breath.

Then, with his fingers and palms still pressed to the glass, he looked up to see smoke billowing into the night sky. *That will show 'em,* he stated, then scooted across the street to crouch behind one of the yew bushes in front of the high school.

He waited and watched as the fire slowly caught, its flames leaping higher and higher, lighting up the late evening sky.

Curfew. Everyone home. Everyone asleep, he assumed. *No one see fire. No alarm. Gateway gone.*

He began to rant.

Fire and fury. No whisky for me. No stores for them.

Jimmy Brazille had been up late, pouring over the latest issue of *National Geographic Magazine* when he just happened to look out of his second-floor bedroom window.

Newly married, he and his wife had recently purchased the modest three-story twin on Fifth Avenue. When they first saw the brick and wood-frame house across from the pharmacy, both he and Diedre instantly fell in love with it. Perfectly located in Phoenixville proper, it was a mere five-minute walk through the small Gateway parking lot to the high school where he taught chemistry and physics.

Jimmy was startled when he saw the flames rising from the roof of the pharmacy, lighting up the night sky. He glanced at his Seth Thomas pocket train clock kept in the vest pocket of his dark grey baggy Edwardian suit. Nine-thirty. He blinked twice, shook his head, then opened the sash to lean out the window.

Yellow sparks and orange and red flames hurdled into the sky. He couldn't believe it. *Gateway on fire? So close to us?* he asked himself, then hastened back down the hallway to wake up Diedre. She was curled up under a thick, tufted homemade crazy quilt in their Early American colonial-styled double bed, already sound asleep

"You've got to see this, Dee," he said, rubbing her shoulder. "Looks like the whole of Nutt's Avenue is on fire."

"What? Huh? Oh, Jimmy... I was dreaming... What did you say? A fire?"

"Yes, my love. Come see."

Jimmy waited until his wife donned the soft shearling housecoat that matched her pink flannel nightgown and, taking her hand, led her into the small front bedroom he used as his library and study.

"Look," he pointed. "Fire in the sky."

"What is that, Jimmy? Gateway Pharmacy? Oh, dear, that's too close for comfort."

Jimmy put his arm around Diedre's shoulders. Despite the cold, he thought he could feel the heat of the conflagration seeping through the window screen.

"Did anyone call the fire department?" she queried?

"Not that I know of... I didn't hear the horn nor sirens..."

"Somebody else must have..."

Jimmy started to comment when they both saw a section of the roof, all aflame, lift up off the store and break apart. Large chunks of it floated up and westward.

"Egad!" Jimmy exclaimed. "They're flying over Nutt's Avenue. Like sheets... caught in the hot gas drafts caused by the fire." They watched as the large burning pieces of tarred shingles and tile shards wafted and floated upward like so many grey geese fluttering across the night sky.

"Oh, my God," Diedre sobbed. "Where is the fire department?"

"I don't know.... But there is a fire box a block or so down on Main. I could, um, drive down there and sound the alarm."

"Oh, Jimmy... My dear. Do be careful."

"Don't worry, Dee. Our Model T is very trustworthy... And the firemen will be here in a jiffy. They'll be able to put the fire out ..." Jimmy sighed again, not so sure that what he promised his wife was really going to happen. The fire was burning hotter and faster as he raced out of the house, leaving Diedre to continue to watch alone in fear and apprehension.

"I certainly hope that is true, dear. I'd hate to have it spread towards us..." she whispered as her husband left, her hands pressed against her cheeks as she watched in horror out the window.

It seemed like an eternity before Jimmy was able to crank up the car; ever since he had purchased it second-hand, the Ford was temperamental at best. Three minutes later, however, he was carefully driving east on Fifth to the intersection of Fifth and Manavon. He turned right onto Main and a few moments later was at the red alarm box mounted on a telephone pole across from the hospital.

The Claxon horn started blaring a mere two seconds after he pulled the lever. He sighed, knowing he had done the community a good deed, and got back into his car. He turned it around and started back down Main Street toward home. His wife, he knew, was home alone, scared, and distraught. He needed to be there to comfort and assuage her fears. There was nothing else he could do.

"Two-seven," Stanley mumbled, still half asleep, as the Claxon horn sounded in the distance and the bell clanged in the steeple on top of the hose drying tower. He clambered out of the ancient rope bed, donned denim trousers and a flannel shirt over his long johns, and raced down the stairs.

"Nutt's and Main, Nutt's and Main, he recited as he ran out the front door to the back entrance of the Phoenix № 1 fire station.

When Stanley ran into the equipment room, Nat White was already in the driver's seat of the Brockway combination truck, turning the magneto ignition switch. He grabbed his helmet and galvanized trench coat and quickly climbed onto the back along with Doc Kimshaw, Billy Szabo, and Lou Double, the newest member of the force. The Fire Chief shouting, "Go! Go! Go!" was climbing into the seat next to White as two other firemen slid open the large double-doors.

The firetruck sped west on Church Street and then left ono Main towards Nutt's Avenue. The streets of Phoenixville were empty and dark, lit only by the fading moonlight and gas lamps mounted on garish blue poles sporadically placed along the sidewalks. As the firetruck sliced through the dimly-lit silence, Stanley had the eerie feeling of riding on the back of a maniacal banshee keening through the night.

They could see orange-red flames leaping from the pharmacy two blocks away as Nat White expertly turned right onto Nutt's Avenue. Gusts of winter wind lifted shards and sheets of burning tar paper and white-hot embers up through billows of black smoke.

As Stanley, Kimshaw, and Szabo hooked up the 2½" hose to the fire hydrant less than twenty-five feet away on the sidewalk next to the store, Fire Chief Mendowski and Nat White broke through what was left of the pharmacy's glass façade and entered the burning building in search of victims. Frank Ecock, the Chief, knew, was fond of closing up the store and then working late into the wee hours of the morning, rearranging stock, taking inventory, balancing the books.

By the time sirens were heard in the distance – and getting closer by the second – Jimmy was back home, his wife weeping in his arms as he stared, mesmerized, out the window.

"Wait, look... Those silvery streaks..." Jimmy finally whispered. "That's water being pumped over what is left of the roof. Looks like the brave firemen are at last trying to contain it..."

Nat was the first to leave the building. Coughing and sputtering, he managed to relay that Chief David Mendowski had been trapped behind a falling beam.

"I tried to lift it, but it's too heavy..."

"Hose here!" Stanley directed Kimshaw and Szabo, pointing directly into the smoke billowing out of what was left of the front door. "Cover me!" he shouted, running alongside the stream of water, directly into the line of fire.

"Spoken like a true hero," Billy Szabo chuckled, confidently aiming the powerful nozzle as carefully as he could toward the fire, trying not to hit Stanley. The pressure of spewing water from a 2½" hose could easily knock any man, however strong, into unconsciousness.

Nat took a deep breath of cold night air, then followed Stanley in, shouting, "Over there! He's over there!"

Jimmy and Diedre stood spellbound, watching in horror as two men dashed into the burning building and then, after a while, one came out. Then another ventured in, looking as if he was propelled by a spume of water. The fireman who had just run out, ran back in.

"Where is the other man?" Diedre asked, her voice quaking with dread.

'Don't know... In there somewhere..."

'God help them all," she prayed.

Then, as if her prayers were immediately heard and answered, Nat White and Stanley Martinez emerged from the lessening smoke into the cleaner. cooler outside air. Fire Chief David Mendowski was between them, his arms draped across their shoulders as they helped him hobble out.

"I'm okay," he coughed and sputtered, dropping to one knee. "You... saved my life..."

Nat wanly smiled, shook his head, then walked away. Stanley grinned, although tears were in his eyes as he continued to hold on to one of the Chief's arms.

'I couldn't let you die in there... David," he said. It was the first time that he, as an adult, addressed the Fire Chief by his given name. "I mean, Chief Men..."

"No, son. Stan. It's fine. Tonight, you've earned the right to call me Dave."

When the flames had died down and disappeared from the midnight sky, Jimmy once again gently took the hands of his sleepy wife into his own sturdy ones.

"Come, dear Dee. The danger is over. The fire has been contained. The brave firemen are safe. There is no longer any threat of it spreading to us... Or to any place else..." He gently led her back to their bedroom. "And, I think that we've had just about enough excitement for one night."

A few minutes after the Brazilles had crawled into bed and Chief Mendowski had been dragged out of the smoldering Gateway Pharmacy, the roof, which had caved into the second floor, caved in again. This time into the first floor. The flames blazed up once more, spreading to displays of flammable liquids, books, greeting cards, and yesterday's newspapers.

The valiant volunteers of Phoenix № 1 did the best they could to contain the fire, but it took another exhaustive and exhausting hour to extinguish it completely.

Ecock's Gateway Pharmacy, reputed to be the pharmacy of the future, was completely gutted. Only two of the brick and stucco walls remained standing. And they were on the verge of tumbling down.

Back at the firehouse, the Fire Chief rasped, "See any tracks in the dust, Stanley?" Not quite recovered from his ordeal, he was still concerned about the cause of the fire. It was, after all, his job. He clutched but didn't acknowledge the pain in his left shoulder once again bruised when the wooden beam had fallen, just barely grazing it. The Chief was sure his old war wound, once thought healed, would never be the same again. And he had doubts that even Doctor Galen Hall would be able to fix it.

"No, sir," Stanley sighed. "It was too dark by the time the fire had been doused and we packed up the hoses and gear and drove away."

"No evidence then..."

"Unless something is found in the rubble."

"I'll leave that to Constable Tucker. And Detective Hoolmes. A shame the pharmacy was totally destroyed."

"But," as the undaunted Frank Ecock, who had insured the building and its contents to the maximum allowable amount, would later say to Constable Luke Tucker, "rebuilding will be an opportunity to implement the newest pharmaceutical technologies."

Always, Tucker smiled to himself, remembering as a young lad, when Henry Ecock had built his prior establishment on Bridge Street in 1893, *the eternal optimist.*

The figure crouched behind the tree on the high school grounds had watched the fire truck arrive. Angered that someone had sounded the alarm, he gritted his teeth and clenched his fists, pounding them against the side of the school building until nails dug into his palms drew blood and welts rose on the sides of his palms.

No! No! No! No! Not supposed to happen.

Then, when he watched the Fire Chief enter the blaze and, moments later, Stanley rushing into the burning building, he cheered.

"Toast. Martinez and Mendowski toast!" he brayed in a slurred whisper. Elated, he slinked off into the darkness to find what remained of the bottle of scotch he had left on the kitchen counter.

He did not see Stanley Martinez and Nat White almost miraculous rescue their Fire Chief.

Two days later, Stanley permanently moved his personal belongings into 176 Prospect Street. Already furnished, albeit with mostly an antiquated bed, bureau, and a rickety maple desk and chair, all he needed, besides his clothes and books, were a set of bed linens and bath towels. His mother, understanding her adult son's need to be on his own, graciously gave him what was necessary to equip his new home. Rosalina, however, had teased him mercilessly about have a "hope chest", joking about his "new trousseau". Her brother, of course, didn't think it was all that funny.

"I'm just moving closer to the fire station, not marrying the company," he scowled.

"Yes, but..." she faltered, then said, "I'm going to miss you, Stan-Stan. Especially at dinner."

He winced at her continued use of his old nickname. "Well, I trust you'll keep the ol' home fires burning," he tried to quip, paraphrasing the now popular slogan used by doughboys overseas. "Besides, if ever you need me..."

"Thanks, but tell that to Samantha. Or, um, is it Rebecca these days?" Stanley feigned a punch at his sister, which she deftly sidestepped. "Sam and Stan-Stan sitting in a tree," she chanted. "K-I-S-S-I-N-G!"

"Stop!' he laughed. "You are, Rosie, totally incorrigible."

In a moment of generosity, as Stanley was lugging his footlocker out the door to the 1917 Woodie gas-powered wagon he had borrowed from Billy Szabo, Carlos slipped a hundred dollars into his son's shirt pocket as he walked out the door.

"No need, Papi. The rent is free 'cause I'm a member of the company and..."

"I don't intend it to be for rent," Carlos said gruffly, although Stanley noticed a hint of sadness in his voice. "Buy yourself that fancy chess set I failed to get you for Christmas"

"You didn't fail me, Papi..."

"I tend to be practical and you did need the dress shoes."

"Yes, I did."

"You got them packed?"

"In the trunk," Stanley tried to smile. He knew his move was especially hard on his mother, but didn't think it would affect his father so much. "I even polished them before putting them in..."

"Dyanshine?"

"The very one..."

"I sell a lot of that in our, er, my store. Gives a great glean to any leather. It's used almost exclusively by the military, you know."

"No, I didn't." Stanley's voice grew harder, colder. He didn't want to be reminded of the war or what would have, could have been his part in it.

He was quickly reminded, however, of the letter now packed under his socks in the scuffed-up truck in the back of the car. He still hadn't opened it and probably, at this late date, wouldn't.

His father, sensing that the old tension between them had returned, step back. "Yes, well. If ever you need more..." Carlos reached out his hand to his son. A warm hug, he knew, would not be welcomed. "I am here."

"Sure, Papi, sure." Stanley wondered why his father refrained from the usual parting hug. But, then again, they hadn't hugged in a long while. "Well, I best be going. Got to unpack and get settled... I'm on call tonight, you know."

"Sure, *mi hijo. Por supuesto.* Sure."

Stanley Frances Martinez turned and walked away from the house, the home he had grown up in. Now, as an adult, it was time for him to further grow up into his own life.

Later that evening, Samantha Higgins Rouleaux showed up on the doorstep of Stanley's new home. A cold bottle of Chandon Brut champagne in one hand and a large picnic basket in the other.

"Time to celebrate your long overdue freedom, fireman," she said, pushing her way past Stanley into the sparsely furnished parlor.

More than surprised, Stanley was taken aback. *How did she find out so quickly?*

"My, my, isn't this quaint?" she smirked, slowly turning around, taking in the faded settee askew at a right angle to the dusty, seldom used fireplace. A rickety mahogany end table alongside a high-backed overstuffed green leather wing chair was already piled high with some of Stanley's collection of literary masterpieces. "I trust you have flutes, my dear?"

"Flutes? Why would I have flutes... I don't play. The piano, a bit. Surely, you don't think I can play the flute."

Samantha laughed maniacally. The sound reminded Stanley of Lenny Lochmann screams just before he punched his nose.

"Glasses," she squealed, "silly fireman. For the champagne."

He gave her a blank look, much like those he had seen on Lenny Lochmann.

"No matter," she sighed, picking up a warn, leather-bound copy of *David Copperfield* by Charles Dickens. "I didn't think so. I brought two of my own. That is, my aunt's friend's... 'Borrowed' them," she winked. "Just in case." She tossed the book aside and laughed as it landed, covers splayed, onto the broad-board hardwood floor.

"Hey, watch it. That's a first edition," Stanley said, rushing to pick up the cherished old tome.

"Well, then, so it's old. Doesn't matter."

"That's not the point." He vacillated. It would have been fruitless to try and explain to her what the point really was. First editions of Dickens were worth a lot. A whole lot. And that particular one, with its leather binding, gilded page edges, and ink and pen full-page black and white illustrations, was actually not his, but purloined from his father's library. He paused, looked at Samantha in her pencil-slim ankle-length dark blue linen skirt and fashionable stark white blouse with balloon sleeves and then inquired, "Why are you here, anyway?"

"Like I said, time to celebrate."

Stanley watched as she took two tall tubular glasses, obviously crystal, from the basket, set them onto the coffee table, and then expertly popped the champagne bottle cork. It flew across the room and bounced off a far wall. Champagne spewed onto the small frayed Oriental rug in front of the hearth and splashed onto the settee.

"Oops," she said, giggling, pouring more foam than liquid into the flutes. "Sorry, but I've already... No, no. Don't tell. No harm done," she laughed, holding up the bottle. "Not to worry, there's another one in my car." She handed a filled flute to Stanley. "Here, have a sip. Or two."

"I'm on call. On duty."

"Then get off... of it." She drained her glass and refilled it. "Oh, c'mon, fireman... A little drinkie-poo ain't gonna hurt you..."

"If I'm on duty and the alarm goes off, I have to be at my best... most alert. And it's 'isn't' not 'ain't'."

"Geez, picky-picky. Lighten up, will ya, fireman?" She took another healthy gulp, then plopped herself onto the settee. She patted one of the now slightly damp cushions. "Well, at least come here and sit close to me. We've lots to talk about... And do. Now that you've moved in here. On your own."

Stanley stood stock still in front of the fireplace, watching as she crossed her legs, suggestively inching the pencil skirt high above the low-heeled Edwardian two-tone pumps obviously fashioned by his father. A few inches of pink bare flesh were exposed. Embarrassed, he looked away.

"I think... I think you need to go," he half-heartedly suggested.

"Oh, not yet. I've brought dinner. You hungry?"

He had to admit that he was.

"I thought so. Moving away from home gives one an appetite. I know it did me," she laughed again. "Many times."

She got up and walked over to the basket. Inside were a large tin of Russian caviar, a box of wheat crackers, assorted French and Dutch cheeses, two long baguettes, a small wooden tub of butter, a paper sack filled with eight hard-boiled eggs, tiny silver salt and pepper shakers, and a china soup tureen stuffed with cold, yet crispy fried chicken.

"Oh, dang," Samantha said. "I forgot the tomatoes and Calamari olives. Oh, well!"

Stanley watched, the still untasted champagne in his hand, as she somewhat clumsily, but effectively, carried the repast to what served as a dining room and laid it all out on the small drop-leaf table against the back window.

"You've knives and forks?"

"Even napkins" Stanley leered, salivating at the largesse. He went into the kitchen to fetch the utensils, vowing that once they had eaten, Samantha Higgins Rouleaux and her overwhelmingly, overpowering commanding ways would just... simply... Would simply have to go.

An hour or so later, after what he had to admit was a somewhat satisfying supper, Stanley managed to escort Samantha out the door and into her car. It took a bit of cajoling, but she had finally left.

But not before she had covered his face with slobbery kisses and long, clinging, hugs.

"Geez," he had said, pushing her away. She had drunk most of the champagne and exuded a fetid aroma reminiscent of the inside of The Columbia Hotel bar on a busy night. "Get off me," he managed to say, wiping a sleeve across his mouth. "You're drooling like a basset hound in heat..." He turned red, instantly regretting the off-color comment.

"Oh, I may not be a basset hound, but I am... In heat? Hah! Hah! Yes, sure as Bob's your uncle. I desire... You, Fireman! You!".

When she reached for him again, he stepped aside. Samantha stumbled and fell against the front door jamb.

"Damn!"

He had then clasped her arm and practically shoved her out of what was his house. His own home.

Crumpled into the driver's seat, Samantha seemed to be alert enough to drive. Even if she wasn't, Stanley vowed he wasn't about to offer she sleep it off on the settee. Or anyplace else, for that matter, at 176 Prospect Street. He had a reputation to uphold and a job to do that required his full concentration. And had nothing, he firmly decided, to do with Samantha Higgins Rouleaux.

When she reluctantly, finally left driving at almost breakneck speed down Prospect Street, Stanley cleared up the remains of supper, washed the flutes, stowed the wicker basket in the hall closet, and wearily went upstairs to bed.

He hoped and prayed that the great and loud Claxon horn wouldn't blare nor that the firehouse bell would toll out an alarm so that he could catch an hour or so, maybe more, of sleep

He'd unpack the footlocker and the rest of his belongings in the morning.

And, maybe, he'd think about giving Rebecca Hope a call.

Maybe.

As he drifted off, he realized that the still unopened letter postmarked "Washington, D.C." wasn't in the trunk under his socks. He had meant to pack it, but had forgotten it.

It was still in the now empty sock drawer of the bureau back in his old bedroom in the house that he just had left.

FEBRUARY 1918

On February 18th, during a three-pronged offensive, the Central Powers broke through the remains of the Russian Southwestern Army Group and captured Zhitomir, then secured Kiev a few weeks later, facing no serious resistance as German troops came within one hundred miles of Petrograd, forcing the Soviets to then declare Moscow as their new capital.

"You could call it a railway war," Captain Whitaker said, chatting with his troops during a Friday afternoon training session. "The rapid advance has been described as such," he pronounced, "because German soldiers used Russian railways to advance. I heard this was ascribed to the German General Hoffman..."

In reality, Hoffman had written in his diary that *It is the most comical war I have ever known. We put a handful of infantrymen with machine guns and one cannon onto a train and rush them off to the next station; they take it, make prisoners of the Bolsheviks, pick up few more troops, and so on. This proceeding has, at any rate, the charm of novelty.*

The entry, Whitaker smiled, had been leaked to a French newspaper by an infiltrator.

"If only fighting battles on our side were that simple," he said.

Edmond could only smirk at the carelessness of the Germans and the naiveté of the Russian soldiers, who had claimed to be the allies of the American Expeditionary Forces. But he did not appreciate the German general's sarcastic comments, however true they might be. He was still angry that his artillery unit, along with members of Company, were still ensconced in Camp

Hancock and not in Europe fighting whom he thought were Hessian thugs.

That night he wrote three short letters back home; one to Rosalina, one to Stanley, and the third to his parents. In all three he expressed his anger, his displeasure, and his disappointment. His missive to Harold and Gwendolyn Hope was published two weeks later in *The Daily Republican* under the headline LOCAL ARTILLERYMAN DECRIES DELAY.

Lenny had overheard his father and his cousin talking in the parlor. Otto was seething something about "an unpatriotic American soldier who questioned orders".

"*Hätte ich nur das Privileg, das er hat...* his privilege to serve," he said. "*Wenn ich das wäre...*"

"But it is not you," Hermann replied. "And you don't have the privilege. *Du bist zu alt und zu deutsch...* too old, too German. Why would you even want to fight for Americans? *Sie sind unser Feind.* Our enemies."

It was the longest Lenny had ever remembered hearing his father talk. And the first time he had heard him express his true feelings. Although he didn't understand the German spoken between the two older men, he was able to sense its meaning.

Curious who the soldier was, he went into the room and stood directly in front of Otto's chair.

"Tell me!"

"Tell you what?" Otto asked, smiling up at his second cousin. He was growing quite found of Lenny, even if he was, as Hermann continued to call him, a *dummkopf*.

Lenny pointed to the paper. "Who?"

"Who what?"

"The soldier not fight..."

"Edmond Hope," his father sneered. "Your patriotic friend."

Lenny shook his head, pounding his thighs with his fists. "Not my friend! Not my friend!"

Hermann looked away from his only son and reached for the sports section of the newspaper. The only way he could handle Lenny was to ignore him.

Otto, however, asked "Why isn't Edmond your friend, Lenny?"

"I have reasons. He not fight. I fight. I want to fight. I want fight for Americans," Lenny exclaimed. "Not enemies. Stanley, Edmond Hope. Enemies. No one lets me. I follow orders. I obey."

"All well and noble... and good, Lenny. But, sorry, you were... um... *Deklariert nicht für Service.*"

Lenny looked confused.

"Unfit to serve," his father said without looking up from the local football scores. "Unfit to fight. Unfit. Like everything else in your life."

Lenny frowned at Herman and Otto, then angrily lumbered out of the parlor and up the stairs. On impulse, he had decided to fetch money from his hidden cigar box and ride his Motor Wheel to Kettleman's to buy a real torch and a bottle of gasoline.

Once again, Lenny Lochmann had a plan. A big plan. Only he had the best plans. And his plans were the only ones that mattered.

Harold prided himself on the lovely well-kept large Victorian twin on Main Street that he had inherited from his father, Isaiah Hope. He also inherited Isaiah's small fortune made by pouring what little extra money he had into railroad stock. He had also inherited his congregation.

Harold Hope was actually The Right Reverend Harold Hope, the current pastor of St Peter's Episcopal Church on Church Street. Built in 1840 on land donated by Samuel Reeves and Samuel Whitaker, the church's first assistant pastor was Reverend Isaiah Hope. "The calling," as Reverend Harold Hope often quipped from the pulpit, had become a family legacy. A tradition. And he had, pardoning his own eponymous pun, hopes that his son, Edmond, would follow in his footsteps.

Once, that is, he returned from the war.

And while his election to head the congregation in Phoenixville came with the smaller, cramped manse next to the stately stone mini-cathedral that Harold had grown up in, he and his wife preferred the larger Victoria house five blocks away. Built in 1870, the three-story five-bedroom brick house with white shutters and blue trim sported large side and back yards. "Big enough for a baseball game," Edmond, as a young lad, had once said.

It also sported three large wooden porches. One, in the back just off the kitchen, was used for summertime dining; the second was a screened-in second-floor sleeping porch; and the third, also roofed, was wide and deep. It spanned the entire width of the Hope home and wrapped around the side. The front as well as a side door leading from the formal dining room opened onto it.

The brown wicker settee with its green and grey striped cushion on the side porch was FrankieBernard's favorite late-afternoon-before-supper napping spot. Which is where he was half listening to and sniffing the clamor and aromas coming for the dining room as Rebecca, Edmond's younger sister, and Lizzie, their live-in maid and cook, bustled about setting the table. Gwendolyn Hope, the vicar's wife, was in the kitchen putting the last touches of herbs and spices on a succulent rib-roast. It was the basset hound's most preferred treat.

That particularly warm late afternoon, Reverend Hope had returned home from counseling and consoling the parents of young Reginald Warner. The navy man, fresh from training at Cape May, New Jersey, had been lost at sea when his troop ship was torpedoed by a German U-Boat as it entered the Irish Sea on its way to Liverpool. The pastor entered the front yard through the wrought iron gate and stopped to inspect the Primroses planted last year along the porch railing. They were just beginning to bud, a harbinger of an early spring. Then he mounted the four steps and chuckled at the sight of FrankieBernard sprawled upon the settee.

"Ah, there you are, my pudgy friend," he said. The basset hound replied by slightly opening one eye and huffing through his drooling jowls. "Well, okay, then. Enough said. I'll let you continue your nap."

Reverend Hope entered his beloved home through the side door. He did not see the man in the flannel jacket on the shiny motor bike stop in front of the house. Nor, once in the house, did he hear the heavy thud of a club thrown onto the front porch. The basset hound, however, stirred and woke up long enough to snuffle and sniff the air. Not quite sure of the scents, he then turned around in place and settled back down.

And, then, suddenly, he was wide awake.

The Hope family were just about to sit down to dinner when FrankieBernard, whose uncanny sense of smell was forty times greater than any human's, started baying and scratching at the side door.

"Gwendolyn, dear, did you forget to feed him again?"

"He eats after dinner, my dear. You know that..."

"And often tend to forget," Rebecca smiled, impatiently waiting for the ensuing Grace before supper to end before passing a warm plate of asparagus roasted in garlic and butter.

"Such largess already," she commented. "Our Victory garden will be especially bountiful come March and April."

Last fall, before the first frost, she and her father had tilled over a patch of the back lawn, dedicating it to growing fruits and vegetables. It was their family's contribution, like many of the families in Phoenixville who followed suit, to the war effort. Growing their own meant that fresh produce could be purchased in bulk by the government from large commercial farms and shipped directly to the men fighting overseas instead of to local grocery stores.

The rack of ribs now steaming in the center of the table came from a young steer locally bred and butchered on the Cornett farm and then sold at Eyrich's Market for the almost inexpensive price of 65¢ a pound. And the government's temporary ban on grain alcohol products did not affect grape growers and wine makers. The red wine accompanying the meal had been made locally from grapevine cuttings brought over to America by a large Italian family now living on Scape Level who now had a small, "fashionable" local vineyard.

The Fenella Family's Fine Wines was slowly gaining in popularity. Besides selling at Gateway Pharmacy – before it burnt down – Kimshaw's Pharmacy, Kettleman's Food Emporium, and Eyrich's Market, the Fenellas supplied restaurants not only in Phoenixville but beyond Borough borders. Spring City, Royersford, Norristown; even Pottstown. Thus, the Hope family purchased their wine directly from the Fenellas.

Daniella Fenella, a friend and neighbor of the Monticellos, was also an active member of the knitting group headed by Dolores Martinez. And a frequent visitor to Gwendolyn Hope's kitchen, where they both labored to put up preserves to stock their family shelves and to also send to local men stationed overseas.

Sipping his favorite Fenella deep red rich burgundy, Reverend Hope commented that the war had caused stringent economies. He savored the velvet wine's taste as he inhaled and swallowed. "Ahh... It's almost a sin, being so frugal."

Rebecca, his daughter laughed. She had often said, "It's nothing more than tightening one's belt or sash, Father." She grinned at the double-entendre. Her father a Father in the church. She never tired of teasing him about it.

FrankieBernard continued to scratch at the door, his constant howling rising to a merciless pitch.

"Leave him, Harold," Gwendolyn commented when her husband started to leave the table. "Sit back down. It's the middle of dinner. He will soon quiet down."

"But, I've not heard him put up such a fuss in the past. There must be something bothering him."

"Hunger, perhaps?" Rebecca shrugged, tucking into a juicy morsel of meat. "The roast is particularly succulent this evening... I am sure he has had a deep whiff of it."

The Reverend smiled at his daughter. "Perhaps, but I sense something else." He rose again in defiance of his wife and opened the door to let the hound in. But, instead of eagerly bounding into the dining room searching for orts from the table, he barked at the Episcopal priest and ran down the side porch to the front of the house.

'FrankieBernard, you come back here!" Harold Hope shouted, walking briskly after the wayward dog. He was glad there was secure fencing all around their home, lest the basset's infamous nose got the better of him, causing him to wander about the neighborhood in search of rabbits. But FrankieBernard stopped short of the small fire now creeping along the porch floor toward the front wall of the house. He howled incessantly as if to say, "Do something! Do something!"

Earlier that day, Rebecca had cleared her father's study of a wealth of old newspapers and had Lizzie stack them outside to be picked up by the Boy Scouts who collected rubber, metal, rags, and paper for the war effort. She should have placed the pile at the backyard gate for pick-up, but Lizzie was a bit of a lazy sort, and opted for the expedient path of least resistance as she went about her daily cleaning chores.

"Gwen!" the Reverend shouted at the top of his lungs, enough to be overheard over FrankieBernard's din. "Call the fire department!" He then tried to stomp out the fire which had already burned through the porch floorboards and had ignited the newspapers. But it was a futile attempt. He could put out the fires in men's souls, but not those threatening his own home.

Without asking why, his dutiful wife raced into the Reverend's study off the large front parlor and picked up the receiver of the graphite desk phone. She pressed the cradle three times and waited for a response.

"The fire department!" she shouted when the operator finally answered. "Now!"

By the time the Brockway combination chemical pumper and hose truck had pulled up in front of the house, a good portion of both the front and side porches had been destroyed. The flames were licking up the side of the Victorian's first floor brick over wood frame walls.

Rebecca had the forethought of shutting the double-hung front windows Lizzie had left open to air out the room full of "wintery mustiness". She dutifully sealed shut the doors as well. But smoke from the fire and fury was encroaching into poorly-sealed sills and window jambs of the front parlor. Rebecca worried about the artifacts and treasures in her father's study. They were too valuable to be destroyed.

Stanley had happened to be on his way home from work when he had heard the alarm and even though he was not on call, he raced to the station and hopped aboard the firetruck next to Nat.

Lenny realized that it had been a mistake not to throw the burning torch soaked in gasoline onto the roof. But the house was four stories high and included a steep pitched attic roof. After a full day at work he did not have the strength nor agility to throw a lit torch that high. Setting fire to the porch seemed a better and safer option. Although his aim was not as true as it had been before. A now slightly crooked arm that had not healed properly inhibited that.

But then he saw the pile of newspapers. A perfect target. He wanted to hit it directly. But coming any closer into the yard might have roused the large dog that snoozed on the wicker settee. Lenny considered himself brave, very brave. He was afraid of only just a few things. And a big drooling hound was one of them.

His Smith Motor Wheel safely parked on the next block over on Third Avenue, he watched from across the street as the fire began to spread and the ugly dog wake up to lead the Reverend to the fire. He grinned, proud of his big success. Thoroughly soaking the torch as well as its bound rags in gasoline rather than kerosene seemed to have done the trick. Despite his misplaced aim.

Certain that the fire would destroy the Hope house, he slowly sprinted down an alley and started up his motorbike. He was putt-putting up Second Avenue toward Main Street as Nat White was speeding into a right-hand turn. Ignoring the fire truck barreling down, Lenny continued to cross the intersection.

"Stupid idiot," Nat cursed. He didn't have enough room to swerve away and barely missed hitting the bike.

"That was Lenny Lochmann," Stanley remarked. "I wonder what he's doing on this side of town?"

As they pulled up in front of his best friend's home, he jumped off the back and, without thinking, directed Kimshaw and Lou Double to hook up the hose to the chemical pump and aim it directly at the base of the fire. Then he stormed through the front door in search of the family.

Rebecca greeted him in the narrow foyer as if he was an expected, welcomed guest.

'Hi, Stan. Fancy meeting you here," she smiled.

"Hello, Rebecca," he said crisply. Then he turned to the smoke seeping out from under the parlor double-wide pocket doors. "What are you doing in the house when it's on fire?"

"It's just the front room. Everything else is okay. At least... will be now that you are here." She lowered her eyes and then calmly led him back to the back of the house. "Mom and FrankieBernard are in the kitchen."

"But you all need to get out..."

"But our darling pet needs to be fed."

Stanley shook his head at her folly. She always was a willful little girl and he still thought of her that way. Even though she was grown-up and would have been married to Campbell Wheatley by now had not the war broke out and he had not bit the mud in France. He pondered why he had even considered asking her out before Campbell beat him to the punch. There, for a while, they seemed like the perfect couple. For a brief instant, he reconsidered, remembering the evening they had had together before Christmas when he had vowed he would eventually marry her. Eventually.

Stanley sighed and followed Rebecca to the back of house.

While his fellow company volunteers fought the fire in the front of the house, he waged his own small battle in the large, well-equipped kitchen.

'You need to evacuate," he pleaded with Mrs. Hope.

"The fire is contained, is it not?" Stanley nodded. "So, when Frankie is finished eating," she said, pointing to the large red and white hound feasting on bits of still-warm rib roast, steamed green beans, and mashed potatoes. "Then we'll consider leaving. Maybe."

The Hope hound barely looked up when Stanley entered the room. The rather short man in the canvas tunic and rubber boots was no threat to his dinner, served in a large blue and white Limoges bowl, that he was now greedily consuming. His was a familiar face and smell. An all too frequent visitor to his domain when Edmond was a youth.

"But that may be too...."

"All clear," Chief Mendowski called from the hallway. He peered into the kitchen. "Stanley? You in here?"

"Here, Chief."

"Why are you hob-knobbing in here with the Hope ladies? You need to finishing up overhaul of the area impacted now that the fire has been extinguished."

"Yes, Dave, er, sir. Rolling hoses, too."

"Right. To your post, son."

He nodded at Gwendolyn Hope then smiled at the basset hound still happily chomping his food, heedlessly unaware of the humans around him. The Chief tilted his head at Rebecca, then turned and walked back up the hallway. Embarrassed in front of Edmond's mother and sister, Stanley meekly followed.

"I only meant, sir... David..."

"No problem. We brave firemen always turn the pretty face."

Stanley's face reddened. He couldn't remember the last time he had felt so flushed, except when he had a fever as a child. And when he had made the rash inappropriate comment to Samantha that evening when she had stormed into his new home with champagne and an over-the-top gourmet meal.

"But I wasn't turning..."

"Sparkling blue eyes... Luxurious shiny hair... Great figure... Why wouldn't you turn your own eyes toward her, Mendowski? As she did toward you?"

"But..."

"Heard you were courting her. Again. You could do far worse, you know... Like that Rouleaux girl."

"Samantha..."

"I've known Rebecca all her life. Salt of the earth. You be her pepper." The Fire Chief smiled. Stanley shook his head in disbelief. It was the first time he had ever heard David joke or make a comment about a company member's personal life. "Now that other woman... of yours..."

"She's not mine, sir... Not anymore."

They were outside on the porch now. Doc Kimshaw and Nat White were talking to the Reverend, trying to figure out how the fire might have started. Lou Double, a slight, slender lad, struggled with rolling a hose by himself.

"Good to hear. She's water poured on a grease fire. Know what it does?"

"It sinks to the bottom and evaporates, spreading the flaming oil everywhere."

'Yep. It burns faster... hotter, consuming everything in its path. If I were you, I'd get rid of her. Stay with the one who lights your fire. The right way."

Stanley frowned, his cheeks still a dark red. He stood silently, listening to the Fire Chief uncharacteristically waxing eloquent; so unlike his normal taciturn self.

"Seems obvious to me, Martinez, she's smitten with you," he nodded at the house, then paused. "And you with her." He smiled wryly as he walked up to Nat and Doc. "Too good a chance to miss, if you ask me."

Stanley continued to frown as he nodded, then walked over to Double. As he helped to roll up the hose, he asked himself, *what chance do I have with Rebecca? She was in love with Campbell... and now Campbell is dead... We had one date since then and that was okay, but...* He shook his head, wiping further thoughts from his mind, half-heartedly listening to the semi-muted conversation conducted just a few feet away.

"Apparently a stack of old newspapers against the wall," Harold Hope was saying. "But I have no idea how it ignited..."

Nat White held up the charred remnants of a sanded-down baseball bat. "Could this be it?" he inquired. "Looks like the same ones we found..."

"Yes, yes," the Fire Chief pronounced. "Exactly. Here's the culprit, Reverent Hope. How do you supposed it got here?"

"I haven't a clue."

'Hmmm... but I do. Nat?"

"Seems," he sniffed, "to have been heavily soaked in gasoline."

"Any 'funny' tire tracks? In the street?"

"Recently paved... I doubt it, but I'll look."

"What are you getting at, Dave?" the Reverend Hope asked the Fire Chief. He and his wife, Susan, were regular members of his congregation. He had baptized all three of their sons and conducted the funeral of Susan's mother who was the first director of the Borough's Library. The Reverend had great respect, if not admiration and affection for Dave, as well as for the whole illustrious Mendowski family. His word was as good as pure 24-karat gold.

"Series of unusual fires in the Borough the past year. We suspect an arsonist. An arsonist with an agenda... A vengeance."

"Who? Why?"

"Not sure.... But we have our suspicions."

Harold Hope nodded. "At least my home is reasonably, um," safe." He waved at the burnt-through front porch floor and the blackened bricks. Lord knew what smoke and water damage lay inside the parlor. "Thanks to you. I am extremely grateful, David. To you and your men."

"Only doing our job. But the damage?" He looked at the house's façade. "You're lucky. Extremely lucky. Could have been worse."

"Easily repaired. Lost lives, not so much."

"You called in time..."

"FrankieBernard sounded the alarm..."

"Ah, yes, your basset hound," the Fire Chief nodded.

"I have a firm belief. Always trust your dog."

"Yes, well..." Chief Mendowski murmured, then shook the Reverend's hand. "I'll leave you to it."

"See you and Susan in church?"

"Yep. Next Sunday. For sure."

As the Brockway drove away, Stanley looked back, wondering if he should return to the Hope house later that evening to make sure everyone was okay.

Whom am I kidding? he asked himself. *I'd be going back to see if Rebecca was okay.* And, he had to admit, *to ask her out again.*

And, so, he did.

The next day Stanley pedaled his Schwinn one-speed racer up Starr Street and then onto Second Avenue to pay a call on the Hope family. His secret agenda, as he had admitted, was to see Rebecca once again and ask her out. He also had to admit, he just couldn't resist, as much as he tried, her sparkling blue eyes and down-to-earth staid and sane practicality.

A welcomed, refreshing change from the erratically unstable and unseemly behavior of Samantha Higgins Rouleaux.

"You know, I am getting fed up with all the fires," Fire Chief Mendowski sighed. He was sitting in Constable Tucker's office alongside Detective Hoolmes and Stanley Martinez whom he had asked to accompany him to the meeting. Stanley was honored to be there, although he wasn't sure he had anything more to offer than a shallow knowledge of Lenny Lochmann's disturbing personality and actions. If, in fact, Lenny turned out to be the arsonist.

"Four heads are better than one," the Fire Chief stated. "Let's pool our resources and forces and solve this rash of crimes."

"Agreed," the Constable said, rubbing his face with both hands. "We could use all the help we can get. Um, but what did you have in mind?"

"I don't think the fires were started by a German spy or enemy sympathizer."

"But the rumors persist," the Detective said. "And our evidence does lead us to believe that the fires were planned and not random acts. For one, they all, except for the ones in the foundry and on the Hope's porch, were started on the roof... And there could be more than one perpetrator..."

"I doubt that, Simon," the Constable interjected. "The patterns are too similar. There is, I am sure you will all agree, definitely a method to his apparent madness. But, first, let's rule out any residents of the Borough who might be sympathizers to the cause of the Central Powers." He opened a folder on the side of his desk. "I've an updated list of residents of German and Hungarian descent..."

"Why must they, be German or Hungarian?" Stanley asked. "Anybody of any other nationality could easily have... I mean, I'm Mexican-Irish. What makes you so sure the arsonist wasn't, isn't me? Many firefighters are thought to be closet arsonists, you know."

"You're right, Stanley. I didn't mean to be discriminatory, but there is a war going on. And our enemies just happen to be German and Hungarian."

"And Italian. And the Russians are in on it, too."

"They were, are on our side until they withdrew after their Great Revolution," the Fire Chief explained.

"Yeah, I know that... but, still..."

The Chief turned to the Constable. "Who is on your list, Luke?"

"Well, as I said, all residents of German extraction. All the ones that registered, that is. Some are not on the list. Yet." He scanned the two pages, then frowned. "I had my men conduct a door-to-door survey and just about everybody here in Phoenixville complied with the law that requires that those of German extraction to identify themselves. They all registered. And all of them are upstanding citizens. Foundry, mill, iron works, bridge and steel company employees... Steady jobs. Even some of their sons enlisted... On our side." He quickly read down the list again. "However, Hermann Lochmann's name is still not here."

"I knew it! He's a spy!" the Detective exclaimed. "He's our man. He set those fires..."

"Please don't go jumping to half-baked conclusions, Simon." He wanted to say "half-cocked", but refrained. He knew better than to accuse his ace Detective of being rash and hasty in his decisions. "Just because he's not on the list..."

"But he broke the law! Federal law."

"Yes, he is guilty of a minor felony, but that's it. No cause to arrest him..."

"Luke," the Chief said, "We've been over Lochmann's status and his failure to register time and time again. It's irrelevant. Why don't we," he suggested, "take a look at the rest of the evidence. What do you, er, we have so far?"

Constable Tucker consulted another typed list on his desk. He began to tick off items with a well-worn pencil stub. "First, charred torches, all except two found on roofs, or what would be left of roofs. The others under a bush and in the ashes of the fire at Kimshaw's. Sacks labeled PERSEVERANCE KNITTING MILL..."

"Which the perpetrator used to collect cotton fibers, scraps of cloth..." Detective Hoolmes added. "Easily obtained by a janitor at the mill..."

"Lenny?" Stanley asked. "I know it's Lenny!"

"Yes, easily could be," the Constable stated. "We, Simon and I, visited the mill back in November. Spoke to the very gruff foreman." He consulted the small notepad neatly placed next to the list to refresh his memory. "A one Mr. Nick Letterman, although by his thick Russian accent, I don't think that's his real name..."

"Probably Leterwonski. Or Leddermanyowski," Hoolmes quipped.

"It doesn't matter, Simon."

"But you were the one who brought it up..."

"Anyway," the Constable shrugged, "he told us that Lenny might be pilfering sacks filled with lint and cloth. He never counts them; leaves that up to the janitor. Letterman didn't seem interested in the details, just in getting the day's quota met." He ticked off another item on the list. "And, get this, Lenny isn't the only one who putts around on a motorized bicycle..."

"They're beginning to call them *motorcycles* now, Luke."

"Simon, if you don't mind... I'd like to continue here..."

"Just trying to help."

"Well, just this once. Don't!"

Stanley chuckled at the friendly repartee between the two police officers. At least it seemed "friendly". He knew from stories his father told him that Luke Tucker had a mean streak. A narrow one, but mean just the same. The stories were confirmed as the Constable continued scowling at Detective Hoolmes.

'Seems one or two other workers at the mill drive motorized wheels, er, motorcycles, too. But apparently larger than Lenny's."

"Any of them with nubby tires?" Stanley couldn't refrain from asking.

"That, I don't know. At least one employee is from Norristown..."

"Shouldn't matter, Luke," the Fire Chief interjected. "Easy enough to revisit the mill during working hours."

"Yes, well, good suggestion, Dave. I considered that," he frowned. "But Doc Kimshaw was certain the vehicle he saw was a small motorized bicycle going down Church after the fire at his pharmacy. Most probably Lenny's. The driver wore a plaid flannel jacket. Like Lenny's."

"And Stanley and Nat White saw him speeding up Second Avenue from the Hope house..." Mendowksi turned to Stanley. "Tell them, Martinez."

"Nat, Mr. White, nearly ran him over..." Stanley shook his head. 'I wondered why Lenny was in the area, that late in the afternoon..."

The Constable nodded vigorously. It seemed all the pieces of the local arson jigsaw puzzle were finally coming together. A picture, as it were, was forming in his mind. He took a deep breath, then waved a hand toward Decretive Hoolmes. "And... the crowning touch are the handprints and fingerprints found on the plate glass window of the Gateway Pharmacy."

"But, the building was destroyed..." the Chief frowned, shaking off the memory of the trauma he experienced being trapped by a smoldering beam in the building and the embarrassment of being rescued by Nat and Stanley. His shoulder still smarted from the bruising. And, as Doctor Hall confirmed, it always will.

"Only partially," Hoolmes explained. "As you know, part of the front and a side wall were, are still intact. I took it upon myself to go over there the day after the fire and do a little snooping around. And I got these."

Stanley watched with great interest as Detective Hoolmes held up the large smoked glass plate sandwich. He listened avidly as the – he now had to admit – ace investigator took a few minutes to explain the technique of lifting and matching fingerprints now commonly used by most criminal investigators across the country.

"Pure genius," Stanley marveled. He had read about the procedure in a few of his fictitious crime mysteries, but was pleased to see it in real life and used locally.

"Ah, yes, but are they Lenny Lochmann's?" the Chief asked.

"Then there's my brass rubbing of the tires." Hoolmes held up the impression he had had made of the motor bike tire taken at Perseverance Mill. Stanley?" he asked. "Recognize this?"

"Lenny's. Same as at The Knoll House. Exactly like Lenny's bike at Doc Kimshaw's."

"Well, then," the Detective smirked. "That proves my theory."

"Ahem, Simon."

"Oh, sorry, Luke. Our theory."

"Ah, but we don't know that for a fact. Yet," the Constable said. "

"But it's irrefutable! The game's afoot!" Detective Hoolmes quipped stabbing a forefinger into the air. "And we are going to find out!"

Lenny's gonna be toast, Stanley thought, rubbing the side of his cheek and nose where he had been punched out by the big German. *There is no way he is not guilty.* Despite the fact he had tried numerous time to be friendly – at the very least... kind – toward Lenny, he sighed. *I certainly do not want to be around when he's finally arrested.*

Stanley's thoughts, however, would prove to be all too prophetic.

At the annual meeting of Phoenix Hose, Hook & Ladder Co., No. 1 Board of Directors with the Phoenixville Borough Council, Fire Chief David Mendowski reported that in the year 1917 the company had taken in $2,249.03 from various fund raisers, including a few sales of homemade ice cream and strawberries during the summer at several establishments along Gay and Main Streets. The company's total expenses were $1,917.17.

"And we've a net gain in cash of $331.87," he stated proudly.

"Then you have total assets... total cash on hand," Burgess Mosteller added up the figures quickly in his head, "of $696.34."

"That's about right," the Chief smiled, amazed at Mosteller's innate mathematical abilities. He turned to another page in the leather-bound ledger he had opened before him. "We responded to fifty calls, most of them brush fires or minor house fires. Clogged flues," he began to tick off the list of fire causes. "Chimneys, spontaneous combustion of oily rags, piles of old newspapers. Those kinds of things. We had five or so major alarms, and about ten false alarms. Kids playing pranks, testing out the new call boxes..."

"About those five or so 'major alarms'," one council member interjected. He consulted a folded piece of paper. "Gateway

Pharmacy, The Knoll House, Reverend Hope's home, Kimshaw's Pharmacy..."

"Kimshaw's was minor..."

"Someone threw a lit torch into Doc's display window. I don't call that minor... Two almost fatal fires at the foundry..." Councilman Owen Sinclair shot back.

"What are you getting at, Sinclair?" the Burgess asked.

"Simply this, Mr. Mosteller. We have an arson in our midst. Setting all those fires." He turned to the Fire Chief. "What are you doing about catching him? Mr. Mendowski?"

"I and my men fight fires, sir," the Chief responded. "I am not a crime investigator. However, I and members of the company are working closely with Constable Tucker and Detective Hoolmes..."

"Any leads?"

"A few..."

"Care to elaborate?"

"Not my place. I suggest you chat with the proper authorities."

"Oh, I intend to," Owen Sinclair smirked. "I intend to."

In other matters, the Council decided to continue the annual $1,000 stipend to Phoenix № 1 and to authorize the purchase of another one hundred feet of 2½" hose, as per Fire Chief Mendowski's request.

The vote was nearly unanimous, save one.

Councilman Owen Sinclair, sporting a red and blue plaid jacket, had abstained.

March 1918

Harold LaBronsky snapped open *The Daily Republican*, then settled into his favorite chintz-covered winged-back easy chair to scan the headlines.

PEACE AGREEMENT WITH GERMANY SIGNED BY LEON TROTSKY
GERMAN ARTILLERY BOMBARD US TRENCH POSITIONS

"They're still at it," he muttered to himself. Thankful that his son was not in the trenches, but supposedly safe on board a Navy destroyer somewhere in the middle of the Atlantic Ocean, he flipped to the comics to see what the Gumps were up to. The constant diet of dire news about the Great War, now in its fourth year, was wearing him down. He, like many of his neighbors, needed a diversion; anything to take his mind off his worries and concerns. "

The two alarms were received simultaneously from Gamewell street boxes 32 and 34. Startled by the incessant loud blasts of the Claxon horn, Sarah nearly dropped the small roasted chicken she had just taken out of the large woodstove oven.

"*Fardinen es!*" she exclaimed in Yiddish. "When will they stop scaring all of Phoenixville and figure out a quieter way to sound the alarm?" she asked Harold as he walked into the kitchen. "I nearly lost your supper!"

"Because there isn't a quieter way," he said, reaching for his tweed jacket hanging on a peg near the back door, "to notify the community..."

"And just exactly *where* do you think you're going? Supper's ready..."

"To see where the fire is."

"But it's *Shabbat* and I need to light the candles and say the *Kiddush*." Harold smiled. His loved his wife for her strict adherence to the traditions of her faith, but curiosity was getting the better of him.

"Three-two and three-four," he stated. "I bet it's the Phoenix Paper Box Company on Morgan," he said as he left. "Don't worry, I'll be back soon."

Sarah sighed heavily and returned the chicken to the cooling oven. *It will be burnt to a crisp by the time he returns,* she sighed heavily. *Yet another Sabbath dinner ruined.*

Harold was correct. The paper box company was on fire. He watched from the corner of Bridge Street as men from Phoenix № 1 laid their lines; two from hydrants and another from the Brockway combination chemical and hose truck. Flames licked up and smoke spewed from the roof of the brick building. Fascinated, Harold crossed his arms and leaned against a telephone pole. He was so entranced by the intense scene unfolding across the street, that he did not notice the hulking figure in the plaid flannel jacket hastening past him.

As Fire Chief Mendowski later noted in the company log, 40 gallons of chemical were used. And, despite the size of the conflagration, the department was only able to raise 22 feet of ladder.

"New ladder truck needed," he wrote, making a mental note to ask the company volunteers to do a bit of fund-raising. With the war on, however, and the financial hardships it was causing, he doubted that Borough residents, with needs of their own, would be able to spare any extra money for that of Phoenix № 1. After all, it had taken a bit of cajoling to even get his request for another length of fire hose approved.

He paused for a moment. Then, under the heading CAUSE OF FIRE, he wrote, "Questionable".

The German bombardment of American trench positions near the French village of Baccarat claimed the lives of 22 men of the 165th Infantry Regiment, part of the 42nd Rainbow Division, originally the New York National Guard. The tragic account was later reported in newspapers across the United States, including the *Atlantic Nightly News*, copies of which were delivered sporadically to Camp Hancock.

During a lull in the monotonous, never-ending artillery drill, Edmond Hope read the article aloud to Hans and a few other members of their regiment.

The twenty-two men, including their platoon commander, First Lieutenant John Norman, were assembled in a dugout when a German artillery shell landed on the roof of the dugout. There was a rescue attempt made my Major William J. "Wild Bill" Donovan, but their efforts to dig out the men were hampered by mud-slides and continued enemy shelling.

Only two men were saved and five of the dead recovered before efforts had to be halted. Voices of the other men could be heard for a while...

Edmond stopped reading for a moment and shuttered. He knew what was coming next.

"Such are the perilous misfortunes of war," Walter Caffrey, one of the artillery unit members opined. Edmond glared at him, shook his head, and continued reading.

But the remaining fifteen men died before rescue efforts could resume. A poem, "Rouge Bourque", also entitled "The Wood Called Rouge Bourque" was written by the poet Joyce Kilmer to commemorate those soldiers in his unit who had died during the barrage on the trenches. He read it at the memorial service held on the battlefield a few days later.

"That guy that tried to save them, Donovan..." Edmond started to say.

"Good for him!" Caffrey exclaimed. "Now, that's a Croix de Guerre, for sure." He looked around at the group. All but one frowned and shook their heads. "You know, the French War Cross. For bravery in the line of fire... What? What did I say wrong?"

One-by-one the men ambled back to their training posts.

"I think you insulted their bravery and intelligence," Edmond said solemnly. "Saving two men and five bodies while many others died... is not act of heroism. Even if the guy was facing enemy fire..." He folded up the newspaper and stuffed it into his ditty bag, then slung the bag over his shoulder. "I, for one, think it was rather foolish of him. Now, if that were me..."

"But it wasn't you, Hope. *Est-ce que seul est capable de...* And it's apparent you're only capable of complaining of not being where we really ought not to be," Walter laughed.

Edmond shook his head again. There was no use or meaning in arguing with a fellow Battery member from Phoenixville, even if he was young and eruditely insulting.

"*À chacun ses goûts,*" he fired back as he, too, turned heel and waked away. "Each to his own, indeed," he muttered, going back to his own post.

More than anything else, Edmond wished he and his unit, his regiment, the whole fucking division would be shipped overseas tomorrow. Then, there, in the bowels of the French trenches, he'd show Caffrey and even Captain Whitaker what true bravery was all about.

Stanley finished reading the latest letter from Edmond while standing in the small foyer of his home at 176 Prospect Street. Just back from a long day at work at the Iron Works and, blessedly, not on call that night for Phoenix № 1, he was looking forward to a relaxing evening with his books and, perhaps, a bottle or two – or even three – of cold beer.

Even though there was a "voluntary" prohibition on distilled "grain products", a few of the local pubs and restaurants brewed their own ales and lagers. The Columbia Hotel, for one, had a small brewery conveniently located in the cold, dank basement, with syphon pumps leading from the vats up to the taps in the barroom above. Stanley had eight bottles of its Phoenix Special, purchased earlier in the week, waiting in the ice box.

He folded the lengthy missive, stuffed it back into its envelope and then casually tossed it onto the small oak hall table where he kept his keys. Over the table was his favorite photograph: an ash-framed picture of "The Reeves Park Baseball Club". The shining bright expectant hopeful faces smiled back at him as he lingered before it. Edmond Hope, poised with a Louisville Slugger recently purchased from Meadows Toys and Sporting Goods Emporium; next to him, Hans Gruber, with his sardonic half-smile; Frank LaBronsky, his fist caught in the act of punching his freshly oiled leather glove; himself, brandishing a bat and glove in one hand, a well-worn baseball in the other. And, to the far right, Campbell Wheatley, the eldest, who simply stood, his hands clasped in front of him, as if in prayer.

Stanley sighed. He still mourned the loss of Campbell, their ace left-fielder. But, outside of letters from Edmond, had not heard from or about the other three. *What had, will become of them,* he wondered. *Will they come home safe? And sound?* He closed his eyes and bowed his head in a second or two of a silent prayer of his own, then looked up at the photograph again.

While Stanley loved the picture of his cronies, he was more enamored of the image of the young girl kneeling in front of the five club members. Rebecca Elizabeth Hope. He could also see the brilliance of her sparkling blue eyes and hear her laughter as the photographer told them to hold still "just for a minute or two" and say "cheese".

With the weather finally turning warmer after an unusually long, cold, snowy winter in Phoenixville, Stanley thought Rebecca might once again welcome an afternoon or, perhaps, an evening out. *I'll call her after dinner,* he vowed, kissing the tips of his fingers then lightly touching the glass. *No, why wait? I'll call her right now.*

Just as he was walking down the hallway into the kitchen to use the wall-mounted phone, the distinctive roar of an Oakland Model 38 Sportster once again came barreling down Prospect Street and, with a screech of brakes, stopped short in front of the house. There was no mistaking whose car it was.

Stanley stopped in mid-step and turned back toward the front door. He waited for the click and subsequent clunk of the car door opening and then closing. A scowl crossed his face. He had thought that their last time together had been just that. Their last. But, it seemed, Samantha Higgins Rouleaux had other ideas. After their last encounter in January, Samantha had, apparently, driven back home to New York. What she did there, Stanley did not know. Nor did he care. He had other things on his mind and plans for his future. Miss Rouleaux was no longer part of them.

But Rebecca Hope was. A major part.

He headed back toward the kitchen.

Maybe this time if I just ignore her, he thought, popping open a bottle of beer, *she'll go away.* He was barely able to take a sip when he heard pounding on the door.

"Hey, fireman! Open up! I know you're there! Let me in! Let me in!" Samantha's words were slightly slurred. She was obviously intoxicated.

Still clasping the cold bottle in his left hand, Stanley reluctantly started back up the hallway. About to open the front door, he hesitated, took a small sip of his cold beer, then backed away. *No, I won't,* he thought. *The last time was the last time. Period.* He turned away and resolutely walked back into the kitchen. The pounding continued as he lifted the phone's earpiece from its cradle and turned the side crank for the operator.

"Phoenixville Exchange," the women's voice crooned. "Number, please." He was about to ask for the Hope house when he realized it was Rebecca on the other end of the line.

"Oh, hello."

"Is that you, Stanley?" Rebecca asked. "With whom do you wish to be connected?"

"Well, you, actually," he chuckled. "I mean. I was going to call you at home, but... there you are."

"Yes, here I am. What can I help you with?"

"Well, how about dinner?" he blurted out. He hadn't meant to be so blunt, but there it was. His mother always said that with women, the direct approach was always best. He smiled when Rebecca started to laugh.

"Stanley, that is so very sweet, but it is rather short notice and I am working tonight."

"Open up, fireman! I want to talk to you!" The pounding continued. Stanley did his best to ignore it, concentrating on Rebecca. He just wished Samantha would stop yelling and go away. He took in a deep breathe, held it for a second or two, then exhaled.

"No, not tonight, Rebecca, but... How about this weekend? I'm on call Friday night and all-day Saturday, but Sunday? How about late Sunday afternoon?"

"That would be lovely, Stanley. Thank you for asking."

"Great! I'll pick you up at three," he stated, not quite sure in what vehicle, since he no longer had access to his father's Underslung touring car. *I'll figure that out later,* he mused as he said good-by and hung up the receiver.

"I swear, I'll break down this goddamn door if you don't answer it!" Samantha screamed even louder than before.

Realizing she wasn't going to stop until he answered the door, Stanley once again went back to the front door and opened it just wide enough to tell her to stop yelling—"You'll wake the neighbors!" – and to "go away".

"Ah, c'mon, Stanley. Let me in. I came all this way soooo looking forward to a perfect evening with you. Drinky-poos, dinner... Maybe even a show at the Colonial. Whaddya say? My treat?"

"No." He pressed hard against the door, hoping she wouldn't try to force herself in.

"Why, Stan, Stan the fireman... Stan-Stan," she laughed, leaning against the door.

"Don't ever call me that again," recalling his younger sister's cherished pet name for him. "And..." He started to press the door shut "Don't ever come here again. You are no longer welcome!"

"Why, fireman..." she said, tilting her head in surprise. "You got guts. Didn't think you had them in you." She laughed again, this time hiccupping as she tried to stifle a cough. "Damn cigarettes. Speaking of which, you got one?"

"No!"

"Well then," she said. "Just let me in." She tried forcing the door open. Stanley tried to shut it closed. He mustered up his strength, clenched his teeth, and tightly pressed his lips together. He was no longer going to tolerate her abuse nor abusive nature. Either to him or to herself.

"Go away!" he shouted again. "Don't you get it? Enough is enough. We're done, we're through." He sighed, running a hand through his thick jet-black curls. He lowered his voice to a restrained growl. "I have a promising life to live. A future that doesn't include you. Understand?"

"Well, I never!" Samantha Higgins Rouleaux, her ego bruised by whom she thought of as "the sexy dark little stocky fireman". She again pushed hard against the door. Stanley realized that if he didn't let her in, she'd yell and scream all the more. *What would the neighbors think?*

Still clasping the cold bottle in his left hand, Stanley reluctantly stepped back and with a mocking bow and wave of the beer bottle, gestured for Samantha to come in.

But this will be the last, the very last time, he said to himself. *The very last.*

"Say, a cold beer!" she exclaimed, grabbing the bottle from him. "Don't mind if I do." Samantha took a long, somewhat healthy draught, then wiped her mouth with the back of her hand. She handed the now nearly empty bottle back to Stanley. "Ah, that was good. Thanks, fireman. What else ya got?"

She staggered into the parlor and plopped down on the well-worn settee, her arms once again splayed seductively across the horsehair camelback. Raising one foot above the other, she kicked off her two-toned canvas sandals, then crossed her ankles on the small table in front of her piled high with books, newspapers, and back copies of *National Geographic,* idlily pressing her knees together and then opening them.

"Still reading, I see," she commented. "Huh. Waste of time, if you ask me."

"I wasn't," Stanley said quietly. He wiped the bottle mouth against his sleeve, then took a small sip. The beer – what was left of it – was now flat and unappealing. The refreshingly cool taste he had being enjoying had disappeared. And, so, too, it seemed, gone was his long-anticipated quiet evening at home.

No! He furrowed his brow. *She has got to go. Now!*

"Listen, Samantha," he began.

"Well, shit. Ain't you going to get me my own drink?" she demanded, scratching the sole of one foot with the big toe of the other. "I'm getting a bit thirsty here. Fireman." She laughed. Her words slurred together. Her eyelids started to droop.

Stanley stood steadfast in middle of room, his own eyes glowering.

"No! I mean... Get out, Samantha!" he grimaced. "Get the hell out."

"Why, fireman..." she opened her eyes and tilted her head in surprise. "What a display of, what is it? Guts? Balls?" She shook her head. "Like I said, didn't think you had 'em." She laughed again, hiccupping as she tried to stifle a cough. "Damn cigarettes. Sure you don't got one?"

"No!"

"Well, how's about we drive down to Kettleman's and buy a pack. I prefer Chesterfields, but if you're a Camel sort of guy, I can handle that."

Stanley mustered up his strength, gritted his teeth and tightly pressed his lips together.

"No! Get out!" he said again. "Don't you get it? Enough is enough. We're done, we're through."

"Ah, c'mon. Why ruin our relationship? Such a beautiful thing." She rubbed a hand across her chest, her fingers lingering on the thin, lacy bodice of her shirtwaist dress. "Wait, it's that Rebecca girl, isn't it?" She stood up and staggered toward Stanley, took the now lukewarm bottle from his hand and finished off the dregs.

"What's she got that I haven't... Oh, I see," She looked into Stanley's eyes. He looked away. "Both virgins, huh? Well, we can easily change that..."

"Stop it!" he shouted, removing her hand cupping the front of his trousers. Holding on to it firmly, he then twisted her arm behind her back, turned her around, shoved her out of the parlor and into the hallway. "Get out!"

"Why, Stan, Stan... Stan-Stan Stanley the FIreman," she laughed. "You're hurting me."

He opened the front door and shoved her outside. "Don't ever come here again. You are not welcome!"

Samantha Higgins Rouleaux stumbled out the door and fell down the two concrete stoop steps. "Damnit!" she exclaimed, fingering the tears in the knees of her stockings. "Look what you've done! Fireman!"

Stanley sighed and with a strong resilience he had never thought he had had before, quietly, and resolutely, closed the door after her. He leaned against it, waiting for the roar of the Model 38 driving away. He sighed. *Hopefully, that is the last I'll ever hear of or see Samantha Higgins Rouleaux again.*

He walked back into the kitchen to deposit the empty bottle into the trash and retrieve another cold beer from the ice box. Exhausted, he took a long draught, then trundled upstairs to his bedroom. As he crawled under the red and white starburst quilt his mother had made for him years ago, he suddenly realized that he not eaten any supper.

Doesn't matter, he exhaled drifting off to a fitful sleep. *I've lost my appetite anyway.*

Constable Tucker thought he had another way to obtain Lenny's fingerprints.

"C'mon, Simon," he said, walking out the police headquarters just behind Borough Hall. "We're going for a ride." The Detective gave him a quizzical look. "Don't worry. I'll explain on the way."

"That's an interesting plan, Luke" the Detective mused in the passenger seat of the shiny Torpedo limousine. "But do you really think, especially after last time, that Hermann Lochmann is going to let us get anywhere near his son?"

"If we're polite, he just might. We'll explain it's to protect his son, not accuse him."

"He'll never believe that. You should have obtained a search warrant from the Judge. Then you could go through the kitchen and find a glass Lenny might have used, rather than asking him to get us a drink."

"Yes, but I intend this to be a social call..."

The Detective could only smile at the feeble excuse of a plan as they walked up the steep stone steps and knocked on the front door of the Scape Level House. Hermann answered, a gruff look on his unshaven face and his German Luger PO8 semi-automatic pistol in his hand.

"What do you want now?"

Hoolmes, standing on the step below the Constable, reached into his inside pocket, fingering his own M1917 department-issued revolver. The small gun was considered the most effective police weapon at the time. However, it was, again, no match for the semi-automatic. In addition, he and Luke were once again in point-blank range and had, once again, failed to don their bullet-proof vests.

"No need for the gun, Mr. Lochmann," Constable Tucker was saying. "We're not here on business... No, not really."

"Then why are you here?"

"Well, I thought we'd have a little chat with Lenny. To get to know him better. Is he, um, here?"

"No."

"Know where he is?"

"*Nein*. What business is it of yours?"

"Like I said, we just want to have a little chat."

"Then chat with this," Lochmann said, raising his gun and pointing it at the Constable. He wagged it back and forth, then shifted his aim to Detective Hoolmes. "As I told you before. Get off my property or I shoot the little runt."

Hoolmes stretched up to his full height of five-foot six. "I beg your pardon?"

"You'll be begging for more than that..."

"Okay, Mr. Lochmann," Tucker whispered. "We'll leave." He turned and stepped in front of the Detective. "Turn around slowly, Simon," he said over his shoulder, "and walk away."

"But... he threatened you. Me... Again. Why is that still not a felony..."

"We'll consider it once again a forgotten misdemeanor. For now. Okay? Now, go."

At the bottom of the steps, Luke Tucker turned and called up to Hermann Lochmann. "By the way, I noticed you still haven't registered as a German sympathizer. Know when you'll be doing that... Anytime soon?"

"Luke, for God's sake! Why are you antagonizing him like that?"

"Oh, don't worry. He won't fire," he said opening the driver's side door of the Torpedo. "He didn't last time, remember? And he knows he's breaking the law. Federal law. Shooting a police officer would only compound his situation."

Hermann Lochmann stood for a moment at the top of the steps, the PO8 still aimed at the policemen. "I should have shot them when they first showed up here looking for my son. *Des policiers fous*," he swore, then walked into the house, slamming the door behind. "The *dummkopf* is going to be the death of me yet."

April 1918

The German bombardment of French artillery that began the last week of March continued relentlessly into the first two weeks of April. Mud resulting from heavily teeming Spring rains hampered the movement of the heavy wagons. Horses sank to well above their hocks; men could only slog slowly through the often-knee-deep muck. A spot of relief did come, however, when a great number of Germans troops were finally routed in the Battle of Lys, part of the Spring Offensive that was dubbed Operation Georgette. Then began the second Battle of Estaires, a phase of Operation Georgette. It was quickly followed by the Battle of Messines and the Battle of Scherpenberg, the final phase.

But the men of Battery C, one of the overly trained artillery units that would later prove to be the major lynchpins in the turning tides of artillery battle, were still mired in the sweltering heat of Camp Hancock just outside Atlanta, Georgia.

As land offenses mounted, the advantages of air combat rose to prominence when the British Royal Air Force was founded by the joining of the Royal Flying Corps and the Royal Naval Air Service. The Air Force was bolstered by the purchase of bi-planes manufactured not only in England, but by Wilbur and Orville Wright in their two factories located in the northeastern United States.

Still a part of an American fighter pilot regiment, Frank LaBronsky, having completed his training in Cork, was assigned aboard the USS FANNING, a Paulding-class destroyer based in Queensland. Her job, he and other Naval firefighters were told as they were transported down the River Lee to the ship, was to patrol the Eastern Atlantic, escorting convoys and rescuing survivors of sunken merchantmen whose boats had been attacked by German U-Boats.

Stowing his gear in a small foot locker under his assigned canvas hammock below decks on his first night onboard, he was introduced to Yeoman Walsh, whom, Frank was surprised to see, was a woman.

"Don't be so astonished, sailor," she laughed. "Nothing in the U.S. Naval Reserve Act says 'qualified persons' enlisting in the Naval have to be, um, just men."

"No, but I haven't... I mean," he flustered, "all my months in training, not one woman..."

"No need for training," she replied, her voice a husky alto. "We're called 'reservists'... Help out with clerical work and the like."

"So, you're a typist?" Frank was curious why one was needed aboard a destroyer.

"No, sir. I and other yeoman operate our two radios."

"He a woman, too?"

"You betcha," she winked. "When you've settled in and got your sea legs, come on up to the radio room and I'll show you around."

When she left the crew's quarters, Frank laughed out loud. "Wait until I write home about this!"

Frank's shipboard duties, along with those of six other firefighters, included being on call both above and below decks. He spent a week or so learning the location of the fire stations located in various parts of the destroyer and how to hook up the 2-½" hoses to the small pumpers that syphoned up sea water. In addition, he was to stand watch, taking turns with other crew members, scanning the seas for enemy periscopes, vessels, and any Allied ships in destress.

After a month, he decided that being on call for two days every three days was a bit boring. He spent much of his free time in the radio room, chatting with Yeoman Walsh. But Ensign First-Class Frank LaBronsky loved being on watch. He enjoyed standing high in the forecastle, breathing in the salt-scented night air, sea spray licking at his cheeks as the swift ship clipped through the ocean swells.

It reminded him of his days at the shore with his parents, languidly sailing or leisurely swimming back and forth in the surf, paralleling the beach. It also reminded him of how homesick he was and, despite the teasing, light-hearted attentions of Yeoman Loretta Walsh, how lonely he truly felt.

Mail postings and deliveries were non-existent while the USS FANNING was patrolling at sea. Frank had no way to keep in regular touch with his parents or Stanley, whose letters, when he was on dry land, he was used to receiving every two or three weeks. At best, he'd hoped there would be a stack of them waiting back at Queensland relaying news of the safety and welfare of their other friends, Edmond and Hans. *Were they still in Georgia or were they finally somewhere in Europe? Still alive?*

Frank sighed and continued to scan the horizon with his binoculars.

The air that night was cool and crisp, the sea calm and nearly serene. As the destroyer slowly slide through the quiet waters, Frank glanced over the starboard side. The shape was unmistakable. He watched as the submarine lingered for a moment, then slowly and silently turned so that its bow faced the destroyer's hull.

And then it turned around again.

Stanley's mid-March Sunday date with Rebecca had, he thought, gone really well.

He had taken her for an early Sunday supper at the Mansion House on Bridge Street, two buildings away from the business offices of the Phoenix Iron and Bridge Corporation. Not exactly his favorite place to eat, but it did have the freshest oysters in town. Which Stanley savored either on the half-shell with lemon or fried in a beer and egg batter. Rebecca had been delighted. it was the first time she had tasted the crustacean and had begged for seconds, washing them down with dainty sips of Canadian Ale served cold in a frosted Pilsner crystal glass.

After a leisurely dessert – chocolate mousse and French roasted coffee – he drove her in the black Model T he had borrowed from Detective Simon Hoolmes – who admitted he had "no real plans for the evening" – across town and then east on Nutt's Avenue to Valley Forge State Park. Near Washington's Headquarters, neatly preserved near the railroad tracks running along the broad Schulykill River, he asked if she cared to stroll for a while or would she prefer "to sit on a nearby bench and enjoy the sunset?"

"I'd prefer a stroll," she had smiled. "Such a wonderful, but filing supper." She patted the wide waistband of her mid-calf length dark grey linen skirt, topped by a white toile blouse and a dark red embroidered bolero jacket. "I am fairly bursting," she laughed, gently sliding her hand onto Stanley's forearm.

"Then a walk it shall be." He took her hand in his and guided her down the path to the small railway platform. They then turned right past the red and green wooden station house. "There is a paved circle with a branch to a memorial site," he said. "I don't know for whom, but..."

"We could go see," she said. "And it would be a perfect place to watch the sun set." He agreed. And, clasping her hand even tighter, led the way.

They talked about books they both read and liked and disliked; the latest movie playing at the Colonial Theatre; the Red Cross fund-raising drives for the war effort; their mothers' participation in the Phoenixville Home Comfort Association that provided heavy field boots – most crafted by Carlos Martinez in his small shop on Bridge Street – and heavy woolen underwear to the troops overseas.

"I don't see why," he quipped. "Considering it's nearly summertime here. I can't imagine how warm it is in France…"

"The Comfort Boxes were sent for Christmas, silly, when it was mostly cold."

"Ah, yes," he said, guiding Rebecca around the small stone marker, onto the path back toward the station. He walked slowly, savoring his moments with her. Savoring the hint of lemon verbena in her hair. Savoring the touch of her soft hand in his.

"Stanley?"

"Yes?"

"Do you regret, er, miss… being over there?"

"Over where?"

"In Europe. Fighting with your friends. Are you disappointed you couldn't go? I mean, your nose and left eye and all…"

"Rebecca, I am not blind. I can see just as well as the next man. And my nose is fine. Nearly, almost."

"But not enough for you to be drafted, right?"

"Well, yes. I mean, no. Not enough."

She was so proud of her brother now training to fight in the artillery. Would she have any reason to be as proud of Stanley. He didn't have the heart to tell her that he was like a little less than half of the population of Phoenixville: Pacifists who did not believe in conflict of any kind, especially war. *What would she think of me if I told her the truth?*

"Well, yes. But you are, you are fighting in other ways," she stated flatly. "Fire. You are bravely fighting fires. To keep us here at home safe." She paused, placing her right hand on top of his, holding her left. "And that, Stanley, is just as, if not more important." When she smiled up at him, he had melted into her deep, dark sea-foam green eyes. "And that's just fine by me."

"Well, if that is the case," Stanley said solemnly. "We could do this again next Sunday. That is, if you're free."

"I think I can be... available," she laughed. Her light soprano lilt touched the thinly frayed edges of his soul. "Maybe even Saturday night, too? But something different, I think."

"Hmm... Both are possibilities. What would you suggest?"

"I'll let you decide, Stanley," she said coyly. "But whatever it is, knowing you, I am sure it will be most interesting."

So refreshing, he thought. *And so different than Samantha.* He had sighed with relief that he would never have to see her again and now would ever be able to be with Rebecca.

The following evening after work, he had stopped by the Phoenix Nº 1 station to say hello to Nat White and the Fire Chief and to check on the duty roster posted for that week. He scanned the list, noticing that he was scheduled for both Saturday and Sunday.

He'd have to rethink his plans for next weekend with Rebecca Hope. Or did he? Miffed that he had to be on call that weekend, Stanley decided to go ahead with his plans. Firefighting, while he enjoyed it, was becoming a burden on his social life.

He had already planned to take Rebecca to the Colonial Theatre Saturday night to see Ethel and John Barrymore portray scenes from various Shakespearean plays. The Theatre had paid a fortune to have them appear and he had paid a handsome price for the two advanced tickets. Two Orchestra seats. Fifth row, center.

It would certainly be a damned shame, he mused, *if the Claxon horn alarm went off in the midst of the performance.*

The ensuing week at work went by swiftly. The call for patterns had increased since the Phoenix Bridge Company had opened branch offices in major cities across the Continental United States. Municipalities could order pre-fabricated bridges simply by leafing through a catalog and providing design specifications and dimensions by mail or, in a few cases, by phone. The parts, appropriately labelled, would eventually be shipped to their destination and erected, much like a pre-fabricated Sears house, by local engineers and contractors.

Exhausted from the stepped-up production demands and the long overtime hours for which he did not expect much more pay than he normally earned in a sixty-hour work-week, Stanley retuned late that Friday night to his home at 176 Prospect Street. He popped opened a bottle of Phoenix Special and settled into the wing-backed chair in the parlor with a well-worn and well-read copy of *A Tale of Two Cities* by Charles Dickens.

Frank watched with intense interest as the slender tube moved at a safe distance alongside the destroyer, keeping pace as they both sliced through the rolling swells. His mind went blank with fear when he realized his ship might be dogged by a German U-Boat.

He scanned the deck, saw no one, and hesitated before deciding to leave his post.

"Ensign, aren't you supposed to be up top watching for..."

"There's a submarine portside," he interrupted.

"You sure?" Yeoman Walsh, the radio operator on duty, asked. Her blue-green eyes sparkled. "Could be one of ours, you know, helping to protect us and the waters around us."

"Can you contact them, if they are?"

"Get back to your post before the Officer of the Deck sees you're not where you're supposed to be. We don't want to be thrown into the brig for the rest of our tour, now do we?"

"But the U-Boat..."

"If that's what it is. Get out of here. I'll handle it."

Frank had managed to scramble back to his post and was eyeing the steel cylinder when Lieutenant Walter Owen Henry stepped out of the bridge and confronted him.

"Ensign LaBronsky. I understand you spotted something out there?"

JUNE J. MCINERNEY

Frank pointed to the periscope, now slowly drifting further away from the USS FANNING, but still keeping pace. "There, sir. Yeoman Walsh says it might be one of ours."

Henry shook his head.

"She tried to raise contact. First in English. No response. Then in German." He chuckled. "And did get a response. In German. Yep, you're right. It is one of theirs. The captain thought he was talking to one of his own female dispatchers back in Brest." He called down to six crewmembers, manning two of what he had learned in training were depth charge launchers. "Bomb it the hell out of the water!"

Frank watched with mixed horror and fascination as a barrage of large explosive canisters was unleashed. One of them hit its mark. Within minutes the submarine, identified by Lieutenant Henry as U-58, broke the surface. Members of her crew were pouring onto the deck from the conning tower, their hands raised in surrender.

"Bring them on board," Lieutenant Henry ordered. The USS FANNING then maneuvered to pick up the prisoners as the damaged submarine — its diving planes and main generator destroyed — sank. It was later reported as the first of two U-Boats to fall victim to US Navy destroyers during the war.

Lieutenant Henry ordered Yeoman Walsh to come up on deck, asking her to act as translator.

"You speak German, too?" Frank snickered as she walked by. "Is there anything on board you can't do?"

"Can't piss in a pot standing up," the Chief Petty Officer smirked back. "But, other than that," she shrugged, "Just about everything else. If not more."

Frank was clearly taken aback by her blunt comments and mentioned it to the Lieutenant. They both watched as she confidently strutted up to the demoralized German crew, huddled together near the bow of the destroyer. She took no time in starting a conversation.

266

'Don't take it personally, Ensign. Walsh had to quickly learn to be gruff and direct when she was commissioned a Chief Yeoman last March. She's just living up to her middle name."

"Which is?"

"Perfectus," he laughed. "You'll get used to her. After a while."

Frank smiled wanly. "Hmmph," he said. "I doubt it."

"I speak quite good English," one of the Germans muttered to Yeoman Walsh. "But not with a woman on board ship. In my country, that is bad luck. *Verboten*".

"Well, it's allowed in America," Walsh frowned, obviously insulted. "But if you prefer someone of a different gender, I am quite sure we can accommodate you."

"*Nein. Das is gut.*" Like her shipmates, he, too, was taken aback by her directness and charm. Or lack thereof. He looked at her more closely. His eyes roaming up and down her curvaceous figure. "You... officer?" he smiled.

"I am. Chief Petty Officer. *Chef-Unteroffizier*... And you?"

"*Der Kapitän,*" he said proudly.

"Well, then, *Der Kapitän,* if you would so very kindly round up your crew, we'll try and find you something to eat and some place to sleep. Unless, of course, you'd rather a man escort you."

"*Nein, Fraulein. Das es gut,*" surprised that they were to be treated as guests aboard an enemy ship. "It's all good. *Danke.*"

"*Bitte.*"

The Barrymores, in Stanley's estimation, were amazingly good, although their rendition of the balcony scene from *Romeo and Juliet* was, as Rebecca whispered, "a bit outré. Considering they're both decades older than the supposedly young lovers." Stanley tried not to laugh out loud. He recalled Mr. Cricksham, his high school English teacher, saying that the two tragic "star-crossed lovers" were supposed to be barely fourteen. And, both parts – male and female – were originally played by young boys.

"In Shakespeare's time," he had said, it was natural for young men and women of that age to wed." *Mere children,* Stanley had thought, barely older than fourteen himself.

He turned his head to whisper into Rebecca's ear.

"But not too old to be in love. As I am with you. Deeply."

"Why, Stanley!' she exclaimed. Members of the audience shushed them. The two actors on stage stopped in mid-line. "I love you, too," she said. "I always have."

"Really?"

"Yes." He scrunched down before her on one knee, squeezed between the seats. "Then... Will you marry me?"

The silence in the Colonial Theatre that night, Ethel Barrymore later related in an interview captured by *The Daily Republican*, "was deafening. There was more drama going on in the audience than on stage. Everyone waited with baited breath for her answer. Which, of course, was, 'Yes!'."

Stanley was elated. He took Rebecca's hand in his, clasped it close to his chest, and nodded to the Barrymores on stage. "Sorry 'bout that... Please. Continue"

"We will," John Barrymore laughed. His deep baritone echoed throughout the proscenium. "But, first, we must congratulate you both." He started clapping and was joined by thunderous applause, cheers, and laughter. All directed at the newly engaged, but now embarrassed couple.

As the audience quieted down and the Barrymores resumed their dialogue, another sound blared.

"Damn it. Five-one," Stanley counted under his breath. "Main and High." He turned to his fiancée. "I am so sorry, but I have to go." He abruptly stood up and rushed out of the theatre to answer the call of duty.

As the only witness reported, the Oakland Model 38 just seemed to suddenly career out of control and slam into the abutment. Chief Mendowski and Sebastian Saulman, the owner of Saulman's Bakery, were standing on the north end of the High Street bridge, watching as Doc Kimshaw and Billy Szabo spewed chemicals from the Brockway combination firetruck onto the burning remnants of the long low, squat automobile.

"It just hit and flipped," the baker shuttered.

"Did you happened to see the driver?"

"A woman? Hard to tell. It's dark, you know." He looked up at the dimly-lit cobalt blue gas lanterns that lined the bridge. As if to burn the image of what he had just witnessed out of his eyes. "I'm on my nightly walk... Every evening after dinner, you know... From my home on the alley behind St. Peter's, down South Main. I cross the bridge to High Street, then turn back toward home."

Chief Mendowski nodded.

"It's peaceful. Hardly anyone is out after dark... The curfew and all... but I manage to get my walk in before that... Every night." He shook his head. "Well, it used to be peaceful. Now... this."

"Where were you when the accident occurred?"

'About here, heading back when that car flashes past me out of nowhere. Hell bent for leather... Then, whoomph! Slams right into the bridge."

"You called in the alarm?"

"Yes, sir. Soon as I see the car crash and sparks of fire. Then I run back here to... um, watch."

The Fire Chief thanked Saulman, then walked back up to what remained of the burning Oakland Sportster. He was dismayed to see Stanley Martinez's agonized look.

"You all right?"

"Yes... Um, no, Dave. I'm not." He glanced down at the fireman's canvas tunic and worn woolen blanket partially covering the driver's remains. Arms splayed across the concrete roadway; one shoeless foot poked out. Its two-tone canvas sandal lay ten feet away on the sidewalk. "It's Samantha Higgins Rouleaux."

269

"You sure?"

"I never forget a face, Dave. Or what is left of one." Stanley was not one to be outwardly emotional, but unwelcomed tears streamed down his cheeks. "I never meant for this to happen..."

'It wasn't your fault, Stan. What we know of her, she was probably drunk."

"Could be. But... Never saw a woman who could hold her liquor like she could." He sighed again. Then he pointed to the charred sawed-off baseball bat by the passenger side of the overturned car. "It could have been thrown in..."

"...and distracted Samantha... She lost control and slammed into the abutment."

"Yes. Then gas leaking out of the side tanks caught fire... and well..."

"Who would do such a thing?"

"I think you have your suspicions, sir..."

"Lenny? That doesn't make sense... He didn't know Samantha."

"But he did know I was dating her... Or, rather, her, me. Just about everybody in town knew."

"Yes, but... Why?"

"He's been jealous of me and Edmond ever since we were in grade school. And... look at all the fires, all of them... The places, the people... all have some connection one way or another with me and Edmond."

The Chief sighed. "A valid point, Stan. We need to chat with Constable Tucker again. He and Detective Hoolmes may have more than arson on his hands. They may also have a murder case to solve."

"Dear God," Stanley scowled. "What is happening to our fair Borough? It never used to be like this..."

Frank and Yeoman Walsh carried tin trays of sandwiches and coffee from the galley to the make-shift containment area in the lower after decks of the destroyer.

The U-Boat prisoners, *Der Kapitän* translated, were profoundly grateful for the food. Although they weren't so sure about the cold sliced corned beef.

"We've eaten only canned foods... not fresh meat, for the lasts few months," he explained.

"Must be difficult living for so long... in a tube," Frank commented.

"You don't want to know," *Der Kapitän* said

"Ah, but I do. You see, I've always been interested in the sea."

Yeoman Walsh laughed at Frank's pun, attempting to explain it to the German seaman.

"*Ach*, but, *ja!* I do understand. *Das ist lustig,*" he chuckled. "*Ja!* That is funny." Obviously several years older than Frank and obviously a much more seasoned sailor, he said, 'And I, as well. What intrigues you the most?"

The conversation between the young American Ensign and the older German U-Boat *Kapitän* lasted hours after the Yeoman had passed around the sandwiches and coffee and had left to continue her radio room duties. It was evident that the two men were fated to be good friends. Subsequently, Frank LaBronsky made it a point to spent as much of his off-duty time as he could with *Der Kapitän,*

"Please, Frank," he said after a particularly long discussion about the "ill thought out" politics behind the war. "My name is Kraus. Gunther Kraus."

"Frank LaBronsky."

"Yes, I have heard. Good to meet you, Frank LaBronsky."

"Same here, Herr Kraus."

"Gunther, please," *Der Kapitän* chuckled. "So, now, Frank. Please tell me about your hometown."

Frankie couldn't expound enough about Phoenixville.

"It's a small steel town" he said, explaining its early history and the expansion and naming of the Phoenix Nail Works by Lewis Wernwag in 1812.

"Ah, a German!"

"Yes. But he escaped Germany to avoid military conscription. Back when Germany was actually many disparate Germanic States…"

"*Ach*, you know our history well!"

"My mother's family… escaped the Russian pogroms. She made sure I learned my European history." He paused, trying to figure out Gunter's frown. *Was it because I was raised in the Jewish tradition?* He frowned back, then continued. "Okay, so Wernwag came to America, changed his name, and started building the most incredible bridges…"

"And then founded your town of… Phoenixville?"

"No, someone else actually did that long before he arrived. But that's another story. Wernwag just developed the nail works into the largest employer…built up the factory… Called it the Phoenix Nail Works after he saw its furnace flames rising into the night sky like…"

"The bird from Greek mythology. *Ja*?"

"*Ja*! I mean," Frank chuckled, "Yes."

"It's okay, Herr Ensign. If I can learn English, you can learn a bit of German, *nein*?"

"No, *nein*. I mean… Yes. *Ja*!."

"Ah, yes, just as a German would…"

"But not just Germans. But there were others. Irish, Italians, Hungarians… Polish, like my father's family… Even Mexicans, like Stanley's father… You name the country… and I think there's at least one family that came from it."

"Interesting. Tell me more about the terrain. It sounds much like my small town. Wesel. Also on the confluence of two rivers, the Lippe and the Rhine. It, too, was somewhat industrial, but we were more exports of German goods…"

"We have three: The Schuylkill River, French Creek, and Pickering Creek, which is a misnomer since it is more like a river. And we now export bridges."

"*Ja.* Someday, maybe your Phoenix Bridge Company will build a bridge over one of our rivers."

"After the war. That certainly is a possibly."

"*Alles ist möglich.*"

"I guess..."

"After the war, Frank LaBronsky, you will come visit Wesel, yes? I will, how do you say? Show you around. You will feel, I am sure, very much like it is your own home. And..." The thin craggy lines in Gunter's face crinkled into a huge smile. "I have a younger sister whose company you also just might enjoy."

Frank didn't know what to say. While thrilled at the invitation to visit Germany after the war – even if that country was his country's enemy at the moment – he was chagrined at *Der Kapitän's* suggestion that he might be interested in his sister. *I mean,* he thought before responding, *there are prospects back home. Sarah Hertzberg, the lanky girl who works in her father's drapery shop at the corner of Main and Bridge... Claudia Cohen, Esther Leibowitz... All members – single members of the shul on Nutt's Avenue where he attended Hebrew lessons as a young boy and later had his Bar Mitzvah. What does Gunther Kraus' sister have that they don't?*

"Um, sure," he said. "Your sister?"

"Greta Kraus. About your age. *Sehr hübsch.* And, Ensign LaBronsky," *Der Kapitän* leaned in closer so that he couldn't be overheard by the other prisoners. "Do not worry. We are Jewish, too. Only," he faltered, "please do not tell anyone..."

"Not to worry," Gunther," Frank repeated. "I won't tell a soul. Your secret is not mine to tell." He slowly smiled. "And, um... Greta, our sister, she is, um pretty?"

"*Ja!* Very pretty. *Wie ein Bild.* Just Like a picture."

May 1918

It was official.

After eight months of grueling training in the almost insufferable heat of the deep south, Battery C Artillery, now both part of the Keystone Division of the 28th Contingent of the American Expeditionary Forces, was to set sail from pier 31 in Brooklyn, New York for Liverpool, England. Once there, the contingent would be shipped to Le Havre, France, where, they were told, they'd be marched to an unknown spot behind the lines to further train with a French artillery unit.

"How much training do they think we need?" Edmond Hope complained to Captain Whitaker. "I mean... We've been at it here in Georgia for nearly eight months and... nothing." He pointed out that Company C had consistently performed impressively and had been rated as the highest of the Pennsylvania artillery units.

"At least we're going overseas, to be closer to the action. Please try to be patient a little longer, Hope." The Captain tried to smile. But, like the newly-commissioned Sargent, he, too, had begun to run out of patience.

Edmond, tired of the endless repetitive drills, could only shrug. He could load and fire any of the French 75-millimeter cannons only so many times. He could harness and unharness horses from the caissons that pulled them in his sleep... only so many times

"Dammit! Enough!", he cursed. "Goddammit! Enough is enough!"

Hans, on the other hand, was content to continue with the training. Harboring a secret phobia of horses, he tried to cope being around them in the safety of regimented drills. But he did not fully trust what they would do in the chaos of battle. Especially the ill-trained and unkempt Belgian drafts.

Artilleryman First Class Thomas Taggart, also a native of Phoenixville, was reassigned to the unit. He had been nicknamed "Tommy Top Gun" because of his acuity with the newer French 75-millimeters just recently brought into service. A steam and pipe fitter by trade, he quickly learned the gun's secrets and peculiarities and adroitly put his knowledge to good use. A cannon under his capable hands, Edmond and Hans would soon learn, never misfired and very rarely missed its mark. Thus, tall, fair-haired Taggert, with the brightly sparkling blue eyes, was a welcomed addition to Edmond's home-grown unit.

The boys from Phoenixville were about to show the Jerrys "over there" what real war was all about.

The members of Company D, training on the other side of Camp Hancock, had become familiar with new military equipment and, under the tutelage of both French and British officers, learned how to operate as a team in large military formations. Unlike the Artillery, who specialized in firing various cannons, the infantry drilled in the use of bayonets, automatic rifles, machine guns, and the "art", as one of the English lieutenants joked, of entrenchment. They, too, received high marks in their efficiently and skill. as well as Battery C, Company D would also soon set sail from Pier 31 in a large convoy also bound for Southampton.

A now not so very disgruntled Edmond Hope sauntered toward the mess tent after yet another grueling yet boring day of training. He stumbled upon another trainee hunched on a barrack stoop. The insignia on his military tunic clearly indicated he was a member of Company D. With the long hours of training and drilling, he hadn't had the time to get to know any members of the other assimilated National Guard Unit from Phoenixville.

He walked up to the soldier who, with his head in his hands, was clearly despondent.

"Need a cigarette, buddy?" Edmond asked, fumbling for his half-empty pack of Camels. He fished out two cigarettes and handed one to the infantryman.

"Thanks, but I... Yeah, okay. Thanks."

Edmond struck a wooded match and lit both their Camels. As he watched the other man inhale, Edmond was positive he had seen him before. A cherry-round pale baby-face with deep-set brown eyes was topped by a short shock of curly dark brown hair.

"You from Phoenixville?" he asked.

"Yeah, how'd ya know?"

"You look familiar."

"You, too. Name's Collier Cornett."

"Edmond Hope."

"I heard of you. The baseball player, right?"

"Yeah, I played some."

"Some?" Collier took a deep drag then blew a ring of smoke into the air above his head. "You were the best pitcher on the high school team. I saw you once execute a perfect no-hitter against Royersford... Boy, was that something."

"No big deal," Edmond said apologetically. He remembered the game quite well, played when he was a junior in high school. Back then, he had hoped to be good enough to try out for the Philadelphia Phillies. But that never happened. Instead, he found himself working at the Phoenix Iron Company as a master puddler.

"You play?" he asked Collier.

"A little. When I was a kid."

When he was a kid. He still is. Edmond smiled to himself. *He couldn't be more than fifteen or sixteen. How did he manage to be accepted into the military when the minimal draft age was twenty-one?* Suddenly, Edmond felt like a hardened, experienced much older adult. Seasoned by the ravages of time and boring, grueling training.

"So, what are you doing here?"

"I'm a fireman in Company D."

Like Stanley. Edmond sat down next to Collier.

"So, why so sad?"

"You have to ask? We're about to ship out to England and then France... to be killed!"

"But, son, that's what we signed up for..."

"You might have, but I did not!" Collier Cornett suddenly turned from being friendly to being hostile and defiant. "And, I ain't your son! I'm twenty-three. Probably older than you are... And I didn't 'sign up' for anything. My father forced me to register. 'It's the law', he said. Then he marched me to bloody Company D and commanded me... Commanded me, mind you, his only son, to voluntarily enlist."

He took another deep drag then continued with his tirade.

"The infantry... Blast! They're the first ones to be killed, you know that? Marched up to the front lines ahead of everybody else... and ordered right into the line of fire... and... killed." He started to sob. "I don't want to die."

"Nobody does," Edmond said softly. "But we've a war to fight... a battle for our freedoms. We all, each and every one of us, need to do our bit. To go over there and fight for what is right."

"Maybe for you that's right. But not for me." Collier flicked the half-spent butt of his cigarette onto the gravel path in front of his feet and angrily stomped it out.

"What do you mean?"

"It means, Hope, I ain't going." Exactly what Stanley had said.

"But you, um must."

"Bullshit. I ain't must anything! It's against my will... You can submit and be ferried across the pond to be killed by them Krauts, if you like. But I won't. See? I just won't!"

"What, um, then what are you going to do?"

277

"Come first light, before reveille, I'm booking outta here. I got me enough money to purchase a train ticket back home... And no one, not even you, is gonna stop me."

Edmond didn't ask how the young-looking soldier was going to sneak out of the heavily patrolled camp. Collier was obviously more than just angry and upset and it probably wasn't Edmond's place to try and stop him. Yet, he was so much like Stanley and Edmond, in his heart, would do anything to help his friend. Even if it meant convincing him to go to war. He knew in his heart and in his mind that it was the right thing to do and he didn't quite understand anyone else who thought otherwise.

"Look," Edmond said, "I know that you're upset. We all are... the training was hard and long. Exorbitantly long. But..." he sighed, "we're on our way now to using all that we've learned. If you go AWOL, you'll just throw away all that time and effort. Besides, if you get caught..."

"Yeah, I'd be labelled a deserter and then shot."

"So, why get killed? For nothing when..."

"When my death overseas would be worth something?" He hissed. "For whom? The British? The garlic-assed French?" He stood up. Despite his baby-face looks, Collier was lanky and wiry; a good two or three inches taller than Edmond's own six feet.

"That may not happen... You fight for a few weeks, maybe a month and the war will be over. Then we all come home. By Christmas."

"Fat chance," Collier said. "Sorry, but I ain't buying it." He paused, then walked away. "I gotta go. Thanks for the smoke... Edmond."

"At least think about it!" Edmond called after him. He shrugged. "Well, at least I tried."

Just before dawn, like he boasted, the young infantryman, dressed in dark blue dungarees and a pale-yellow chambray shirt with a small knapsack slung over his shoulder, snuck out of Camp Hancock and made his way to the small train station in Atlanta,

Georgia. He had left his uniform and military accoutrements behind. He was, he hoped, on his way home to safety.

But Obie Coldpepper, the stationmaster, who told him the next train north wouldn't be for another six hours, had other ideas. He had seen enough Yankee soldiers pass through the station on their way to training at Camp Hancock to recognize that the young lad – even out of uniform – requesting a ticket to Philadelphia PA was one of them. He had a sixth sense that the soldier was a deserter. And crotchety old Mr. Coldpepper had no use for deserters.

"Go back to base," he drawled. "Go fight the war for us elder gents who can't. Don't be branded a coward in the face of what might be your finest moments."

Collier scuffed, shifting his knapsack from one shoulder to the other. Homesick for the cooler lush fields of his parents' farm on the outskirts of Phoenixville, he was determined to leave hot and dusty Atlanta. Edmond Hope couldn't stop him. Why did an aging trainman think he could?

"Go 'wan," the stationmaster said. "Get outta here, or I'll ring for the local constable. You'll get locked up."

Collier stood his ground, insolently glaring down at the wizen southerner. "Make me," he sneered, then sat down on one of the wooden benches lining the station platform. Obie Coldpepper shook his head and went back into the office. Moments later, he quietly returned with a sawed-off shotgun and aimed it at Collier's chest.

"You either go and do your duty and risk the chance of being shot over there or be killed right here and now."

"You'd be arrested."

"No law says I can't defend myself and my station from trespassers and robbers. It's wartime, ya'll know."

"Hah! You won't."

"Don't tempt me," he said, cocking back both barrel hammers. "Now, git!"

Collier tried to stare him down. But the stationmaster was crusty and hard and set in his ways. He finally realized the old coot meant business. Clutching the strap of his pack, he put up his other hand in surrender. "Okay, okay, don't shot. I'm going." He slowly backed away toward the end of the platform, jumped off, and ran as fast as he could back to camp. He made it just in time for rollcall.

That afternoon, after he had finished packing in preparation to finally being shipped off to war, Corporal Edmond Hope wrote a letter home.

Dear Stanley, he began. *Do you know a guy – maybe one, two years younger than us – named Collier Cornett?*

Companies C and D, now part of the much larger and all-encompassing American Expeditionary Force under the command of General John J. "Black Jack" Pershing, were transported by train to Pier 31 in Brooklyn. On May 18th, Battery C Artillery unit left New York on a converted passenger ship, the USS SATURNIA, part of a convoy destined for Southampton.

It was a long and boring voyage, with only twice-daily lifeboat drills to break the tedium. Hans, not used to the rolling seas, was seasick, and spent much of his time in his make-shift bunk below decks. Edmond, who had spent many a hot summer afternoon swimming in the Schulykill River near Lock 60, as well at at the shore, suffered a mild case of nausea, taking only a day to gain his "sea-legs". He spent his time either gazing out over the rolling seas or in one of the passenger lounges writing letters to Rosalina.

Sargent Thomas Taggart befriended Walter Caffrey and made it a point to spend time with the young lad discussing books and the more cultural aspects enjoyed by those living in Phoenixville. Besides the Library, there was the Colonial Theatre, soirées at the Columbia Hotel, various church groups... The Union Athletic Club, the Rotary, Kiwanis, Elks, and the Royal Arcanum. All offering residents – young and old alike – varied and diverse opportunities to socialize and share intellectual, sporting, and civic pursuits together.

Caffrey agreed that once he got home, he'd "investigate" a few of the groups.

"Take it slow and easy," Taggart advised. "At your age, you've got plenty of time to enjoy just about everything our fair Borough has to offer

Caffrey agreed. Then, at one point, he told the kindly Sergeant about his older cousin who had married a Taggart.

"Could we somehow be related?

"I believe so," Taggart replied. "We'll sort it all our when we return home."

"And if I don't?"

"Don't be silly. Hope and I will watch out for you. I promise. And before you know it, we'll be in the Library together searching out new books to read."

Caffrey grinned. Oh, how he wished the Taggart and Caffrey families could somehow really be related.

On the eleventh day at sea, the men of Company C found their ship surrounded by yet another convoy of ships pursuing a German submarine. Both Edmond and Hans, feeling well-enough to ventured up on deck, watched the maneuvers with mounting dread, hoping they would not suffer the same fate as their friend, Frank LaBronsky. Before they shipped out, Stanley had written to Edmond telling him that their buddy's ship had been torpedoed. Stanley noted that he hadn't heard anything more.

I presume he was lost at sea, the letter said.

Edmond and Hans watched as two of the convoy destroyers in the distance off the port bow launch what looked like steel canisters the size of oil drums from their decks.

"What are those?" Hans pointed.

"Depth charges," Edmond explained. He had read in *The Daily Republican* about the British invention. "Filled with TNT explosives ignited by a spring-loaded trigger."

"How do they know where to drop them?"

"Good question." He scanned the horizon hoping to spot a periscope or even the U-Boat itself.

Multiple explosives erupted where the depth charges had been cast. Plumes of water and clouds of smoke jettisoned in to the sky, then disappeared back into the waves.

"They got 'em!" Hans shouted.

"Let's hope so," Edmond smiled warily. "I also read that those weapons are not all that effective. Probably just scared the Huns off..."

Hans shrugged as the SATURNIA veered to starboard and picked up speed, continuing its final leg of its journey to Liverpool. "Well, at least it's something to write home about."

Collier Cornett and the other men of Company D aboard the USS OLYMPIC were also bored by endless days of doing nothing more than fire drills. They were nearly desperate for something to break the monotony. And they, too, were not disappointed.

Just as their convoy was about to enter the English Channel near Falmouth, a German submarine, later identified as U-203, suddenly surfaced in its midst. Excited, the infantrymen of Company D rushed to the rails of the troop transport to watch as two escort destroyers opened fire upon the submarine, quickly disabling it. They cheered loudly as thirty-one of the U-Boat crew were captured.

Collier, morbidly glad that both Edmond Hope and the old stationmaster had convinced him to stay in the service of his country, was thoroughly enjoying the scene being played out in the open waters near the OLYMPIC. Seeing it up close for real suddenly excited him about the prospect of fighting. He was now eager to get his own digs into the Germans.

PHOENIX HOSE, HOOK & LADDER

How bad could it be? he asked himself. *I'll do my part... put out a few fires... maybe kill a few of the enemy... Then, as Edmond said, the war will be over and I'll be home.*

Collier lit a cigarette, relieved that he was making the right decision.

"Put that butt out, soldier!" a sergeant yelled behind him. "Why aren't you at your lifeboat station instead of daydreaming?"

Collier looked around at other members of his unit, also cheering as the last of the destroyed German U-Boat crew were being pulled aboard the destroyers.

"Nobody else, sir, is..."

"Still being defiant, Collier?" The sergeant turned and shouted at the rest of the men on deck. "Get to your lifeboat stations, men! Nothing to see here. Get going! Now!" When most of the infantrymen ignored his command and continued to mull around and crowd the railings, the sergeant shrugged. He tended to agree that since the danger of being blown out of the water had passed, it was useless to continue any semblance of getting the men to obey. He shook his head, then lit a Camel of his own.

Even if I did try, he smirked, *it'd be like herding cats.*

Company D of the 28th Division of the American Expeditionary Forces landed in Southampton and were promptly transported to Dover. They crossed the English Channel and, on May 14, 1918, landed in Calais, France. A week later Battery C landed in Liverpool, England. But it would take yet another month or so of training before the members of either unit would face the ravages of enemy fire.

The Third Battle of the Aisne, reported as Operation Bücher-Yorck, was the third phase of the Triple Entente's Spring Offensive. The German advance, while enjoying initial gains, had finally been halted by the combined military forces of England, France, and the United States.

283

But not before Edmund Hope and Hans Gruber had entered into the fray. Still in Liverpool at the end of May, their regiment was visited by a representative of King George V. Reviewing the troops, the royal adjutant personally handed each man a pocket-sized *New Testament*. He then spoke about the many dangers they would face and then saluted. The next day the men of Battery C boarded a train for Southampton where they sailed across the English Channel to LeHavre, France.

"Finally," Edmond Hope sighed as their small ship approach the shore. "We'll see some action."

But he would once again be disappointed.

Hermann Lochmann was decidedly miffed. He had not received copies of *Jugend,* the weekly magazine dedicated to German art and life, for at least a month.

"Perhaps, with the war, they are no longer publishing," Otto had suggested.

"*Nein.* I think it is more than that. No newspapers, either. The American mail, like everything else in this country, has failed us."

"So, why don't you go down to the post office and find out?"

"*Bitte. Gut idee.* I go at once."

Gabby Forresta, the postmaster, could offer no more information than what was on the proclamation posted on the bulletin board. Hermann squinted in anger as he read the notice. The United States Post Master General, it said, has stopped distribution of "foreign language publications interfering with the conduct of the war".

"*Mein Gott. Jugend* is about art and daily life. It has nothing to do with the war. *Nicht eine verdammte Sache.*

"But your German newspapers do."

Hermann looked beyond Gabby's beefy shoulders. "You've got copies, my copies, stacked up in that little storeroom of yours? Give them to me."

"I can't do that, Mr. Lochmann. Simply because they are not here." He took a deep breath. "If they were not confiscated by the government at the main sorting stations... we're ordered to burn them."

The angry German huffed and sputtered, barely understanding the irony of American citizens in Phoenixville burning the property of its own German residents.

"I guess you'll have to settle for *The Daily Republican,*" Otto smirked when his cousin stormed into the front parlor and told him about the US Government's edict.

"Harrumph. That rag? *Ich würde lieber die Opernlibrettos meiner Frau lese ...*"

"*Ach! Ja...* But remember, Hermann, you told me that right after she died, you burned the operatic librettos, too."

Constable Luke Tucker and Fire Chief David Mendowski finally agreed that Lenny Lochmann was, in fact, the probable perpetrator of the many fires that had occurred in Phoenixville during the past year. Based upon the compelling compiled evidence, the Constable and Detective Simon Hoolmes were able to secure a bench warrant for his arrest.

But it took a bit of doing.

"Arson is a major felony," Judge Anthony Piccolino stated in his chambers on the second floor of Borough Hall. He cursorily reviewed the typed list of evidence that Tucker, Hoolmes, and Fire Chief David Mendowski had put together. Tossing it upon his desk, he asked, "Are you sure? Arresting the young man because of, because of that?"

Tucker's shoulders slumped slightly. He thought he, Dave, and Simon – with input from Stanley Martinez – had tied up all the loose ends. It was disappointing to have their thoroughness questioned, even by a judge. Even more demoralizing was that, after serving twenty years as Phoenixville's Constable, his judgement was still not trusted.

Judge Piccolino had been the one who had, twelve years ago, refused to issue a warrant for the arrest of Mabel Hopper, whom Tucker had suspected of strangling Nellie Fitz in a second-floor room of the Columbia Hotel. "Speculative circumstantial evidence," he had said, off-handedly dismissing the case and the crestfallen constable.

"I just need to ensure that your facts are correct," the judge stated. "After all, it will be my name on the warrant, based upon what might be your 'supposed' evidence."

"We are police officers." Detective Hoolmes pled. "We have no reason to present you with falsehoods, Judge." "We've worked too long and hard on this case for it to fall short because of some local legal technicality." He wanted to say "arrogance", but, out of respect for the bench, not the man occupying it, he refrained. "For all we know, Lenny is out there starting yet another fire. Each day, each hour we, you delay, puts our community, its residents in jeopardy."

"I understand your dilemma, Mr. Hoolmes, but it's the best that I can do." Piccolino adjusted his wire-rimmed glasses, their stems resting crookedly on large wide-splayed ears. He looked like an aging nearsighted elf about to fly away. Ruffling a few papers on his desk, the Judge said impatiently, "I'll think about it. Give me a few days."

"Days?" Tucker questioned. "I, we, were hoping we could arrest him, um, this afternoon. With all due respect, Judge, as Hoolmes said, we need to bring him in. Now."

"As I said, I'll consider it. Now, if you'll excuse me..."

"No, I will not excuse you!" Detective Tucker was about to explode. "You stonewalled me before on a major case that ultimately allowed a killer to get away. I vowed that I was not going to let that happen again. And this is a major case. More than six major fires in a year... People injured, animals put at risk..."

"No one was killed, Constable."

"Not true. A woman was! Read the part where a torch was thrown into her car as she drove over the High Street Bridge. Probably by Lenny."

"Probably. Not solid proof No evidence that he did."

"Fine, Piccolino! You wanna wait until someone else gets burned up in a fire – and I can prove it – before you issue a warrant for someone's... No, Lenny's arrest?"

"No, but I..."

"But, you... What?!"

"How dare you get huffy with me, Tucker! I said I would consider the matter. And I will. All in good time. And, it's *Judge* Piccolino to you!" He slammed his gavel down.

Clenching his fists tightly, the Constable bristled.

Hoolmes put a restraining hand on Tucker's arm. "Please. Calm down, Luke," he whispered. "Let me handle this." Tucker looked away as the younger police officer spoke.

"Look, Judge. Sir. I, we understand *your* dilemma. You're a busy man and it takes time to review a proposed set of evidence, but I firmly... Luke and I firmly believe that our community is in danger. And we firmly believe that Lenny Lochmann is the prime, the only suspect."

He squared his shoulders and furrowed his brows, trying his best to look authoritative, if not intimidating. Although, truth be told, he was the one feeling intimidated.

"What you are doing, pardon me for saying so, *Judge* Piccolino," Hoolmes announced in his best defiant voice, "is obstructing justice."

Judge Piccolino peered over the top of his glasses.

"How dare you?!"

"No, how dare you?! Constable Tucker here and I... We came here in good faith, facts in hand, hoping that you finally had enough faith and trust in him, me... In us! Your own local police force... that you should be supporting whole-heartedly and not backstabbing..."

"I am doing nothing of the sort..."

"... and backstabbing your, our community as well. You live near Reeves Park, don't you?" The judge nodded. "On Second Avenue, if I am not mistaken, in one of those large Victorians with painted eaves and gabled roofs. Right? Well, what if?" He inhaled deeply. "What if..." He paused to exhale slowly, gathering his thoughts.

"What if Lenny Lochmann is out there right now, throwing a kerosene-soaked torch onto your own grand, wide wooden porch? Right now? Right this very minute... And we couldn't arrest him for destroying your home, your own home, because you refuse to issue a warrant? In a timely fashion?"

Judge Piccolino stared at Hoolmes for a few moments, then finally said, "Well, that was an impressive speech. You've missed your calling. You should have been a lawyer and not a detective."

"Thank you, sir. I'll take that as a compliment."

The judge looked at both men standing expectantly in front of his desk. He hemmed and hawed for a few minutes contemplating his next move. It seemed that, as in a good chess game, his opponent – the dynamic team of Constable Luke Tucker and Detective Simon Hoolmes – had him in an inescapable checkmate.

"I'll issue a warrant this afternoon."

Constable Tucker looked up and was about to say something when the judge held up his hand.

"No, don't talk. Just don't talk," he sighed. "Just get out of my chambers."

Tucker grimly nodded his thanks and then, with Hoolmes following in his footsteps, quickly left.

"He was right, you know, Simon. You should have been an attorney."

"Nah. Not exciting enough. Besides, that would mean I'd probably have to work with or, God forbid, someone like Tony Piccolino."

"Probably true..."

"Besides, Luke, I am having a hell of a lot more fun with you."

Edmond Hope and the rest of the Battery C compliment had been marching for miles, leading inexperienced Belgian draft horses as they pulled caissons mounted with the newer, but ineffectual French artillery over rutted roads and through dense mud. In Camp Hancock – it seemed like years, rather than months ago -- Edmund had been the most vocal about training with substandard equipment under wounded and callous French officers. Now, after more than three weeks of training yet again by French officers who were more concerned about saving their own lives and countries than the proper care and treatment of horses and American soldiers, he was more than livid. And, once again, he bitterly complained to Commander Samuel Whitaker.

"We've slogged through this shit for days," he said, pounding his fists against his now thinning thighs. Weeks of short rations and increased training exercises had begun to reduce his once strong and hardy frame to a lesser shadow of his former robust self.

Captain Whitaker listened quietly, understanding this soldier's reason for his outburst. Hope's wasn't the first; he had also heard the same from Taggart and Caffrey. And it wouldn't be the last.

"The horses are skittish under fire; the too-small harnesses chafe against their flanks, causing sores," Sergeant Hope was saying. "Their rations are minimal and half the time – you've seen this, sir – they have to pull and pull and pull... hours on end with no relief. And several of them have already dropped dead... in harness... under fire... Any no one cares. That is just... Just not right!"

Edmond searched for the right words to try and explain about the gross maltreatment and malfeasance of the French army toward their equine as well as human comrades in battle. But he was too upset, too tired to think anymore of the right words. Too frightened to think what will happen to the horses assigned to their regiment once they advanced to the front lines. Putting their artillery unit, other artillery units in grave danger. Samuel Whitaker bowed his head in agreement. He had no words to explain away the atrocities – on both sides – of the treatment of the animals who so valiantly, and unwittingly, served.

"I know," he finally said, trying to calm down the angry soldier. "But, unfortunately, there is nothing I can do..."

"Nothing?"

"Nothing. We are now part of the of the larger 98th Division and whatever it is commanded to do, we do. No questions asked.

Edmond snorted. "No disrespect, sir," he said, clenching his teeth. "But that is totally unfair and unacceptable."

"Maybe to you, Hope. But that is the military way and I'd rather you keep your opinions to yourself. No need to upset the men..."

"Our morale has already gone downhill. Sir," Edmond responded. "You know that and I know that. Everyone in our unit knows that." He then gave a half-hearted salute and walked away.

In the meantime, as Battery C did its best to trudge onward through the mud – the air filled with the miasmic metallic stench of blood – French and English forces pushed German forces back across the Marne River. During their retreat, the Allies erected a pontoon bridge across the river. Troops of the 111st Infantry were the first to cross. Other units of the American Expeditionary Forces would soon follow.

Including those of Battery C.

Later that afternoon, with a warrant for Lenny's arrest in hand, Constable Tucker deftly wended the police car along the streets of Phoenixville on the way to Scape Level. As they drove by, both he and Detective Hoolmes took note of banners hanging in the windows of many homes. Felt gold stars, a few with black ribbons, were hand-stitched on wide red and blue stripes. Each star represented someone overseas in the service of their country.

"There are a lot more of them these days, Luke."

"A lot more husbands and sons serving overseas."

"How many...?"

"I don't know the exact count, but I think close to three, maybe four hundred of our finest... Don't ask me how many injured. Or worse. Just one is one too many."

Hoolmes nodded. "The war is a bitch," he said under his breath. "If I wasn't a deferred police officer, I'd be over there right now serving my country."

"Don't sell yourself short, Simon. You're serving it now, being here. More importantly, you're serving this community."

"By arresting Lenny Lochmann for arson?"

"Preserving and protecting, son. Saving lives is saving lives, whether you're here or over there."

"Doesn't look like anybody is home," Hoolmes observed when they stopped in front of the rundown stone house on Canal Street.

"Well, it's supper time. They're probably back in the kitchen eating." He slowly got out of the car and walked up to the wooden door, no longer broken. Its cracks had been neatly patched and it now sturdily hung on new wrought-iron hinges. The detective stood a few steps behind him prepared to thwart Lenny should he decided to run away. He clutched his small, but trusty M1917 police piston in his left hand.

"Police! Open up! Police!" Luke Tucker shouted as he pounded on the door. He waited a few seconds. When there was no response from inside the Lochmann's house, he shouted and pounded again. "Open up!"

"*Ja, Ja. Halte deine Pferde!* am coming!" Otto Schlemmer shouted as he opened the door. He looked far better than when Constable Tucker last saw him. He was clean-shaven and wore a freshly-laundered yellow Chambray shirt and dark light-weight flannel trousers. He had come a long way from being a homeless vagrant sleeping in the Reeves Park pavilion and being suspected of setting fires. His second cousin had begrudgingly allowed him to stay, provided Otto paid a modest rent – Hermann claimed he needed the money – and did a few household chores. One, it seemed, was mending the front door.

"*Was ist es?* What is it? Am I in trouble again?" Even after securing a job as a pipe-fitter for the Phoenix Bridge Company and establishing himself as a "good citizen" in Phoenixville, Otto Schlemmer was still a bit paranoid. He did not want to spend another night in Constable Luke Tucker's jail. No matter how accommodating it was.

"No, no, Otto. Not you. But we are here on official police business," Constable Tucker stated, showing Otto his badge. "Is Lenny home?"

"*Nein.* He left just before supper..."

"Do you know where he is?"

"Said he had to do an errand. An important errand..."

"Did he take anything with him?"

"A bat. He loves baseball. Maybe he is in the park, playing.

"What is going on?" Hermann Lochmann asked, coming into the hallway from the parlor. "Now what do you want with Lenny?" he scowled.

"We have a warrant for his arrest, Mr. Lochmann."

"Why? *Um was geht es hierbei?*" Otto said. "Is he in trouble?"

"Arrest?!" Hermann Lochmann shouted. "What do you mean, 'arrest'?!"

"You know about all the fires being set around town?" Detective Hoolmes queried, stepping up to stand alongside the Constable.

"Lenny has nothing to do with them."

"We have evidence to the contrary, Mr. Lochmann. Hence, the warrant."

"Where is Lenny?" Tucker asked. "Do you know where he went on... his errand?"

"My son is an adult. I no longer keep track of him."

"More's the pity, because Lenny is in a heck of a lot of trouble right now..."

"Get out of my house!" Hermann shouted, shoving Otto aside to slam the door shut.

"I wouldn't do that, if I were you, sir," Hoolmes said, brandishing his gun.

"Oh, for God's sake, Simon. Put that thing away..."

"But, Luke..."

"You have no right coming again and again to my house, threatening me with your puny *Polizei* guns,' Lochmann shouted again in his thick accent, reverting to his native German. "*Sie ficken die amerikanische Gestapo!*"

"*Nein*, Hermann," Otto said. "*Amerikanische Polizei*. They are the good guys."

"Bah!" Lochmann managed to slam the door on Tucker and Hoolmes. But not before he spat into the Constable's face.

"Well, that went well."

"Shut up, Simon," the Constable sneered, wiping phlegm off his nose and cheek.

"If Lenny is out running an errand, where do you think he is?"

"I haven't a clue. But wherever... whatever he is doing, I bet it's not playing baseball in Reeves Park."

Lenny had an affinity for hamburgers fried with onions in butter and olive oil. The greasier the better. At work during the sultry June afternoon, he had a hankering for just that. A large, thick slab of ground beef, its outside quickly seared nearly to a crisp, its inside juicy, pink and blood-red. Stuffed between two think slabs of Italian bread and smothered with the sautéed onions.

His father refused to cook them, even though he claimed the food was first invented in Hamburg, Germany (hence its name). Hermann insisted on cooking the same monotonous fare of bratwurst and sauerkraut for dinner; day in and day out except when Mrs. Marcelino occasionally favored them with her homecooked lasagna or chicken parmesan. Ever since she had spent those two months last fall taking care of Lenny while his broken arm was healing, she had taken "quite a shine" to the two "Lochmann boys". She enjoyed sharing her home-cooked Italian meals with them.

There was only one place in the Borough where Lenny could get his favorite hamburger and that was a concession stand at the Bonnie Brae Amusement Park just outside of town. So, when cold leftovers were once again served, Lenny left the table. He offered Uncle Otto and his father no other reason for skipping supper except that he "had an errand". He did not hang around long enough to listen, once again, to his father's tirades about him being ungrateful.

Lenny, lately, had learned that he could do whatever he wanted to do. Whenever he wanted to do it. Even if it was harmful to others. And neither his father, or anybody else for that matter, could do anything about it. The truth was, his father didn't care and thus ignored his son.

With a growing gnawing in his belly, Lenny sped up toward his destination, impatiently skirting around the Toonerville Trolley slowly clattering its way westward along the tracks. As usual, he had a box of matches, a thick wad of lint, and a fistful of cash from his cigar box savings stuffed into his pants pockets. A sanded-down baseball bat was slung across the handlebars of his shiny Smith Motor Wheel with its nubby tires. The image of himself devouring a greasy hamburger smothered in fried onions on a thick Italian roll occupied his mind.

"So, he left before dinner," Constable Tucker pondered, steering the Tornado limousine across the High Street Bridge. "A big bruiser of a guy like that is always hungry... I wonder why he didn't eat first."

"Maybe he had an errand too important that kept him from eating," Detective Hoolmes offered. "Unless... unless his errand had something to do *with* eating."

"Good point." Tucker thought about it for a while. Then ventured, "Anyone know Lenny's favorite food?"

"His father might?"

"Also Mrs. Marcelino. She took care of him after his accident..."

"The day of the Price's book store fire, Simon."

"Yes. Anyway, we could drive back to Scape Level and ask her?"

"And run the risk of being seen again by Hermann? No, I don't think so," Constable Tucker shuddered. "I have a better idea."

"Harrumph, Luke. You always do."

An operator always manned the main switchboard in the Bell Telephone Exchange a block up from the Post Office on Gay Street. When the company began installing phones and erecting the many telephone poles that dotted the community, Borough Council, back in 1906, had insisted that services be available all day and night. Phoenix Nº 1 joined in the demands, requesting that call boxes and signal wires of the new Gamewell electro-mechanical fire alarm system be strategically mounted on poles. This ensured that the fire department, the police, as well as the hospital's new ambulance service could be called by phone in case of emergencies. As the local Constable, Luke Tucker had the privilege of using the telephone company's services whenever he deemed it necessary. And concerned that Lenny Lochmann might be "out there somewhere" about to start yet another fire, he deemed it necessary this evening.

"Please connect me with the Marcelino's up on Scape Level," he asked the operator on duty.

"Just a moment," Rebecca said, her blue eyes sparkling in the blaring ceiling lights of the windowless room. She pulled a plug from the array in front of her and inserted it into a small metal switchboard socket.

Recognizing Edmond's sister, the Constable smiled wanly. He knew her engagement to Campbell Wheatley had been tragically cut short back in July when he became the first soldier from Phoenixville to be killed in the war. Tucker judiciously refrained from mentioning Rebecca's loss.

"Hello, Mrs. Marcelino? Yes, yes, hello." Her voice crackled through the line. "This is Constable Luke Tucker of... Yes, Mrs. Marcelino. No, no. Nothing is wrong." He paused. "Well, maybe something might be..."

He listened as she exclaimed few choice Italian expletives, then tried to continue.

"Mrs. Marcelino? Do you know Lenny Lochmann's favorite food? Yes, your lasagna. Anything else? Ah, chicken parmesan. My favorite, too." He listened patiently. "No need to do that, Ma'am. But thank you. You don't need to cook for me." He listened again. "Anything else that Lenny might like?"

With a thick accent, Anna Marcelino shouted into the phone mounted near the back door of her well-stocked kitchen. "Hamburgers. He loves hamburgers. Especially Grappas, the ones my friends made out at the fair."

"The fair?"

"Si, si. Bonnie Brae. But," she said, "they get the flu this winter and die ... The stand... It's a still there, but closed."

"Okay, thank you, Mrs. Marcelino," The Constable said and hung up. He nodded to Rebecca as he hastened out of the exchange to Simon Hoolmes waiting anxiously in the Tornado. "I know where Lenny went. I'll explain on the way."

The large yellow door of what used to be Grappa's *Buon Cibo* – Good Food – was nailed shut.

"No! Not closed!" Lenny yelled at the top of his lungs, pounding on the door. "Grappa! Grappa! I want Grappa!"

Adults, as well as children, hoping for a pleasant evening of light-hearted fun and amusement to distract them from the constant daily horrors of the Great War overseas, gathered in a crowd around him. They alternately booed, laughed, and cheered at and for Lenny. Inwardly enraptured by all the attention, he outwardly ignored them and continued yelling for "Hamburger! Grappa, Grappa! Hamburger!" as loud as he could.

Constable Tucker parked his shiny police car as close as he could to the stand. "Disperse them, Simon," he said. "Last thing we need is for him to get... violent. Especially when we arrest him."

"Done." Hoolmes got out of the car and started waving people away from the scene. "Go, go back to the midway. There are no fun and games here, folks. Just police business. Go away." Slowly, the crowd began to disperse, walking away toward the merry-go-round and a whirly-gig where the barkers promised free rides for everyone.

A portly gentleman wearing a red and white stripped vest sidled up to Constable Tucker. A ragged straw hat tilted jauntily on his bald head. His left cheek just below a blood-shot eye was slightly swollen, slowly turning black and blue.

"I tried to stop him," he said. "but he hauled off and slugged me with that baseball bat." He pointed to the Louisville Slugger laying at Lenny's feet. "There's no stopping him."

"Well, we're going to try," the Constable said, flashing his badge and introducing himself. He then took out his trusty small notepad and pencil stub. "Your name?"

"Thaddeus P. Barnum."

"An ominously curious name," Tucker chuckled as he wrote it down.

"P. T. was a distant forebear. Grand entertainment... Show business runs in the family."

"I see," although Luke Tucker couldn't quite fathom how the Bonnie Brae Amusement Park could qualify as "grand entertainment". To him, it was just small potatoes on a supposedly larger scale. "So, you're the manager?"

"And proprietor." Barnum spread his thick, burly arms wide. "All of it. Ain't it just amazingly wonderful?"

"Yes, well... Um, Mr. Barnum, if you'll excuse me, I need to take care of this, er, situation." He stowed his notebook and pad in his tunic pocket and edged his way toward the closed concession stand. Lenny had stopped yelling and was now sobbing, his forehead pressed against his crossed arms on the door.

Tucker put what he thought would be a reassuring hand on the young man's shoulder. "Lenny Lochmann? I think we need to talk..."

Lenny whipped around and flailed his arms in two wide circles around the Constable's head.

"What?! Who are you?!" he rasped, his throat clogged with tears. "You Grappa? Open up!"

"No, son, I am not."

Lenny glared blankly at the Constable.

"You know who I am, Lenny. The local Constable and I have... I have a warrant for your arrest."

Lenny glanced at the official-looking folded parchment paper in the policeman's hand. Then he reached into his pocket and pulled out his book of matches.

"NO!" He screamed and fumbled to light a match. The Constable quickly grabbed Lenny's hands and tightly held them together. Lenny struggled, trying to wrest himself away.

"No use fighting this, Lenny. You have to come with me."

"No! I! Don't!"

"Sorry. It's the law."

Lenny spat into Luke Tucker's face as Detective Hoolmes walked up alongside the Constable.

"Like father, like son," he declared, trying to suppress a chuckle. He grabbed the matches from Lenny's hands, then restrained his arms as the Constable clapped a pair of handcuffs onto Lenny's wrists. "Looks like you are coming with us, son," he said. "Prison awaits."

"I do nothing," Lenny wailed as he was dragged to the limousine and then shoved into the back seat. "I want Grappa!" He began sobbing again as Tucker started up the Tornado's eight-cylinder engine. "I hungry. I eat now."

Bouncing along on less than smooth hard-packed, winding dirt roads, it took them less than an hour to travel the 15 or so miles to the county courthouse in West Chester. An hour or so later, a judge indicted Lenny on six counts: four felonies for suspected arson; one felony assault of an officer of the law; and a misdemeanor for attacking a public servant – if Thaddeus P Barnum could be called that. There was no mention of the supposed murder of Samantha Higgins Rouleaux. That, the judge explained, would have to be a totally separate case.

Lenny Lochmann was refused bail and, pending trial, was remaindered to the nearly eighty-year old Chester County prison at Market and New Street. As per the law, he was not allowed visitors, although he was allowed one call home.

"No phone!" he screamed.

"Don't worry, son," the prison guard said as he escorted Lenny to what would be his home away from home for a while. "We'll try to figure out a way to contact your parents. Let them know where you are."

Lenny nodded, then tried to smile.

"No mother. Father on Scape Level."

"Okay. His name"' the guard asked, disinterested.

"Hermann Lochmann. And Uncle Otto."

"Those German names, huh?"

"Yes, we German," Lenny offered. "You?"

The guard did not answer. Instead, he grunted and then shoved the hulking oaf into a dank and dirty cell and slammed and locked the door shot. The guard then instantly dismissed Lenny's father's name and address from his mind.

"That guy in cell 27?" he said, tossing a ring of keys to the attendant sitting at the desk at the end of the cell block. "He's a bit dim-witted Kraut. Would be a waste of money to spend any time taking 'proper' care of him" He paused. "You get my drift?"

The attendant nodded.

"Yeah, sure," he mumbled with a slight French accent. "I get it. Fucking Boches."

After a few more weeks of training in France, Battery C finally entrained to the front on August 9th. They arrived close to Chateau Thierry four days after a major conflict, marching through the debris of buildings and supplies destroyed by battle, then crossing the pontoon bridge over the Marne River into the town of Roncheres.

Edmond was the first to spot the two graves just over the bridge on the side of the road. He pulled Private Longacre aside. Lean lanky Longacre stooped down and slowly read one of the inscriptions.

"An Allied pilot. Probably shot own... Name's Quentin Roosevelt. Related to President Theodore Roosevelt..." He stood up, rubbing his chest and coughing as if to clear up painful congestion.

"Hey, you okay?" Edmond asked. "Not catching cold, I hope. I won't wonder with all the wet mud we've been forced to..."

"No, no... Eddie. I'll be... fine."

"So, what about President Roosevelt? This fella a relation?"

"Yeah," Longacre said, "If I remember correctly... His youngest son."

"Hmmm... Well, now I wonder who the other guy was."

"No clue. Just a blank wooden cross." The Private bowed his head, said a silent prayer, then made the Sign of the Cross. "Rest in peace," he whispered.

"C'mon, Longacre. Don't dawdle. We've got a war to fight."

The next day, Edmond, Longacre, Hans, along with Caffrey and Sergeant Taggart, found themselves engaged in a battle that would last five days. Their guns were strategically placed near Revigny, inside the Eshelon Woods; almost perfect camouflaged positions from which to fire upon the enemy.

On the first day, Sergeant William Clarke commanded Longacre, whom he had designated the number one member of his crew, to "Do the honors. You be the first to fire Battery C artillery in the war."

Edmond Hope handed Longacre the lanyard used to trigger the 75mm cannon. Longacre vigorously pulled and a few seconds later, the gun fired and then recoiled on its caisson. "Well done," the Sergeant said. "We are finally in this war, men." One by one, the rest of the Battery C gun crews followed suit and soon the whole artillery unit was embroiled in battle.

Six days after the battle, won by the artillery unit, Battery C was once again on the move. As his gun crew was settling into its new location, Longacre motioned to Edmond, grabbed his chest again, and then dropped death of a massive heart attack. Private Edward Longacre, a native Phoenixville son, had fired the unit's first shots of the war and was the first of its men to die in combat. But his fellow soldiers did not have time to mourn their loss.

Battery C was immediately ordered to relocate just outside of the small Belgium town called Ypres.

Hermann Lochmann was furious when he heard his son had been arrested and was awaiting trial in a dank prison cell in West Chester. Wielding a sanded-down baseball bat of his own, he stormed into the police station and demanded to see Constable Luke Tucker.

"You don't know what you've done!" he shouted, slamming the blunt end of the bat against the side of Tucker's desk.

"Oh, I think we do," the Constable responded calmly. He stood up and came around to the front of the desk. Lochmann raised his bat, threatening to strike again. Only this time, it would be the police officer, not the desk.

"Don't come near me! Or I'll... I'll..."

"You'll do what?" Detective Hoolmes said behind him, reaching up to seize the bat from Lochmann. He stepped back and motioned to the Constable. "All yours, Luke."

"Thank you, Simon." He turned to Lochmann and pointed to a small Windsor chair. "Now, why don't we both sit down together and rationally... and calmly talk this out."

Hermann Lochmann reluctantly sat down. His back ram-rod straight, his eyes looking not at the Constable, but at the wall behind him.

"Mr. Lochmann... er, Hermann... Let me explain that your son..."

"Imprisonment will kill him." Lochmann lapsed into his thick German accent. "He cannot cope... being pent up... confined."

"Unfortunately, that's his situation. And will likely be for a long time." The constable paused. "Do you have a lawyer?"

"*Nein*..."

"Then I suggest you hire one." When Hermann Lochmann shook his head again, the Constable realized that Lenny's father could not afford one. "Or the court will appoint one for him... But he may not get the best defense..."

"Lenny is not guilty, Tucker!" He stood up and pounded a fist in the air "Lenny. Did. Not. Set. Those. Fires!" He shouted. He paused and turned to leave the policeman's office. "He's *dummkopf. Zu verdammt dumm...* Not bright enough to be a common criminal."

To make matters even worse, Lenny's Smith Motor Wheel had been recovered from the Bonnie Brae Amusement Park and had been impounded as evidence by the County Sheriff. It meant that Hermann Lochmann did not have any means of transportation to go see his son incarcerated in the prison just outside of West Chester. Even if he wanted to. Or was even allowed to.

In mid-August, Stanley received a letter from Edmond. He had written to his friend just a few weeks ago, telling him about the fires and both Chief Mendowski's and Constable Tucker's suspicions that Lenny Lochmann was the arsonist. He didn't expect Edmond to respond so soon.

Dear Stan, the letter began, *I don't have much time to write, so I'll try and make this short... and sweet. I was heartened by your last letter and proud that you're doing your part keeping Phoenixville safe. I won't put it past the Fire Chief or police that our "good friend" Lenny is the culprit. So, have they arrested him yet?*

"Just wait until you hear the latest," Stanley said aloud. "He's in the clink..."

We fought long and hard at [crossed out] and were moved much closer to the front. The conditions are terrible. Not only are we fighting other men, but the weather as well. Heavy rains every day make roads muddy ditches. It's nearly impossible for us to slog along and twice as difficult for the large draft horses to pull our artillery. The mud is so deep in the trenches, that if your boots aren't tied on tight, they're sucked off. Along with the mud, there are rats everywhere. Lice – cooties – infest clothes, jackets...

Stanley shuttered, absently-minded scratching his arm as he continued reading.

We're okay, but other units in our division, especially Company D, were hit by a poisonous gas attack yesterday, hid by dense fog. Many of the men, including the young lad Collier Cornett that I wrote you about a while ago. Apparently, he didn't see what hit them. Badly burned, I was told. Was being shipped back behind the lines to a field hospital... I guess he'll be sent home... If you come across him...

Stanley made a mental note to watch out for the tall, stocky farmer's son. The Chief had mentioned in passing that two days before he was drafted Cornett had volunteered to be a fireman.

I've been lucky so far, Edmond concluded. *Remember when I was so gung-ho about joining up and fighting? Well, I am now much more eager to come home. Safe and sound. Gotta go... our Artillery sergeant is barking orders about harnessing up our horses again... Stay safe, Stan. Give my love to Rosalina... Pray for me. Your best buddy, Eddie.*

Stanley said a silent prayer, then carefully folded the letter and placed it with the stack of other letters from Edmond, Hans, and Frank in his sock drawer. Alongside them, still hidden under read and blue Argyles, was the unopened envelope postmarked WASHINGTON, D.C. he had retrieved from his parents' home after last Sunday's dinner; relieved that no one had found and opened it. He considered finally opening it, but reasoned that since he had received it back in July no military officials had come knocking on his parent's door looking for him. After such a length of time, he was probably safe. At least for now.

When the alarm sounded on the last afternoon of August, Chief David Mendowski had been dozing in his office. His head, sandy hair tending to greying flecks, was slumped on one beefy shoulder. The Claxon horn blaring in the distance, then, seconds later, the clang of the bell atop the hose drying tower, startled him awake. He jumped up and without thinking, grabbed his red helmet and wool-lined canvas tunic and barreled out of his office.

"Where?" he asked Nat White as he jumped up onto the driver's seat of the Brockway Combination firetruck.

"I counted five, one. Main and High."

"Isn't that Friendship's area to cover?"

Nat cranked up the powerful in-line six-cylinder engine as Billy Szabo and Lou Double opened the two wide double doors. "They're responding, too!" he stated, carefully guiding the long truck into a right turn onto Church Street. "Must be a big one!"

The Pennsylvania House Hotel had been built several years before the turn of the century. A large, four-story wood and stucco building with a shingled Mansard roof, it spanned the half-corner where North Main Street ended at High. The hotel featured moderately priced single rooms and small suites for rent – daily, weekly, or monthly. Catering mostly to single men working at the Phoenix Bridge and Iron Companies, it was also a starting point for young couples venturing into their first year of married life. Most of the young men, however, had been drafted and were now fighting oversees. Half of the rooms were empty and the hotel's owner, Victor Flanagan, was slowly losing, rather than making, money. He had been heard lately in town threatening to "close the damn place down".

The fire broke out in on the third-floor, in a room overlooking the roof of the wide covered side porch. Flames and clouds of black smoke leapt out of the window and sparks fell onto shingles; some started to smolder through tar and wood laths. By the time Nat had driven the Brockway to the front of the hotel, the flames were flicking upward under eaves painted with intertwining flowers.

A few men from the Friendship Fire Company were already spraying water from its pumper. Their 2½" hose had been hooked up to the red fireplug installed in front of the hotel's side entrance. But the fire resisted. And persisted. As Nat guided the gleaming apparatus into the side alley, Doc Kimshaw jumped from the back and, as it unwound, began aiming the 2½" hose at the base of the window. Billy Szabo had already started the chemical reaction in the pumper. Water and foam from both companies' hoses mixed in the air thrust into the broken window and fell onto the burning porch roof.

By the time Stanley Martinez had arrived – running most of the way from his pattern shop in the large foundry building across the Main Street Bridge across French Creek – the fire was almost half-way contained.

"Anyone inside?" he called to Nat, standing next to the hotel's proprietor. Flanagan's arms were crossed tightly across his thin, boney chest. His right foot tapped impatiently on the hard-packed dirt. One of the Friendship Fire Company's older firefighters was also standing beside him. Stanley recognized him as Sebastian Peters, one of the veteran members of Phoenix N° 1 who had joined the new company on High Street when it was formed in 1906. His face and hands were blackened with soot

"Rooms on this side are mostly empty," Flanagan called back before Nat White could answer. "Both a curse and a blessing."

'What rooms are still occupied?" Stanley asked, reaching for a leather helmet and a fire coat from the side of the Brockway.

"We've already checked, son," Peters commented, wiping his forehead with a damp cloth. "Didn't find anybody."

"It won't hurt to check again," Stanley responded. "Now, sir, if you could tell me which rooms are still..."

"Rabble-rouser, all of them," the hotel proprietor sneered. "Won't miss any of them if they were all burnt up... Some not even paying their rent. Smoking and drinking in the rooms... Drunken whores everywhere...That's what caused the fire, I tell ya... Lit matches... carelessly flicked. Coals burning in cast-iron pots on bare oak floors for heat... Sonsabitches..." The tirade when on for another three minutes. Each word and phrase more accusatory and profane than the last. Peters nodded his head in agreement as Flanagan began to dance in place, hopping from one muddied foot to the next. He tapped the side of his temple and winked at Stanley.

"Been like that for a few years, now. Crazier than a one-winged loon in heat..."

"Sir?"

"Ah, c'mon. Everyone in town knows it..." Peters explained. "That's why the hotel is losing money. Who wants to stay in a place run by a batshit nutcase?" He paused. "Wouldn't be a bit surprised if he didn't start the fire himself..."

Frowning, Stanley moved aside, whispered something to Nat, and then walked around to the front of the burning building.

Chief David Mendowski was descending a flight of narrow stairs in the lobby, leading a frightened group of two young women and three older gentlemen who, by their shabby dress and disheveled appearance, looked like they had seen better days. Much better days. The Chief's face was dusted with ashes, his long tunic powdered with grime. A concealed charred taper was up his sleeve.

"No need to go upstairs, Martinez," he said. "Here's all who were left..."

"Didn't they know enough to leave?" Stanley unconsciously registered seeing the tip of the torch, but prudently said nothing.

"No one tells us the bloody house was on fire," one of the men said in a thick Irish brogue. "That Flanagan," he spat onto what once was a rich velvety-hued carpet, now frayed and thread-bare. "Didn't say a word. Ups and runs out, I bet. Nary a word to us trapped upstairs like rats in a locked pantry..."

The two women, coughing back tears, nodded vigorously. Bambi Bates and Christie Turnbull, who had taken over Mabel Hopper's "establishment" when she had skipped town in the darker hours of one spring morning, flanked the elderly Irishman's side. Stanley had heard stories about them from his father, but had never met them. Nor had he the desire to.

"Scalawag," Bambi, the younger of the two, said, shaking her head. "We ought to sue..."

The Fire Chief chuckled. "I doubt, given your, um, reputation, that anyone would take your case." The women bristled as he ushered them and their three gentlemen friends out of the hotel. "Good luck, boys," they waved as Stanley and the Chief watched them all saunter arm and arm up High Street and across the bridge.

"You saved their lives!" Stanley exclaimed. "And they didn't even thank you?"

Mendowski shook his head, tightening his lips together. His brow knitted into a frown. "Well, such is the life of a firefighter, Stanley. C'mon. Let's go assess the damage."

Back at the firehouse, Stanley lingered to help Nat White and the other fireman clean the hoses and shine up the vehicles. It was too late to go back to work and he was curious about the Borough's latest conflagration. Especially since he had seen the make-shift torch the Fire Chief had carried into his office.

"Think it was arson, Mr. White?" He was vigorously rubbing wax onto one fender of the Brockway, remembering how he had often rubbed Harry's already sleek coat as the horse, with a cagey sense of humor, tilted his head and bared his teeth in a mawkish grin as if waiting for his driver's answer.

The red and white Brockway stood stock still, silent and unaware of the conversation. *It just isn't the same,* Stanley shook his head, holding back from once again voicing his displeasure at the unfair disposition of the two talented

Percherons. He rubbed the fender more vigorously, as if he rubbed hard enough, the truck would simply, as if by wishful thinking and magic, disappear. Or, better yet, morph into Duke and Harry.

"I don't know, Stanley. We found no evidence of... foul play. Or did we?"

"Mr. Peters from Friendship found a blackened cast-iron skillet in the room where the fire supposedly started."

"Doesn't mean a thing. And I am sure he mentioned that to our Chief."

"Yeah, I guess. Besides, Lenny Lochmann is locked up, safe and reasonably sound. Right?"

'He may not be the only arsonist in town, Stanley." Nat White dribbled a few drops of Neet's Foot oil onto the section of hose he was cleaning. He thoughtfully paused, watching Kimshaw and Szabo clean the nozzle and the couplings. "And not the only one who uses torches to set fires. It could very well be Mr. Flanagan, the hotel owner. For the insurance..."

"Yah think?"

"Or, just another accident." The driver shrugged his shoulders and continued to clean another section of hose. He, too, rubbed almost too vigorously as if the leather hose could miraculously turn into a black leather horse harness.

In his office, Chief Mendowski was on the phone with Constable Tucker.

"Too coincidental. The sawed-off, sanded-down baseball bat just outside the room..." he said. "It's badly charred. Like the others. But Lenny is in prison awaiting trial... How can this be?"

On the other end of the line, the Constable shook his head. "Yeah, I thought we had this all sewn up, too. But, apparently, another arsonist is on the loose..."

"But... Who?"

"And... Why?"

The figure dressed in a black and red plaid shirt and fading denim trousers nearly tripped and fell on his way down the narrow stairs of the Pennsylvania House Hotel. He had barely made it to safety. Luckily, he had had enough presence of mind to fan the fire out of the window he had opened. *No one is going to be hurt*, he promised to himself. *Just a small message to Constable Tucker... He ist unschuldig. Iinnocent. Innocent.*

He slipped out the back door onto St. Mary's Street and briskly continued onto Dayton and up then along Freemont. The piercing laughter of two women in the room across the hall from the one he had just been in still ringing in his ears.

The next day, Victor Flanagan gleefully called Tyler Frees, his local insurance agent, to report the fires.

"One of my transient tenants had been drinking and smoking in bed," he claimed.

"A foundry worker?" Tyler had asked. The Pennsylvania House Hotel had been insured for a considerable amount of money. To verify and process Mr. Flanagan's claim would result in the payout of hundreds, if not thousands of dollars. It would make or break his fledgling firm.

"Yes. The tenant in room 303."

"Home during the day? And not at work?'

"Yes, he claimed he was sick, but I saw..." Flanagan lied again. "I saw him earlier in the day walking back from Kimshaw's Pharmacy carrying a brown paper bag..."

"Could be anything..."

"And... And he was smoking in his room. Against my rules."

"Since when?"

"Why, Mr. Frees. Are you questioning my authority to run a proper establishment?"

"No, Mr. Flanagan. Just your ethics." Tyler paused. "I'll contact Fire Chief Mendowski and the local Constable and see what their report says."

Victor Flanagan mouthed a string of profanities, then slammed the phone receiver into the cradle of the wooden box phone mounted on a lobby wall. He knew full well that the young renter in Room 303 was a train engineer and had been shuttling bits and pieces of bridges between the Iron Company and the Bridge works all afternoon. Hence, he was, of course, not home at the time of the fire and was not responsible for it. "But whoever did it," Flanagan smiled to himself, "actually did me a favor."

That evening, two men arrived at the not-quite-delipidated house on Scape Lever's Canal Street at the same time. One was dressed in a black and red plaid flannel shirt and faded blue denim trousers, the other in a light-blue chambray shirt and light grey twilled trousers. One carried an empty small flask smelling of gasoline; the other a leather satchel filled with tools, nails, and various plumbing supplies.

'Where have you been?" they both asked at the same time.

"To fetch some things... to fix the leaks in the kitchen and put in an indoor bathroom," one said in a thick German accent. "I am tired of using the smelly outhouse.

"*Klage dich*. Suit yourself," the other grunted. His voice, too, tinged with Germanic overtones. "I was on an errand." But he did not offer his cousin any further explanation.

Hermann Lochmann, with a smug smile on his face, headed into the kitchen to heat up yet another batch of overcooked bratwurst and stale sauerkraut. Otto Schlemmer, eager to fulfill his end of the bargain while living with his cousin, bounded up the stairs to begin transforming the small storage room at the end of the hallway into a usable bath and toilet.

Once again, Battery C was in the direct line of fire. Edmond Hope and Hans Gruber were knee-deep in mud in the sordid mist of the third battle of the Somme, a small northeastern region of France with small access to the English Channel. It would prove to be one of the most decisive battles of the war.

Edmond's unit was positioned on the left flank, just slightly behind the front line to protect the advancing infantry which included members of Phoenixville's own Company D. He couldn't recognize any of them, but was able to see blurs of their insignias through the haze of smoke and the light shroud of drizzling rain. He thought of Collier Cornett and wondered if he had made it home okay.

Hell, he thought as a stray bullet whizzed by. He ducked behind the caisson, hoping to avoid the fate of Campbell Wheatley. *Hell! Will even I make it home okay?*

In the early days of his marriage to Dolores Murphy, Carlos Méndez Martinez had begun to cultivate a liking for poetry. He was enamored of its mathematical precision and elegance, of its profound expression of emotions that he, with his Latino background, was eager to express in a culture that lately had begun to frown upon overt displays of affection. His wife, stoically Irish, cautioned him about being publicly passionate. Yet, she shared his eagerness to read and embrace all literary genres. Hence, his vast collection of books now filling up the small room in their large house that served as their library.

He had, of late, begun reading the works of Yeats, Ezra Pound, and e. e. cummings, whose free-form verse lacked capitalization and punctuation. "Most annoying," Carlos said, "but I like his implied rhymes." One particularly favorite poet was the up and coming Joyce Kilmer, who had written a simple poem, "Trees", in 1913 that extolled the beauty of nature.

"There's one by him in today's paper," Dolores suggested one evening during dinner. It's entitled 'Rouge Bouquet'. Perhaps you'd like to read it aloud later?"

"Wait," Carlos responded. "That was published last April... Why again?" He scanned the accompanying article in *The Daily Republican*, reading with sadness that Kilmer had died two weeks ago on July 30th during the Second Battle of the Marne. The same battle, the paper reported, in which several members of the Battery C artillery unit, a regimental part of Pennsylvania's 98th Division, were also slain.

With Battery C in the throes of heavy fighting just outside a small village in France. Edmond Hope, now thoroughly scared and fearing for his life, struggled to keep his wits about him as he maneuvered horses and a caisson into firing position. Behind him, Caffrey was humming a catchy tune as he started to unload a wooden ammunition case.

"Will you please shut up," Edmond whispered. "That tune is driving me nuts. Besides, the Germans might hear you."

"Over this noise?" He waved his hand, indicating the deafening roar of cannons and the constant rat-a-tat of rifles and Luger pistols. "*Chance génial.* Fat chance, *mon ami.*" He continued to hum, then whistle.

"Stop it!"

"Okay, okay. Why don't I just go over there a ways and take a look-see. You know, *Jouer dur.*"

"War is not a game, Walter," Edmond said, walking the horses, still harnessed together, further back behind the artillery line. "But, if you must, yes, go stand guard." *Anything to get the young erudite fool out of my way.*

Seconds later, as he and another artilleryman were loading the French 75mm cannon, Edmond heard his name being called.

"Hope! Hope!" Caffrey exclaimed in surprise as the sniper's bullet slammed into his chest. Edmond rushed to his side, trying with his bare hands to stanch the flow of blood seeping through Caffrey's woolen tunic.

"Hang in there, buddy. We'll get help."

"Too late," the fallen soldier gasped. "Too late."

Three days after Caffrey was killed, Edmond wrote a letter to Stanley, which he read two weeks later as he leaned against the fence surrounding the statue of David Reeves. Lately, it had become a place of refuge, where he could relax and think and enjoy the late summer evening cooling breezes. It was also where they had had their last soul-searching chat before Edmond was transported down South for training. Reading his latest letter, Stanley felt as if his best friend was sitting right beside him once again, tossing up and catching a well-worn baseball.

I am writing this before a huge stone fireplace that was once part of a house in the old town part of the France capital. Most of it has been leveled and us soldiers are living amongst the ruins. Not the way I thought I see Paris...

Anyway, there was this guy in our unit...a real smarty-pants... a few years younger than us... from Spring City, I think, Emond had written, *who kept on quoting arcane philosophers and asking us dumb questions. "Did you read this, read that? What do you think of Socrates?" The kid was French – name of Walter Caffrey. Blue eyes, blond hair. I, we, most of the members of our unit treated him pretty badly. Teased him unmercifully about his high fa-looting quotations and archaic little-known facts. That's what Hans said they were. "High fa-looting". Hah! Hah! When Hans decides to say something, he's just as wise as young Caffrey.*

He, Hans, and I, spent two nights in Paris together and Caffrey was so impressed by the sights and lights... and the women... He called it "all the bright life". And I scoffed at him. Ignore him. Laughed at him for being so young and naïve. Never thinking... that a month later...

Anyway, Caffrey got hit by a sniper a few days ago. Sad to say, he didn't make it... Took him less than twenty minutes to bleed to death. There was no one there, under such heavy fire, to treat him, let alone take him back behind the lines. He died with a smile on his face. Looking up at me like I was his long, lost best friend. Which I wasn't. Just another artilleryman who had wished the kid would just go away. Poor kid. He was only 19... Lied about his age when he enlisted. Damn. I did the best I could, but I had my own duties to perform. Fighting for freedom, you know.

But Caffrey, because of me, is no longer. And that's just the thing, Stan, I told him to go away. He was humming this silly song in the midst of battle... a happy tune. That was the kind of guy he was. And it bothered the hell out of me, so I told him to go stand guard. And that's when he took the two sniper pills to his stomach. And died. He died because of me. He didn't have to, but I was so annoyed...

The letter continued with more self-recriminations. Stanley finally finished it, folded it up and stuffed it back into its envelope.

"I am sure your buddy forgave you, Eddie," Stanley said, standing up and brushing a few early fallen leaves from his denim work pants. It had been an unusually cool summer, foreboding an early fall. "At least, I forgive you. As I hope you, too, will forgive yourself."

He related Edmond's story about Walter Caffrey's premature death to Nat White the next day.

"I didn't know him. But Edmond did," he sighed.

The kindly driver could only bow his head.

"Being in the line of fire, my young man, whether you're fighting fires here or an enemy there in war over there... No matter where you are, it's pure hell."

317

Constable Tucker shook his head. "Damn. If I can just figure it out."

He and Detective Hoolmes were seated in Chief Mendowski's office.

"I told you it was that Otto Guy," Hoolmes stated. "And you let him go. Hah! We arrested the wrong bloke."

"Couldn't be him," Mendowski chided. "He's quickly become a pillar of the community... Even came in and wanted to know if he could be a volunteer."

"What did you tell him?"

"I gave him an application to fill out. Then," he smiled, "I got him to replace the bathroom faucet and unclog the kitchen sink."

"A man with a trade earning a decent living is too busy to be running around town setting fires," the Constable agreed. "Besides, Lenny Lochmann is snug behind bars. At least for now."

"Then who set the last fire?" the Chief queried.

All three men looked up as Stanley knocked on the door and walked in.

"Sorry to disturb you, Chief, but..."

On the morning of September 2nd after a heavy battle, Canadian Corps seized control of the western edge of the Hindenburg Line. Heavy German causalities were inflicted and more than 6,500 unwounded were taken prisoner. The Germans had been decisively forced back to the Hindenburg

Line, from which they had launched their offensive in the spring. A key part of the German supply line ran parallel with the front. This second 1918 battle around the Somme was part of a strategy designed to push parts of the German line back behind this main supply line so that cutting it would make impossible the efficient maintenance of the German forces on the front.

Edmond Hope and Hans Gruber were in the thick of battle once again. Both fought side-by-side in the battle of Bapaume as the unit moved as one with the Artillery Regiment of the 98th Division toward the Somme. The Belgian horses, now more used to the sounds of cannon – although a few were still wary, skittish, and restless – strained against their braces as they slogged through the mud pulling the heavy caissons. On the third day, within just a few miles of the Hindenburg Line, Edmond once again suffered the loss of a close comrade.

I am not sure what happened, he wrote to his sister. She was reading her brother's sad words in the narthex of St. Peter's Church, holding vigil as local school children arrived singly or in groups of two and three, to drop off their pennies for the Relief Fund to Aid Little Ones in the throes of war.

Headed up by Loretta Coffin and Catherine Norris, the fund had been started to help provide the "real necessities of life" for children overseas. Public school children as well as those attending the Sacred Heart parochial school had been asked to donate a penny or two to the cause. They had, according to an article in the local newspaper, "responded magnificently". But more monies were need. Collection boxes had been set up all over the Borough; at Martinez's Shoe Shoppe; Eyrich's Meat Market; as well as other locals, including the vestibule of the local Episcopal Church.

Ten-cents, the children had been told, would keep a child from starving for one day. Rebecca had already counted 250 pennies that afternoon. Twenty-five children in war-torn lands would not go hungry. At least for one day...

One minute he was in back of the caissons, helping to shovel mud and dirt onto the flammable spent shells, the next he was next to one of our horses, trying to calm him down. Hans, you see, was deathly afraid of horses and why he was still allowed to continue with an artillery unit that depended on horsepower is beyond me... And because of some duty officer's ineptitude, Hans Gruber is now beyond us all.

She looked up and nodded to three young parishioners, each holding a parent's hand, walked tentatively up to the box to toss in their pennies. One, two, three... No matter how small the donation, each penny was counted in the larger amount to save other children. Rebecca wiped back the tears from her eyes and tried to smile "Thank you!" to each of the donors.

"Come now, collecting money shouldn't be a sad thing," Stanley laughed in his now familiar not-quite-deep bass voice. "Or are you saddened by taking pennies from children?"

He sat down beside her and took her hand. The engagement ring, a half-carat diamond in a gold solitaire setting, sparkled on her finger. Each time he looked at it, he was ashamed he could not afford anything larger, but also proud that she was, one day soon, going to be his wife.

"The children have been very generous," she whispered. *How am I going to tell him about his buddy, Hans?* Stanley, she knew, would be both devastated by the news, but relieved that it wasn't Eddie who had been trampled to death in the Somme mud by a frightened horse.

"It isn't that, she indicated the box, steadily filling up by the steady stream of generous children. "It's... this." She handed him the letter, then grasped his hand even tighter as her fiancé's face turned white.

"Hans?" he choked back a sob. "He was the last person I thought would... He was so quiet, so wise... So..."

"So, Hans," she tried to smile. "Edmond says he was trying to hold the horse steady... Well, I'll let you continue reading."

I was directly behind the caisson, between it and the horse, unloading an ammunition box. The procedure was to get the gun in position and then unload. Many times we don't have the option to unharness and move the horse to safety. Lock, load, fire, and be ready to move to another position... Then the bomb went off nearby... Hans was just a few feet away when the horse – We call him Brutus because he's absolutely huge and as black as night – spooked. Without thinking, Hans grabbed the bridle and that's when Brutus reared up in his traces and kicked him down... then ran, caisson and all, over Hans. He didn't have a chance...

"Geez. Goddamn. What a way to die," Stanley swore under his breath. "Edmond had written Hans was planning on joining Phoenix N⁰ 1 when he came home." He paused, wiping his wrist under his nose. "When he came home... He would have been a great addition to the company..."

"It's okay to cry, Stanley," Rebecca whispered behind her own tears. "I know Hans, quiet and stalwart as he was, was such a good friend... And ever so kind."

"Yes, and now, ever so gone."

"But... he did save Edmond's life."

Once again, Edmond did not have the time to recover the body of his buddy or even to say a proper good-by. After firing off just a few more rounds, his regiment was ordered to a new position. He had to leave Hans to the devices of medics. As he rode off sitting next to the driver, mercilessly whipping Brutus on, he only had a moment to quickly glance back to wish his dear friend, "God speed."

Lenny still awaited trial. Even after being locked up for two months in a Chester County Prison dank and dark cell, his trial date had not yet been scheduled. The guards, indifferent to his screaming outbursts and sobs racked with fear, largely ignored him except to pass him tin trays of cold, watery food. And rarely was he allowed time in the small exercise yard for a breath of fresh air. Even worse, his father had not even tried to come to visit him. Or so Lenny thought. In fact, Hermann Lochmann tried many times. But because he had not registered as a German with the Government, he was denied access to public government facilities. Which meant he could not visit his own son.

He did, however, with Constable Luke Tucker's help, manage to secure a court-appointed attorney. A one Mr. Jeremy Sloth, who lived up to his name. He did only the barest minimum to protect his client, spending the least amount of time to build a flimsy defense.

"I read the evidence presented to Judge Piccolino, son," he tried to explain during one of his rare, brief visits to Lenny's dimly-lit cell. "Clear cut, open and shut case.You're guilty... All's I can plea for is a minimum sentence..."

"I not guilty!" Lenny protested, although he knew in his heart that he was guilty of setting some of the fires that ravaged buildings in Phoenixville. But not all of them.

"Then, there's this matter of the young woman dying..." he flipped through the messy pile of papers in his briefcase. "Yes. This one," he pronounced. "Seems a one Samantha Higgins Rouleaux was driving across the High Bridge... in Phoenixville..." he cleared his throat. "Fire Chief Mendowski says someone threw a lit torch into her car which spun out of control..."

Lenny's face went blank. He turned away from the lawyer in an ill-fitting, wrinkled Edwardian suit and stared straight ahead at a stone wall. He did not hear Sloth's next words

"Tragically, she died, crushed and burned by the overturned car that burst into flames. What do you have to say to that, Lenny?" He frowned, tapping Lenny's shoulder, trying to get his attention.

Lenny shrugged him off.

"Lenny? Lenny, you in there?"

Lenny continued to stare, but mumbled, "I not do that. I not hurt nobody…"

"Well, someone did. And whether you are that someone or not, looks like a separate case. But, still, you're going to take the rap for it."

"No!" Lenny was, by now, seething inside, but refused to express his emotions. He continued to stare at the wall.

"Well, you think about it. Arson is one thing, but murder could easily get you hung." He shoved the papers back into his briefcase, stood up, and placed a fraying black bowler hat on his balding head. "Well, guess that about sums it up. I gotta go see a paying client… See you in court. Whenever that's going to be."

Lenny continued to stare straight ahead. As the guard slammed the cell door shut behind Sloth, his blank look suddenly collapsed into a miasma of tears.

"I not kill lady," he sobbed over and over. "I not kill lady. Someone… help me, please." He crumpled onto the filthy unswept concrete floor, folded into in a fetal position, and wrapped his arms around his stomach.

"I only want Stanley like me… Father to love me… Please, someone…. Help me."

A guard walking past the cell heard Lenny crying aloud. But after fifteen years of being a prison guard, was inured to men sobbing and screaming. "Probably nothing to worry about," he sighed and, choosing to ignore prisoner 1918-66784, strolled on by.

Fire Chief David Mendowski was finally able to breathe a sigh of relief. Except for the usual brush fires and kitchen flare ups caused by carelessness, there were no longer any major fires in Phoenixville. He tried to discount the latest, mysterious conflagration at the Pennsylvania House Hotel as "just a fluke. A coincidence." But he wasn't entirely convinced that it was. Mendowski's initial thought was that Victor Flanagan, losing money on his latest business venture, had set it for the insurance money.

Then again, he thought, *Frees did do an exhaustive investigation before he awarded the owner the payout. He would have reported it if he suspected fraud.*

Yet, there was the charred torch in the third-floor hallway. It was too similar in shape to the ones found at earlier fires. The ones everyone now knew Lenny Lochmann had set.

The Chief shrugged his brawny shoulders, rubbing the left one to ease the constant dull pain.

Oh, well. Hopefully, we've no more major fires to contend with now. And, hopefully, won't in the near future.

In Belgium, northeast France, and along most of Germany's border, artillery barrages against the Allies were constant. But the Allied forces pushed back. Slowly, ever so surely, most of Central Powers troops were finally starting to lose ground.

Edmond Hope, who once was eager to step on to the field of battle, was slowly tiring of the boredom of battle and found himself anxiously anticipating a return home. By the light of a small hearth fire in the rubble of yet another stone farmhouse destroyed by exploding shells, he wrote yet another letter home.

My dear friend Stan, he began, *I can't wait to come home again. It's been only a few months, but it feels like years. I've lived a lifetime of memories here... and seeing Hans die like that, I've lost the joy of living in danger.*

The first thing I want to do is see Rosalina, then have a beer with my buddies. And then shag a few balls in Reeves Park...

Say, have you heard anything from Frank at all? Last I heard he was on a destroyer out in the middle of the ocean...

And Collier Cornett, the young man I wrote you about. Did he get home safely?

I often wonder about him... He was so much like you...

October 1918

Fighting on the Western Front had finally subsided.

Captain Samuel Whitaker decided to offer his men of Battery C a bit of respite, hoping to bolster the low morale of the Allied artillerymen from the Keystone state.

With the fighting in hiatus, Edmund and two other members of his artillery unit went a few miles behind the lines to the small Belgium town of Poperinge in West Flanders. There they coerced, in their broken French, a house frau and her husband to allow them to bathe. The Bergens proved to be more than just hospitable. Frau Hilda Bergen, when she learned of Edmond's Germanic heritage on his mother's side, cooked endless amounts of sauerbraten, waffles, and *Carbonade flamande,* a version of the French *du Boeuf Bourguignon.* It was made with home-brewed beer instead of wine.

While the American solders slept in their barn loft, she washed and ironed their uniforms. Her husband, Herr Geoff Bergen, cleaned and polished their boots. After dinner, he plied them with copious amounts of brandy. Where the Bergens were able to secure such largesse in a time and place of war when and where other families in the area were destitute, Edmond wondered, but did not ask.

"I have my ways," Herr Bergen smiled in English, as if reading his guest's thoughts. His accent was thicker than the stew his wife had served for dinner. He raised his beef stein in salute, declaring,

"War, if you know how to work with and not fight in it, can be very profitable."

Assigned to escort and patrol duty for the duration of the war, the USS FANNING plied the seas along the European coastline. No sooner had the destroyer reached the icy waters of the Irish Sea, when it would turn around again, dock in Le Havre for fuel and supplies, then head south again, skirting France, Spain, and cruising through the Straits of Gibraltar before it once again turned around and headed back north.

While he enjoyed being at sea, Frank was still finding it tediously boring. He spent his free time between trading stories with Yeoman Lorretta Pefectus Walsh when she was off duty and talking with *Der Kapitän* Gunther Kraus, learning as much as he could about the small German town of Wesel. And his sister, Gerta Kraus. And *Der Kapitän* Kraus learned as much as he could about the small Borough of Phoenixville nestled snuggly in the foothills of the Appalachian Mountains in Pennsylvania, the United States of America. After each of Frank's visits, he dutifully recorded his "findings" in a letter back home.

I think it will suit you just fine, Gunther wrote to Greta. *Meine geliebte Schwester. Just fine.*

Hans Gruber's Aunt Esmé was attending the memorial services for her nephew and two other fallen comrades at Central Lutheran Church when the line from her house to the sewer conduit under Second Avenue burst. Since the line was on her property rather than under the street, the Borough Council deemed it her responsibility to repair it.

"In a timely fashion," Burgess Mosteller had stated when she appealed to the Borough Council during its last monthly meeting. Unmoved by her sigh of defeat and helplessness, he had rapped his gavel twice on the table.

"But... Who, if not you... our elected officials... can I turn to for help?"

Councilman Edwin Soto, in a common characteristic moment of concern and kindness, offered to call Otto Schlemmer on her behalf. "He's, in my opinion, the best plumber in town," Soto smiled. "The Borough has used him for a few projects…. And, well… He is quite reasonable." Esmé Gruber brighten at the prospect of help and eagerly consented to the Councilmen's generous offer.

"Yes, I'd be most grateful," she said, vowing to bake her best Kugel for both Otto the Plumber and Councilman Soto. Once, of course, the repairs had been made and paid for.

Otto Schlemmer was just as Councilman Soto had said he was. Efficient, inexpensive. And kind. Aunt Esmé was also smitten by his good manners and, well, his rugged good looks. And she wasn't ashamed to admit it.

"Why, Esmé," Dolly Martinez had commented during the last knitting session of the Phoenixville Home Comfort Association. "I didn't think…"

"Just because I am an older woman, doesn't mean that I don't... have feelings," Esmé retorted. Her fair complexed face turned beet red. "I m-m-mean," she stammered.

"We all know what you mean," Gwendolyn Hope smiled. "Know what I think? I think… You should go for it. Er, him. He's too good a man to be stuck living with his be'er-do-well cousin up on Scape Level. I say…"

"Yes, Gwen," Dolly smirked. "Coming from a minister's wife…"

"And what of it?"

"Just saying…"

"Ladies," Esmé scowled. "I get the point." She signed. "He's coming tomorrow to finish the job. Guess I'll just have to happen to be cooking some sauerbraten and stuffed cabbage to celebrate. Now, won't I?"

Both Dolly and Gwendolyn laughed aloud.

"And Kugel!" they said in unison.

Like Esmé, Otto, too, was smitten. But he was also shy. Having had to spend years taking care of his ailing mother, he hadn't many chances to meet women of his own age. Let alone court them. When Esmé Gruber invited him to stay for dinner, he was astounded, astonished, and nervous. As well as inwardly pleased.

"I am... *ziemlich schmutzig von der ganzen Arbeit...*"

"Not to worry. You're not that dirty. And you can wash up upstairs. There are soap and clean towels in the bathroom. And, thanks to you, lots of water..."

He didn't have the heart to tell her that her repaired sewer line had nothing to do with the flow of clean water into her house. Yet, after a few moments of reflection, he looked into her kind, gentle green eyes and agreed.

What harm would there be, he asked himself, *in staying to eat one dinner?*

It did not take Otto Schlemmer long to realize that Esmé Gruber was not only a good cook, but the love of his life. He proposed three weeks later during yet another scrumptious dinner. This time she roasted pork chops served with buttered noodles and a tossed salad. Otto, on a whim, brought a bottle of Riesling.

"I know what you're going to ask," she said, noticing how he had squirmed all during dinner. "And my answer, to save you the embarrassment, is yes."

Otto took a deep breath, then sighed in relief. He was not the sort of man to get down on one knee to anyone. Even if it was the woman – and a good-looking woman at that – who was about to become his wife.

A month later Esmé Grube walked down the aisle of Central Lutheran Church bedecked in a light grey moiré suit and feathered hat carefully chosen from the local seamstress shop two doors down from the Columbia Hotel on Bridge Street. With no close relatives in the area, she chose Dolly Martinez as her Maid of Honor. Otto reluctantly had to choose Hermann Lochmann as his best man. Despite the mismatch in bridal party partners, the wedding ceremony went off without a hitch. Afterward, Stanley Martinez danced with his mother at the reception held in the upstairs ballroom of the Columbia Hotel.

"Hans..." he said with great difficulty, "would have like this. I wish..."

"I know," his mother said, "how much you miss him. And Edmond, I am sure that wherever Hans is... He's happy for his aunt. And for Otto, too."

Stanley hugged his mother closer.

Grateful for her understanding.

NOVEMBER 1918

The first time since the company's inception in 1874, the alarms that sounded in the Borough did not involve a fire.

Shortly after midnight on November 11th, Phoenix № 1 had received a telegram that Germany had signed the Armistice.

The Claxon horn atop the Iron Company Pipe Mill began to blast. The bell atop the station tower incessantly chimed. And as the alarm sounded, as Fire Chief Mendowski quipped later, the news spread like wildfire.

Finally, The Great War was over.

Almost instantly, a celebration started that was to last nearly eight hours. The only cessation in the din and racket was between 5:00 and 7:00 when residents regrouped to plan an even larger celebration for later in the afternoon. And, as if by magic, flags appeared all over town, hung by both Patriots and Pacifists alike.

Startled awake by the Gamewell Diaphone horn, Stanley raced out of 176 Prospect Street to the station. He was about to pull on his canvas tunic when Billy Szabo, who happened to be on duty that night and had initially received the telegram, chuckled.

"There is no fire, Stanley," he said.

"But the alarms? Isn't there an emergency?"

"No... Unless you consider the end of the war an emergency..."

After congratulating other fellow firefighters, Stanley ran all the way to his parent's house.

"We, they did it!" he cheered as he bounded through the door. Carlos and Dolly, groggy from being awakened from a sound sleep, still had not heard the news.

"*Qué está pasando, mi hijo*?" Carlos asked. "Why are you here so late... So early?"

"What did you do?" Dolly asked, fully prepared to defend her son against his father, regardless of what he may or may not be guilty.

"What is happening, Papi," Stanley exclaimed, "is that we are no longer at war. Germany signed the Armistice."

"Finally!" both parents sighed in relief.

"What's going on?" Rosalina appeared at the top of the wide staircase. "Edmond..." Nearly in tears at the thought, she timidly asked, "Is it Edmond? Is he...?"

"No, dear sister," Stanley laughed, racing up the stairs to hug his younger sibling. "The war is over. He is coming home! Everyone is... coming home!"

Burgess Mosteller, along with the other member of Borough Council, declared a holiday. Industrial establishments, schools, and the Post Office were closed. The churches, however opened wide their doors so that Phoenixville residents of all denominations could come in and give thanks.

"In many homes," *The Daily Republican* noted, "there was not only rejoicing, but a spirit of thankfulness... expressed in prayer. Many women received the news with tears in their eyes; others sobbed."

Two celebrations were held; one "rehearsal parade" up Bridge Street and the other what was reputed to be the largest parade ever held in Phoenixville, led by Burgess Thomas O'Brien as Chief Marshall.

There were more than 4,000 people all marching all around town, Stanley later wrote to Edmond. *It was amazing You should have been here to see it....* He laughed to himself as he wrote. *Silly... of course you'll be here. And there'll be another celebration. Bigger and better than ever. Take care of yourself!*

It was probably the best day of Frank LaBronsky's life. At least the best in his whole short-lived Naval Career. Having completed its tour of duty in the Atlantic, the USS FANNING was called back to its home port in Queensland, Ireland. But that wasn't what caused Frank's excitement.

It was the prospect of meeting President Woodrow Wilson.

Yeoman Loretta Walsh had received the transmission ordering the destroyer to Brest Harbor in Brittany. The Commander-in-Chief was to be aboard the troop transport ship, the USS GEORGE WASHINGTON on December 13th, when he would review the several American ships that served in the war on both the Atlantic and Irish Sea.

It was all Frank could do to contain himself. Especially since he and the crew were also informed that after the ceremonial parade of ships, theirs would layover in Brest until the following year. That meant he'd be able to secure shore leave and visit *Der Kapitän* Gunther Kraus – and Greta, his younger sister -- in their small town of Wesel, Germany.

For the second time in his young life, Lenny Lochmann was deemed unfit. This time he was considered incompetent to stand trial for the six felonies and misdemeanors he was allegedly accused of committing.

The circuit judge who held the preliminary hearing in a small West Chester courtroom was none other than Anthony Piccolino, who had, back in June, issued the warrant for Lenny Lochmann's arrest. He gave no reasons for the delay in scheduling the hearing nor did he, outside of Lenny's slovenly appearance and blank stares all through the proceedings, give any rationale, legal or otherwise, for dismissing the accused.

"Leonard Lochmann..." Judge Piccolino said, adjusting his wire-rimmed glasses and tapping the bench lightly with a gavel. "Since there is nothing but circumstantial evidenve against you... You are to be released and placed in your father's custody and home, where you are to remain for the rest of your natural life. No more shenanigans," he commanded both father and son. "If I hear of any more suspicious fires in Phoenixville, you'll be taken to Pennhurst State Hospital and *there* you will spend the rest of your natural life in solitary confinement." He banged the gavel again. "Get that?"

Hermann Lochmann nodded his agreement and thanks. He was grateful for Judge Piccolino's leniency, but not for the fact that he'd have his son to deal with for the rest of his life.

Lenny stood uneasily, slowly swaying his now unhealthy gaunt body, shifting his balance from one foot to the other. Four months confinement in cruel conditions had taken its toll. He stared blankly at the oak-paneled wall behind the judge, giving no indication that he even barely understood what was going on around and about him. All he knew was that his father was by his side, squeezing his arm so hard it hurt. And that he was finally going home.

During his confinement, he had made yet another big plan. The best errand ever. Now he was free to show them all that it was just he that mattered. No one else. Just Lenny Lochmann.

"Shenanigans! He calls setting five or six major fires... 'shenanigans'!" Detective Hoolmes snorted as he, Constable Tucker, Fire Chief Mendowski, Stanley Martinez, and Nat White left the courtroom. "It's a downright travesty, I tell you..."

"Calm down, Simon," the Constable chided, then sighed. "It's probably all for the best. Besides, we didn't get his fingerprints to match..."

"We could have, Luke. Asked the warden to get them..."

"Too late now, Simon," he sighed. "Too late."

Constable Tucker was disappointed that, once again, he had been, as he thought, "robbed" of solving yet another major case in his career. Lenny Lochmann was not proven guilty of setting fires, nor was he proven innocent. *Stalemate again.* Tucker thought, shaking his head. *I wonder how long it will take Lenny to set yet another building on fire?*

"And he didn't even address Samantha's murder," Stanley observed.

"Separate case," Fire Chief Mendowski said "Besides, there wasn't any evidence that Lenny was the culprit."

"But the torch..."

"Like so many others we found... Like those at fires set while Lenny was in prison. We'll never know for sure..."

Stanley shrugged, willing to take Dave's comments at face value. But Chief Mendowski was still not sure if the matter was truly settled. Yet, he did mention to Stanley, by way of assurance that, "With everything sorted out... Perhaps life in our fair village can get back to a reasonable sense of 'normalcy'." He was surprised when Stanley chuckled in response.

"Honestly, Dave, with all that's been going on... Do you really think there is such a thing in Phoenixville?"

On the Saturday evening after Thanksgiving, the Woman's Auxiliary of Phoenix № 1, in conjunction with the Phoenixville Home Comfort Association, held a benefit dinner-dance to raise money for the injured members, and their families, of Battery C and Company D.

"No real occasion," Sue Mendowski explained as she tied and straightened his black bowtie. "With the war finally over, the fires ended..."

"We hope..."

"Yes, well, for now they are. The women of the Borough just wanted to celebrate and help out at the same time."

When the Fire Chief frowned, squirming uncomfortably in what he called a "monkey suit", she chided, "It's a worthy cause. Now, keep still while I get this... just... right." Finished, she patted his burly chest. "There, now, dear. Don't you look just handsome?"

"I would have been more comfortable in my dress uniform." Then he smiled "And just as handsome, if not more."

The large ballroom of the Phoenix Hotel, Stanley Martinez noted as he escorted Rebecca, dressed in her new silk dress copied from one she saw in the latest issue of *La Mode*, through the double-wide swinging door, was bedecked with red, white, and blue banners and multi-colored balloons. Heavy, thick white linen table clothes and crisply starched napkins graced the round tables that, in turn, encircled the shiny squared parquet dance floor.

"Phil McGinty and his Phabulous Philly Five," he said, guiding his fiancée to their table shared with his and her parents and the Fire Chief and his wife.

"Where's Rosalina?" he frowned. "She promised she'd be here."

"I guess she'd rather not be a loose end..." Rebecca offered. "Without her own betrothed... I imagine she would think it rather awkward..."

"Ah, yes. Edmond," Stanley smiled. "But I would have danced with her..."

"And leave me sitting alone with my future in-laws?," Rebecca jested, wrapped her arm around his and leaning into his shoulder. "Not a chance."

"But she is my sister..."

"We left her in the library," his mother commented. "With her beloved Martha Finley books and halfway through yet another letter to Edmond. She'll be fine."

"Um, *mi hijo*," Carlos asked softly. "Will there be a double wedding? You and Rebecca," whom he smiled at warmly, "and Edmond and Rosalina? All together at the altar?"

"Carlos!" Dolly reprimanded. "No woman wants to share her wedding day with another bride..."

"Yes, but think of the savings on the expenses of two weddings in one family."

Dolly put a hand her husband's arm.

"Carlos... I don't think we should put money above our children's happiness..."

"Actually," Rebecca smiled again "We are planning a December wedding. Christmas Eve, perhaps. Maybe before then. My father, of course, will do the honors. And my mother will plan the reception. Probably at the Columbia..." She took a small sip from the champagne just placed before her, then turned to Stanley. "Is that okay, dear?"

"First I've heard of it. But, um, yeah, I guess it's okay." He squirmed a bit in his seat. *Reminds me of Samantha. What she used to do... Take command. When do I have my own say in the matter?* He did not want to be controlled ever again like he was by the niece of Estelle Griffin Higgins. Regardless of how influential in the community she, they, both had thought they were. He patted Rebecca's hand, then said, "I want Edmond to be my best man. We'll have to wait until he returns home."

"But that could take weeks... Even months..."

"But still... He is my best friend. And your brother. The least we could do is wait for him... Yes?"

Rebecca bristled, looking around the table for support. None came. She then saw the determined look on Stanley's face.

"Oh, okay, Stanley," she signed. "Anything you say."

"That's my girl," he smiled, patting her arm. "That's my girl."

The dinner-dance festivities progressed well into the late-night hours. Just before midnight, Constable Luke Tucker made his excuses to the hostesses and then walked to the Police Station where he had a few odds and ends to take care of before retiring for the night.

As he approached the station glass-paneled doors, he thought he saw movement inside. At first, he thought it was Detective Hoolmes, then realized Simon had driven to Lancaster earlier that afternoon to visit relatives. He wouldn't be back until late Sunday evening. And the ten other policemen on the force, save two who were on duty patrolling the Borough proper, were off for the evening.

Tucker moved to the side of the building where an electric streetlight, one of many recently approved by Borough Council, shone obliquely through two windows. He peered in and watched as the hulking figure moved slowly in and out of the shadows. It seemed, whoever it was, was looking for something. As the figure passed by one window, the Constable dunked down under the sill. He waivered, trying to decide whether to go inside and accost the intruder. *What if he's armed?*

He patted the left side of his chest and smiled, assuring himself. *Not a problem.* His own M1917 police special was safely holstered under his arm. *Good thing I never leave home without it,* he smiled wanly, then withdrew the small handgun.

Suddenly, from inside the station, a loud crash and a piercing scream cut through the semi-darkness.

Wasting no time, Tucker raced back to double-doors and, without hesitation, kicked one in.

"Who's here?" he called out, venturing into the semi-darkness. The acrid order of kerosene and smoke filled the air. The figure, surprised, suddenly turned around, poised to throw the lit torch at the policeman.

"Stop, or I'll shoot!" the Constable warned and then, in a moment of panic and self-defense realizing a split-second later that the torch was about to strike his shoulder, fired not once, not twice, but three times. His aim was sure and steady, even if he wasn't sure of his target. The torch, still lit, clattered to the floor. Tucker kicked it aside, his pistol still aimed at the hulking figure now dropped to his knees, clutching his chest.

"I told... Not shoot!" a familiar, halting voice cried. "No shoot! Father hit me again."

The stunned and speechless Constable Luke Tucker watched as Lenny Lochmann fell on his side to the floor. He tossed the M1917 onto his desk, then dropped to his knees beside Lenny. Blood seeped through Lenny's familiar fraying plaid flannel jacket. Foam bubbled out of his mouth. He looked up at the Constable, the glint of surprised anger fading from his usually dull eyes.

"My father... Fires... I want him... Love me," Lenny said and then died.

"Oh, dear Holy Mary, Mother of God," Constable Luke Tucker moaned. "What have I done?"

He would come to regretfully live over and over again the last few moments of Lenny Lochmann's life for the rest of his own.

But, now, at least, he ruefully thought in the wee hours of a November Sunday morning as he stomped out the lit torch and called the local ambulance. *At least, I managed to solve at least one major crime in my career as a police officer.*

Or so he thought.

The alarm sounded at 4:30 in the afternoon, the day after Leonard Lochmann was laid to his final rest in an almost forgotten corner of Morris Cemetery. "Four, one!" Fire Chief Mendowski called as he climbed aboard the Brockway Combination Chemical and Hose truck. He watched as Billy

Szabo and Doc Kimshaw quickly slid open the wide double doors, waving to the new volunteer trainee. "C'mon, Cornett! You're coming too. Move it!" He turned to Stanley Martinez, now the new paid driver. "Okay, Stan. We all aboard? Hit it!"

It took nearly two hours to stem the raging fire in Klotzbach's Funeral Home on Gay Street. Chemicals normally spewed from the Brockway were ineffectual against the flammable formaldehyde stored in large vats in the embalming room. It seemed someone had opened the safety valves, flooded the room, and then tossed a torch, fashioned from a baseball bat, onto the liquid. The fire caught instantly and within minutes the better back half of the funeral home was consumed. Due to the fire's magnitude, Phoenix Nº 1 had to call for backup from both Friendship Fire and the West End Bridge Companies.

"Haven't seen one like this since we put out the Pennsylvania Hotel," Sebastian Peters commented as he and Billy Szabo manned the 2½" hose hooked to a fire hydrant across the street.

"You weren't there when Gateway burned to the ground," Szabo stated. He had been a member of the company for several years when Peters, as he begrudgingly said, "jumped ship" in 1906 to join the newly-formed Friendship Fire Company No. 2. "We didn't need any assist to put that one out. And it was much larger than this..."

"But as hot?"

Szabo had to admit as he helped aim the nozzle into the white-hot flames, that while it had been a larger fire, Gateway's conflagration was at least one hundred degrees cooler than this one.

"Chemical fires are a bitch, Peters," he agreed. *Which is why fire companies like ours are here. To save lives.*

"In a funeral home?" Peters laughed as if reading Szabo's thoughts. "C'mon, Billy. You've got to be kidding."

Despite an exhaustive investigation, Mendowski and Tucker could not fathom who had set the fire at Klotzbach's.

"Could have been revenge by Hermann Lochmann," Tucker suggested. "But there was no love lost between him and is son."

"Maybe, Luke. Just maybe Hermann really did love Lenny. In his own way. Maybe more than we realized."

Despite his wanting to postpone the wedding until Edmond Hope returned home, Stanley Francis Martinez really couldn't wait. He loved his best friend's sister more than life itself. And, so, he married Rebecca Edwina Hope on the first Sunday of Advent in St. Peter's Episcopal Church. Her father, of course, not only gave the bride away, but officiated at the ceremonial rite.

Intensely proud of his new position in life as the paid driver – Nat had retired to raise Percherons – and now a member of the company board, Stanley wore his Phoenix $N^{\underline{o}}$ 1 dress uniform. Replete with the shiny new black leather shoes his father had custom made and gave him last Christmas. He was even more proud of Rebecca as she walked up the aisle, tightly clasping her father's arm, wearing a tightly-fitting silk and lace dress fashioned by herself and her mother – once again straight out of one of the French fashion magazines she insisted on reading.

After a small reception in the newly built hall on the second floor of the fire station – Chief Mendowski insisted on hosting the affair, although both Reverend Harold Hope and Carlos Martinez footed most of the bill -- they left for a brief honeymoon in Washington, D.C. A week later, they settled into a small house in Mont Clare along the Schuylkill River canal on Port Providence Road.

Stanley had purchased the Sears kit home a month or so before the wedding with his share of his and Rosalina's war bonds. It required a bit of fixing up, but Stanley knew just the right man for the job. And Otto Schlemmer had agreed to waive part of his costs as a wedding present to the young couple.

It looked as if everything in life was coming together for Stanley.

The Great War was over; there was no fear of being drafted or sent to foreign shores to die what he thought would be an ignoble death. Deemed a hero for saving several lives, he became a pillar of the community; even esteemed by his father who now welcomed him and his new wife with open arms to the Martinez family's Sunday dinner table.

"*Mi hijo! Mi hijo. Mi querida hija,* Carlos gushed, warmly hugging them both as they visited him and Dolly upon their return from Washington.

"But I am your *daughter-in-law,*" Rebecca corrected.

"No! No! You are married to my son. You are now part of the family. *La familia. Nuestra familia*. You are now *mi hija*. My daughter."

"Come, come in," Dolly said warmly. "Tell us all about your trip."

"Well, the firefighting museum at the Smithsonian was awesome..." Stanley began. "The Chief would have loved it."

I won't be able to make it home for Chanukah, Frank LaBronsky wrote home to his parents. *We are laid over in Brest for a few months. The ship won't be crossing the Atlantic anytime soon.*

"But wasn't he due for a discharge?" Sarah asked, putting the letter aside.

"He upped for two years," her husband explained. "He's got another six or seven months to go..."

"But, but that's... that's next year, Harold!" Sarah exclaimed, heartbroken that even with the war over, she probably wouldn't be welcoming her son home any time soon.

"I know, dearest. But the war is over and he is quite safe..."

"But if his ship is still in Europe?"

"They'll probably fly him home."

Sarah shook her head. "That won't do at all. You know he's afraid of flying."

On its way back to Queensland, Ireland from Brest, the USS FANNING stopped at Le Havre, then Dunkirk before it sailed up the Netherland Coast. It was Yeoman Walsh who reluctantly told him about the unique rail service into the interior of Germany.

"Most of it miraculously survived the war, Ensign. I am sure you could find your way to Wesel."

When the destroyer moored offshore of The Hague, Frank secured a four-day shore leave. He was about to start the third leg of his life's journey.

With the Great War over and most of the 420 men and women who left to fight it expected home, the Holidays in Phoenixville that year were especially joyous.

Mr. and Mrs. Stanley Martinez put up their first Christmas decorations as a couple. Rebecca, already adept in the kitchen, did wonders with a five-course meal featuring a standing rib-roast from Eyrich's. The temporary ban on distilled grain products now lifted, Stanley stocked a small pantry with wine, Irish Whiskey, and an assortment of locally brewed beer, including the Columbia Hotel's Phoenix Special brew.

And while fireworks were set off during the last week of December to celebrate the coming New Year as well as a hard-fought Victory, Phoenix № 1 had, thankfully, no major fires to contend with.

Greta Kraus was prettier than Frank LaBronsky had expected or even anticipated. Soft, long plaited blond hair, crystal blue eyes, and a smile that lit up the darkest corners of his heart hardened by grueling, boring months at sea.

Her parents and, of course, Gunther, her older brother, welcomed him with open arms, almost as if he was already a member of the family. For three days, Frank enjoyed the best food Mrs. Kraus could offer, given the devastating shortages caused by the war. While not as good as his mother's, it was far better than the stale fare aboard ship.

Frank just couldn't help himself. He became enamored of Greta Kraus during long morning walks around the countryside and during afternoon tours of Wesel. A small German town that, he had to agree, was very much like Phoenixville. The more they got to know one another, the more eager Frank was to show Greta his own hometown.

"Collier Cornett?" Stanley asked the Chief the weekend after his had returned from his honeymoon. "Edmond wrote me about him getting caught in a wave of mustard gas. Isn't he... I mean he did well on our last call, but I didn't get a chance to... I mean... His face..."

"Yeah, I know. His face, his neck," David Mendowski explained. "Right side of his torso, as well. Caught in a wave of mustard gas in the Somme Valley. But he survived. He was shipped home after two, three months in the hospital."

"I am sorry... But..."

"Stan, he's doing fine. Here. With us. I know the scars are a bit, um, off-putting, at the very least but... deep inside..."

"Yeah, I know. He's a good guy and a great firefighter. Trained by the best. The American Military forces overseas."

"Look, Stanley, You are now a company leader. You'll take care of him. Show him the ropes... Er, the hoses?" he chuckled.

Stanley hesitated, remembering his promise to Edmond that he'd watch out for... their fellow resident from Phoenixville. He nodded slowly, then said. "It would be my honor, Dave. It would be my honor."

345

Edmond stood on the Philadelphia Railroad platform and took a deep breath of cold air still tinged with ash and the metallic scent of smelted iron. The foundry of the Phoenix Iron and Bridge companies was, he was happy to note, still in operation.

Music from the Phoenix Hose, Hook and Ladder Co. No. 1 Fife and Drum Brigade wafted toward him as the parade of welcoming friends and family marched east on Bridge Street to the station. He laughed at the shared joke he and Stanley had about the brigade. Not one volunteer of the fire department brigade was a member.

"Us members of the fire company," Stanley had to admit, "are not that musically inclined. As a matter of fact," he had explained. "we hire the brigade to play at various functions and festivities. And please don't ask... I have no idea who they all are..."

Listening to the familiar strains of *The Star-Spangled Banner*, Edmond stood at attention, searching the crowd for his parents and, of course, Rebecca. And he thought he saw, in the distance Stanley's unruly mop of dark curly hair.

And is that my sister draping herself over his arm? He hadn't realized it before, but Rebecca was a few inches taller than his best buddy. *But why was she clinging to him so closely?*

Other members of Battery C standing nearby were also searching the crowd. The stalwart Sergeant Thomas Taggart nearly collapsed with joy at seeing his own younger sister.

"Winnie's going to have a baby," he said. "I'm gonna be an uncle."

"Congratulations, Tom," Edmond smiled. Having grown up with Rebecca and her seemingly stiff prudish nature, he doubted he would share the same destiny. He extended his hand. "I just wanted to say... Um, it's been an honor serving with you."

"Likewise, Hope," the older artilleryman said, shaking Edmond's hand. "Oh, um, I gotta go. There's Caffrey's parents. I have a letter for them, from him... You know, in case he..."

"Yeah, I know. I wrote one myself." Edmond patted the inside pocket of his now worn and fraying woolen tunic, still stained with the blood of former comrades and the caked mud of French soil. He had tried to clean it as best he could, but there was no way he was able to restored the discolorations left by his vigorous repeated brushings.

"You take care of yourself, you hear," Taggart called over his shoulder as he elbowed his way through the throng to Walter's grieving family.

Stanley's embrace was almost embarrassing.

"You made. You made it home! Welcome back, Black Bess," referring to Edmond's favorite childhood penny-dreadful hero.

"Well, it's damn good to see you, too, Stan. What's new?"

Stanley turned toward Rebecca and hugged his wife.

"We're married," he grinned sheepishly.

"Without me?"

"I... er, she just couldn't wait," Stanley laughed, squeezing Rebecca's waist.

"Not true," she sternly stated, pulling away. 'It was you..."

"Enough!" Edmond interrupted. "Come here, Sis. Give your heroic older brother a big welcome-home hug."

"Mom and Dad are back at the house," she said, lingering in her brother's arms. "Mom's readying a big feast for you and Dad... Well, you know Dad. He's got a stash of Fenella's wine hidden somewhere in the house. He just can't wait to crack open a few bottles with you."

"Ugh! I can't stomach that stuff. Frizzy tart grape juice. Now the wines in France..."

"Well, you're just going to have to suck it up," Rebecca laughed. "He's been talking about spending time with you ever since your last letter saying you're coming home."

"Don't worry," Stanley smiled. "I'll be there with you. At least for the first bottle."

"Gee, thanks." Edmond searched the crowd again. "Where's Rosalina? I thought she'd be here, too."

"Back home with our parents, Eddie. You know how she is with crowds. And I think she wanted to welcome my new bother-in-law home..." Stanley slightly waved toward the crowd now amassing in front of and on the train platform, "in a, um, more private, er, intimate setting."

Later that evening over dinner at the Hope residence, Edmond refused to recount or relive any of his wartime experiences. He was glad to have been able to finally soak in a suds-filled tub, cleansing his body, as well as his heart and soul, of the last sixteen harrowingly gruesome months. Clad in a new starched cotton shirt and dark blue serge trousers, he looked around the table at his friends and family.

"Some things," he muttered, "are best left unsaid. I'd rather learn about all the goings-on here at home." He turned to Stanley. "Tell me about all the fires."

"Not much to tell anymore. Lenny – remember Lenny?"

"I've only been gone a year or so, Stan... Of course, I remember the big lummox. How is he?"

Covert glances passed around the table between the dinner guests. No one wanted to tell Edmond about the final fate of their one-time childhood classmate and fellow Borough resident. After a few moments of awkward silence, Edmond cleared his throat, took a small sip of the insipid Fenella Family's red, and dabbed his lips with his starched linen napkin.

"Let me guess," he offered. "Lenny is in jail..."

"He was," Stanley said softly.

"So, he's at large again, lighting more fires?"

"Um, no. He's..."

"Dead," Rosalina exclaimed. "What don't you just tell him, Stan-Stan? Lenny Lochmann. Our local arsonist is dead!"

Edmond Hope bowed his head.

"He was a good guy. At least I thought he was. At least he tried to be. What happened?"

"Constable Tucker shot him the Saturday after Thanksgiving," the Reverend Harold Hope said to his son.

"What?"

"Apparently, he was attempting to set the police station on fire... and the Constable walked in on him. It was self-defense," he said. "He threw a lit torch..."

Edmond was more than upset at what he had heard. While, as a child, he had distanced himself from Lenny Lochmann, he did try, at times, at the urging of Stanley to try to be nice to him. But still... the fact that he, for whatever reasons, had set fire to several places in the hometown he had spent months overseas fighting to protect... Well, it was a bit too much for the war veteran to accept

"Okay, Father, I've heard enough," he scowled. "So be it. Lenny is dead. May he rest in peace. And... There have been no more of the fires Stanley's written me about?'

"None since. Well, none so far..." he hesitated. Then, "Well, there was one..." Stanley stated. "One at Klotzbach's in November... but..."

"Who set that one?"

"No one knows," Rosalina started to sob. "No one knows."

Carlos and Dolly Martinez did their best to try and comfort their daughter. She had been on edge, visibly upset ever since her father's shoe shop had been set on fire. And Edmond had gone off to war.

"I am so sorry, Gwendolyn," Dolly offered. "We did not mean to ruin this, your dinner... celebration the homecoming of your son... our soon-to-be son-in-law. But... Rosalina... ever since... Well, she's more than just upset."

"I'll take care of this," Edmond said, rising from the table. He took the hand of his fiancée and led her from the table into his father's study. What transpired between the engaged couple, no one would know nor would anyone dare to ask. When they both returned to the dining room to partake of dessert, Stanley's sister was all smiles and congeniality and Edmond was suddenly strait-laced and in total command of the room.

"Our wedding" he pronounced, "will be in two weeks this coming Saturday afternoon. Father, I mean, Reverend Hope, I presume you will officiate?"

"It will be my honor, son."

"But we're members of Saint Mary's," Carlos protested, clinging to his wife's hand. "If you're to marry my daughter, then..."

"Then... If I am to marry your daughter," Edmond said softly, "you will abide by her... by our wishes."

Stanley was overjoyed. His sister was going to be wed to his best friend, who would truly become his brother. The venue of the event did not matter to him. What did matter was that the Martinez and Hope families would be finally cemented together, doubly joined by marriage. Just as, growing up, he had hoped it would be. It was the best news ever. He took a large gulp of the acrid red wine, ignoring its acerbic aftertaste.

Everything is going so well, he smiled. *What a great life we all now have here in our peaceful little town of Phoenixville.*

He looked around the table at his new soon-to-be extended family. "I, we are all so truly blessed," Stanley whispered to Rebecca. "I will remember this moment for years to come."

The fire alarm sounded just as Stanley and Rebecca were saying their good-byes to the Reverend and Mrs. Harold Hope. Carlos and Dolly had already left, saying their own thanks and good-byes earlier before driving up Second Avenue in their American Underslung touring car. Edmond and Rosalina had also made their earlier excuses and were taking an evening stroll around the neighborhood.

They have, Stanley said to himself as they left, *much to talk about.*

He stood with his wife on the porch of the Hope home counting the blasts from the Claxon horn blaring across town.

"Four, three," he sighed. "Bridge and Nutt's Avenue."

"Do you have to go, Stanley?" Rebecca asked clinking to his arm. "It's been such a special night..."

"Sorry, I really should see what's going on... If I could help..."

"But, dearest, you're not on duty," she cajoled. "I was hoping..."

"Please. Stay here with your parents, Rebecca." He paused and shuddered as if he had a small glimpse into the future. His future. "Until I return."

The dark blue Sussex two-seater was a wedding gift from his father. Now Stanley no longer had to borrow cars or ride

351

his old bike whenever he had to go somewhere. He was proud to drive the sleek sports roadster, escorting Rebecca around town. Tonight, however, he was on a different errand. A different reason to speed down Main Street, following the Brockway Combination apparatus and the old horse-driven American LaFrance steamer now towed by a Ford Model T truck.

In order to keep up on the now burgeoning demand for cotton goods, the owners decided to run the Perseverance Mill around the clock. That meant two extra shifts. One in the late afternoon to midnight; the other, the swing shift, from twelve to nine in the morning when the regular day shift started. And, for what they thought was for the safety and protection of their workers, the foremen, including the stocky surly Nick Letterman, were ordered to keep all the doors locked.

Letterman, who wished to ingratiate himself with the owners, used every trick in the book to save and make more money for them. So, when Lenny Lochmann died, the crusty manager reneged on hiring a replacement custodian. To save the wages, he would do the work himself. He did just about everything Lenny had done, even rethreading the machine needles, running errands, and cleaning the small, dingy break room. Almost everything. Except for sweeping; a dirty chore he deemed beneath himself.

Piles of loose threads and bits of lint had collected in the corners of the large workroom. The women complained bitterly of the thick layers on the floor; the loose ends clinging to the hems of their work dresses; worming their way into their canvas-topped shoes.

Letterman, more interested in the quantity of their work, ignored their pleas for improving the quality of their workplace.

"Besides," he slurred, spitting out a wad of tobacco juice onto the debris-littered floor, "they're just women. What do they know about management?"

On the night of the fire, forty women, mostly inexperienced young girls and several much older women, were toiling on the dimly-lit second-floor at their various sewing machines. It was piece-meal work. Paid by the amount not the excellence of their efforts, the women, mostly Mexican, Afro-Americans, and Hungarians – daughters, wives, and mothers of local steel workers – their small wages helped to eke out a meager living for their families. The more sleeves, collars, completed shirts, and pajama sets they made, the more money they brought home.

Each one intent on besting the other in production, they did not hear nor see the door to the rear stairwell click open. No one saw the hulking figure in the almost new plaid jacket enter, light the torch, set it onto the floor littered with lint and thread, and then leave. No body heard the door lock click shut again.

Nor did they see the flames flicker and flare until it was too late.

By the time the complements of Phoenix Nº 1, West End and Friendship arrived on the scene, the back half of the mill had been consumed. The stairway, with the door to the first and second floors locked, was inaccessible to the workers frantically seeking to escape the smoke and flame-filled rooms. Workers on first floor, where large bolts of cotton were cut into the various-sized pieces to be sewn together upstairs, had managed to break windows and crawl out to safety before the fire above drifted down to them. They escaped with only minor cuts and bruises

Most of those on the second floor, however, were not so lucky.

Without thinking, Stanley careened his Sussex into the empty side lot of the mill, barely crashing into the Brockway. Billy Szabo and Doc Kimshaw were already hard at work trying to contain the fire. He counted three more firemen, including Lou Double who was furiously working the steam pumper. The Fire Chief barked orders from halfway up the ladder, a live firehose slung over his shoulder.

"Where's Collier?!" Stanley shouted over the din.

"Took an axe and went inside," Szabo called back.

"Damn fool," Stanley hissed. Grabbing a tunic and hat from the back of the Brockway, he raced to the entrance; its door neatly smashed in.

Billows of black smoke filled the stairwell. Stanley could barely see a hand in front of his face, let alone Collier at the top of the stairs trying to whack through the door.

"Collier!" he shouted. "It's no use, come back down..."

"I'm almost in!"

Stanley heard the crunch knocking down what remained of the door, releasing more billows of smoke and flames.

"Collier, come back!" Stanley called, mounted the now burning stairs two at a time.

I can't let him die in there, he thought. *Not after what he's been through...*

Collier appeared at the doorway just as Stanley was reaching the top. He had a young girl gasping for breath slung over his shoulders.

"Here, take her. There's more inside..."

Stanley turned, the girl in his arms, just as Lou Double came up the stairs manning a 2½" firehose, spewing water through the doorway.

"Get her out of here!" Double shouted. "I'll try and dowse this bitch of a blaze out."

Stanley carried the frightened mill worker down the stairs to safety. It was, he realized the fifth life, including that of two horses, he had saved in nearly two years on the force. *But,* he chuckled, deeply inhaling fresh night air. *Who's counting?*

'I've another!" Collier screamed as he came out of the now burning stairway. He put the older woman down next to the younger one Stanley had carried out. "But there's more inside! Many more!"

Stanley and Collier didn't hear the steady putt-putt of a Smith Motor Wheel on Buchanan Street speeding away. Nor did they see the manager sidle up beside them.

"They're jumping out the windows in droves," Nick Letterman spat close to the two women, now coughing and panting for breath.

"Dropping to hard ground from the second floor.... That'll kill them or sure..." Stanley said.

"Better than being burnt to a crisp," Collier muttered. "Believe me, I know." He turned toward Letterman, who recoiled then spat, again repulsed by the sight of the ex-infantryman's face. "Yeah," Collier grinned through his twisted scars. "The Somme was a bitch."

Without warning, Stanley headed back toward the building.

"Stanley! No!"

He met Lou Double halfway coming down the stairs, with the nozzle turned off.

"It's no use, Stanley. The flames are too hot for one man to handle. And the stairs... they're about to collapse. Let's get out before..."

But Stanley Francis Martinez did not listen.

"I can't let innocent women die..." he whispered. "Turn that damn hose on again and aim it high into the room." He waited until Double obeyed, then disappeared into the smoke and fire before Lou could stop him.

Stanley managed to carry out four more mill workers until, overcome from heat, smoke inhalation, and pure exhaustion, he collapsed trying to save an older woman who, when he dropped to his knees in the smothering ashes of what was left of the second floor of the mill, died in his arms.

Their bodies, even as hard as Lou Double tried, could not be recovered.

Constable Luke Tucker was more than frustrated. He was angry and distraught. He thought he had once again nearly solved one of, if not the major case of his career. He cursed the ineptitude and misguided leniency of Judge Anthony Piccolino. If Lenny had not been free, he wouldn't have been lurking in the police station trying to set it on fire. And the Constable wouldn't have shot him. Lenny was caught red-handed and should have been in prison... And now he was dead.

Worst of all, fires were still being set in Phoenixville. With Lenny Lochmann gone, who was now – or was it still? -- setting them?

Frank LaBronsky had arrived home on an extended leave the day before the funeral. He had six more months to serve in the United States Navy, but he'd still be on the USS FANNING, now docked in Annapolis as a temporary training ship for the Academy cadets. He welcomed the time home and the opportunity to explain to his beloved parents that he had met "the one". They'd be happy to hear that she wasn't a German Lutheran, but Jewish. He knew his mother would be pleased. And he hoped that once they met, Sarah would fall in love with Greta, now his fiancée.

But he'd tell them all about the young pretty *Fräulein* from Wesel later. Now he had more somber things to take care of. Like meeting his buddy, Edmond Hope, in the barroom of the Columbia to hoist a few in honor of their fallen comrade.

"I stopped by the firehouse," he said, sipping a cold Phoenix Special, Stanley's favorite. "The Fire Chief is willing to take me on once I'm discharged."

Edmond stared sullenly into his double scotch.

"Yeah, now that there's a vacancy."

"Oh, c'mon. Yes, it was a foolish thing for him to do, but he saved lives."

"How many times the Fire Chief told him not to rush into flaming fires... That isn't, wasn't like him. Such a coward, I thought and here he turns out to be more of a hero than we both were..." Edmond took another sip. Swallowed it hard. He couldn't ignore the lump in his throat. He squeezed his eyes shut, rubbing them with his fingertips, trying to stop the tears.

"Look," Frank said. "I know it's the wrong thing to say..."

"Say it anyway."

"I'm sorry for you, for me. For his parents... For the whole town... But..."

"For Rebecca, too?"

"Yes, especially for Rebecca, too."

Edmond took another sip then looked directly at Frank. "She's pregnant, you know."

"Good for Stanley!"

'He'll never know his child... And that's the saddest thing about all the whole goddamn fiascos of this past year. Not the war. Not the loss of Campbell and Hans... It's this...those. The goddamn fires."

"Which I'll fight when I get back. I did that during the war, you know. Aboard a ship... Maybe not the same, but the techniques..."

"Yeah. Yeah, right." Edmond chugged down the rest of his drink. "Yeah, you do that, my friend," he said, walking away from the bar. "You fight your damned fires. But, you know," he patted Frank on the shoulder as he left. "You'll never be the fireman that Stanley was."

357

Stanley Francis Martinez, age twenty-three, was buried with full fire service honors including the "Last Alarm" Ceremony. The large brass station bell was personally run three times by Fire Chief David Mendowski symbolizing that Brother Stanley had completed his task, his duties well done, and had answered his last alarm. Then, over an urn containing what was they thought, hoped to be Stanley's ashes, he solemnly spoke.

"Many of us close to him knew Stanley adamantly refused to face the fires of an unknown enemy overseas on foreign land. Yet, here, on his own country's soil, he faced far more dangerous flames and made the ultimate sacrifice..." The Fire Chief took a deep breath, wiping the top of each cheek. It would be unseemly for a man in his position to be seen crying in public.

"Which, um, which his friends and comrades had offered. Two were privileged to make that sacrifice... dying while saving the lives and freedoms of many... But Stanley, chosing to fight here rather than oversees, more than exemplified the values of his friends and fellow countrymen."

He cleared his throat, then looked at Carlos, Dolly, and Rebecca. Edmond and Rosalina sat behind them. The Fire Chief couldn't help noticing Edmond's redden eyes.

Well, if he can cry. So can I.

He then let his tears flow freely. Through them he said:

"Stanley Francis Martinez was a much braver, a far braver man than he thought he was or ever hoped to be. He was – and still is – an asset to our company and to our community. He was and shall be forever a hero. A true hero of Phoenixville. The very best that our fair Borough can offer."

Later, at Stanley's small plot in a shady corner, on the opposite side of Morris Cemetery from Lenny Lochmann, his father noted through uncontrollable tears that, "There are battles fought inwardly and outwardly. Both overseas and here on our own soil. I am proud of Stanley. *Mio hijo.* My son. I loved him more than my own life. I wish I had had more opportunities to tell him that..."

Edmond Hope, standing beside Carlos, with Stanley's wife on the other side, whispered, 'I think he knows that, Mr. Martinez. I think he always did."

#####

REFERENCES

Citizens of Spring City, *Welcome Home Book,* September 1, 1917
(Courtesy of the Historical Society of the Phoenixville Area)

Ertell, J.R., "Phoenixville's National Guard Units in World War I",
Newsletter, The Historical Society of Phoenixville, September
2008. Phoenixville, PA.

Ertell, J.R.," Phoenixville Soldiers in the Great War", *Newsletter,* The
Historical Society of Phoenixville, June 2017. Phoenixville, PA.

Meadows, David B., *Phoenix Hose, Hook & Ladder Company No. 1,
Phoenixville, PA: A History Commemorating 125 Years of
Service 1874-1999.* ©1999 Phoenix Hose, Hook & Ladder Co.,
No. 1. Phoenixville, PA.

Marshall, Susan, "Phoenixville's Brilliant Fire Horses", in archives of
The Historical Society of Phoenixville, Phoenixville, PA.

PHHL1 Fire Reports, 1881-1914 & 1920. Phoenix Hose, Hook &
Ladder Co., No. 1. Phoenixville, PA.

Sanborn Sectional Maps of Phoenixville 1903 -1920.

Williams, Keith, "F.Y.I.", *The New York Times,* Sunday, May 7, 2017.
New York City, NY.

Various articles culled from *The Daily* Republican 1917-1920 on
microfiche at the Historical Society of the Phoenixville Area,
Phoenixville, PA.

Various online sources including Wikipedia, Facebook postings, and
other incidental sites.

Acknowledgements

It may "take a village" to raise a child, but it also takes one to write a novel. This fourth historical novel of my Novels of Phoenixville... series would not have come about without caring, supportive, and considerate residents of the small yet expansive Borough of Phoenixville. And, of course, to the village itself, whose rich, vibrant, and diverse history has been carved through the annals of history ever since Charles Pickering, searching for silver in 1693, first set foot on the shores of the creek that now bears his name. He found, and founded, I believe, more than mere metallic treasures.

Treasures... treasured stories which I am dedicated to write about my adopted hometown.

First, I'd like to thank Betty Weber who started me on this second vocation and passionate avocation with her encouragement and abiding friendship.

Then there is David Meadows, the past president of the Phoenix Hose, Hook & Ladder Company, No. 1, who inspired this novel. He unselfishly dedicated his time and efforts to assiduously help me pour through the many fire records of the company while unstintingly and generously telling me stories of his own experiences as a firefighter. I will always appreciate his endless array of pictures, photographs, and other memorabilia first on display at the Historical Society of the Phoenixville Area in October 1916. As well as those he carefully scans into the HSPA archives and is so eager to share with me.

It was the exhibit as well as Dave's history of Phoenix Hose, Hook and Ladder Company No. 1 that caused me to conceived the idea of writing a novel about Phoenixville's fire department during the tumultuous era of the Great War. I had planned to have it published in time to augment the June through October 1917 HSPA exhibit ("Over There, Over Here") commemorating the centennial of the United States' entry into the war. But, alas, like The Great War itself, the writing of this fourth tome went way beyond its anticipated completion by last Christmas. But, a year plus later, here we are.

I also thank Dave for his astute perusal of my several drafts and for his expert assistance in selecting and then helping to design the cover.

This is his novel – as well as that of the members – both men and women – of Phoenix Hose, Hook & Ladder Co., No. 1, as much – if not more – than it is mine. Oh, and I have to say this: My "buddy" David Shellfish and his companion, Marshall Hosehook also thank you and Susan, your wonderful wife, too. I just couldn't have written this without you both. Thank you, Dave!

I'd be remiss if I didn't also thank Jack Ertell and Sue Marshall of the Historical Society. Both are most supportive in my writing endeavors. I've learned a lot from them about local history – as well as customs and mores – while writing my Novels of Phoenixville, especially during my afternoon research sessions pouring over documents and many hours sifting through reel upon reel of microfiche newspapers in the Museum's library and archives.

Also, importantly, thanks to my ace, number one writing buddy, Sarah Peppel, who took countless hours out of her time while campaigning for Borough Council to read early drafts and proofread later and final ones. Sarah, not only are your proofing skills spot on, but your plot, continuity, and "tell" suggestions were suitably applicable. I've incorporated them all. I am also most appreciative of our growing friendship and mutual support of each other's literary endeavors.

And, lastly, my unbounded thanks and admiration for my readers, both in the Phoenixville area and beyond! I even have a few in England and Ireland!

Yes, it does take a village. But its borders, I am finding are endless and go way beyond the limits of my own imagination. Thank you all for reading this as well as my other novels.

Enjoy the read!

ABOUT THE AUTHOR

June J. McInerney is an accomplished literary critic, free-lance editor, as well as a talented author.

Her seminal debut novel, *Forty-Thirty*, set in a small New York village in the 1960s, tells the story of a young woman coming-of-age as she learns the game of life by playing the game of tennis.

June has also penned several collections of short stories, including *The Basset Chronicles* and *Cats of Nine Tales;* two volumes of poetry; and books and lyrics for three musicals that have been produced over the years by various theaters across the country.

Originally from New York, she holds a dual Bachelor of Arts in mathematics and English Literature as well as an Associate's Degree in Theology. She currently resides with her loving family in Phoenixville, Pennsylvania, where, as a member of the Historical Society of the Phoenixville Area has written the occasional article or two for its newsletter. Phoenixville, that, she has often said, is still very much like it was during the era of the Great War.

Phoenix Hose, Hook & Ladder is the fourth in her *Novels of Phoenixville...* historical series of fiction, her eighth work of fiction, and her sixteenth published work.

Please visit June at June's Literary Blog.
www.JuneJMcInerney.com